SPARK

OF FIRE AND SHADOWS

KRYSTA MARAVILLA

DEDICATION

To all my nieces and nephews—anything is possible.

CREDITS

<u>Editors</u>
Parisa Zolfaghari
David Farland
Diann Read

<u>Proofreaders</u>
Elizabeth Thompson
Evis Asterwyn

<u>Writing Platform</u>
Bookcicle

<u>Book Cover Designer & Map Maker</u>
Natasha MacKenzie

<u>Writing Coach & Editor</u>
Kelly Chausovsky

I've learned so much from each one of you.
From my heart space to yours,
Thank you.

AUTHOR NOTE

Spark isn't a story that looks away from pain.

After years in the mental health field, I've seen what trauma can do—how it lingers, distorts, and shrinks a life down to survival.

I wanted to write a story that doesn't erase that pain, but faces it head-on. *Spark* is about surviving the unsurvivable, and holding onto what matters—even when it feels like a lost cause.

It's the beginning of a character-driven series where darkness isn't the end, but the starting point of transformation.

If *Spark* leaves you with anything, I hope it's this: **You're not broken. Your pieces are just being rearranged into something stronger.**

Stay marvelous,
 —Krysta

ACKNOWLEDGMENTS

To the high seas, stars, and flipping earth, I've birthed my
book baby!
The gestation of this book took four long years. I swear at
one point it was crowning and instead of popping out, it
clawed its way back in and latched on like an alien baby
leeching the life from me. In the darkest hour, when I
thought it would succeed in stilling the heartbeat of my
dreams, it did a weird thing. It transformed me, changed the
rhythm of my soul song, and in its birth, it gave me new life.
Now to the thank-yous!

Eulalie. You are my rock. I love you.

To my brother-in-law, Mike, you've seen firsthand my crazy
and yet I think you still like me. Weird.

Without you, Kelly Chausovsky, my writing coach and so
much more, I'd still be stuck on the second rewrite. With
your support and guidance, you helped me craft the
foundation of my book (may Fabio be a success) and
supported my shaky confidence in different ways
(sometimes literally by the force of your belief in me) on my
writing journey. Thank you. Thank you. Thank you.

To my editors, Parisa, David (may you rest in peace), and
Diann. I learned so much from each of you on how to write,

it's incredible, and not a single one of you crushed my creative spirit. Thank you for your kindness in your editing (Parisa), in your patience with my constant missing of deadlines, and in teaching me how to craft a story.

And, just when my spirits were the lowest, fear clogged my lungs, and paralyzed my fingers, I met Pamela Hart. You are an angel, and our meeting is nothing but miraculous. Your willingness to read my work, chapter by chapter, and spend hours reviewing it with suggestions, is invaluable.

Thank you, Elizabeth Thompson, Evie Asterwyn, for last-minute proofreading, Rob Gadkey, Jake Huckaby, Sami C., Jennifer E., Christine M., and Leslie E.: you all offered me consistent encouragement in your own beautiful ways. To all those who've stuck with me on this wild ride, I love you. Like, a lot.

To every person who heard the storyline of my book and told me I'd be the next J. K. Rowling or Stephanie Meyers, you uplifted my burnt-out soul. You kept me going. Now, let's see if your predications come true (wink, wink).

To every author, thank you for having the bravery to write and share your stories.

And, if you haven't heard it today, *you* are marvelous.

AETHRA
IHL OCEAN
BYND SEA
SHALEXUM
ARIAS
TRYST FOREST
Y ALUNA
XIHERIA HIGHLANDS
AGLIZAN
DEGALDUR
GALVENOR
FAYSTAR
PIOPINA
ESBURY HILLS
VAETELA
JAGGED WILDS
XYBELL
UANNAS
PROMERE RAINFOREST
EZURA
NEN
INABELLE
OCEANID
DRYKZ FOREST
SRYLN SIERRAS
SPIRITVALE
XAFARA
UKLESA
HAZELMAC
N
S
E
W

PROLOGUE

The swaying motion of the carriage gives a false sense of soothing, and I fight the lure of sleep weighing on me. Mama had signaled for silence when we'd entered this part of the forest, her tension seeping into the closed space of our horse-drawn caravan. My chest tightens with anxiety, and I resist the urge to fidget. Moving would wake the sleeping baby in my arms, and that would only distress Mama.

Light streams in from the edges of a large covered window, making the colors inside glow even more vividly and decorating the cramped space we call home. I focus on LaLora. She's sitting at the rear of the wagon, peeking past the curtain. At almost eight years old, LaLora's the eldest, older than me by six months. Our grandma calls her a cat for her insatiable curiosity.

Swaney, my two-year-old brother, is lying on Mama and Papa's bed at the opposite end, trying to figure out a wooden horse toy that comes apart and clicks together. My gaze swings diagonally to my other sister, Jezzie, four years old. Head tilted down, hair tucked behind her ears, she concentrates on learning her letters at our small table. I peek at the sleeping bundle in my arms, eight-month-old Jayden. His sweet face is serene. I gently trace the line of his cheek.

All of my siblings are considered beautiful within our community of travelers. They have light brown hair, deep brown eyes, and a pale white complexion, courtesy of our parents.

I look completely different. My chestnut-brown hair feels drastically darker than everyone else's and it curls around my face, framing my light olive-colored skin and reaching to my mid-back. Yet it's the streak of silver growing a little off-center to the left of my forehead marking me as other. My eyes aren't brown either. They are honey colored. I am not one of them.

I was abandoned as an infant, a tiny baby girl left crying in a basket with a name pinned to it. Everyone calls me Anala except MaJaJa. She uses my other name, the one that meant darkness. It was MaJaJa, the leader of the caravan, who found me and placed me in the care of Mama, her daughter, since she was already breastfeeding LaLora. But the real reason was because MaJaJa wants me close to her. She has a *feeling*.

The caravan's normal noises fade into the background. The clopping of hooves, wood creaking, leather stretching— all a symphony to our travels. Normally it was accompanied by jests and laughter or bird song, vocals to the track. Right now, the quiet feels like an oppressive blanket.

My skin tingles, and my gut twists.

"It feels like we're being watched," LaLora whispers, visibly shuddering. Her finger holds the curtain to the back-door open a sliver, and she stares out intently.

The drape next to Swaney twitches, and Mama's bejeweled hand comes through, signaling for complete quiet.

LaLora huffs and rolls her eyes. I can tell she thinks Mama is being overbearing—again. We share a smile. Mine is tight as apprehension fills me.

A shout breaks the silence, immediately followed by the sound of clanging metal and the frightened shriek of horses. The symphony shatters. We're pitched forward as the wagon abruptly stops, and I barely stay seated.

Mama ducks her head into the window, the bright light blinding for a moment as the shade is shoved aside. "We're being attacked." Her fierce eyes scan us, expression grim. "Stay inside until we tell you to leave." Her eyes narrow in on me. "Anala, care for them," she commands, then disappears behind the screen, thrusting the caravan back into darkness.

Swaney drops his toy. He glances from the window to my face.

"Come." I motion for him to sit next to me, and he scrambles over quickly, jostling me. Thankfully, Jayden has not awakened. Jezzie seems frozen with wide, fear-filled eyes. She clutches her pencil so tightly, the tip snaps against the table.

We wait tensely, listening to the sounds of battle. LaLora seems transfixed, half-sitting, half-standing, staring open-mouthed out the window. None of us make a sound.

"They're burning the wagons," LaLora whisper-shrieks.

I twist, knocking Swaney with my elbow, and shove aside the heavy curtain behind me. It's hard to see at this angle, but the smell of burning reaches us and smoke climbs skyward.

Movement catches my attention. Papa lunging forward, engaged in a sword fight with a woman dressed in rags. Her face is gaunt, with hollowed cheeks and the crisscross of visible veins, and her limbs are gangly.

It's her eyes that cause me to freeze.

There is no white to them. Just pure blackness.

A horseman comes careening down the path, a torch in his hand, and someone hanging off his side. It's hard to tell who. A swift punch from the horseman and the person falls, leaving a knife protruding from the horseman's leg. He doesn't seem to notice, intent on sweeping the wagon's curved roof with his torch.

I gasp; my heart stops. His black eyes lock onto mine as if he heard me. A grin spreads across his thin face, and he throws the torch at me.

I dodge immediately, dragging Swaney from the window. Both of us topple over; the impact jolts Jayden awake, and he screams.

Jezzie scrambles, the torch barely missing her as it lands on the cushioned bench. Flames lick up instantly. Jezzie's dress ignites. Her cry is high-pitched, panicked.

LaLora has plastered herself against the carriage door. I shove Swaney behind me.

"LaLora! Open the door," I yell.

She glances at me, then at the flames.

"Open the door!" I shout, desperate. Heat shoots up my arm as I smack one-handed at Jezzie's dress, shoving her toward the exit.

LaLora unlatches the door and jumps.

"Jezzie, jump out!" I command, pushing her. She throws herself through the door, and I hear the thud of her landing. "Roll around, Jezzie. Roll!"

Without looking to see if she listened, I grab Swaney's collar and drag him in front of me, dropping him outside. I don't wait, but launch myself and Jayden out, landing hard and almost falling. Swaney is crying, and LaLora's missing.

My gaze locks onto Jezzie. I drop next to her rolling form

and hit the flames with my free hand, ignoring the pain. Together, we extinguish them just as LaLora returns with a bucket of water. She throws it on Jezzie and me, drenching all of us. Jayden wails louder.

Swaney's hands wrap around my waist, latching onto me. My breath is ragged, my heart beating in my throat. I shakily try to drag Jezzie closer. My hand isn't working right.

Noises rush in.

Children crying.

The stamping of hooves.

Horses neighing.

Metal clanging.

People yelling.

The crackling of wood burning. Then the smell of fire mixes with the aroma of incense, the familiar musky scent of sandalwood, and cooking spices. People are fighting within the tight confines of the road and burning wagons, the trees hindering the battle.

We shuffle off the road and try to hide behind the nearest tree. It's not big enough.

A man grabs Swaney by his collar, violently yanking at him to dislodge him, shaking and dragging me in the process. I shove Jayden at LaLora, who's kneeling next to Jezzie's whimpering form. Swaney's grip on me is gone, and I lunge, grabbing Swaney's still-outstretched limbs. Agony radiates from my burnt hand as I force it to lock around Swaney's arm.

No one is taking my family. No one.

With a hold on Swaney's forearm, I dig my feet in to slow the man down. My hold is tenuous, my nails breaking skin, my injured hand slippery and weak. Swaney's mouth is open in a silent scream. The man glances at us, and I catch sight of his black eyes. My breath seizes. They're vacant, yet . . .

The next moment, metal is arcing toward me. I'd been too distracted to notice the man had pulled a sword. Reflexively, I shut my eyes and hunch my shoulders up, dreading the impact.

An unnatural screech assaults my ears. Nothing hits me. I open my eyes as the resistance on Swaney is suddenly gone. We smack into each other, toppling backward.

Without stopping, I crab crawl with Swaney toward Jezzie. She cries out as I fall onto her. Shifting to her side, we all huddle together, and I realize the man we'd been struggling with was on the ground, unmoving.

My heart sinks. Xan, our horse, is rearing, trying to break free from the burning wagon.

I shift Swaney from me to Jezzie. "I've got to help Xan," I mumble.

Jezzie whimpers as Swaney transfers his grip to her midriff. LaLora seizes my arm with a shake of her head. "Anala, don't go."

I break from her grasp and crawl, clutching my injured arm to my chest as I stay low and make my way to him. I stand and my legs wobble. Trying to figure out how I can help, I inch closer.

Jezzie screams.

I swivel.

Xan moves at the same time, knocking me down. All air leaves me when I hit the ground. I try to scramble away, but a frantic hoof catches me in the ribs, sending me flying.

Barely managing to prop myself up, I try to suck in a breath and nearly double over with the pain. It hurts so much, and I'm bleeding. The ground vibrates under me. My vision locks on my siblings. They are fighting to stay together. The edges of my sight blacken, tunneling my focus. *I can't help them. I need to help them. To wrap them in their own protective bubbles.*

Almost as soon as I think it, I see something forming around each of them. I blink, trying to clear my vision. It doesn't disappear—instead, it crystallizes into bubbles—into shields. Then I notice a pulsing in the shields, like a heartbeat, only they expand with each beat.

A lightness spreads through my body. Heat creeps into my belly, extending to my limbs. I pick up a hand to drag myself forward and a trail of blue light follows it, connecting me to the earth.

What stops me is the orange and red sparks. *Are they coming from my hand?* I gaze in fascination, the hard-packed dirt rough on my cheek.

Scorching heat ignites where my body connects with the ground, and the colored cords solidify. The searing inferno pushes past the limit of my skin.

What is happening?

The weight of my arm is too much; it drops. I glance at my siblings as another sweltering wave sweeps through me. The spheres throb, and the men holding my siblings go limp. My siblings run to me. Swaney and Jezzie snuggle into my sides, shaking, and LaLora tries to move me. She can't.

I'm too heavy.

A third rush hits, the bubble expands outward, growing, encompassing. I lose track of it as it goes past my narrowing vision. I only care about my siblings. *Must keep them safe.* A fourth swell pours into me, and my heart flutters. It's going to burst.

My vision is a haze of darkness I try to see past. Shadows sweep in from the trees, tendrils of darkness reaching for me.

A whooshing noise jars me. Blinking, I glance in its direction. A blue light strikes a woman heading toward me, trapping her for a moment in its terrifying beam. Her body gives out.

Her head lifts, oily, matted hair sticks to her cheeks, and she spears me with her bulging black eyes, unnaturally craning her head. Grotesquely, she drags herself closer to me with single-minded determination. She's close.

I can't move.

Another bolt of light strikes her. The ground trembles.

My vision pinpricks. I fight to stay conscious when an upsurge pummels through the woman, engulfing her in blue light, her body quivering under its attack. I stare in horror as darkness captures me.

1

Phe woke, her vision filled with two pairs of fear-filled brown eyes staring at her, feeling the vestiges of their bodies pressed into her. She blinked, clearing the image from her head.

She was sweating, her hair matted to her neck. She mopped her forehead with a forearm, leaving her arm pressed against her hot face for a moment. The leather amulet bracelet she wore dug into her temple, the drop of water suspended in it, cooling.

A shudder raced involuntarily across her body. *What is it about this dream?* It unfailingly left her emotionally raw.

She tuned into her breath, calming her pounding heart.

To her relief, the sensation of little bodies huddled into her lessened. An intense heaviness settled in her chest. Was it sadness? Fear? Hurt? Or was it not an emotion at all, but some type of weight on her heart? She didn't know, but every time the dream came, it felt so real, disturbing. *Who is Anala? And why do I keep having this dream?*

Abandoning any pretense of sleep, Phe focused on the surrounding sounds. She could hear rhythmic breathing in the other rooms. The soft, irregular snoring coming from the room next to her told her Finian, a teammate of hers, had chosen the bed on the other side of the shared wall. She smiled. He adamantly denied he snored.

Slowly and cautiously, she started shifting. The bed frame creaked, and she froze, hyper aware of the soft sounds she made. They were all light sleepers.

She quietly slipped into clothing and shoes, opting to dress in darkness rather than risk the light. She assessed her exit strategy as she pulled her long brown hair into a quick bun at the base of her neck.

She hopped onto the ledge of the window she left open. The stone underneath her was jagged and rough, making it an easy climb down.

She took a moment to envision wrapping herself in shadows, a habit she'd formed years ago when all she'd wanted was to hide. She knew it was only in her mind, but just the thought made her feel both invisible and soundless whenever she "cloaked." Then she flipped around and carefully lowered herself out.

The cool air felt refreshing on her heated skin as she deftly made it to solid ground and slipped away. She kept her footfalls silent until she was far enough away she could relax, feeling confident she wouldn't wake anyone. This was one of the cons of partnering with an elite military unit for team training. Sneaking away was always a challenge.

Then she ran—as if a pack of bloodthirsty hounds were nipping at her ankles.

Phe quickly left the cobbled streets of Spiritvale behind, the roads narrowing and switching to rock as they crept into the mountain, until she was past the last house. The tapered footpaths stretched into the darkness of the woods.

She knew the path so well, darkness was not a deterrent

to her. She was not afraid of the noises or a happenstance animal encounter. Nothing in these woods would make her pause.

Phe rounded a corner and stepped off the footpath onto what she liked to think of as her own trail. It wove around the mountain to various destinations, branching continuously. Eventually, it dead-ended into a bramble of thicker trees and bushes.

Without hesitation, she squeezed through the shrub until the path cleared and an opening emerged. It wasn't much, just a slab of rock extended out toward the city.

After a large storm a few years ago, a tree had fallen. The impact had cracked the rock extension. A portion of the cliff had crumbled with the force, and a crack ran through the entire shelf now.

She liked the crack. It reminded her of herself—broken, yet filled with dirt and life.

Phe strode to the end of the overhang and dropped to a seat at the edge, her feet swinging into space.

She breathed in deeply, feeling the burn in her lungs. The woodsy scents of dirt and pine forest wrapped around her, soothing her, and she let go of the shadows she hid within. She didn't need them here. She had a special relationship with the silence of forests.

This nightmare had been creeping up in frequency, distressing her. Why had it returned to plague her sleep? The question of who they were always stumped Phe. Why did she dream of people she didn't know?

And the colors—she had never seen such vibrant colors in her day-to-day life. Even her other dreams were dull in comparison. At first, Phe had thought it was because she hadn't seen much of the world, but as she grew, she had been exposed to different lands and people. She still had never come across luminescent colors like those anywhere. In fact, all colors were muted and drab in comparison. She marveled at what the world would be like if colors existed the way they did in her nightmare.

The horizon lightened, going from midnight black to shades of dark blue. A cloud drifted in front of the moon.

Phe shifted on her stone seat, feeling conflicted, and tugged a corded braid on her amulet bracelet for comfort. Kyra, her best friend, had created the amulet for Phe years ago, after Phe had gone missing for almost a year. As a Water Nymph, Kyra was able to use the suspended drop of water to locate Phe.

Phe sighed heavily. Her life was complicated.

Kyra, also known as Her Grace, was the last surviving Water Nymph, and as such, she upheld her family's sworn oath to protect their island country, Xafara, and its people. Kyra's mother, Thetis Theanora, had died during a visit to Shalexum while they were exploring the Xiheria Highlands. A blizzard had ravaged her last known whereabouts, leaving behind no trace of the parties existence. No one knew who Kyra's father was.

Kyra was intricately connected to the waterways of Xafara, as her family before her had been. With her ability to communicate with water, to work with the sea surrounding them, Kyra could control who came in and who left, could purify water for people to drink, could water the land, and more. Her role, and the responsibility of her family before her, afforded her General Bastion's elite guard protection, as well as made Kyra an integral part of the government and social echelon in the capital city of Oceanid.

Many coveted Phe's friendship with Kyra, believing the position gave her a life filled with luxury and ease. In many aspects, they were right. Phe lived in House Nereid, Kyra's enormous palace in Oceanid, and benefitted from its luxuries. When at home, Phe never wanted for anything material.

In Oceanid, however, Phe was someone different. She couldn't help it. The moment she entered the empty carriage that would return her to Kyra's side, her shoulders crept toward her ears, spine concaving, and her stomach churned.

Over the years, she'd discovered that the gilded carriage, with its plush navy-blue lining, had the power to evoke the younger version of herself. The one who didn't speak because silence was safer and who felt every sensation skittering across her skin, remnants of pain from Grum's caretaking. In Oceanid, she was forced out of the shadows she hid in, and instead of receiving the acceptance she'd craved when younger, she was ostracized for her place in the limelight.

She could understand why Xafarians did this, but it never lessened the sting. Phe was grateful they didn't know the full story, only the censored version of her past. Otherwise, life in Oceanid would be worse.

What they knew was Phe, a homeless ten-year-old, had risked her life to stop an attempt to abduct Kyra, killing the Shalexum perpetrator in the process. This wouldn't have created strife in and of itself if Phe had disappeared afterward, an absent hero. But she hadn't. Kyra and Phe's friendship had formed from this event.

How could a murderer be welcomed into their ranks? Socialize with their children?

The scrutiny only intensified on Phe herself. Averse to touch. Odd. Empty-eyed, yet cunningly observant. Even the way she moved or didn't was critiqued, and they couldn't forget Phe's lack of proper social etiquette.

Her heroic act—tainted by murder—melded with her homelessness and bizarre behavior, branded her as unsavory.

Then there was the fact she was a foreigner, and this was the nail in her societal coffin. She was from a country on the mainland, Shalexum. The same one as Kyra's would-be abductor.

They weren't told Phe had been brought over from Shalexum by the perpetrator, Grum, a criminal mastermind who had been her guardian. Nor did they know Phe had spent the last three years as Grum's slave, forcibly molded into an instrument. Or that Grum's hadn't been the first life she'd taken. General Bastion deliberately withheld these details, as he saw her as a tool to wield for Kyra's safety.

A prickling sense pulled her to the present; someone was approaching, reminding her that her time with Shadow Unit had ended, her "treatment"—the cover story for her many absences from Oceanid—over.

General Bastion had welded her into a lethal weapon, an assassin.

Due to the secrecy of her training, General Bastion and Phe primarily trained alone. In this way, he privately—and brutally—honed her skills across the spectrum of hand-to-hand combat, weaponry, and outdoor wilderness survival excursions. To further refine her expertise beyond solo work, he'd paired her with this unit years ago. His rationale, even though her role was a tightly-kept secret, was to prepare her for team situations. Training sessions with Shadow Unit were yearly, and she wouldn't see them again unless she was called and asked to assist them with a mission.

This was bittersweet for Phe. This team knew her capabilities, had witnessed her growth, her sweat and blood. Her drive. She'd earned their respect. She could be herself with them, show both her dark and light sides, her strengths and weaknesses. And they helped her to improve so she could be the best weapon in Kyra's arsenal. One no one would be prepared for.

Once, she'd asked why they were called Shadow Unit. They'd explained to her it was because when they did their work, they weren't seen. They were shadows.

Phe resonated deeply with this. She walked with shadows too.

She would start her return to Oceanid today, a full two-day journey, as she was expected to attend a ball with Her Grace, Kyra. Phe normally despised large social events. Yet this was a coming-of-age celebration for Princess Attiva, and she wanted to be there. The royal family was the exception to her social experiences, welcoming and nurturing.

A footstep sounded behind her, her normally stealthy interloper announcing his presence.

Phe sighed, shifting, so she was partially hanging off the rock ledge with one leg dangling, the other tucked up and under, to face where her visitor would appear.

He wasn't clear of the bushes when he called out. "One day I am going to clear a path so wide—" Roar grunted, "—I will tiptoe through here in total silence."

She huffed.

Roar threatened this whenever he followed her out here.

He sauntered toward her. His deep auburn red hair, dull compared to the reds in her nightmare, popped for a moment under a ray of moonlight. He'd pulled it into a tight little bun. She could just make out his slightly crooked nose and powerful jaw. She couldn't see his dull blue eyes with the shadows still encasing them, but she knew they'd have a dancing energy to them, with smile wrinkles at their edges.

She always wondered how, with their line of work, he had those at all. But then, working with him and his team, it was hard not to laugh with them.

Roar was over six feet tall, so when he sat next to her and scooted close, he towered over her. She straightened her spine, giving herself a few more inches, and pretended her fluttering heart wasn't because it was him sitting next to her.

"Roar," she warned, watching as he dropped his feet off the ledge. His arm nudged her.

An uncomfortable heat tingled up her arm, the skin he'd brushed hyper-aware. She fought the instinctive urge to move, not sure if she wanted to lean into his touch or away. Normally, she avoided touching others, except for Kyra and Jallia—Kyra's lady's maid; resonances of Grum's violence.

"I'm fine. It was a nightmare," she finished, not missing a beat.

Even though she couldn't actually see the deadpan expression he gave her, she felt it.

Roar sighed deeply and, with a rehearsed and resigned tone, replied, "If it was just a plain old nightmare, you wouldn't sneak out and run as if a pack of wolves were chasing you, absconding to the woods to brood."

Brood? She pinned him with a piercing stare.

In the past, she'd denied her reactions to her nightmares, citing instead a restlessness and need to move. She'd stopped this denial years ago—after her time in Drykz Forest—where she'd worked on acceptance and healing from her past. Since then, all but one of her nightmares had dissipated. She hadn't told Roar this, nor had she shared her tormented dreams.

She shifted to watching the wakening sky, with the

muted hues of light blue, orange, yellow caressing the horizon. "Roar, you worry too much," she muttered as she repositioned, and noticed they were close enough she felt his warmth.

"Someone has to," he replied. He scooted closer to the edge too, so they sat within an inch of touching, and more of his heat seeped into her.

Phe smiled sadly, no longer wanting to engage with him, and toyed with a braid on her wrist amulet.

Roar had stopped trying to push her to talk in these moments, opting now to follow her lead, share her space, and allow her to be. His presence merely said, "I am here for you."

Phe turned her attention to the view. She liked to run through the geography, a visualization practice she'd found helped to calm and ground her. From their vantage point, they overlooked the bustling community of Spiritvale.

Spiritvale was a major trading post and a midpoint in the country. It held the crossroads to the rest of the island. Though it was not geographically the center of Xafara, one would never say such things to the people who lived there.

Since Spiritvale was the hub of the connecting roads, it had the best markets in Xafara—except for Oceanid, of course—and the townspeople boasted of their diversity. They sold wares from each of the four other major cities of Xafara's island. With so many merchants traveling through, the city also pulsed with an element of danger and excitement.

Phe took in the city's overview. She could make out the large oval where the four major roads connected and trace in her mind's eye all four roads unraveling in their separate directions.

Phe narrowed in on Naid Road. This led to Oceanid, the

capital city of Xafara, named in honor of the water nymphs who had lived there.

Getting to Oceanid, a trip Phe would start this morning, took two days. Once she cleared Spiritvale, she would ride all day and come to the outer edge of Drykz Forest, a haunted wood.

The forest could only be entered during early morning hours, as travelers needed to exit it before dark. If they didn't, they were never seen again. When traversing the forest, the hair-raising feeling of being watched never vanished, and combined with the eerie sounds erupting from its depths, it always made for a creepy journey.

Oceanid was the only international port in all of Xafara. Therefore, the city was extremely busy and diverse. Long ago, Water Nymphs had created a security system for Xafara. They'd delineated an area around the island and worked with the water systems to manage the water traffic access.

Roar leaned back, placing one of his arms right behind Phe as she contemplated her returning.

When she was away receiving "treatments," secretly training or working, Phe was strong and powerful. She'd survived all of Bastion's—the bastard's—training. She was confident in her abilities and skills.

She glanced at Roar. Even when she didn't speak, Shadow Unit listened. In Oceanid, if she spoke in social situations without Kyra present, she was ignored, shunned.

A bird tweeted nearby as colors spread across the skyline. Phe reclined, then straightened quickly at the warmth along her spine. She'd bumped into Roar, and her skin sparked where they touched. Heat flooded her cheeks and neck.

Again, she battled the odd yearning to lean in.

"It's okay to relax," Roar gently coached, reading her mind.

Phe cleared her throat uncomfortably, letting her silence answer as she dislodged a small rock loose from the crack and rolled it between her fingers.

"We need to return. General Bastion has called a meeting."

Tension filled Phe. "I didn't hear a missive come. How do you know?"

"It came as I was leaving."

She took a last, quick look at the sunrise, her brow furrowing. She had sensed no one in the streets as she'd left. This wasn't the first time the team had received a "missive" Phe hadn't noticed come in. Her senses may not be perfect, but she wouldn't miss messengers.

Roar stood and held out his hand to help her.

Not wanting to believe he'd lied to her; Phe shook the feeling off. She eyed his hand, debating refusing it, then dropped the rock as she wrapped her hand around his calloused palm and hopped up, releasing it quickly. Only a slight burning at their hand-to-hand contact occurred, sending a pleasantly unnerving tingle up her forearm.

Roar had withdrawn, yet they were so close their breath mingled. There was a tired, sad smile on his face, and for a moment Phe thought he might say something. As if he knew she was aware of his lie.

"No rock?"

She gave him a wan smile, subtly shaking her head.

His glance swept her face, no doubt noticing the distance between them now, and the corners of his mouth sharpened. Somberly nodding, he turned on his heel.

Unsettled by her reaction to him, Phe flexed her tingling hand as she watched him disappear into the shrub. She wiped her still-warm hand on her leg and jogged after him.

General Bastion met them at the door. He appeared wide awake, as always. He had a clean-shaven face with a scar running from his hairline to mid-cheek. The strikingly pale scar tissue against the tan of his leathery skin was always eye-catching. His five-foot-ten-inch, barrel-chested frame blocked the doorway for a moment as he opened it for them. Then he stepped aside to let them in. Bastion acknowledged Roar with a stoic nod.

"Thank you, sir," Roar said as he passed. To Phe, Bastion scowled. Phe fortified herself. Their relationship was tenuous.

Bastion shut the door hard once they were inside.

They shuffled into the small kitchen, which was unsurprisingly full. The team was up.

A small round table stood in the center of the room. Finian and Kirzia were sitting at it, Orc hovering around them, and Ihrone off to the side.

Kirzia, with her long black hair pulled into a severe bun at the nape of her neck, turned too swiftly, glaring at Finian. She was the only person in full uniform and ready for the day. Phe caught Finian's wink at Kirzia, his brown eyes laughing at something only he thought was funny, and Kirzia's stiffening.

Ihrone was in a kitchen chair he'd pulled away from the table and propped on two legs to lean on the wall. His short cropped, wiry black hair was still wet from his shower. Sipping coffee from his precariously balanced position, his dark gray eyes studied Bastion.

Orc grunted noncommittally, moving away from the

small group to Roar and Phe, coffee in hand. "You missed out on the coffee," he muttered around the rim of his mug. Mossy green eyes, bright with delight, watched them as he sipped from the steaming cup.

"Finian," Roar called, watching Orc's demonstration.

"Yes, Commander Maverick," Finian responded, stiffening a little and, for Bastion's benefit, calling Roar by his rank.

"Coffee?"

"On it, sir," Finian responded, though his glance at Roar communicated disdain at being tasked with the job.

Phe bit the inside of her lip softly, refraining from teasing Finian.

Orc repositioned himself on her other side, distracting her from observing Finian. Orc was the unit medic. There was an ease to him that settled Phe's nerves. "Dream?"

Phe's "Mmm" response was lost as Bastion spoke.

"There has been a change of plans. There have been disturbing reports of people with black eyes sighted in Oceanid. You're to report there immediately."

Heaviness settled into the room.

Phe didn't have a moment to process her team's reaction. One moment she was in the room with them, the next, she was staring into a man's bulging black eyes as he clutched Swaney. Veins crisscrossed his gaunt face and those empty eyes, vacant yet not.

Her heart skipped. Her chest constricted.

She closed her eyes, smelling smoke mixed in with musky sandalwood incense and spices. She saw the emaciated face of the woman who'd dragged herself closer and closer to Anala, malice radiating from her in waves.

Her breath stopped.

Roar bumped into her. The skin-to-skin contact dragged her to the present. A tingly burn. She blinked. The room reappeared.

She'd missed whatever Bastion had been saying.

Forcing a breath past the vise in her chest, she made herself ask, "Sir, could you please clarify what's the problem with someone having black eyes?"

Bastion's penetrating gaze landed on her.

Holding his gaze, she kept her posture relaxed. It was never good to make movements a predator could mistake as weakness or fear. Stiffening would have shown him he affected her, and she was not willing to give him any power over her.

"It's a sickness," Bastion finally responded, "and it's not black coloration we are worried about. The whole eye," he circled his own, "including the white, is black."

The small sparks of hope she'd had extinguished with those words. Dread's piercing claws gouged its way up her throat. *There is truth to the dream.*

Bastion continued. "We are calling in specific units and considering the threat level high."

She swallowed, shoving the sour, coppery tang of trepidation aside. *I need to pull myself together.*

Roar stepped forward to take a cup of coffee from Finian. He turned slightly toward her, offering the cup.

She declined with a small head shake. She didn't need coffee, it would only exacerbate things. Phe focused on Bastion's voice, trying not to think about her nightmare.

"... We will travel as a unit, except for Phe."

This didn't affect Phe at all. She couldn't be seen traveling with others or even staying at any type of establishment when the people of Oceanid thought she was receiving medical treatment. Bastion's rules. When they trained and had access to safe houses, such as this one, she could stay. When she traveled, she camped alone along her routes.

She straightened as Bastion's intense chestnut-brown eyes locked onto her.

"Phe, you're to return to the center. Your carriage will arrive on its normal schedule."

On the far outskirts of Oceanid, there was a healing center with individual cabins for some of their more prestigious guests. Somehow Bastion had permanently reserved or purchased one of them for their ruse. He managed all the details, and whatever he was doing worked, because there was never any speculation.

"Yes, sir," Phe replied.

"For everyone else, I will give you fifteen minutes to get yourselves in order. Dismissed."

Phe bolted, running upstairs to snatch her packed bag.

In the stable, she found her horse, Edva—a rescue like Phe—eating hay. Edva's body was strong and healthy, a contrast and relief to how Phe had found her years ago. A foal, emaciated, with jagged edges of broken rib bones that protruded into her skin, her knees double the size of Phe's fists, and her hide a patchwork of whip lashes.

Edva's light brown coat seemed to shimmer under a ray of light, an oddity Phe loved about her. Edva was not a normal horse. Her deep, intelligent, mocha-colored eyes tracked Phe, and when Phe was close, Edva tossed her long black mane.

Edva snorted her "Hello" happy snort.

Phe dropped her bags outside the stall and stepped close to be nuzzled, petting Edva's neck while cooing. Touch from animals never caused the same reactions in Phe as being touched by humans. She allowed herself to relax into Edva for a second before she started gathering Edva's gear. She wanted to make quick work of tacking up, primarily to forestall any contact with Bastion, the bastard.

With the creak of the opening door, she captured Edva's muzzle, locking gazes. "Be nice," she commanded sternly. Edva disliked Bastion with a vengeance.

Edva gazed innocently at her.

"Don't you give me that look. Be nice," Phe ordered sternly.

Edva huffed, concentrating on who was entering.

"Hey, Phe," Kirzia said as she approached her own steed.

"Morning, Kirz."

Phe liked Kirzia. She was a no-drama, get-things-done kind of woman. As the only woman in this group of elite soldiers, she had the patience of a goddess in Phe's eyes. They'd developed an easy back-and-forth over the years, once Phe had started speaking to them. That was another reason Bastion had paired her with a team. Phe selectively spoke until she was thirteen, and even now, she preferred non-syllable responses when possible.

Edva returned to eating hay, nonplussed by Kirzia's presence.

"Early morning run?" Kirzia asked politely.

Phe's dreams weren't a secret. They'd been haunting her for as long as she could remember. When she was younger, they came every night. She'd had an aversion to sleeping, doing it only in small bursts. Each dream had held parts of her brutal past, only dissipating once she'd stopped running from it. All except the one. The one that wasn't a memory of hers.

"Dream." Phe threw the saddle blanket onto Edva's back, dragged a stool over, and climbed onto it with the saddle.

She hefted the saddle into place, smoothing out any kinks in the blanket.

"Want to talk about it?"

"Not really. Have you heard of this black-eyed sickness before?" Phe attached the cinch to the saddle, tightening it while ignoring the constriction in her chest. She *needed* to get to Kyra.

Edva stopped eating, her body tensing at the sound of the door opening. Phe didn't need to peek around Edva to know who it was.

"Kirzia, could you give Phe and me a moment?" An order phrased as a question.

Kirzia immediately headed for the door. "Yes, General Bastion. I'll keep the others out until you're finished."

"Thank you," Bastion said, all manners.

Phe sighed. She'd really been hoping to avoid Bastion. She tacked faster.

General Bastion was the reason for Phe's cover story, as he'd poisoned her multiple times when she was younger, resulting in her being sick. His training was brutal. Not only had it included all types of weaponry and different forms of hand-to-hand combat and fighting styles, he'd also tried to kill her during training. Sometimes he'd left her so broken, so vulnerable, it shocked her that he hadn't.

What amazed Phe was her inability to die—as she'd danced closely with death on more occasions than she'd ever admit—or at least it seemed that way. Then there was the matter of her ability to heal more quickly than others, an anomaly she had to carefully hide from those outside of her inner circle.

Bastion had been her commanding officer until she was sixteen, but that changed after he'd ordered her into Drykz Forest, at night, in punishment for endangering Kyra. He hadn't expected her to survive. She nearly hadn't, and the incident had served as the catalyst for change.

"Yes, sir?" She kept her voice level.

Edva swished her tail and continued to eat, warily watching Bastion approach. Phe didn't stop her preparations.

He stopped out of Edva's reach. His sharp chestnut-brown eyes latched onto Phe. "Last week, an embassy ship from Shalexum arrived with two ambassadors."

Phe's shoulders tightened, and her skin tingled. Shalexum was Phe's home country, a place she didn't want to return to. Only terrible memories remained of her life there.

"The ambassadors," Bastion continued with a demeanor of deference, which was oddly out of place, "have requested to meet with Her Grace, and you." Bastion paused, glancing at Edva distastefully. "They've expressed curiosity about your heritage."

Phe waited for him to continue.

"You will answer their inquires," Bastion commanded. "And remember, they are important to us as liaisons with Shalexum. Behave appropriately."

"Yes, sir." Phe's hands trembled, and she shifted to make sure Bastion didn't see. She'd long ago discarded trying to find anything about her heritage, and the realization that Bastion condoned this line of questioning rattled her. It was normally taboo because of her past. *Why? And why now?*

"Why are they interested in my heritage?" Phe braved.

"Apparently, they've heard about you and your plight and are curious."

"You know I don't remember anything before Grum." When Bastion shrugged nonchalantly, she continued. "Why are they requesting to speak with Kyra?"

"They're very interested in creating a partnership with Her Grace." This was common; many sought to cultivate relationships with Kyra.

Phe slowed her tacking. "What about the illness? Do we know how it spreads?" *Will meeting with them endanger Kyra? Are they the source?*

"I'm not concerned."

She stiffened irritably. She *hated* when Bastion withheld information, something he did all the time. He clearly knew details and wasn't sharing. "What aren't you telling me about this illness?"

"For now, what you know suffices. When you need to know more, you will." Bastion continued, "Velimir has been staying at House Nereid."

They shared a mutual dislike of Velimir, and when he came about, they subtly worked together to disrupt the man's intentions.

"While you have been away," Bastion said, "he moved to the room adjoining Her Grace's, and they have been inseparable."

Phe's heart sank. Velimir was slimy. He had been trying to wriggle his way into Kyra's affections for a long time. Phe checked her tacking once more.

"Good to know. Has she taken him to her training room?" Allowing someone into her private, secured training room was a tremendous step for Kyra, one she didn't do often.

"Yes," Bastion said grimly, his scar blanching.

Phe frowned. This wasn't good news. There was enough going on without having to manage Velimir too.

By the time Bastion reached the stable door, Phe was on Edva's back, trotting up behind him, tugging her hood over her head.

Bastion swung the doors open and stepped to the side. The entire unit was outside, milling about, waiting for entry.

She nodded in the unit's direction, leaned forward, and whispered into Edva's ear, "Home." Edva took off, leaving dust in their wake.

2

As Phe approached Drykz Forest, she felt its familiar pull. It was as if she had a tether attached to her stomach, and whenever she was within five miles or so, it tugged.

She had tried to ignore the tug over the years, but its intensity would only increase to the point of unbearability. The only way to relieve it was to visit the forest. Once close to its edge, the feeling would dissolve. As though the forest summoned her, and was only satisfied when she answered its call.

Edva picked up her pace, sensing Phe's discomfort.

As the forest approached, tension eased from her stomach. An odd reaction when the forest permeated such a sense of foreboding. The wood on the perimeter was thin and spindly, a combination of saplings and shrub. The forest canopy was thick with dark green oak leaves, occluding light. Branches reached unnaturally into the adjoining meadow, heavy with greenery and vines that draped like snakes, adding to its ominous presence.

As Edva approached the edge fearlessly, daylight faded,

lighter hues of orange and yellow replacing the bright sun and bringing with it relief from the heat. They left the road to travel parallel to the forest's edge, heading for Phe's campsite.

For a mile or more, weeping lovegrass claimed the area between the forest and a neighboring farm. Scattered patches of purple, orange, and blue wildflowers bloomed in waves within it. The green scent of the oak forest permeated the area.

Phe inhaled deeply, its calming balm disintegrating the call of the forest.

She hadn't always had this reaction to Drykz Forest. It had only developed after she had barely survived traversing it. A feat considered impossible. A death sentence. Yet, at sixteen years old, she'd defied the impossible and had emerged, changed and tethered.

Edva stopped as they reached the campsite, slightly obscured by trees. Phe wasn't worried about being seen. Her location was tucked away from the road, and she was sure no one would see any light she'd create while cooking or warming herself. No one would brave the forest's edge, even if they saw the flickering of her flames. It was simply too dangerous.

The campsite wasn't much, but its grass was ankle length and soft, unlike the unruly lovegrass—an abnormality she was grateful for—and it was close to a stream.

She untacked Edva, setting her to graze, and piled Edva's tack neatly before peering into the depths of the forest, using her senses to discern the wood's danger level.

The hair on her neck rose. If the forest was sentient, it was fixated on her. No danger emanated from it, though.

Phe stepped into the woods, deciding to collect the pack she'd stored there for when she traveled through. She had stashes similar to this along all of her well-traveled routes, allowing her to travel lighter through Xafara's countryside and easing Edva's load.

An eery sensation slithered down her body, her warning system activating. The chirping of crickets and soft birdsong ceased; the forest held its breath.

She didn't hesitate—danger could arise instantaneously—and grabbed her backpack, hauling it over her shoulder. It was heavy.

The watchfulness morphed into anticipation.

Back in the meadow's safety, her rucksack hit the ground with a thud. She stared at the forest, wondering for the millionth time why she was sensitive to it and what it meant. *What would it be anticipating?*

Nothing moved within its perimeter to give her any indication.

She knelt on the soft grass, giving the meadow a quick glance. Edva was by the stream, her head down, chewing on lovegrass. Nothing looked amiss. Phe examined the sky. There was no threat of rain, only fading colors of blues and purples. No need to go through the hassle of setting up a tent. She'd fall asleep staring at the stars.

Phe plucked apart the knot at the top of the pack, then unpacked some of its contents, laying them around her. A change of clothes, a pot. The rough blanket she used for padding she tossed closer to the saddle, followed by her journal and wax pen, then she replaced the unneeded items, tying the pack up.

Spreading the blanket, the soft grass cushioning underneath, Phe propped herself on her saddle and relaxed into its leathery smell.

There was a niggling sense of guilt and urgency. She should be with Kyra right now. Protecting her.

Yet she wouldn't risk entering Drykz Forest at night.

She opened her notebook, contemplating how she hadn't trained today. Briefly, as her fingers fumbled through the coarse pages, her eyes strayed to the forest again. To the location she kept her training staff.

She'd left it inside the forest's perimeter, and while she'd been away, it had fallen and rolled partially into the meadow. She fought the urge to push it into the forest.

She used her notebook for many things, sometimes uncensored streams of thought when she was trying to manage an overwhelming feeling or process something. She memorialized memories with the unit she found touching or hilarious. Other times it was to leave herself cryptic messages, reminders.

She opened to the last ink-filled page, writing, *What does my nightmare have to do with this illness?* Then she answered the question. *Nothing, yet everything. In my dream, they didn't act sick, but they looked sick. Gaunt, visible veins, and those eyes.*

She tapped the page with her wax pen, reflecting. *A heaviness had filled the room. Right before my memory hit, Shadow Unit reacted. They'd known about this illness and its significance. Gah! Why is Bastion withholding from me? Especially when this concerns Kyra's safety. I should know everything. Why didn't I ask more questions? I should've asked what the symptoms are, other than black eyes. Stupid, stupid flash. If I hadn't had it, I would've asked more questions. I wouldn't—*

She stopped herself. If she rode the stream of those thoughts, she'd find herself in a sea of self-deprecation. Beyond how she'd feel in its depths, the reason she wouldn't allow herself to go there was Kyra. It would distract her from her purpose.

Frustrated, Phe scrubbed a hand across her face and toyed with her amulet wristlet. It grounded her. She rolled one of the three leather corded braids, following it until the single band merged into the main leather bracelet.

She listened to the night's song, searching within its beats for warnings.

The waning moon a sliver in the sky, barely emanating light. Stars sparkled in a thick cluster above her, a celestial river of light.

A soft rumbling broke the forest's symphony, the sound wavering, captured her attention. She strained to hear it, the sounds of the meadow fading as darkness surged around her.

Elzac's wrinkled face coalesced, his white hair a contrast to the darkness of his skin. His eyebrows furrowed, face tense. His mouth moved, yet his words were muffled.

Elzac lived deep in Drykz Forest, in a hidden community called Ligeia. A village no one outside of the forest knew existed, other than Phe. It had been eight years since she'd seen him—though she thought of him often.

She leaned in closer, trying to decipher what he was saying. Warm breath touched her chilled cheeks. His whisper was indiscernible.

She focused on his mouth, narrowing her gaze, attempting to lip-read.

His eyes flared white and hands gripped her biceps, startling her. Fingertips dug into her muscles, and his words solidified. "Phe, you must awaken!"

She jolted, heart pounding, and rubbed her face. Gads, she must have fallen asleep.

You must awaken! echoed in her mind.

She rubbed her arms, her skin tingling from the visceral remembrance of his grip.

Awaken?

Little shocks ran along her skin. Why did she have the feeling he wasn't demanding she physically wake?

The sensation intensified to a throb, and she got up, clenching and releasing her fists, trying to dislodge it.

Her skin felt uncomfortably alive, prickling with awareness. She slowly paced the meadow, shaking her limbs until the feeling dissipated.

She tried recalling more of the dream. Nothing.

She focused on remembering Elzac's face. His warm brown eyes, radically white hair, sun-wrinkled dark skin, lips tight, worry narrowing his eyes.

His brown eyes, not white, Phe admonished herself, trying to displace the weird feeling she had when she replayed the moment his eyes flashed white to match his hair. She could not shake the last image.

It is a dream, that's all, she told herself.

First her reoccurring nightmare, and now this. *What is my subconscious trying to tell me?*

She kicked a small rock, watching it arc toward the forest edge. A niggling feeling clawed at her. She was missing too many pieces to this puzzle.

Phe stared up into the sky, scrunching her face in frustration. She exhaled loudly, reminding herself, *I've been lucky*.

Her life had been one unrelenting hardship after another. Stumbling into Elzac in Drykz Forest had been serendipitous on many levels.

Meeting someone who helps you save yourself from yourself was a rarity, but in the forest? Where no one was supposed to survive, or live? It was a miracle. Phe didn't let herself reminisce. Transformative as it was, it was a story all unto itself.

She settled herself on the ground again, gathered her

journal and wax pen, and started writing out her thoughts. She wrote uncensored, not caring if she was sensical. Steadily, she released the uneasy emotions bottled within her mind, impairing her objective. *Kyra.*

When she was done, Phe ripped the pages into tiny shreds, which she scattered like ashes in the forest.

3

Edva had wandered into the meadow, her sleeping form a large dark mass. The surrounding grassland thrummed with sound. Chirping crickets, wind ruffling the grass, and tree branches creaking, creating a soothing melody.

Normally, Phe would search for constellations and dream of being lost in the stars as she drifted to sleep. Not tonight. Dreaming of Elzac, with his flashing white eyes, had rattled her.

Her senses stretched in all directions. Her skin was sensitive to the feel of her clothes, the well-worn leather pants she wore constricting, her sheaths tourniquets.

Something shifted in the woods.

Phe swiveled toward the movement. Her senses heightened, skin tingling. From one moment to the next she became intimately aware of everything around her. Edva's soft breathing. The delicate rustling of grass under a slight breeze. The musky scent of the woods, the absence of insect chatter, and the malodorous smell of an unwashed person.

She scented the air again, confused. Trepidation rippled through her, the scent heavy.

Edva—who'd awoken with the sound—raised her head sharply. Her ears tipped forward stiffly, and her nostrils flared. She stomped a warning.

Phe cautiously crouched and slowly inched toward her staff, scanning the grassland. She didn't have far to look. A group of people stood, where a moment ago it was empty. Menace radiated from them. Automatically, she counted. *One, two, three . . .*

She entered the forest's edge, her hand locating her staff. Grateful she hadn't kicked it further in. *Seven, eight . . .*

Movement behind her had Phe shuffling forward, the faintest touch of a vine tickling her ankle. She glanced down. The vine hadn't followed her. *Fourteen. How have they crept up on me?*

Phe took a deep breath, feeling adrenaline rush through her, sharpening her awareness. A wave of calm followed. This? She trained for.

She grasped the smooth surface of her staff and stood, feeling the extra weight of its metal-tipped edges. She used the staff for training, wanting the additional weight and challenge, striving to best Bastion one day. She'd never used this form of weaponry in the field.

The sheaths of her weapons felt heavy, reminding her of their presence. The two on her calves held small throwing daggers and two wicked knives were strapped to her thighs. She hadn't worn her twin blades to avoid extra scrutiny. She tightened her grip on the staff, grateful it allowed her to fight at a distance, and rested her other hand on the pommel of a knife.

Edva charged the nearest person and delivered a strike. The thud reverted into the tense silence. Then she planted herself between Phe and the group, muscles rippling.

"Edva!" Phe commanded. "Safety!"

Edva trumpeted, extremely displeased with the command. As she passed the group, she fake charged them, before hovering at a distance, watching.

The horde—unfazed by Edva—stepped forward in synchronized movements, black eyes locked on her. Eyes that bulged out of emaciated faces with pale blue lines visible under pallid skin. Images similar to those that haunted her sleep. *Anala.*

She blinked and her chest tightened, making it hard to breathe.

"There you are," the group proclaimed, their monotone voices blending lifelessly. "We've been searching for you. Master claims you, and we are to bring you home. "

Phe focused on the nearest man, who showcased discolored and missing teeth. Underneath a patchy beard, his cheeks were hollow and, despite its brown tint, his skin looked ashen. His clothes hung loosely from his frame, holes in the seams of his arms, and legs. *Like my dream.*

"Who is your master?"

Ten fanned into a semi-circle around her, the others right behind them.

"Djall the Great Father," the group flanking her right side responded.

She scoffed. *The Great Father?* The tingling in her skin became an itch. "You can tell D-jay I am not a possession he can claim," Phe said, deliberately mispronouncing his name.

"D-Jall," they corrected her in unison. The closer they got, the stronger the smell.

She breathed through her mouth.

"Wayward child, voluntarily or not, you're coming with us."

The pressure under her skin was building painfully.

"Why would D-All want me?" Without taking her eyes off the men, she tossed her pack into the woods.

"D-Ja-ll adopts and embraces all with magic," a rearward man replied.

Phe laughed dismissively. "Magic doesn't exist." She ignored her twang of doubt.

She'd been told, repeatedly, magic didn't exist. But she'd also experienced unexplainable things, such as the forest at her back, House Nereid's tunnel system, or how Kyra could manipulate water.

They'd explained Kyra's abilities stemmed from her lineage. The house and forest were ancient, riddled with history and haunted by it. And so she had uneasily accepted long ago there was no magic.

The horde laughed in unison. It was creepy.

"So convenient," they drawled. "They've done half the job for me—hiding what we are—what you are. Leaving you and that princess of theirs," they paused as if searching for a name—and Phe didn't miss the change in their pronouns. "You know the one all you Xafarians bow to. Her Grace, Ms. Theanora the *Last*." They hissed mockingly, "Water Nymph, defenseless."

Phe's heart hardened. "Are you threatening Her Grace?"

"Ohh," they switched to a soothing, condescending tone. "Does that bother you?" They paused, then said, "Don't worry, you'll soon meet. I have a plan to bring her to the hearth as well."

Not if I have anything to say about it.

Their semi-circle tightened around her, placing them precariously close to the forest's edge. The ones on the side angled themselves toward her, their limbs loose and ready. She recognized fellow warriors in their movements, yet they were shaky. Weak.

"How did you find me?"

"Magic," they sneered.

The man to her left lunged.

She slammed her staff into his belly, then shifted quickly to hit him in the head. His lip split, blood splattering the forest as he tumbled over. A growl emitted from the woods behind her. The ground at her feet trembled with it.

She dropped to a crouch, barely avoiding being tackled by a woman, and jammed her staff into her legs, knocking her down, then hammered the staff into her thigh. Phe heard a crack, and the woman screamed, rolling into the forest and away from the fight.

They converged on her.

Phe bounced up, time slowing down for her. She used her staff as support and ran up the closest body. At his head, she twisted and delivered a roundhouse kick. His head whipped to the side as he fell. Phe stayed in the air with her momentum, kicking her way through the small huddle. When she dropped to her feet, five men and another woman were on the ground.

The woman's cries suddenly cut off.

One man stumbled to his knees, holding his head, and she rammed her staff into his neck. She shuffled forward, freezing when vines brushed past her ankles.

They rapidly wrapped around those on the ground, dragging them into the woods. In a matter of seconds, eight of Phe's attackers were gone.

Her skin was now burning as if she was on fire from the inside out.

The remaining woman charged. At the last second, she rotated to the right, rapidly kicking. Phe blocked the kicks with her staff, her arms vibrating with force, and side-stepped into the woods.

Before Phe countered, vines shot down from branches with baffling speed, wrapping around the woman's neck and hauling her up. Phe lunged around the woman's swinging legs, trying to avoid the same fate.

Vines brushed her arm and neck, their leaves moving with unnatural awareness. Phe hopped out of the forest. Her skin was blazing.

Three men were on her immediately. She had to fight the instinct to turn toward the greater danger, the forest.

She slid into a lunge, her staff an extension of her right arm, and jabbed the closest hip, swatting his lower spine with the metal point, then his head. Using her momentum, she jumped and twisted around the staff, clearing the first man to back-kick the second and land in a crouch again.

She then erupted up to strike down the third man. When she turned to finish the other two, they were already being pulled away, embraced by a mass of moving greens.

One left.

"You are well trained," he said with a grin, his flat tone incongruent. "I am eager for you to join us." He raised his hands and spread his fingers wide, aiming his open palms at her.

Her skin flared white-hot.

Vines wrapped around her, hauling her behind a tree as a burst of light left his hands. The tree trunk exploded, toppling toward her.

Phe fought to get to her knives, the mass of vines coalescing around her. She could barely move. The vines yanked her further into the forest's depths, scraping her painfully against protruding roots and rocks. *I'm going to die.*

An enraged roar detonated. It was all-encompassing, overwhelming. The ground rolled, or was she quaking? The heat pulsing inside her felt pressurized, threatening to burn her from the inside out.

The vines released her.

She scuttled across the forest floor, bursting into the clearing on her hands and knees.

The ground was moving, dirt bubbling up from the earth and refilling a hole. A void where the last man had stood.

Phe stopped at her overturned saddle and forced her legs under her. They shook. She gripped the saddle horn as her gaze roamed the heath.

"Seas! What was that?" she exclaimed, her voice octaves higher than normal.

A vine crawled up the side of her leg, and she stilled, one hand on a knife pommel when it tapped her shoulder. Hesitantly, she glanced at it.

Two vine leaves gently held her chin, the green blades fluttered with her breath, while other leaves nuzzled her neck. She barely breathed, waiting, as leaves brushed up and down her body as if checking for injury. When they finished, the vines withdrew, noiselessly reentering the forest.

It was moments like this Phe believed the forest was a sentient place.

She dropped to her knees, exhausted.

4

Phe opened the windows of House Nereid's carriage, letting in a breeze while she watched the wild fields surrounding Drykz Forest pass. The breeze did nothing to relieve the tension thrumming in her veins or stop the pulsing walls of the carriage from closing in on her. She slid her sweaty palms down her thighs, flattening the fabric of her day dress. Early this morning, she'd changed at the healing center while waiting for the carriage.

Magic wasn't real.

Yet one moment, the meadow had been empty, and the next, it wasn't.

How had her attackers appeared so suddenly? What was the light the man had created? How had he exploded a tree?

Phe forced herself to not fidget, to breathe through her urgency to get to Kyra's side and ensure she was safe.

Please, seas, let her be safe.

Bastion would have announced if something had happened. He'd redirected Shadow Unit and probably others to Oceanid to protect Kyra. He knew about the threat. She'd been safe yesterday.

But what if something happens today?

Guards surrounded Kyra, who lived in a palace of water. Water Kyra could use to fight.

Phe gulped. *Nope. Kyra is fine.*

Magic. Her attackers had thought Phe had magic. *They were crazy.* There was nothing special about Phe, other than her friendship with Kyra.

Now with Kyra, she understood their fascination. What Kyra could do because of her lineage was incredible. She understood how they could believe Kyra had magic. If she hadn't endured years where it had been drilled into Phe that magic didn't exist, she'd be a believer too. She'd accepted long ago that magic only existed in fairy tales.

Phe shifted to ease her discomfort. None of it made sense.

Djall may have plans for Kyra, but those people are dead now. Kyra should be safe.

Yet Phe had the distinct feeling there were more than the fourteen who attacked her. A lot more in his *fold.*

Who was Djall? Why would trained warriors let themselves deteriorate into such a state of weakness?

Phe looked out the window and the landscape passing by. She swallowed, recalling how the vines had slithered into the meadow, past the perimeter of the forest. *Had the forest helped me?*

The forest was chaos and brutality, capable of destruction and death. Yet it could also heal, grow, and create life. It was abnormal and haunted, yes. What it was not was protective, interactive, or sentient—the reality was it was just a forest.

Soon enough, the carriage was passing worn farmhouses and silos, fields filled with large stalks of corn, ankle-high bundles of lettuce, and more. When they reached the orange groves, she steadied herself by focusing on their rich fragrance.

As the carriage entered the city proper, the houses changed from single-story wood farmhouses to two- to three-story stucco and stone houses, stacked one on top of the other, so close Phe could run along the rooftops. The road adjusted from packed dirt to cobblestone, the clopping of horse's hooves now a sharp, hollow sound.

The city of Oceanid had been built on a hill, curving downward into a crescent-shaped port. The smell of the sea drifted in the breeze, accompanied by the occasional screeching of seagulls. At the wharf, wide stone roads had been built to accommodate transporting large amounts of commerce and food. Smaller streets and alleys interconnected, like a spiderweb, for townspeople to avoid the traffic.

The carriage took a series of turns, making its way to House Nereid. The homes they passed as they grew closer displayed their prosperity with green lawns and gardens growing in size. Rows of blossoming magnolia trees greeted Phe as they entered the grounds to House Nereid, the sweet scent filling the carriage.

She dug her nails into the dress material on her thigh, feeling the warmth of a knife hilt press into her skin.

Only a few more minutes.

Automatically, Phe's shoulders reached her ears, and she slouched forward, making herself smaller. Her internal struggle reared its ugly head, spiking her anxiety. She wanted to be fierce in Oceanid, unshakeable. But the younger, traumatized aspects of herself always seemed to overpower her, and she let them. So much so that Bastion had tested her intensively in Oceanid, concerned with her ability to perform.

But protecting Kyra was different from defending herself

against the nasties in Oceanid. She would do anything for Kyra.

When it came to herself, though, she's found herself trapped in a complex web. Her younger self, the version who was weak and sickly and had experienced years of trauma and shunning and social cruelty, was the person she was in Oceanid—except for behind closed doors with Kyra and Jallia.

Breaking this role was out of the question, even if she had to squeeze herself into the misfitting skin—which was feeling harder and harder to do. Maintaining her Lady Orphne image was the keystone to her role of protecting Kyra. It ensured she was underestimated and overlooked.

The cruel people who encircled Kyra made Phe feel small, helpless. Their method of attack was predominantly one she had no defenses for: words and exclusion, waves of judgment. Maybe it hurt because their malicious comments had reflected Phe's own thoughts and beliefs. Or maybe, deep down, she really wanted to be accepted. To belong. Instead, her younger version had silently fractured with every insult and sneer, and every time she returned, the echoes of those fissures vibrated through her.

It was a price she willingly paid to protect her best friend.

She closed her eyes, collecting and centering herself.

The carriage stopped. A horse nickered. When wood scraped, Phe opened her eyes, squinting into the glare of the sun.

Rosea's dull, reddish-brown hair captured her attention, the guard's upper body framed in the light, her features obscured in shadows. Rosea was Phe's personal bully in House Nereid.

Welcome home.

Phe lowered her gaze, caving further into herself.

"Lady Orphne, welcome back to House Nereid," Rosea's honeyed voice greeted, offering a hand to assist her out.

Phe didn't respond as she stood and gathered the front of her skirt, bracing herself to touch Rosea.

The contact felt like razors scraping her skin, biting into her and skittering up her arm. Her breathing hollowed.

Rosea held on tighter, and Phe fought the urge to wrench her hand free.

When Phe's foot was in the air, Rosea yanked.

Phe slammed into the hard cobblestone, hissing from the impact. Pain burst up her hands and knees, radiating through her.

The transformation from lethal to vulnerable cleaved deeper every time.

"Lady Orphne!" Rosea exclaimed. "Are you—"

"Oh my goodness! Phe! Are you all right?" Kyra said, her normal singsong tone deepening in concern.

Relief flooded every pore of Phe's body, drenching her in gratitude. *Thank the seas Kyra is safe.* Phe moved slowly, sitting on her heels, then shakily, she pushed the hair from her face.

"*Still*, I'll help you up," Rosea said. Hands grasped under Phe's right arm, the fabric pinching her, and roughly dragged her up.

Even with the layered clothing barrier, an uncomfortable burning sensation spread. Phe shrugged, trying to dislodge Rosea's grip.

Then Kyra was there, sliding a supportive arm around her waist. "You can let go. I've got her."

Rosea released her, tweaking her tricep painfully. "Lady Orphne, I am so sorry."

Phe bowed her head, swung her arm across Kyra's shoulders, and closed her eyes, frustrated with Rosea's false sincerity.

"You're injured!" Kyra sharply sang, her voice naturally lilting. "Rosea! Why is it that whenever you're around, Phe's injured?"

"Your Grace, I—"

"No, I'm not interested. I'll be speaking to Commander Elex. I don't care where he sends you, you are not welcome here. Leave." Kyra tugged Phe toward House Nereid's entryway, murmuring, "Let's attend to your injuries."

House Nereid was palatial, the glare of the descending sun reflecting off its white surface. The palace was a masterpiece crafted by Water Nymphs many generations back. The three-story structure was essentially one continuous fountain, with water flowing not just around it, but through every room.

"Jeez." A corner of Phe's mouth tilted up, cradling a scraped hand to her chest. "Your talons are out today."

Kyra's lips straightened into a compressed line. *Something's wrong.*

"I know you said it doesn't matter," Kyra nodded at Phe's hand, "that it's nothing, but she drew blood *again,* and I bet you have bruises. I know you have a role to play, and believe you have to endure this, but it doesn't mean I have to stand by and watch. Your silence is hurting you . . . and! I take offense to talons. If I were a creature, I'd be an octopus, and I just slapped her with my slimy, sticky tentacle."

Phe clamped her lips, swallowing the rising smile. "Slimy tentacle?"

"That's what I said."

Phe tightened the arm around Kyra's shoulders, warmth blossoming in her chest.

Kyra sagged into her. "Two months is too long. I don't know what crazy things the bastard makes you and your unit of—"

"Not my unit."

"—studs do."

"Don't forget about Kirzia."

"How can I? She's riveting and gorgeous and—"

"Yes, yes. If she ever gives you the eye, you'll reconsider. She even scares me."

Phe allowed Kyra to guide her under the archway, water cascading on either side and disappearing into the ground, continuing on to the large fountain in the middle of the drive.

"I'm not worried." Kyra squeezed Phe's waist, quieting her voice. "I got you."

"Always," Phe promised as her eyes landed on Velimir, who was leaning on the large, open mahogany door, watching them. He wore a salty, soured expression. She wondered if he was the reason Kyra's *tentacle* came out.

Phe understood Kyra's physical attraction to him. He was handsome, with an oval face, chiseled chin, short-trimmed blond hair, brown eyes, and a stunning smile he used often. But that is where his appeal stopped, or so it seemed to Phe.

"On that note, Bastion will be here soon. We're going to need to talk privately," Phe finished in a whisper.

Kyra let out an unhappy sound and pouted. "The bastard is coming?"

"Yes." Sunken faces with protruding black eyes fluttered by her vision. Phe shivered with unease.

"Welcome, Lady Orphne," Velimir greeted stiffly.

Phe weakly smiled in return. "Hello, Velimir. How lovely to see you."

"Vel," came Kyra's soft admonishment.

Phe glanced between the two. Kyra appeared to be imploring him, her green eyes wide. Velimir's jaw tightened, his own stare intense.

"I'm so glad to be home," Phe filled the silence, breaking their standoff.

"How did your treatments go?" Kyra inquired, subdued.

Phe shrugged, visibly sagging. "As expected."

"One day, I hope you won't need them anymore. I worry—"

"Your Grace, Lady Orphne!" a deep male voice yelled.

Kyra twisted, a brilliant smile lighting up her face. "Someone missed you," she whispered conspiratorially.

Phe sighed, suddenly finding a plant holder extremely captivating, and dreading any matchmaking maneuvers.

Kyra's tone swiftly changed. "Commander Elex, I'm glad to see you. Saves us time. Rosea Rosenthal, your second-in-command, is no longer welcome here, nor do I want to work with her again. Please see she leaves immediately."

"Your Grace, she is packing as we speak. Lady Orphne, are you all right?"

Phe peeked up at him.

He was tall at six-feet two-inches, well-proportioned, and every bit of him was muscle. His naturally tanned complexion was dark, enunciating his olive undertones and sun-bleached blond hair.

Phe met his hazel eyes for a moment, before timidly dropping hers. "I'm fine."

"I'm sorry you were injured. Are you feeling unwell? Unsteady?" Commander Elex persisted.

"Commander," Kyra patiently stated, "you're an observant man. You have, I'm sure, noticed that the only time Phe's injured is when Rosea is involved."

Commander Elex's stoic expression gave nothing away. "This will be addressed, I assure you." His gaze softened when it landed on Phe again. "Do you need your chair? Or shall I carry you?"

At Kyra's sudden sharp breath, Phe rushed to answer, "No need. I'm steady. See?" She detached from Kyra quickly to show exactly that, anxiously wrapping her arms around herself. "I'll be fine, thank you."

Kyra leveled Commander Elex with a look. "This problem should have been addressed well before now. Make sure it never happens again."

"Understood, Your Grace." Commander Elex paused, scanning Velimir a moment. "General Bastion has requested to meet in the Blue Parlor when he arrives."

"Then we'll wait for him there." Kyra linked arms with Phe, patting her hand. "Come, I'd like to order refreshments. I imagine you haven't eaten all day, Phe, and we've already had our dinner."

"Your Grace, I will escort you."

Kyra led them into the house, white marble floors with all shades of blue tiles depicting waves and encasing moving water. The house was a visual splendor. Twin staircases, one on each side of the room, met on the second-floor balcony, its railing made of intricate gold designs with sapphires sweeping up both stairways, across the landing, and open hallways on either side. A large chandelier hovered in the open space, its lights always on.

"Glendoll, would you please send for a tray of refreshments?" Kyra requested, spotting her butler. "Phe hasn't eaten, and I believe the general will be here momentarily as well."

"Yes, Your Grace. Where shall I have it delivered?"

"We will be in the Blue Parlor. Thank you."

The Blue Parlor was aptly named, decorated as it was in varying shades of blue. The room was large, prepared to hold social events of varying kinds. Enormous windows lined the wall, allowing the dimming evening glow to flood the space. Sconces and lights were lit, balancing the shadows.

Kyra steered them to the seating area in front of the magnificent fireplace, wood stacked and ready to be burnt should the need arise.

Phe sat on the large couch and watched Kyra drift to Velimir, pressing up against him and giving him a kiss. They quietly murmured to each other.

Phe heard the sharp clatter of horses approaching the house. Shadow Unit and General Bastion had arrived.

Elex squatted in front of Phe. Again, she felt as though he was scrutinizing her. "Where are you hurt?"

Phe pressed into the couch as far as she could. "It's nothing that won't heal. Truly, I'm fine." She met his gaze, forcing herself to keep it until he seemed satisfied.

He stood. "I will greet the general."

Phe nodded, watching him leave.

A part of her was relieved Bastion was here. That was a first. Even though he was a bastard, they shared the same goal, protecting Kyra, and he was extremely competent.

Phe glanced over at the couple cozying up together, wishing Velimir would leave. His presence meant they couldn't openly talk.

The door to the parlor opened, and Roar entered first, his deep auburn red hair disheveled from the ride, his clothing dusty. Phe felt Roar's scrutiny and ignored him, watching Bastion instead. His scar was taut, making it even more pronounced as he stalked into the room.

Bastion zeroed in on Velimir. "You, leave us."

Kyra's forehead wrinkled. "Bastion—"

"Your Grace, this is non-negotiable." His tone could freeze ponds, Phe thought. "He leaves. Now."

Velimir, clearly shocked, sputtered. "Excuse me, sir."

Bastion emanated cold aggression.

Phe watched. It was fascinating to see Bastion in action, especially when he wasn't directing his hostility at her.

Velimir huffed, his cheeks reddening. "I'll retire to my rooms," he announced, haughtily striding out.

Kyra straightened, outraged. "Bastion, you didn't have to be so rude."

Bastion's features softened. "Your Grace, this is a matter of your security. It takes priority above the feelings of your current admirer."

Bastion swiveled to Phe, softness replaced with a cold, piercing stare. He dropped to a squat at her feet. Roar moved closer too, both their gazes uncomfortably intense.

"Report," Bastion commanded, grabbing her arms, inspecting the skin of her hands. She had minor scrapes scattered on both palms.

Searing pain emanated from his harsh touch.

"I fell outside," Phe mumbled. She retreated further into the couch, blinking rapidly and trying to dislodge his grip.

"Hm."

Her skin webbed with discomfort, waves of agony rolling up her arm.

Bastion dropped her arms to grasp her neck, holding her still while studying her.

Phe's vision clouded, and her breathing stopped. The opulence of the room bled and faded until what was left was a small dirt hut. She was no longer seated, but suspended in the air, grasping desperately at the large hands wrapped around her throat, squeezing the breath from her. Her tiny fingers clawed at them, scouring the flesh.

Her fist connected with Bastion's jaw, hard, shattering the intrusive memory.

Pain blossomed in her knuckles; this she welcomed. When Bastion didn't immediately release her, she kneed him.

"Bastion!" Kyra surged forward, wedging herself between them. "You forget yourself. She is not yours to command!"

"Don't. Touch. Me." Pure rage infused Phe, prickling her scalp. She sucked in a breath, fighting the vise constricting her lungs, glaring at him.

Bastion rubbed his face. "Are you going to make me repeat myself?"

Phe burrowed further into the couch, avoiding contact with Kyra. "I was ambushed last night."

Kyra flipped around, anger melting to shock. "What?"

Roar's soft blue gaze connected with her. "She's clear to me, sir."

Things clicked.

"Are my eyes black?" Phe scowled.

"What happened? And can't you see she doesn't have black eyes?" Kyra persisted, tension tightened her features. Lines etched themselves into her forehead and the corners of her eyes.

Phe glowered at the men. "They aren't worried about those kinds of black eyes."

Kyra slid into her chair, facing Phe. "I only know of one type of black eye. Explain."

Someone knocked at the door. Kyra sang a little too high-pitched, "Come in!" To the room, she said, "It's our refreshments."

The door opened to a servant, who wheeled in a cart laden with quartered sandwiches, a plate of tiny dark chocolate bites, a large teapot, and multiple teacups.

"Thank you, Vale," Kyra offered, the rumbling sound of the wheels on the wood floor loud in the tense room.

Once Vale exited, Bastion demanded, "Report. I won't ask again."

"Kyra's in danger," Phe blurted, worry pricking her skin.

"From the beginning."

"I arrived at my campsite at dusk. I use a clearing abreast of Drykz Forest."

She ignored Kyra's inhale. Kyra did not want Phe near Drykz Forest because of the incident.

"I'd settled in when I —" Her eyes met Bastion's, "— heard a weird sound." Phe paused, recalling the strangeness of her attackers' appearance. "They came out of nowhere. Fourteen men and women in total.

"Hollowed faces, pale skin and bone. Terrible body odor. Their eyes were the most disturbing. Bulging black masses. No white visible at all."

Kyra shifted, her anxiety palpable. "Ah, black eyes." Kyra delicately picked up the teapot and, without asking if anyone wanted any, poured.

Phe continued. "When they spoke, they spoke as one. As if one person talking through all of them, if that makes sense. It was bizarre. They claimed me as if I was a possession." Phe pinned Kyra in a somber gaze. "They claimed to have plans for you."

Kyra rose, as if she hadn't heard the last sentence, and handed teacups and saucers to Bastion and Roar.

"Thank you, Your Grace." Bastion carefully took the offering. "Did they say anything else?"

"Only that they were there to acquire me, because of

magic, and to bring me to their master, Djall. They attacked, I defended."

"They accused you of having magic?" Roar asked incredulously.

"They did," Phe grimly responded. "What bothers me the most? I do not know what happened at the end. What I saw was the last man create a sphere of light with his hands and throw it at me, but that's impossible." She hesitated, censuring the story. "Yet whatever he threw caused the tree behind me to fall. Then he disappeared. One moment he was there, the next a hole in the ground was refilling itself."

"Inconceivable." Bastion put down his tea.

Kyra handed Phe tea, the delicate china radiating heat. Phe carefully grasped the fragile handle, taking a moment to smell its soft rose aroma before sipping from it, the hot liquid soothing.

"The forest consumed someone?" Kyra arched her eyebrows.

Phe shrugged. "I have no idea, really. He was there, then he wasn't."

"Drykz Forest has been doing the impossible for centuries now," Roar supplied.

Roar sauntered to the window and gazed out, cup in hand. Kyra poured herself a small bowl of water, placing her hand in it, letting the water soothe her.

Phe nervously tugged at her amulet.

"Tell me about their fighting technique," Bastion instructed brusquely.

"Competent." Phe reflected. "They converged on me in small groups, but slow. Starved. If they had been in fighting shape, there's a possibility I would not be here now."

"Did you have skin-to-skin contact?" Roar asked.

"No. But clarity on this illness would be helpful."

"The important question here is, why you?" Bastion inquired.

"I've considered this all day," Phe admitted but she'd ended up nowhere. There was nothing special about her. "I don't know. Do you?"

"I want to understand what the forest did. Tell me more," Bastion commanded, ignoring her question.

She did, censuring out details of how the forest directly helped her. When finished, all she got from Bastion was a distracted, "Interesting."

"Tell me about your attackers," Roar said. "What were they wearing? Describe everything."

Phe pulled up the memory. "Tattered clothing, old, thin, and worn into holes in places. They were emaciated—"

"I want to know about Djall." Kyra interrupted. "What do you know about him? And we need to understand what this *illness* is."

"Your Grace, recently I was informed of sightings with this description in Xafara. Right now, we are information-gathering and once the first reports from throughout Xafara are in, I will inform you." Bastion stood, signaling the end of the conversation.

"For now, I am considering this a direct threat to your well-being. I am increasing your security. Consider all social events canceled until further notice."

Phe was in utter agreement. There had been something very wrong with those people.

"We will attend Princess Attiva's ball. That is nonnegotiable," Kyra said firmly.

Bastion strode to the door and placed his hand on the knob. "It'll be the last event you attend until I deem the threat gone. *Neither* of you are to leave House Nereid. And send Velimir home. Otherwise, I will." His predatory gaze narrowed, pinning Phe. "I'll arrange for the ambassadors to come here for the meeting. I am very interested to see what we'll learn about your heritage. And Phe, I haven't forgotten about your assault." Then he was gone.

Roar pushed off the windowsill, sauntering after Bastion. "Lady Orphne, I'm glad you're okay. I'll take my leave, Your Grace."

5

"Geez." Kyra released a tense breath, pulling her hand from the bowl of water. "He's such a bastard."

"I know." Phe shoved aside Bastion's threat of retaliation. No use worrying about it.

"I hate when he acts all authoritarian," Kyra ranted. "Does he think this is a dictatorship?"

Phe sighed deeply. "I always force myself to remember he does everything for your protection. If he's concerned, we should be too."

"Ugh. You know I hate it when you defend him," Kyra said, flopping her head in her hands.

"Not defending," Phe corrected, palms up.

"Do you think I'm in danger?" Kyra's voice wavered.

"They mockingly named you and said they have plans for you. Yes, I'm highly concerned."

Kyra groaned, peeking faded green eyes through her fingers.

"It's why you have me," Phe reminded her gently.

"Yeah, but I don't want you endangered either. Why is

the bastard arranging a meeting with ambassadors to discover your genealogy?"

"Ah, the meeting is for both of us. He mentioned it to me yesterday," Phe said. "I'm not sure why there's a sudden interest in my lineage."

"I presume they're from Shalexum and the bastard provided no details."

"Your Grace, your deduction skills are superb." Phe winked at her.

Kyra tucked her blond locks away, sarcasm dripping. "I don't know how you manage. He blatantly ignored all your questions while he expected responses to his interrogation. I'd be pulling my hair out."

"He's my greatest teacher . . . and, of course, a bastard," Phe offered, snatching a sandwich. "I think we should search through your books to see if there're any references to magic," she said around a mouthful.

"I hate when you call him your greatest teacher." Kyra slumped into the chair. "I don't want to send Velimir away," she whined. "I really like him."

Phe took a huge bite, chewing slowly and contemplating her response. After the way Velimir greeted her in her own home today, it thrilled her he'd soon be gone. Phe wouldn't admit it, but she was thankful Bastion had kicked him out. She couldn't understand what Kyra saw in him, but then again, when Kyra was in love, she formed blind spots.

Phe would have to talk with her about them and fess up to how much she disliked him. She dreaded it because who knew how Kyra would respond? Would she become angry with Phe? Push her away, creating a rift in their friendship? Phe really didn't want conflict in their friendship when there was a threat looming.

"I'm sorry this is happening." The statement encompassed everything, Phe's sincerity ringing true.

"You know the pressure I'm getting to have children. Yet every partner I find, Bastion drives away. I've been dying to talk to you about Velimir, though."

"Maybe he has another partnership in mind." Phe smiled playfully around her food. "He seems pretty intent on you and those Shalexum ambassadors having a *relationship*."

Kyra laughed violently, tears springing to her eyes. "Seas, Phe! I can't imagine the salty general playing matchmaker."

"Speaking of relationships, it sounds like you and Velimir got really close while I was away."

A brilliant smile lit Kyra's face. "We did," she breathed, sitting up. "But I feel guilty wanting to talk about it now when you've been attacked, are exhausted, survived two months of his training, and had one of your flashes. Are you really okay?" Kyra leaned forward, inspecting her.

"I'm fine. I'd love to hear, don't feel guilty. Let's go to your training room. We can talk more freely, and I want to dig through some of your books."

"Of course. Let me help you."

In the hallway, a small army met them, falling into pace with them. Phe was surprised to see Ihrone and Orc with them. Kyra informed them where they were going and then the only sound was the soft treads of footsteps and gurgling water.

The wide hallway snaked into the depths under House Nereid and dead-ended at a set of massive doors, reaching twenty feet high and fifteen feet wide, with intricately carved designs of waves, sea creatures, and merpeople.

Kyra placed her palm into the indented slot on the door,

her hand disappearing in the curve of a wave. The lock audibly released, and the door opened.

"This is where we leave you for now," Kyra announced.

"Your Grace, we are to accompany you everywhere," one guardswoman said.

"Since no one can access this room but me, I will be safe within. You can wait outside."

Kyra ushered Phe in, then firmly closed the behemoth doors behind them.

The lights in Kyra's training room sparkled into existence.

The first wave of lights resembled stars winking to life within the stalactites hanging forty feet above them. The second surge was more powerful, these lights suspended in an extraordinary display of chandeliers. Even though Phe didn't believe in magic, she had no other words to describe this.

The final awakening of the cave seemed to come from everywhere as if there was a sun that rose every time they entered. Its brightness illuminated the ground. The light below and the twinkling above gave an impression of both day and night in the cave.

They both walked in sacred silence: Phe overwhelmed with awe, Kyra connecting deeply with the water. This was their way each time they entered this space. Kyra started stripping to her ever-present swimsuit as she neared the water.

Brilliantly colored mosaic tiles depicting a scene of a stream corralled them to a pond that led to a large, flowing underground river.

On one side of the circular pond area were bookshelves, housing Kyra's collection of precious books, telling her everything she needed to know about being a Water

Nymph. The fact the books remained in a state of perpetual dryness was another oddity. In front of the shelving was a large conference table accompanied by eight comfortable chairs. Past the tiled area lay a darkened graveyard of rock formations Phe had never explored.

Phe visited the washroom, the only structure in the cave, then disrobed and climbed into a simple black swimsuit. Kyra glanced at her when she emerged. She was already floating. Her wet blond hair fanned out behind her, and her eyes glowed emerald green.

"I've been thinking." Phe walked into the cold water, then dove in and waited for the telltale tingle that signaled Kyra was warming the surrounding water. "What if what you do, and all of this," Phe relaxed as the water supported her as it did Kyra, "is magic?"

"Phe . . ." Kyra sounded a little exasperated. Phe peeked at her and saw Kyra's lips pressed together in a straight line.

"I was ambushed because of *magic*. I think it's appropriate to question."

"You know I don't know the answer to that. If my mother were alive today, I'm sure she'd tell us," Kyra said sharply.

Phe wiped her face. "I'm sorry."

"I'm sorry too. I know you're asking because of what's happening."

They floated, neither speaking until Phe probed, "Do you still want to tell me about Velimir?"

"Yeesss!" Kyra glowed. "Velimir has been amazing," Her eyes softened. "He's thoughtful, considerate, attentive. Interested in everything I do and wants to be with me all the time. It's been so easy to talk to him." Her lips curved into a smile, and her face took on a dreamy look. "I feel this magnetic attraction to him. A pull . . . I want to be with him, touch him, all the time."

"Oh, lust, welcome," was Phe's sarcastic reply, which was met with a small splash of water. Phe sputtered, laughing.

"Seriously, Phe," Kyra playfully scolded.

"By the tides, I missed you," Phe said through her laughter. "I can't help it."

"Tell me about it. I had no one to talk to about all the fun stuff Vel and I've been doing. I'm bursting." Kyra raised her arms, gathering her hair at her neck and twisting it together.

Phe's laughter died when she noticed the finger-shaped bruises on the inside of one of Kyra's forearms. "What happened?"

Kyra glanced at her, frowning. "What?"

"You're bruised," Phe pointed out. Kyra was clumsy, but clumsy didn't leave finger-patterned bruising.

Kyra peeked at the marks, her expression shuttering. "Must have gotten this while he had me up against the wall today." Kyra's normal singsong was off pitch.

Phe took a deep breath. "You're lying to me."

"No," Kyra denied defensively, her green eyes flashing. "I was against the wall today."

"And?"

"We were passionately discussing something, and one thing led to the *other*." Her face brightened, inferring intimacy. Yet her smile was tight, and her joyful, excited gaze was missing.

Phe swam toward the shore. "What I don't understand is your reaction and what you're not telling me. Don't bother denying; I know."

"Grr," Kyra growled, face grim, and went under.

Phe waited. When Kyra didn't reappear, she took a seat on the ledge, letting the water lap at her feet.

Kyra resurfaced, water streaming in rivulets down her face. "Fine," she spat angrily. "It happened right as you arrived. Velimir doesn't like the idea of sharing me, even if it's with my sea sister. He doesn't understand our relationship."

Phe gave her a look. "Sharing?"

"He likes our alone time."

Careful to keep her tone neutral, Phe said, "I'm sure he does. Sharing is hard." *For a toddler.* "I need to know what happened." *Did Kyra's guards see this? Was this the reason Bastion kicked Velimir out?*

"We were coming to greet you. He was upset, he's passionate, and he pushed me into the wall. A guard pulled him off me immediately. You know how they're always around." Kyra cleared her throat. "He doesn't know you yet . . ."

Anger bubbled up inside her, and Phe took a deep breath, trying to settle herself. It didn't work. "No one has the right to shove someone against a wall." Fear slithered its way into her heart. Everything about Velimir screamed warnings, yet Kyra refused to acknowledge this.

Phe gave Kyra a *what-the-hell-are-you-thinking* look. How could her friend be so brilliant and yet so blind?

Over the last fourteen years, she had trained extensively with Bastion to become the last barrier between Kyra and any aggressor.

Phe could easily arrange an accident for Velimir.

But doing anything to Velimir would hurt Kyra. And Phe's heart was telling her there were certain battles she could fight for Kyra, and others she had to watch from the sidelines.

This was one of them.

"He didn't mean to and apologized immediately," Kyra said earnestly, riding the wave of hopeful belief. "He got—"

Disregarding what her heart was saying, Phe interrupted. "I don't care. If he tries something like that again, I'll show him what nightmares are truly made of."

"Phe, don't you think you're overreacting?" Kyra's face slackened with shock as she rose from the water.

"You think I'm overacting? When I leave you, I'm not going to some retreat to be pampered. I've dedicated my life to training with *Bastion* to keep you safe." Phe seethed. "And when I'm gone, someone who professes to care for you bruises you? Because he doesn't want to *share*?"

Phe stood. "And I won't even bring my childhood into this." She crossed to the bookshelf, throwing the words over her shoulder. "It doesn't change the fact that if he hurts you again, I'll make sure he becomes familiar with pain."

6

Phe's jaw was so tight she had to flex it to unclench it, which she did while she twisted her hair and wove it into a knot at her neck.

She blindly grabbed a book, a worn light blue, soft leather cover, with rough, thick black stitching. The leather was indented with stamped waves running along its border. She flipped it open and glared at its table of contents.

Of course, none of the headings were labeled "magic." Instead, there was some nonsense about connection, communicating, understanding the power of, etc.

Phe restrained herself from slamming the book down. Deliberately, she slowed her movements and gently placed it on the table. It wasn't the book's fault she was livid.

Phe avoided looking in Kyra's direction, hearing only the rush of the underground river. She pulled another book, the sage green of its leather cover catching her eye. This time, with a deep centering breath, Phe read the title, *Intricacies of Water*.

She turned to the table and sat in one of its chairs,

setting the book in front of her. If she had to read every book in this library, she would.

Opening the book to a midpoint, she buried her nose into its pages, inhaling deeply. The musky scent of old books always relaxed her.

She ignored Kyra's snort and scanned the book's drawings. They were different depictions of water.

How many different ways does one need to see water?

She systematically skimmed the chapters. She learned water was in all living creatures and a powerful enough Water Nymph could connect and manipulate the water within bodies.

Phe sat back in her chair. *So that's how Kyra saved me that time I nearly bled out. She must have forced the blood back into my body, circulating it.*

Wow.

When she'd finished, she slid the light blue book over. Running her calloused fingertips across the waves, feeling the difference between the rigid, inked leather compared to the rest of the cover. Softness versus hardness, Kyra versus her.

She opened the book and stuffed her nose into it. *Smells so good.* Her tension eased for a moment.

"Are you going to do that to all of them?" Kyra had made her way out of the water and stood at the edge of the table, her swimwear dry. She gave Phe a tentative smile, as if offering a branch of reconnection.

"I might." Phe leaned back in her chair, arms crossed, lips pressed tight.

"It's going to take you forever. What are you looking for?" Kyra's forehead wrinkled.

"References to magic."

"You know," Kyra walked along the table, her half-lidded gaze indifferent, "I have read all of these books, cover to cover, multiple times. There is no mention of magic." She reached the bookshelves and selected several books.

"Maybe not overtly, but what about inference?" Phe persisted, curling her fingers around the top of the book, the edges digging into her skin.

"I am willing to be open-minded." Kyra pulled out the chair next to her and deposited her armload of books. "I've never searched for references to magic; it's possible I missed something."

Phe felt another load of tension lift from her shoulders. "Thank you."

"Puh, don't thank me. I know if I don't help, we'll be here forever." Kyra grinned and opened a book.

A companionable silence descended between them, the song of the river gurgling a relaxing background noise, accompanied by the ruffling of pages. They worked like this until Phe found a sketch showing the exact hand positioning and stance the man from the forest had taken. The caption read, "Assume a combat stance," and was a pose taught to beginners to direct one's capabilities in an attack.

Phe read the book's title aloud. "*Beginner to Advanced Teachings in Water Manipulation.* Look, the man took that exact posture when he did his hand thing." Phe slid the book over for Kyra to see.

Kyra skimmed the chapter. "There's no mention of magic."

Phe's stomach growled, reminding her she'd only had a half sandwich and some nuts. She picked up another book and reread a sentence that had been niggling at her. "I know. In this introduction, it says, 'Learning your elemental capabilities is important and will be tested within and against other branches in regard to enhancing your skills and assessing your levels.'"

Phe tapped the sentence. "Against the other branches? What do you think they're referencing?"

Kyra shook her head, crinkling her forehead in thought. "I don't know. I've never thought about it, but now that you point it out, elemental capabilities implies other elements."

Tired, hungry, and feeling that they were grasping at straws, Phe pushed the book away. The mention of magic was either elusive or it really was non-existent.

She closed her eyes, recalling the attack. Her skin crawled in remembrance of the fireball, and the forest's vines. Tingles rippled along her spine, down her arms and legs, and into her fingers and toes, just like before. "Did I tell you I had this weird skin-tingling feeling during the attack?"

"No." Kyra perked up. "Describe."

"I'm not sure I can. My skin was tingly, and I felt this pressure . . . hard to articulate, and it hurt. I felt on fire and as if something wanted out of my body."

Kyra jumped up in a burst of energy, rummaging through the pile of books on the table. She yanked one out and quickly flipped through the pages. When she found what she was looking for, she started excitedly reading.

"'When someone refuses or is disconnected from their capabilities, there will be somatic symptoms. Many describe this as their skin prickling, or odd sensations traveling under their skin, but not limited to the skin.'

"'Each person has their own unique way of this manifesting in these rare instances, with one consistency. Without their capabilities, there is a stillness within them. Descriptions have included an inner pressure seeking re-expansions.'

"'Other reports," Kyra continued, "include migraines

and debilitating pain in parts of their bodies. One account describes having their capabilities negated as the most painful experience in their life.'

"'One survivor claimed it was as if they were attempting to amputate one limb," she read, "but all were removed. At first, I couldn't do anything. I was on fire, begging for death. For the longest time, there were phantom twinges. It felt as if something wanted to burst through me, yet was kept imprisoned in my body. Pushing at my skin daily . . . eventually receding into bursts of reminders when it was activated before returning to dreaded stillness.'

"'Other changes included how I sensed the world around me. Everything became duller, color appeared faded and drained, the noises muffled, taste bland, everything less vibrant. I could no longer feel my family.'

"'When they neutralized my abilities, they took an essential part of me. I lost access to pieces of myself I never realized were connected to my capabilities and were irrevocably gone. I no longer am whole.'"

Kyra was beaming, green eyes flashing with excitement. "A little more dramatic than your description, yes, but it said the sensations decreased with time. You've complained about this for years." Kyra closed the book and tossed it on the table.

"I have not!" Phe denied. If she had *capabilities*, then she would be special, like Kyra. If she was special, her family would have protected her. She wouldn't have fallen into the hands of someone like Grum. Someone would've loved her, raised her.

"Ah, yes." Kyra tapped her forehead. "All the time, actually."

Phe shook her head, refusing to engage.

"I can't believe I never connected this! When we met,

you complained of it whenever we came in here, and again when you first started working with Shadow Unit. In fact, I bet you experienced it in the water a moment ago."

Phe didn't answer, narrowing her eyes. She'd experienced it. But her having these . . . "elemental capabilities"? No. Phe drew the line there. She wasn't special. Life had taught her this lesson repeatedly and harshly. "I don't like the direction you're taking."

"Please, listen to me. What if my capabilities *are* magic?" Kyra asked, eyes beseeching. "I have the ability to control the element of water, as my books say. But you—and the attacker who created light with his hands—have a different type of capability, *magic*." She bounced in her chair.

Phe balked. *How could I have magic? Impossible. Non-negotiable. Not special.*

"You're struggling with this." Kyra sat on the table, smile dying, eyes dimming.

Phe's chest ached, and a vise tightened around her throat. "I came here to research if magic actually existed, not to hypothesize whether I had it." She flicked imaginary dirt off the table.

"Help me understand what's going on in your head," Kyra soothed.

A memory of Grum's cunning light brown eyes, mob of sandy blond hair, and cruel smile sprung up. The grip he had on her arm, painfully tight as he held her, bruising her. His hot breath scored her neck, and she held completely still, ignoring the blood running down her temple and her pulsing split lip, tensely waiting. *"You could've done better, much, much better."* His disapproval radiated menacingly, his grip intensifying. *"Why do you make me punish you?"* Phe's breathing became labored. *"Look at me, you worthle—"*

Phe cleared her throat and shoved this memory aside,

searching for memories before Grum, only to find a blank, shimmering canvas. She would have mattered to someone if she had magic, right?

Kyra had a tremendous amount of protection and support. She grew up idolized, cherished. Wouldn't Phe have had something similar? People who cared about her? Wanted her?

"If I had capabilities, like you, shouldn't I have mattered to someone?"

"Oh, Phe." Kyra pulled her into a tight hug. "You do matter. You matter to me. I even suspect you matter to Bastion."

Phe laughed disbelievingly. "Really?"

Kyra pulled back, holding her shoulders, and her gaze softened. "I don't think he would ever admit to it, but yes. You forget I observed him when you almost died. He was affected."

"He was probably annoyed."

"Nevertheless, the few people who get the privilege of knowing you see your fire, your resiliency, and your kindness. *But* I want you to see those two aren't related. Your worth as a person has nothing to do with whether or not you have magic."

"I understand what you're saying," Phe started, "but struggle with believing it for myself."

"I will believe for you until one day you will too." Kyra paused, her attention on the pile of books. "Why don't we call it quits for the day?"

"Agreed. I'm exhausted." Phe forced herself to gather books, helping Kyra organize them. "And starving."

Once they'd re-dressed, Kyra slipped her arm into Phe's, and they strolled toward the exit. "Sea sister, I love you. You know that, right?" She squeezed Phe's arm.

Phe smiled sadly. "I love you too."

When they got to the doors, Kyra stood back, gesturing toward the indentation. "I think you should try to open it."

"Kyra," Phe said warily.

"I know, but what if the door opens for you?" Kyra's gaze glistened with hope.

Phe looked from Kyra to the door, then shook her head slightly. "I'm not sure I want to know."

"Could you please try for me? If it doesn't work, you don't have magic, and no harm was done," Kyra rationalized.

"Isn't there a reason I haven't tried this in the past?" Phe delayed, shoulders creeping to her ears.

Kyra shrugged. "Yes, because we never thought this could be a possibility." She widened her eyes and pummeled Phe with her best impression of a puppy-dog gaze, the one Phe always had a problem saying no to. "*Please*, I have a feeling about this."

On a heavy sigh, Phe said, "Fine," then placed her hand into the indentation.

Immediately, her body felt as though she were being torn apart, each limb screaming in agony. Pain exploded through her, and before she could even gasp, her world went dark.

7

Everything hurt. She'd thought her skin had been on fire before, but it was no comparison to the blaze in her veins now. She was wrapped in darkness. Weightless. Connected into the infinity of shadows.

Waves of vibrant colors swirled around her, expanding and constricting with her heartbeat. The raging inferno inside her was both consuming and excruciating.

"Transformation," Elzac's soft voice broke the defeating silence, "can be as easy as shedding layers or as painful as needed to induce and complete the change. The choice is always in the transformer."

"El . . . zac," she wheezed.

"Don't fight it, Phe." The woodsy, smoky smell of Elzac filled her senses. She felt his cold, leathery hand on her face. Two white orbs appeared, glowing. She narrowed in on them. Half of Elzac's features morphed around them, his matching white hair, furrowed brow. Their eyes locked.

Another wave of nauseating heat swept through her. "I'm dying."

"Isn't this what transformation is about? Death of what

no longer serves you, a rebirth?" The cold from his hand seeped into her skin.

The pressure in her chest contracted. Her spine arched in pain. ". . . want to die," she stuttered, wanting the suffering to end. *Why won't the pain end?*

"Some do die when they resist transformation, clinging to old versions of themselves, becoming the living dead. But," he placed his cold hand flat on her chest, "you will live."

There was no pain or discomfort at his touch. In fact, the coolness of his hand was an icy balm. It countered the building pressure, easing the constriction in her lungs and allowing her to drag in a breath, then another, while fire and ice battled within her.

Her hands covered his, holding his hand to her chest. "What is happening to me?"

"You, my dear, are transforming. Awakening what can no longer be suppressed."

"Awakening?" She recalled her dream of him at Drykz Forest. The ice retracted. His gentle hand was now a fist against her chest.

A different searing pain flooded her senses, and the glow of his eyes faded. His response lost.

Light blossomed into her vision, and in place of Elzac, glowing mossy-green eyes hovered closely over her. Hands pressed her into the hard floor, their pressure breaking ribs.

Instinctively, Phe grabbed a hand, twisted it, and slid from underneath the other hand, ignoring the searing pain radiating from her chest through her torso. Her feet made it under her as she captured the throat of the hand's owner. He froze, his pulse beating frantically in her palm.

Orc.

She stilled, too, taking in the vibrance of his eyes, the

light pink flush to his cheeks, his mouth slightly open, the beads of sweat on his forehead and bald head. She released her grip, stumbling backward.

Then the noise hit. So much noise. Water rushing, someone crying, voices, ruffling clothes, shuffling feet—each a dagger stabbing into her.

She clapped hands to her ears and twisted, realizing she was surrounded.

Her gaze landed on Roar, whose deep auburn red hair seemed to shine and his blue eyes glowed so brilliantly it hurt to look at. Kyra was on her knees, tears streaming, mouth hanging open. Phe had never seen her green eyes and blond hair so awash with color. As though they had been dull before, and Phe was only now seeing the true vibrancy of the world.

Why are they all staring at me?

She tried to inhale and couldn't. She dragged a hand to her throat, then chest; pain exploded. Her hand dropped.

Her chest throbbed and her legs gave out, her knees slamming into the stone walkway, jarring her.

Transformation is bullspit, she thought, dropping to all fours, unable to hold herself up.

"Phe!" Kyra's high-pitched panicked singsong forced Phe's attention to her.

The light reflected off of Kyra's hair, and Phe closed her eyes. It was too much light, too much color. She felt the granules of small loose stones under her palms and knees. A chill seeped up from the ground into her calves and hands.

She fought for another breath. Her pain reduced to a pulsing, scorching sensation, fighting to burn through the boundary of her skin. *Is this shedding layers?* It was unbearable.

"Get out of my way," Kyra commanded.

Phe dropped to her forearms, squinting in Kyra's direction. Kirzia was blocking Kyra, her raven-black hair iridescent in the light.

Phe's stomach heaved, the clenching of her muscles around her chest blackened her vision, and the next thing she knew she was on her back, staring up at the starry, ethereal lighting in the cavern.

"Phe." Orc appeared. "I'm going to touch you." She felt cold fingers on her neck, icicles scraping her burning flesh, feeling her pulse.

She couldn't peel her gaze from the ceiling. She searched for the celestial staircase within the twinkling lights.

"Geez, Phe, you're burning up."

Roar crouched next to her, blocking her view, and addressed Orc. "How can I help?"

"Don't block the light," Phe choked out.

"Phe," Roar said, his response edgy, "you are not dying on us."

"We need to drop her temperature," Orc said.

"The river," Roar suggested.

"*You* want to keep *me* from *her*?" Kyra's voice had a touch of crazy to it.

"Your Grace," Orc interceded, "we need to bring her temperature down. Would you call the river to her?"

Water surged toward them, the sound soothing and frightening simultaneously, encircling Phe in an arctic embrace, intensifying every sensation, then deadening them. The water soothed Phe's fire.

Roar slid his arms under hers, dragging her body flush with his, and lifted her chin.

Kyra was there.

"Don't touch her chest," Roar warned.

Kyra's gaze narrowed to daggers. "I know."

"What happened?" Phe uttered throatily.

"I'm so sorry, Phe." Kyra appeared pained. "I'm so sorry. When you touched the indentation, you were thrown." She gulped. "It's bad." Kyra gently washed Phe's cheek, her hand coming away red. Blood.

"I'll be all right," Phe whispered, exhaustion sweeping through her. "I'm just so . . ."

8

The soft chirping of birds woke her. Phe dragged her eyes open. It was dark, with small shafts of light trickling in. She recognized her room. The gilded, wall-sized painting of the most magnificent view in all of Xafara hung opposite her bed. It was titled *Ascension*.

It depicted a night scene from Uklesa's famous terrace, Gateway To The Stars, which overlooked the Sryln Sierras. The striking mountains, with imposing evergreens, were cast in stunning detail. Moonlight cascaded down, illuminating clouds dancing within treetops, and showcasing the spectacular illusion of a staircase of stars leading into celestial paradise.

Often Phe would gaze upon the painting, wishing she could walk up the stairs and into the vast starry universe.

She inhaled shallowly. Bursts of searing pain traveled alongside her breath.

What happened to me?

The sound of rhythmic breathing surrounded her. Kyra was in bed next to her, her lustrous hair splayed on the comforter. A shimmering cyan aura encompassed her.

Phe blinked. The aura disappeared, yet the vibrancy of colors remained.

Craning her neck, she scanned herself, taking inventory. *All limbs present.* She wiggled her toes. *And they work.* Weakly, she dragged a hand to her chest and hissed silently.

Slowly, a memory formed.

She wanted to sink into the contours of the plush mattress, yet the pressure in her bladder created an urgency she couldn't ignore.

She glanced at the two others in the room.

Orc and Roar. They'd pulled chairs close to the bed, positioning themselves to monitor her. A crystal blue aura shimmered around Roar. Phe stared at it, unblinking, and it dissipated.

She shook her head, trying to clear her mental fuzziness.

Roar's head hung slightly to the left, held in an awkward position by the chair's cushioned backing. His legs sprawled wide, arms resting limply on his thighs.

His shoulder-length deep auburn hair had been pulled back into a loose bun at his neck; stragglers had fallen free and framed his face. She could see scruff on his jaw, some of it deeper, more vibrant red than his hair.

He had a strong jaw with matching, proportional features, a small crescent-shaped scar on his right temple, and a slightly crooked nose. It broke up the perfection of his features and enhanced his attractiveness.

The glimmer of mossy green encasing Orc drew Phe's attention to him, yet it was gone before she could study it.

Orc had a pillow crammed between himself and the chair. His mouth drooped slightly, his arms crossed loosely at his chest. He was built wider in the shoulders than Roar, and he looked compressed into the small piece of furniture.

Preparing herself for the onslaught of pain any movement would cause, Phe strained to move her legs, forcing them to drop over the edge of the bed, tangling in the covers. She was panting and sweating and she'd barely moved.

Roar's blue eyes flicked opened.

She froze, caught in his penetrating gaze.

Eyes never leaving hers, he leaned forward and whispered huskily, "How are you feeling?"

"I haven't decided yet," Phe murmured. She shuffled an arm under her and audibly exhaled, the only indication she was in tremendous pain, and paused, needing a moment.

"What are you trying to do?"

Phe glared at him, her vision tunneling. "I have to use the washroom."

Instantly, Roar was on his feet, gently grasping under her arms and tugging her up. "Let me help you."

Dizziness hit. One moment she saw all the colors vibrantly and clearly, the next they swirled nauseatingly. She shut her eyes, breathing to quell her stomach.

"You all right?" Roar intoned.

She didn't answer. *Imagine yourself flying up the Gateway To The Stars*, she coached herself, clenching her jaw.

Orc shifted in his chair, sighing.

After a moment, when things were bearable, Phe reopened her eyes, grunting she was ready.

The journey was torture, the pressure on her bladder intense, her body barely strong enough to stand, let alone walk. She leaned heavily into Roar's side, his arm supporting her. "What happened to me?"

"We don't know." His breath tickled her neck.

Phe humphed but didn't bother trying to speak. It was too much.

Roar braced her on the wall close to the toilet. When he

suggested helping further, she stared at him blankly until he released her.

"I'll call for Jallia." He hesitated to leave. "If you need help, I'll wake Her Grace."

Phe pinned him with a *don't-you-dare* stare, and he left her alone to manage her business.

A light knock was the only warning she had before Jallia slid into the room. In one hand, she balanced a tray with a teapot and a single tea set, clothes thrown over her shoulder, and a pair of shoes dangled in her other hand.

Phe would've grumbled at Jallia had she not been distracted by her aura. It had two colors weaving together around her, yellow and orange, distinctly different. And like the others, it faded too quickly.

Jallia's long brown hair was captured in her signature thick braid that ended at her lower back. Her mouth was compressed, eyes tense, and forehead crinkled.

The woman slid the tray onto the counter, her reflection catching in the large gilded mirror, and dropped the shoes. "You look frightful."

"Way to make a girl feel pretty," Phe croaked.

Jallia simply poured a small amount of tea into the cup. "Drink."

Phe peered impassively at her, not moving.

"I'll help." Jallia brought the cup to her lips. "Drink."

Phe rolled her eyes, acquiescing. Warm liquid cascaded in, tasting of diluted earth. She scrunched her nose in distaste.

"Drink all of it," Jallia instructed, tipping the cup and forcing more into her.

Each sip ignited mini-explosions of sorts in her throat, chest, stomach, soothing her pain somehow. "What kind of tea is this?"

"Aswagandhia, and you'll get used to the taste." Jallia refilled the cup to the brim. She crouched, her brown eyes wide, her mouth clamped tight as if she was holding herself back from saying things, and brought the cup to Phe's mouth.

Phe watched her, silently drinking.

They stayed like this until the cup was empty, Jallia imploring and apologizing simultaneously. Phe wished she knew why but was unwilling to push. They both had their secrets. Slow and steady, Jallia helped her clean up while the tea's effects sluggishly reduced her pain.

Jallia gathered Phe's hair, and Phe tugged a strand free. It was no longer muted and dull, but a vibrant chestnut brown. "Jallia, I can see colors."

"Of course you can."

"No, you don't understand. Until today, everything was muted and dull."

Jallia swept Phe's remaining hair into her grasp, tugging the strand Phe was looking at away, preparing to braid. "I hear when people have close experiences with death, they see the world differently."

Phe regarded her pensively, toying with her amulet. "Maybe this time I was further up the stairway than all the other times," she rationalized.

"I am so glad you didn't complete the journey. You're needed here. You're recovering well, faster than I expected, which, mind you, was already fast."

"I'm always the anomaly," Phe bitterly responded.

"Phe, one day I hope you realize we are all anomalies, and certainly at one point in our lives we are faced with deciding how our differences will impact our role within the world. It can define us, separate us, connect us, create hate or compassion." She paused.

"If this is when you tell me I'm a snowflake . . ."

"Excuse me?" Jallia deadpanned.

Phe clamped her mouth shut, fighting an exhausted smile.

"This is when I tell you we are all created with unique gifts and purposes. Some, like Kyra," Jallia leveled Phe with a compassionate stare, "were born into big roles, their gifts evident from a young age. More commonly, as we age, our gifts emerge and force us to see everything in a different *light*—"

Phe laughed at how Jallia subtly wove in the change to her perception.

"—and propels us into worlds we never knew existed. Even when it makes little sense, you need to trust."

Trust. Phe's stomach rolled, her mouth dried. She coughed. "What do you mean?"

"Trust is—"

The door flung open, and Kyra flew in. Eyes damp and bright, voice tremulous as she said, "Phe?"

9

Phe sat confined in her wheelchair by her voluminous dress. Kyra rested a hand on Phe's bare shoulder, her grip like a talon poking into Phe's sensitive skin for purchase. Silently, they absorbed the surrounding chaos.

The royal palace on a normal day was extravagant, but for Princess Attiva's ball, the royal family's outrageous wealth was on full display. The palace's regularly ornate furnishings had been enhanced. Historical statues and sculptures were showcased, exquisite paintings exhibited, and an exorbitant amount of food was laid out with keen attention to detail. Rows of elegant golden chandeliers reflected their shine on the arched, muraled ceilings.

All around them, women in colorful gowns and men in stiff tuxedos floated by, mingling. Some in quiet admiration at an artifact, others in voracious conversations. The loud chatter merged into a nonsensical cloud of noise, immediately reviving the pounding in Phe's temples.

If only I had that repugnant earth tea.

All of Phe's senses were askew, though she liked to think she managed them better now than when she'd first woken.

She stared at everything, seeing it differently. It didn't matter if she was staring at Kyra's hair, the design on the rug, or *Ascension* and its starry landscape. Everything was so much more *vivid* somehow.

Phe had to blink often to relieve her eyes from the vibrance. Add this to all the mixing perfumes, cleaning products, body odor, food, and countless other scents, and her stomach was in knots.

Phe touched Kyra's hand, glancing up at her. "Can we move away from the food?"

"Yes." Kyra squeezed her shoulder. "Princess Attiva plans to dance in the East Ballroom tonight. Why don't we join the royal family there?"

Guilt nibbled at Phe from Kyra's lackluster demeanor. Phe might despise social events, but Kyra was her opposite: often in the center of all the activities.

Phe reached up, snaking her fingers under Kyra's grip. "Kyra, please try to relax and have fun. I'm okay."

Kyra clasped her gloved hand. "But I'm not."

Phe sighed, squeezing Kyra's fingers. They quietly proceeded. Phe's chair steadily rolled through the palace, pushed by one of Kyra's guards. Her remaining escorts cleaved through the crowd.

"Sometimes I think Jallia can foreshadow."

Phe swiftly glanced at Kyra. "You mean see into the future?"

Kyra met Phe's gaze, her mouth grim. "Yes."

Phe's heart pounded. This was something Phe had often considered, yet it felt too close to magic, and Phe wasn't ready to revisit the possibility of magic. After last night, her skin crawled with angst whenever her thoughts veered in its direction.

No one had been able to explain what had happened.

All Phe was told was that when she'd touched the door, a force had thrown her and she'd immediately started convulsing. Blood had leaked from her eyes and ears, her temperature had spiked, and her heart had stopped. A sliver of Phe briefly wondered why she couldn't seem to die, but the rest of her was just grateful to be alive.

Phe shook her head, clearing it. There were too many things she was still reeling from. Magic was not on the list. Not today anyway. Tomorrow, maybe.

"Why?"

"You can't tell me you haven't noticed. You used to sing her praises every time you'd come back from one of Bastion's unannounced wilderness survival trainings. Remember?"

How could I forget? Phe grunted. "But why now? You've never mentioned this before."

Their clasped hands lifted slightly with Kyra's shrug. "Maybe because of the way she warned me to stay with you tonight? There was an ominousness to it. Or something she said the other day about you and a door . . ."

Phe scrunched her face.

Kyra continued, "But what really cinched it for me today? Your dress. Watching you walk so Jallia could see how the sparks popped or when you twirled, so we could see your fire ignite. All I could think of was a phoenix rising from fire." Kyra's tear-filled eyes connected with Phe's, giving her a sad smile. "And shadows."

Jallia had outdone herself with both dresses.

Kyra was breathtaking in the gown Jallia had created for her; it was a masterpiece of dressmaking. She had exposed Kyra's shoulders, melding fabric to her curves up top, then billowing out around her in unseen craftsmanship. When

Kyra moved, her blue-gray dress shimmered, creating the illusion of moving water.

Jallia hadn't stopped there, always ensuring both girls paired equally.

Phe's dress was equivalently magnificent. The sleeveless bodice resembled armor. She'd chosen a glimmering black cloth that fit like a second skin. A slit on the left side exposed deep oranges, reds, and yellows flowing up her body like fire. The flames circled around, appearing to crawl up the open back of the dress. Jallia had accented her with a jeweled golden belt, laden with daggers.

Kyra murmured, appearing lost in thought. "It's like she knew you were going to die last night."

Phe swallowed the sudden sour taste in her mouth. It hadn't felt as if she'd died, not when every cell in her body had been an inferno of pain. "I'm here, and I'm almost recovered."

Kyra gave her a disbelieving look.

Phe's reassuring smile wavered. Kyra was right. Everything was off. Phe's senses were overwhelmed, every bone in her body ached, her skin itched, and her heart beat unsteadily—as if it were wrapped suffocatingly tight.

"Maybe I'll start calling you Phoenix, instead of Phe, because this is the second time you've risen from death."

And those are just the times you've been witness to, thank the seas. Phe'd lost track of how many times she'd thought she'd died, or maybe more appropriately, felt she'd died.

"I don't know. Seems like more work. Phe. Phe-nix. Phee-nixxx—" Phe dipped to a lower octave.

Kyra snorted. "I get it." After a pause, she said, "Your name is so interesting. I call you Phe, which means bright, and Orphne literally means darkness . . . Light and darkness. Fire and shadow."

"Kyra." Phe sighed. "You're thinking too much."

"I know, Phe. I'm—"

"Your Grace!" Velimir called, separating from the throng.

"He can enter," Kyra said to the guards before turning back to her. "I'm just not okay. If our roles were reversed, how would you feel?" Kyra ducked her chin, her eyes vulnerable.

Phe grunted. *Devastated. Guilty. Overprotective. Sad. Panicked. Grateful.* Phe gave Kyra's hand another squeeze.

"Your Grace, you're utterly enticing tonight," Velimir muttered as he swept Kyra into an embrace, passionately kissing her.

Ugh. Phe tried not to look, but he was so close, his calves brushed Phe's skirts. Phe's eyes narrowed at his display, and she swallowed the tart taste she got with his company. She disliked every fiber of him.

When the kiss ended, Velimir dropped his forehead against Kyra's, staring into her eyes, and kissed her nose. "I missed you."

Phe wanted to punch him.

"I'm glad you're here now," Kyra answered, her talon returning to grip Phe's shoulder.

No, tentacle, Phe mentally corrected herself. *She's a self-proclaimed octopus.*

"We're heading to the East Ballroom, but I want to warn you, I'm not much company tonight . . ."

"I was told there was an incident. Lady Orphne had a spell or something." Velimir probed, wrapping an arm around Kyra's waist, almost dislodging her from Phe's shoulder as he tucked himself close to her side.

Phe happily watched Kyra disentangle herself from him, re-securing her hold on Phe. "I can't talk about it. It was bad."

"Hello, Lady Orphne," Velimir finally acknowledged, peering down his nose at her. "I see you've recovered from your spell," he said, then returned his attention to Kyra. "I wanted to be there for you—you must have been so distraught—but I was escorted home."

Sighing, Kyra said, "I'm sorry." She cleared her throat. "General Bastion believes there is a heightened level of danger for me."

Velimir tensed. "Why?"

"Unfortunately, I cannot discuss the matter."

A wave of spiteful contentment washed over Phe at Velimir's puckered mouth and narrowed eyes.

The retinue stopped at the edge of the partially full ballroom. On the elevated platform next to them, a small army of guards stood at attention around Prince Fynn and Queen Oltha, who lounged on chaises.

"Pardon me, I need to speak with Queen Oltha. I'll be a moment," Kyra stated, releasing her grip on Phe's shoulder. Blood rushed back to the area, pinpricks of pain following its path.

The guard pushing Phe's wheelchair eased her to a stop and secured the chair. Phe watched Kyra walk into Queen Oltha's outstretched arms.

Wisps of auburn hair framed the queen's heart-shaped face, the rest secured in the latest fashion with flowers woven into it. Her clear crystal-blue eyes met Phe's. Her expression was soft.

Uncomfortable with her attention, Phe peered at Prince Fynn, who flicked one of his wild curls aside as he examined his mother and Kyra. Then slowly, he evaluated Kyra's entourage, giving Phe an inspection before returning his attention to the crowd. He rubbed his angular jaw thoughtfully, his intelligent brown eyes seemingly analyzing everything.

A dragon idly surveying his territory. This was a running joke between Kyra and Phe.

Phe stood slowly, carefully, when Kyra and the queen approached, their arms linked.

Phe would never admit it, but today there was minimal acting. She was exhausted. Her limbs were heavy, her head throbbed, and her stomach curdled. Even though she'd significantly improved throughout the day, thanks to her unusually fast healing, it felt as though all her cells were singed.

"My darling, sit. Please don't strain yourself," Queen Oltha mothered, the tips of her mouth dipping into a concerned frown. "I'm conflicted. I'm glad to see you, for it's been too long, yet you should be at home, resting."

String instruments started tuning up in the ballroom.

Phe sank into her chair. "Your Majesty, I would have to be unable to move to miss tonight's events."

"Phe, your illness devastates me. I've watched you struggle for years, and I've patiently and hopefully waited for your recovery."

Guilt tightened in Phe's chest, as it always did. Queen Oltha truly cared about her well-being. Not telling her what she truly did when she was "receiving treatments" rubbed Phe the wrong way, even if she was doing this all for Kyra.

"Yet you're not any better." Behind Queen Oltha's kind gaze was determination. "I know General Bastion believes he has the best doctors working with you, but," she shook her head, her lips tight, "it's time to try something different." Her eyes glistened. "I should've stepped in years ago. Expect my physician tomorrow morning."

Kyra planted her warm hand on Phe's shoulder.

"Your Majesty—" Phe started.

"My darlings," Queen Oltha interrupted, "I will not discuss this further. I cannot. I will become upset. Tomorrow morning, my physician and I shall be there." Her expression saddened and she placed a hand on her bosom. Her voice dipped as she said, "I wish I could hug you."

Feeling the guilt squeeze tighter, Phe focused on Queen Oltha's glittery jeweled bracelet. It was an old family heirloom, with a circular red ruby covering the entirety of her wrist, surrounded by rows and rows of unblemished diamonds.

After another moment, Queen Oltha straightened her spine, her hand smoothing down the fabric of her dress. Phe watched the ruby sparkle with the movement. "Now I am going to make my rounds. Phe, darling, rest." Then she walked into the crowd, guards falling into step next to her.

Phe peered at Kyra. "I'd like to be there when she talks to Bastion."

"Phee-nix," Kyra exaggerated dryly. "I think we'll get a front-row seat."

"Why are you calling her phoenix?" Velimir intruded, having had enough of hovering awkwardly to the side.

"Because she rises from her ashes," Kyra simply stated.

"Don't phoenixes have to die first?" Velimir queried. "Aren't they supposed to die by fire, then they rise from their ashes?" When both Phe and Kyra stared unresponsively, he attempted to soften it. "Let's hope Queen Oltha's physician can discover the cause of her episodes and she can fully recover, so you no longer worry so much about her."

"Vel, Phe and I have a bond that is unexplainable. I literally feel her," Kyra pressed at a spot in her chest, "here. Last night, the bond . . ." Kyra's singsong quivered, and she paused, covering her mouth, then cleared her throat. "I will always worry about her," she finished firmly.

Velimir searched Kyra's features, considering her words. "I understand."

But do you?

"Good." Kyra looked toward the dance floor, where a sizable crowd had formed.

Velimir interlaced his fingers with Kyra's free hand, dropping his voice to an intimate murmur. Phe semi-listened to them. She'd wanted to talk to Kyra about auras, knowing Kyra saw them too, but they hadn't been alone all day. Members of Shadow Unit were always with them. The oddity of Shadow Unit's presence wasn't missed by either Phe or Kyra.

The bastard had dropped by too, reminding Phe again he hadn't forgotten about her "assault." He'd have his vengeance, under the auspices of training, and knowing him, it'd be a "surprise" session.

Phe yearned for a way to contact Elzac, which was an impossibility. She wanted to ask him about, well, everything. The dream, and what happened in what she'd named the void—the in-between place she'd been in last night— neither in this world nor passing on—and how he'd been there.

"I can't answer the meaning of life," Roar interrupted her musings, his tuxedo accentuating his muscular body, hair secured in a small bun, blue gaze searching hers. The corners of his eyes crinkled with mischievousness. "But perhaps I could help you with your brooding."

Phe was unamused.

Kyra squeezed her shoulder.

Phe didn't need to look at her to know that, even upset as she was, Kyra's eyes would be twinkling.

"I've come to regale you with my company," Roar announced playfully, ignoring her unwelcoming response.

"Have you?" Phe asked, reaching her hand up to Kyra's fingers and giving them a *settle-down-matchmaker* pat. "Haven't you got beautiful damsels seeking you out?"

"I do, but Her Grace's guards are holding them at bay. It's quite convenient."

The tingle returned, and Phe's chest tightened uncomfortably. She ignored it as she followed Roar's gaze. Sure enough, a small group of women were, in fact, eyeing him. She shook her head, playing along. "Are you—"

Roar's gaze locked on someone, and he tensed, crouching to whisper in her ear. "Follow my lead. One of the Shalexum ambassadors is approaching. I know you're going to meet with them, and hopefully they can help track down your lineage, but—"

"Commander Maverick," a sharp voice interrupted. "I'm surprised to see you here."

Roar stood, an easy smile lighting his face.

Phe noticed the golden-brown, crystal-clear aura first, then the ambassador himself.

Golden orbs locked onto hers, radiating a cunning intelligence and cold detachment. His sun-bleached hair was wavy and long enough for him to tuck behind his ears. He'd dressed in a brown and tan tuxedo, and the way he was standing—broad shoulders, slightly puffed-out chest, trim waist, hands tucked into his pockets, and powerful legs— reminded her of a hawk.

Outwardly, he looked relaxed and welcoming. Yet something just under the surface raised her hackles. Her tingling increased. She hated the tingles.

"Ambassador Genor," Roar said, offering Phe his hand.

"You have come too late. Lady Orphne has accepted a dance with me."

"Wait! What?" Kyra interrupted. "She has?"

Phe slipped her gloved palm into Roar's, slowly standing. Instead of releasing her hand, his engulfed hers, drawing her close to his warmth. The tingles morphed, becoming oddly delicious somehow as they ran up her arm. Heat warmed her neck.

Phe glanced at Kyra, who looked back at her in shock. Phe couldn't help widening her eyes and giving Kyra a small smile for her reaction, then followed it with a narrowing. A warning to not matchmake.

Would I have taken Elex's hand? Kirzia's? Ihrone's? She squashed the unwelcome thought. *Definitely Orc's.*

Kyra didn't know Roar was saving her from an encounter, nor had she, other than today, witnessed Shadow Unit interacting with Phe. The easy way the unit and Phe had with each other, the banter, was new to Kyra.

"Vel, we're dancing too," Kyra declared, dragging Velimir with her as she aligned on Phe's other side. Linking arms with Phe, she leaned in and whispered, "We're talking about this."

"Are you going to whisk her away before introducing her to me?" The ambassador sounded affronted. His piercing gaze seemed to burrow into her.

"Lady Orphne, let me formally introduce you to Ambassador Genor." Not releasing Phe's hand, Roar gave him a small bow. "Now, a dance is a dance, and I will not have you steal my partner."

Roar guided them to the dance floor. Phe felt Ambassador Genor's cutting gaze track her, her neck prickling, until the crowd engulfed them. Kyra was forced to release her grip and step ahead of Phe. Kyra's guards encircled Kyra and Velimir, separating Phe further from Kyra.

"Why am I avoiding him?" Phe inquired.

"I'm saving you from an unpleasant experience, trust me." The crowd surged into them as Kyra's circle moved further ahead. Roar weaved through the onlookers, carefully creating a path. "Do you feel well enough to dance?"

"I'm exhausted, but it's nothing I can't manage," Phe said, ducking into him to avoid touching a stranger. "A slow song would be best."

Roar tugged her into his chest, throwing his other arm over her shoulder. "Glad to hear it."

Phe let out a light hiss, tensing. His muscled arm was heavy, the texture of his satin shirt, the hard planes of his chest overwhelming. If this were a stranger, scorching pain would be searing through Phe, but it was Roar.

His touch wasn't Kyra's. Not painful, not comfortable, yet a wanting . . . of more. She immediately locked the yearning up, reminding herself she couldn't have what everyone else had. She was a blade crafted for one reason—protection—and nothing, including her thoughts and wanting, would get in the way.

"Would you rather I didn't?" The weight of his arm lifted.

"No," she quickly replied, shuddering at the thought of strangers accidentally touching her. "I'd honestly rather not have this aversion at all."

"We all have reasons for the way we are." Roar's breath tickled the side of her face. "And, have you considered when you're sparring, you don't have any aversion?"

The intimacy sent ripples down her neck and shoulder. Heat rose to her cheeks, and she fought the urge to pull away.

Stop it, she chided herself, clenching her jaw. Phe focused on answering. He was right. When she was fighting, something within her came alive. Her aversion to touch disappeared. "I've spent too many hours of my life pondering it."

They broke through the crowd. Phe immediately sighted Kyra and Velimir a few feet away, ringed by guards and a few friends.

Roar tucked her in front of him, his body shielding her. "Your ability to recover," he whispered, "is incredible. I'm positive General Bastion wouldn't have let you attend if you were in the same shape as this morning."

The pesky warmth crawled up her neck again, flaring brightly in her cheeks. "Bastion is not my caretaker; he takes an interest in my well-being only regarding my ability to perform."

Roar cleared this throat. "I know you don't remember last night, but General Bastion was with us most of the time."

Phe didn't respond, not able to comprehend how someone who'd been so emotionless, brutal, and calculating toward her could care about her, as Roar and Kyra had both implied. Bastion always did things for a reason. There must be one for keeping vigil over her; she just didn't know what.

"Do you think one dance will suffice, or will the ambassador be waiting?" *Or worse, would he demand a dance?*

"I will not abandon you," Roar promised.

Phe shook her head at him. He was being ridiculous. There was no way he'd stay with her all night. "What do I need to know about him?"

"When you meet with him, make sure he doesn't touch you."

Phe's brow furrowed. "Why?"

"Because—"

Princess Attiva landed in front of them, breathless, her eyes alight with happiness. "Phe!"

"Princess Attiva."

A wide smile lit up Princess Attiva's face, brown eyes sparkling. "You're going to dance? Are you sure you should? Does my mother know?" she rapidly fired as she leaned in. Gloved hands reached for Phe's chin, stopping inches from it. "I'm so glad you're here."

Phe smiled back, the princess's energy infectious.

"Princess—"

"And who is this handsome gentleman escorting you?"

Phe turned, gesturing. "Let me introduce you to Commander Maverick."

"Princess Attiva, it is my honor." Roar bowed deeply. When he stood, he tucked Phe into him again, this time leaving a hand on her waist.

Phe bit her inner lip. His light touch settled with the force of a landslide. Her skin sizzled, breath caught. Her body automatically curved into him, and she surprised herself by slipping her hand onto his and wrapping her fingers delicately around his instead of flicking his hand away.

He gave her hand a quick squeeze.

What am I doing? she berated herself, releasing his hand and skimming the crowd. Kyra and Velimir were at the opposite end of the ballroom now. *How did they get so far away?*

"My pleasure as well, though you must be careful with my Phe," Princess Attiva ominously stated.

"We were waiting for a slow song, Princess," Phe inserted quickly at Princess Attiva's pause.

"Then I shall request it for you." Princess Attiva glanced to the side and subtly signaled. A moment later, a servant appeared, and the princess whispered to him. When she was done, he jogged toward the musicians.

"Thank you, Princess."

"Of course. Good luck if Mother sees you dancing. Who knows what she'll do?"

"Banish me to my corner?" Phe offered.

"Or have you escorted to your guest suite and locked in! It'll save her a trip and a fight with the general." Princess Attiva's smirk disappeared. Her gaze intensified as she peered over Phe's shoulder. "Consider Phe a delicate rare flower. She's to be handled with extreme care."

"Phe is a treasure I cherish." Sincerity echoed in each of Roar's words.

Phe's heart fluttered, and heat blossomed in her cheeks.

Over the years, she'd learned a lot about Shadow Unit. Orc was the best cook. He and his long-time partner often created elaborate competitions and coerced—if you could call it that—their respective teams to judge. Ihrone had an adult son who was following in his footsteps and was close friends with everyone on the unit. Finian was the epitome of a ladies' man, and he constantly tested boundaries with everyone; it was amazing he wasn't dead yet. Kirzia could beat anyone in cards, which the team unabashedly bene-fited from on their weekly game nights. Roar had a sister who, through stories, was hilarious, and he was known to be smooth with the ladies too.

Phe'd never experienced this flirty, intimate side to him.

The orchestra stopped mid-song, inciting groans and disgruntled grumblings from the dance floor.

"Hmm . . ." The princess scrutinized Roar. "Phe, take care to not overdo it, okay?"

"Yes, Princess."

"Now," soft slow musical notes began, and Princess

Attiva broke out into another one of her contagious smiles, "we dance." She winked, gesturing them onto the dance floor.

Roar exhaled. "She's a fierce little thing." Wrinkle lines formed around his dancing blue eyes. "I have been warned."

Phe locked gazes with Kyra, who was still at the far end of the dance floor. "Let's line up next to Kyra."

Roar's hand splayed at her hip, his calloused fingers touching her exposed back.

Phe instinctively arched, the sensation not so much painful as unnerving, sending fiery tingles along her nerves.

He repositioned immediately and continued, knowing she hated attention drawn to this. "For a long time, I worried you only had Her Grace and Jallia. Not that either of those two aren't gifts in and of themselves. Now I have a sense of ease. Your Princess just threatened me, and the queen is visiting you in the morning." His voice rose at the end, questioning her.

An impish smile erupted on Phe's face. "Queen Oltha is bringing her personal physician to take over my care and have a conversation with Bastion."

"Haha, I'll make sure to be there."

The nape of her neck prickled. The air stilled.

Roar tensed.

The exhaustion she felt just moments before disappeared instantly, and her heart settled into the first steady, expansive rhythm all day. Her senses no longer pounded uncomfortably. Everything slowed, the cacophony of chatter blanketed.

Lady Orphne's personality discarded, Phe bolted to Kyra, her limbs heavy, acid singeing her muscles with each movement.

All noise deadened for a beat, only to be filled by a

whooshing sound, similar to the one she'd heard in the meadow.

The noise returned in a deafening wave, and Phe saw Roar was keeping pace with her, sprinting toward Kyra.

The sharp sensation along Phe's skin flared anew, and her new, extraordinary sense of smell dialed into the malodorous scent of ripe, unwashed bodies.

Phe tracked Kyra; her guards were rushing her toward an exit.

A scream rang out, the sound too familiar.

Seas, Princess Attiva!

"Roar." Phe grazed his arm, pointing upwards. "I need up."

Without hesitation, he interlaced his fingers, and she stepped into them. Roar launched her. Phe spun, weightless, her dress flaring around her, fire blazing to life, and released one of her bejeweled knives.

The blade lodged into the man's neck. Blood splattered across Princess Attiva's shocked face, her mouth hanging open, her eyes enormous.

Phe landed in a crouch, springing up and dashing to Roar's side.

Mayhem erupted. Screams and shoving bodies swarmed.

They were barreling through the crowd when the air compressed again.

A voice thundered over the chaos. "Abaixo!"

An oozy sensation slithered over her, and everyone in the ballroom fell to the floor. Bodies littered the ground in mounds, seemingly paralyzed, and panicked shrieks hit higher octaves.

Phe stumbled to a stop, yanking knives from her belt. She was the only one standing.

Correction, she and two men with bulging black eyes.

The closest one charged her, scrambling over the people.

Phe dispatched the furthest threat, releasing several knives with her next breath. Feeling the air burst behind her, she swiveled, instinctively stabbing the empty space, yet her blade sank into a wall of flesh. Blood sprayed, and a female with white hair coalesced.

High seas! How are people appearing out of nowhere?

A voice boomed. "Ah, how delightful we meet again! And so soon." More people had morphed into the room. "Bring her to me."

Phe rapidly released one knife after another. Each thudded into their targets, dispatching them efficiently.

She dodged to the side, avoiding the charging man's tackle and slamming her knife to the hilt into his throat.

He fell to his knees. Gasping, blood leaked from the silver tip of the blade.

The bulging blackness faded from the man's eyes. His now clear gaze locked onto Roar's. Unshed tears filled them. "Tell them I love them," he said, barely audible. Both hands gripped the hilt of the dagger, then he yanked the weapon out. Blood erupted, covering Phe.

What?

People started shuffling. The invisible force holding them in place was gone.

"Everyone stay on the ground!" Roar commanded, vaulting to his feet.

Phe snatched her knife. Blood dripped from it. The last two daggers weighed heavy in her hands. She leapt over bodies.

Surges of air erupted around her.

She didn't have enough daggers. One of her daggers

embedded into a woman who emerged near the royal family. The other took down the threat nearest to Kyra. But there were more.

People stood. Those foolish or unaware of Phe's path, she tossed aside. *Why did I let Kyra get so far away?*

The last clear view she'd had of Kyra, she'd been on the ground, her guard standing protectively around her, their legs caging her in.

The crowd waned.

Phe's glance connected with Kyra's as an unnatural wind swept through the hallway. People were yelling.

Phe's blood accelerated to a frantic staccato, her skin on fire.

The air froze again as Phe slid in between the guards' legs, fighting to get to Kyra.

Kyra lifted to her knees and crawled toward Phe, the skirt of her dress hampering her.

Hand outstretched, Kyra reached for her, but a guard grabbed Phe's hair, yanking her.

Phe watched in horror as a pinprick of blackness appeared over Kyra's shoulder. The next instant, it expanded outward, its center a pulsing mirror.

Slamming her fist into the guard's inner thigh, she twisted out of the guard's grip. Phe stretched out, their fingers almost grazing.

Kyra vanished.

"Kyra!" The internal tether she had to Kyra pulled taut, tearing. Phe couldn't breathe.

She dropped to her forearms, vision tunneling. All she saw was Kyra's wide, terror-filled eyes before they blinked out of existence.

The fire within her reignited, its heat swelling up and

engulfing her completely, burning away the last of her barriers. Pressure built as she let it fully consume her.

Phe shattered.

An explosive force burst from her, leveling the hall. A river of shadows flooded the room, flickering red and orange sparks within its depths, cascading into her, around her.

Hands grabbed her, hoisting her up. She blinked, her vision red-tinted, liquid streaming down her face. *Tears? Am I crying?*

Then Bastion was there, as if he too had appeared out of thin air. His scar was stretched tight, his piercing stony gaze latched onto her, his jaw clenched.

Before she could react, he punched her, and darkness descended.

10

Phe didn't wake in her bed.

Her cheek was pressed into cold porous stone, moisture crawling up the side of her face. Or was that something else? Heavy clumps of hair pressed against her other cheek.

Her senses were equally conflicted, all of them nasty. She had a horrible taste in her mouth, and she realized it was open, as if frozen in a scream, and bone dry. Then there was the smell. Urine? Feces? Vomit? Blood? Fear? Despair?

Slowly, Phe dragged her mouth closed, the effort mind-bendingly exhausting.

She was no longer burning, though her nerve endings prickled with new awareness. Her head throbbed to the slow sound of water dripping.

There was a heaviness in the air, an unseeable force blanketing her. It was disconcerting and comforting at the same time.

She tried to open her eyes, but couldn't.

Before she could consider what that meant, Phe's stomach rolled, twisting sharply, and she heaved. She vacillated between gasping breaths and violent purging, barely keeping her face from the bile. *Is this more bullspit transformation?*

When the vomiting stopped and she could muster the energy, Phe flopped onto her back, gulping air.

The chilled floor on her exposed back sent shivers raking through her. Her dress skirt was bunched up, creating mounds of uneven fabric under her lower back. She couldn't round up the energy to cover herself.

Kyra.

Her heart shattered, fragmenting into shards, shredding her insides.

Taken.

The bond they'd shared since the day they'd first met, their tether to each other, was whisper-thin. For the first time in fourteen years, she couldn't feel Kyra. She curled to her other side, her hand wrapped around her amulet.

A door opened in the distance.

Her survival instincts flared, focusing her. She suddenly knew she lay on the floor in a dungeon cell buried in the rock foundation of House Nereid. She knew precisely five people were striding in her direction, their paces even and steady. She knew her cell was locked.

Panic didn't come; detached deliberation did.

Phe needed information. The only way she'd get this was to eavesdrop. Luckily, it would not be hard, because she couldn't move or open her eyes.

The key clanged in the lock, a sharp metallic sound, followed by the screams of the rusted, heavy metal door being forced open. Each noise drilled deeply into the throbbing mess of her head.

"Flipping cripes." She heard rushed footsteps, then felt icy fingers pressing into her neck.

Phe was shocked the skin-to-skin contact didn't elicit an adverse reaction.

"Is she alive?" a haughty voice asked.

"She is," came Orc's terse reply. "You said she'd be fine in here."

"Act-ually," the voice stepped closer, "I said if she was to survive the rebound, this was her only option. I think the room has helped to neutralize some of her power, thus helping her to integrate her capabilities and live."

Soft treads approached. "Let's cover her up," Roar said, followed by a tugging. The mound of cloth flattened from under her, and Phe felt the brush of cold silk on her legs.

Orc slid his hands under her arms, boosting her up. "Commander, will you help move her?"

Hands slid under her thighs. "Where are we going?"

"Over there." Carefully, they lifted her and carried her a few feet, propping her against a wall.

She listed to the side. Someone caught her, careful to not touch her bare skin.

"Her power is immense." Awe coated Ambassador Genor words. "And we're in a muted room. This is incredible. How is she surviving this?"

Hands tentatively skimmed the side of her jawline, cautiously pulling her hair aside. It was stuck in congealed gunk on her face.

Her reaction, or lack of one, stunned her. No searing pain. Only mild irritation, and that quickly dissipated.

"She went through something similar last night after she attempted to open the doors to the Juncture," Bastion stated matter-of-factly.

The Juncture?

The ambassador gasped. "No . . . Didn't she know?"

"You forget, gentleman. People in the world at large don't

know about magic . . . including Lady Theanora. We haven't had to caution anyone on the Juncture because there was no reason to; it only reacts to magic-borns."

"Unfortunate happenstance of misinformation," someone Phe didn't recognize said. The arrogance in his voice was unbounded. "In this case, it's gifted us. Who knew you had such a powerful magic-born right under your nose? Why wasn't I informed of this last night?"

Magic exists.

Pieces of her past clicked into place. House Nereid's haunted hidden passageways. Kyra's capabilities. Kyra's training room. *What had they called it? The Juncture?*

"I do not answer to you, Katoa. As you already know, Phe is abnormal. It's why I'd asked you both to meet with her. I assure you, we were closely monitoring her," Bastion responded, nonplussed. "She had manifested no signs of magic this morning."

"I sensed something about her at the ball, but was not allowed to investigate it; someone wanted a dance," Ambassador Genor jabbed. "I didn't see her aura, so I understand your confusion. I wonder if what she went through was a partial rebound."

"I haven't read of anyone experiencing partial rebounds or multiple. The texts only refer to one occurrence. I should've been here documenting it all. Do you know how rare this is?" Katoa said.

"She is not one of your study specimens," Roar snapped.

"Do not worry, Commander. The accommodations here are subpar and it's too late. I believe the worst has passed, and since she is alive, I'm certain she'll remain that way," Katoa said brusquely.

"Are there stages to rebounds?" Orc questioned.

"Essentially, her body is removing the non-magic

essences from it. A purging, and yes, pun intended," Katoa said condescendingly. "Her body can't integrate her magic without eliminating any aspects unable to bind to it. If this means her body needs to excrete everything she was before to rebuild, it will. It seems everything has been expelled, so I believe what we are seeing is the beginning of the rebuilding."

"Do you know what to expect in the rebuilding? When she wakes, I'd like to be able to explain what's happening," Orc pressed.

"Not off hand." Katoa answered. "I've never witnessed a rebound. All my knowledge comes from my voracious appetite for reading about the rare cases."

"I'm impressed. I'd imagined a rebound would take time to recover from and fully integrate," Ambassador Genor said. "Yet watching her last night, I wouldn't have known. Has anyone sighted her aura yet?" Ambassador Genor queried.

When no one answered, Katoa said, "Someone went to great depths to hide her magic. If she'd been born in the Still community, they wouldn't have known or had the access. We would have found her years ago when her magic emerged. It makes me wonder: where did she come from, and who is she really?"

Phe had been seeking those answers all of her life.

"Gentlemen," Bastion interrupted them disinterestedly, "I don't have time to muse." His manner curt and abrasive, he said, "She's alive. Your curiosity has been satisfied. I now have to meet with the royals and military leaders. Commander Roar, you'll be needed. Medic, stay with her and see if you can clean her up."

Footsteps receded, then she heard Ambassador Katoa,

his voice distant and echoey. "She'll be coming back with me. I can't wait to test her."

After another moment, Orc muttered, "I can't with Katoa."

"Don't worry, Bastion won't let him anywhere near her. I'll send for Her Grace's maid to help you," Roar murmured. "Take care of our girl."

"Yes, sir."

11

The past decade, Phe'd questioned the strangeness of what she could do, what she had seen, and Kyra's capabilities. But all her questions had either been dismissed or ignored or they'd told her this is the way it is and silenced her. A decade of being told her quick healing was abnormal and had to be concealed. A decade of being told that what happened in the secret passageways of House Nereid was all in her head. A decade of being told Kyra's abilities were genetic.

The stab of Bastion's betrayal, of this lie, layered onto all the other lies and omissions, sparked rage. Deep-rooted rage. Sweltering rage. And for Shadow Unit to know and not prepare her for the possibility of encountering magic to protect Kyra weaved thorned threads within the roots of her rage.

Shadow Unit.

Phe reflected, slowing her smoldering anger. *Have I ever talked to them about this?*

Their conversations had been superficial, sometimes dipping into deeper pools when they talked about healing techniques, but never magic. And definitely never anything she'd experienced—not from her childhood, or Bastion's solo training sessions, and her weird encounters with House Nereid and Drykz Forest. They knew only the basics about her. Her friendship with Kyra. The reason she trained with Bastion, but no details. The sting didn't dissolve.

If only I could talk to Kyra.

Phe's chest ached thinking about her. She tugged at the slim thread connecting them to each other, but she didn't feel a response. *Where are you?*

The mad drummer pounding in her head slowed his tempo at Orc's touch. His contact *felt* relieving. Like warm rain water streaming down her face and neck and trickling into the spaces in between her skin. She greedily absorbed the water into her, replenishing.

The noises of Jallia's arrival snapped Phe's careening mind to the present.

"How is she?" came Jallia's breathless question.

Jallia, don't trust them.

"She isn't dead," Orc tensely responded. "And, if Katoa is correct, she's in the recovery stage of her rebound."

Phe's stomach twisted, this time with an altogether different pain. *Jallia lied to me too.*

"Hard to believe with the way she looks."

"Tell me about it," Orc stated grimly. "I can't believe she's magic-born, even though I was *there.*"

No, no, nooo . . . Phe's heart spasmed violently.

"I heard. I wouldn't want to be in General Bastion's shoes right now." A bucket thunked onto the cold stone floor, water splashing. "I don't know how he'll explain what happened to the Xafarians."

Jallia's wet hand traced from Phe's forehead to her jaw. Phe could feel the intensity of Jallia's gaze.

"She's shown signs of breakthrough magic ever since I've known her," Jallia muttered quietly. Jallia rested her fingers on Phe's chin, pokers of searing heat branding her before disappearing.

Orc sighed, his calloused fingers drawing small circles at her temple. "It all makes sense now. Her ability to heal. Her skill level. General Bastion's decision to pair her with us."

"He must have suspected." A pouring noise, the sound of fabric twisting, followed by heavy drops of water sounded. A cloth wrung out. "She's special."

Flipping seas, I am not special.

"It must be the reason Katoa and Genor are here." Orc's icy fingertips migrated down her jawline. "You care about her?"

"With all my heart." Jallia moved closer and laid a warm, wet cloth across Phe's eyes.

"We've been deliberating how we can help." Orc adjusted his touch to Phe's neck, loosely holding her chin up. "They'll tear her apart in Arias."

"You're taking her to Arias?" Jallia lightly scrubbed her left ear with another warm towel.

Orc shrugged, and Phe's chin bobbed. "Those are our orders, and honestly, I'm relieved. We all live there, so we'll be able to protect her better."

"If I had to choose between the five magical cities, Arias would be my first choice. It makes sense. It's the training grounds for Phoenixes, and it's the headquarters for the general's army. Don't the elders reside there, too?"

Phe racked her memory, running through her geography. She'd never heard of a city called Arias. *Phoenixes? Elders? Bastion has another army?*

"They do, and we're worried. Who knows what their reaction will be? She's powerful, untrained. Dangerous."

The cooling cloth swiped her cheek. Jallia's breath whispered across Phe's skin as she spoke. "And she's going to resist, which they don't tolerate. She's endured her conditions over the years because of Lady Theanora, but now?"

"Do you think she'll fight?"

"Definitely."

"I've never seen her defiant." Orc sounded disheartened.

"Bastion's held her on a tight leash." Jallia made another pass at the same cheek, this time scrubbing at Phe's skin a little. "She's going to feel so trapped."

"I know." Orc lifted one hand, then the other, allowing Jallia to clean her neck. "Can't be helped. No one leaves the cities without permission, you know this. And with Djall targeting her? General Bastion will never approve. If she fell into his clutches, with the power she has, even in this muted room, Djall would be unstoppable." Orc paused, adjusting his grip back. "What I can't figure out is how Djall could identify and track her when she was magically bound."

Jallia carefully lifted the cloth she'd left across Phe's brow, then used it to scrub at whatever had sealed her eyes, freeing them. Phe's heart raced.

Does Jallia know I'm awake?

"Who knows with Djall? His abilities have morphed over the last century, and she has shown signs of magic even bound." Gooseflesh rose on Phe's neck. Jallia shuffled toward the bucket of water, noisily cleaning the cloth.

The last century? No one lives that long.

"What have you seen?"

"What do you mean?" Jallia stilled.

"Come now, do you really think we would not have looked into you?" Orc's rhetorical question was lightly laced with condescension. "We know you're an extremely strong clairvoyant, among other notable things."

Phe's throat's closed. *Kyra was right.*

"Humph," came Jallia's unhappy response. The rewarmed cloth swept across Phe's collarbone and down her right shoulder. "There are too many lines of possibilities right now. None of the paths shown to me have cemented. What hurts me is her inevitable loss of trust. I can't fault her. I'd feel betrayed too."

"What were we supposed to do?" Orc slumped, resting his chin gingerly on the top of Phe's head. "We're oath bound to not discuss magic."

"At least you didn't directly lie to her. I had to." The chilled cloth glided across her chest again, this time delving into her corset, making its way to her other arm. "Did you know General Bastion sent her into the passageways? Sometimes for weeks at a time?"

"Noooo." Orc stiffened around her.

"House Nereid's magic was not gentle, and *I* had to tell her magic didn't exist. The general, he told her it was in her head. How could you tell a ten-year-old girl who had bruising and cuts from the house's sentient, overly protective, finicky magic, it was her imagination?" Jallia's voice cut with indignation.

"She was ten?"

"The tunnels and poisoning started at ten. Don't get me started on the rest of his training." Derision dripped from Jallia's voice. "Everyone speaks so highly of him. His atrocious treatment of Phe wiped away the respect I once had for him."

"I've only known him to be an honorable man." Orc sighed, rolling his shoulders, and thus Phe. "I know it's impossible in this room, but I swear, I feel her drawing from me."

Jallia grunted. "Nothing's impossible."

"Katoa wants her, you know."

"Of course, the man covets power." Jallia soothed her edge. "I want to rinse her hair. Could you lean her forward?"

Orc effortlessly crouched, barely disturbing Phe. He slid a hand to cradle her throat and chin, and then tilted her forward. Jallia swept her clumped hair over. The movement launched bursts of pain through Phe.

Jallia dragged the bucket under her, letting the ends of her hair soak, while Jallia's other hand worked on loosening the clumps.

Silence blanketed them.

Maybe they'd leave, and Phe could escape. She would not willingly go to Arias, wherever that was. They'd never let her out. And she had to rescue Kyra.

But how can I rescue her if I don't know where she is?

"So much better," Jallia muttered when her hands ran freely through Phe's hair. "Orc, will you lift her while I undo the skirt of her dress? Then would you mind leaving us while I clean the rest of her?"

Orc adjusted his grip and lifted her, twisting Phe to allow Jallia's apt fingers access to the buttons. "I'm not sure I should leave."

When the waist released, Jallia tugged it to below Phe's hips only. "You can put her down. Why don't you see if there's any new information?" Jallia said as if he hadn't spoken. "It'll take me a bit of time to clean and re-dress her."

"Hmmm, you may need me." Uncertainty coated Orc's response.

"Orc, we'll be fine. Go on." Jallia's voice didn't change in tone, but something threaded the air when she spoke. Tingles burst along Phe's flesh.

"Fine. I'll get you clean towels." He gently leaned Phe against the chilly wall.

Phe listened to the barely audible sound of his retreating tread. The scream of the creaking door echoed loudly, followed by a heavy boom.

"Thank the seas," Jallia muttered, releasing her steadying hold. "You can open your eyes. I know you're awake."

Phe didn't.

"Please," Jallia said, her voice dripping with sarcasm. "I can tell when you're faking it."

Blinding shards of light stabbed into her. *Aren't these cells all dimly lit?*

Jallia hurriedly pulled things out of a bag. "We have little time. Drink this." Phe felt the lip of a bottle against her mouth.

Her eyes cleared, and she reared back, her heart stopping.

Jallia's brown eyes glowed white.

"Phe, it is Elzac. Jallia has given me permission to speak through her. The water will help you. *She* is helping you. You need to get to the forest. Be quick, there isn't much time."

"Elzac?" Phe forced through immobile lips.

Bastion's betrayal was expected. Shadow Unit's hurt. Jallia's devastated. Elzac? That demolished the remnants of her fragmented heart.

Elzac had rescued her. Miraculously found her in the depths of Drykz Forest when she'd all but given up. He'd given her choices and walked with her during her deep healing. She had shared with him her nightmares, her flashes, her shattered childhood. She'd bared everything to him.

"Drink. I'm sorry you found out this way." Jallia pressed the bottle to her lips. "I will explain everything once you get to the forest. You need to drink, dress, and leave."

"You too?" Anguish ladened Phe's words.

"Yes, and you have a choice. Do you want our help to rescue Kyra? Or do you want to be taken to Arias? Because each second you delay determines this."

Her breath caught, and she said quickly, "Do you know where Kyra is being held?"

Jallia carefully tilted the bottle and let the liquid flow. Phe didn't expect the lush, cold water deliciously sliding down her parched throat.

"When you're safely in the forest, we'll talk. You need to drink until it's empty."

The water had the same effect as Orc's touch, only more powerful. The empty spaces in her flooded, saturating the dirt within her.

It took a moment for the waves to reach her muscles, returning her strength in mini-bursts, aches and pains disappearing completely.

Slowly Phe moved, bringing her hands to the bottle and holding it, a feat she hadn't thought possible moments ago. She kept drinking until the seemingly unending water supply was gone.

"Good." Urgency flooded Jallia's tenor. "Move quickly, change." Jallia pulled out clothing from the pack she'd brought.

Phe scrambled out of her dress, catching the wet towel Jallia threw at her and scrubbing her lower half.

"Faster."

Phe tossed the soiled cloth aside, noticing the tremendous puddle of blood that outlined a form curled in the fetal position. Hers.

"How am I alive?" Phe wiggled into her pants, then

slipped into her boots, quickly securing them. "How can I move now?"

"Magic is an anomaly. We don't know why some survive rebounds and others don't. Focus." Jallia handed her a clean shirt. "I must go. My presence is distressing your friend. Take this." She handed Phe a small bottle attached to a necklace. "The moment you leave Oceanid, drink this. *She'll* come to you."

Elzac's glowing white eyes faded, the soft brown of Jallia's eyes bleeding back into them.

"Jallia?"

Phe cinched her knives to her thighs.

Jallia groaned, catching her head in her hands. "I hate people in my head."

How many people has she had in her head? "You okay?" Phe paused to scan her.

"I've survived worse. Don't you worry about me. You need to leave. Edva's in the north pasture."

"Will there be repercussions?"

"Isn't that what life is about? Choices and outcomes." Jallia stood, smoothing her dress anxiously. Again, she said, "Edva's in the north pasture."

The door to the dungeon opened, and hurried footsteps approached.

"You're the best." Relief coursed through Phe. Without Edva's speed, her chances at successfully escaping dramatically narrowed, and she'd feel horrible leaving Edva behind. She might only be a horse to some, but she was much more to Phe.

Phe peeked out of the cell. "Can you come with me?"

Ambassador Genor and several others hurried toward them. *Not good.*

"No, I wouldn't risk getting anywhere near Edva at a

time like this." Jallia scoffed, ushering Phe to the doorway. "And I'd slow you down." Jallia pushed her into the hallway. "Go."

A weightlessness imbued her the instant she was free of the cell. The sensation disintegrated as she locked gazes with Ambassador Genor. A flash of astonishment seemed to flicker over his features before he blanked all expression.

"Don't move," Ambassador Genor commanded, sprinting toward her.

Phe bolted into a vacant cell, slamming the door behind her. She flung herself at the wall, fingers searching for the release.

There!

Heavy footsteps reverberated in the hallway, slowing at the cell door.

The passage door swung open on silent hinges. Phe slipped through the crack, yanking it closed behind her. She caught a glimpse of Ambassador Genor's glowing golden eyes just before it clicked shut.

The door shuddered forcibly.

She turned into the void of darkness, the labyrinth of House Nereid's secret passageways. Taking a steadying breath, she instinctively pulled her shadows to her.

Then she ran—as if Kyra's life depended on it.

12

Edva cleared the last dwelling of Oceanid, sweat coating her, sides heaving. The sweet scent of oranges mingled in the salty sea air and the piercing hollow sound of Edva's hooves became muffled when the road changed to packed dirt. Behind Phe, waves of sharp sounding hooves chased her.

The familiar pull of Drykz Forest tugged at her, a relieving sensation within the discomfort of the forest's call. She could see the ominous line of trees. They were getting close.

Phe risked a glance back.

It was a mistake.

Roar was in the lead, his deep auburn hair glinting in the moonlight. Behind him, the rest of Shadow Unit followed. Others she didn't know were slightly behind them. She twisted back, her chest tightening.

"Can't trust anyone," she apprehensively told Edva, narrowing her focus in the distance.

Drink the vial, Elzac's soft whisper urged her. *She'll come to you.*

Phe grabbed the tiny bottle Jallia, or rather Elzac, had

given her, and thumbed off the cork. The horrid smell of decay greeted her. She fought a gag as she tipped it back.

The slimy, viscous fluid coated her mouth and throat, burning a path to her stomach. It reminded her of the one time Elzac had made her drink his stinkhorn mushroom tea concoction, only exponentially worse.

She spit, trying to clear the abhorrent taste, and yanked the necklace off, tossing it into a patch of lettuce.

Her stomach rolled. "That may have been the worst one Elzac's made me yet," she grumbled through clenched teeth, trying to keep the bile in her stomach.

Elzac. How had he gotten inside Jallia's head? Why hadn't he told her about magic?

They flew by the farmlands, rows of vegetables and trees blurred past until the untamed meadow erupted. Waves of grass shifted in the wind, tipping with hints of color as they crested in the moonlight.

A prickling shiver cascaded from the base of Phe's neck down her back.

She chanced a quick glance behind.

One of the unknown riders had gotten in the lead, a hand in midair. Glowing eyes locked on her. In his palm, a ball of flickering lights formed. He threw it.

It was no ordinary toss. The ball of light zinged toward her, driven by an unseen and unnatural force.

What in the ever-loving high seas?

She veered Edva to the right.

Bam!

The explosive impact to the left pelted them with dirt and rocks. Both Phe and Edva involuntarily jumped, startled.

What was that?

She tuned in only long enough to hear familiar voices

yelling at her to stop. She ignored them, urging Edva to go faster.

There was shouting behind her, along with another ripple of trepidation rolling down the length of her spine.

Every hair on her body rose.

Instinctively, Phe swerved them to the left.

Boom!

A ball of light blasted to their right. A small branch embedded itself into Phe's bicep. Clenching her jaw, she ripped it out.

Almost there.

Edva's coat hardened under Phe. *Odd . . .* She ran her hand along Edva's neck. Long, hard scales had formed. *What in the seas?* Yanking her fingers away, she glanced down. Her fingers had not lied.

Black scales shimmered under a burst of lightning.

Scales? Phe refocused on the road, swallowing her bewilderment that her horse was covered in scales, only to receive another shock.

Lines of horses covered in armor blocked the road where there had been nothing before. Riders, hidden underneath protective gear, watched her, unperturbed that Phe was about to barrel into them.

Phe's heart stopped. *Where—? How had they appeared?!*

Edva reared and screeched.

Phe unsheathed one of her twin blades, assessing. There were at least twenty, if not thirty, horsemen. The odds were not in her favor.

A man at the front pulled his helmet off.

Bastion.

Seas, Phe despised him.

The scar along his cheek glistened in the moonlight. His cold, cunning gaze shackled hers.

She rolled a wrist, comforted by the weight of her twin blade, giving him a death stare. If he thought he could hold her hostage while Kyra was in danger, he had another think coming to him.

Another man removed his helmet. His slick black hair remained perfectly in place. He had thick black eyebrows that crowded his forehead, an elegant nose, and a perfectly balanced mouth that tilted upward at the corners. "General, she's magnificent," he said excitedly, his haughty tone revealing his identity.

Ambassador Katoa.

Phe despised him on sight.

Edva shuffled to the side, stamping her hooves.

Apparently, she agreed with Phe.

Phe leveled her blade at Bastion. There wasn't much time to think of other options. The pounding of hooves grew louder as the riders closed in. The instant they arrived, she knew any fight would be over. She'd be taken.

Phe nudged Edva into a gallop, heading straight for Bastion. Her blade gleamed in the moonlight.

Bastion didn't move.

Katoa's smiled widened, showcasing white teeth.

An invisible force wrapped around her blade, yanked her arm wide and ripped the twin from her grip. Then a vortex of wind struck her.

She flew off Edva's back.

The side of her face slammed into the dirt-packed road. Pain erupted. Granules of dirt scraped across her cheek and neck. The coppery taste of blood filled her mouth.

She leapt to her feet, unsheathed her remaining twin blade, and spat.

The ground tilted.

Edva screamed.

It was hard for Phe to know why. Somehow, she'd landed an absurd distance from her horse, and a row of people blocked Edva from her now. *If they hurt her...*

Phe hissed, eyes narrowed to slits, and sprinted, throwing one of her thigh knives into the fray.

Dead roots shot from the earth to wrap around her. It happened so stunningly fast, she didn't have a chance to brace for impact before being smashed into the hard-packed dirt road. She inhaled a plume of dust that burned her throat and chest, launching her into a coughing fit and weakening her struggle.

Phe didn't have a chance.

Roots bound her, covering every inch.

For a split second, she froze, paralyzed under the mass of earthly roots encasing her. Her heart pummeled against her ribs. Images flashed past: Drykz Forest, vines, imminent death ... Then, her heart lurched heavily, her breath caught, and her survival instinct regained its fighting footing.

One raw breath after another, Phe wildly strained to pry free while trying to keep Edva in sight. *How in the high seas are they doing this?*

The more she fought, the tighter the hold. Spindly, knobby roots forcibly turned her to stare into the awakening dawn sky.

With stiff movements, the roots unsheathed her knives, one by one, and flung them. Even her desperate grasp on her remaining twin didn't stand a chance. The roots cut her fingers as they pried them open.

A waxy, textured thing fluttered at her neck, crawling up her jawline, followed by another.

Phe stilled.

A green viny leaf unfurled and gently nudged her cheek. The musky scent of Drykz Forest washed over her, and the knot in her stomach released. A spiraled leaf rose alongside it, catching Phe's attention; it was riveted at something beyond Phe.

If a leaf could glare, that's exactly what it was doing. And, thank the stars, it was directed at Bastion and his minions.

The roots holding her loosened fractionally, and she squirmed, creating more space. But not enough to free herself.

The intensity of the approaching horses shook the ground.

Phe's body flooded with heat. Every muscle burned as she fought the roots. *This can't be it. I'm so close.* Sweat dripped along her ears and neck, but she didn't stop. Couldn't stop. *Kyra needs me.*

Horses flew by, encircling her. Dust filtered heavily into the air while chunks of earth pelted her. Other horses slowed around them.

"Phe!" Orc was beside her, carefully brushing the debris and roots from her face. The roots moved easily with his touch. "Are you okay?"

Phe's dagger-sharp gaze stabbed Orc. No other response was needed.

"Seas, Phe. We were hoping to have a little time to prepare you." Orc's fingers gently pressed into her temples. "How in the world did you manage this? Last I saw you, you were unconscious, drooling on yourself."

Roar's command, "Stand down. She's one of us," carried to her at the same time a warning shout came from Bastion's side.

Someone scoffed. Others from Shadow Unit encircled her, their backs to her, blocking her view.

"Ridiculous. Get out of our way."

"In that case, we claim the nix too and challenge you."

The ground under her shifted.

"Accepted—" Roar's tone was cutting.

"Shield, we have incoming!"

"—we'll sort it out in Arias."

Noises of struggle ensued, horses neighing.

What is happening?

Phe flinched at a loud whizzing noise as, above them, a brilliant white light formed. It stretched itself over them, becoming a shimmering translucent color. Its edges dropped, creating a dome shape and, from what Phe could tell, encasing the area. When it was at her level, it felt as though a swarm of tiny ants crawled over her.

What in creation . . .

Orc ignored it all, his glowing moss eyes honed onto her. "We can't stop what's happening, but we are going to buffer as much as we can. Trust us."

She slitted her eyes in response.

"Is the forest attacking!?" someone yelled clearly enough for Phe to understand in the wave of sound crashing around her.

The "dome" emitted a low-pitched hum, adding to the jumble of chaotic sounds. Her skin burned as more vines scraped across her.

Orc glanced over his shoulder as Ihrone sidestepped someone. A burst of wind slipped over Phe, sweeping toward them, and then the person was gone. Just gone.

The ground caved under her, and she was yanked to the side, into a tunnel. More dirt covered her. Phe knew these vines, their sentience a dead giveaway. *Drykz Forest.* She relaxed, hope sparking.

Orc dove after her, his grasp on her slowing the vines'

momentum. Some unraveled with his grip, but it wasn't enough to stop her.

The ground beneath her exploded, and she was thrown.

Phe smacked into a hard wall of muscle, unable to stop herself from falling with the roots and vines that encased her. As she struggled to free herself, a collection of rough hands forced her to eat ground, and someone shoved a knee across her shoulders. Phe could tell by their weight, it was Kirzia.

Her brief flare of hope shattered.

Her arms were wrenched backwards. Cold metal slid over a wrist, clicking shut, before her other hand was twisted painfully and treated likewise.

Phe tested the strength of the shackles. As expected, there was no give. She turned her face into the dirt and silently screamed. Dirt and pebbles dug into her, mixing with her blood. *So flipping close . . .* Grief welled in her as quickly as a passing summer storm, its heavy rain drowning her in a sea of despair.

"Check her," she heard Roar command.

Fingers settled on a patch of exposed flesh at her lower back. The warm, soothing energy Phe was now starting to associate with Orc seeped into her.

Phe twisted her face out of the dirt, trying to wiggle from under his touch. "Don't. Touch. Me," she barked.

"Sir?" Orc's touch lightened.

A tremendous *boom* reverberated. Shouts rang out.

"What the flip?!"

"General, we can't hold the shield!"

Phe's gaze pivoted, searching for the source. The dome's translucent covering rippled. A twinge of satisfaction thrummed through her. Drykz Forest was attacking them. For her. Who knew what creatures it pulled from its depths?

"Portal!" An offbeat humming thrummed to life, an additional layer to the already overwhelming sounds.

"Do it." Roar's tone broached no argument, and the press of Orc's fingers on her increased again.

Phe growled, wiggling. "Kirzia, get off me," she grunted angrily, pulling on her shackles again, if only to feel the sting of pain.

"Sorry, girl, can't do."

"Why are you guys doing this? Why aren't you rescuing Kyra?"

Finian fearlessly placed his face next to hers. "Right now we're helping you."

"Me?" she snarled, trying to head-butt him. "I don't need rescuing."

"Really?" Finian took a moment to obviously scan her. "Because it doesn't look that way to me."

Phe sealed her mouth, letting her expression speak for her.

Roar squatted, his glowing blue eyes on her. "You want to rescue Kyra? Going to Arias is the only way you'll be able to. We know who's taken her and what he is capable of. Running off blindly in search of her will get you nowhere fast."

Phe jutted her jaw out, refraining from telling him about Elzac.

"None of us *needed* to touch you to immobilize you. Think about that," Kirzia added from above her, digging her knee into Phe's back one more time, then releasing her.

A blanketed weight settled across her shoulders and upper back in Kirzia's absence, demonstrating her point. The weight wrapped around her sides, pinning her more securely to the ground.

Seas, I despise them. All of them. Why hadn't they used their magic to protect Kyra?

"The only way to rescue Kyra is to learn about your capabilities. Harness them. We'll help you," Roar continued.

Phe grunted. Like she'd trust them again.

"Commander, she's too hot-headed right now." Ihrone said, unhelpfully in Phe's opinion.

"We can't hold the shield much longer!" someone shouted.

"Portals open, go, go, go!"

"Get her across!" Bastion's voice carried over the chaos.

"I'll take her." Ihrone bent, the restraining weight lifted, and he rolled her onto her back. The cuffs dug into Phe more. A few vines fell away, but not nearly enough. "Muzzle her."

WHAT?

An invisible weight pressed across her mouth and jaw.

"Sorry, Phe." Ihrone had the audacity to grab her chin and force eye contact. "I have no intention of being bitten."

Drowning in rage, she closed her eyes as he hefted her into his arms. Each place their skin connected radiated painfully.

"No, I'll carry her." Without waiting for a response, Orc pulled her out of Ihrone's arms and into his soothing touch.

Opening her eyes, Phe cranked her head as far away from Orc as possible.

"We are about to walk through a portal," Orc said, shifting her against his chest. "Think of a portal as simply a doorway from one place to another, but it stretches over vast distances, effectively shortening the time it takes to get from one place to another. It's a capability of transportation magic."

They were heading directly toward a circular opening

hanging in the air like a life-sized painting would on a wall. Phe couldn't capture glimpses of the canvas because people were walking through it, blocking her view.

Then they walked through it.

Her skin crawled, and the temperature changed from warm summer to a crisper chill. The scent of morning dew with hints of fresh grass hit her.

The noise lessened.

Vibrant green lawn stretched as far as—an armor-plated chest intercepted them.

It was Bastion, the bastard. He wasn't alone. Katoa hovered at his shoulder.

"General," Orc acknowledged, his grip tightening.

Phe scowled at them, squirming in Orc's arms, and averted her gaze.

Bastion leaned in, his warm breath skittering like fire ants across her cheek. Grabbing her by the hair, he forced her to meet his predatory gaze. "Welcome to Arias."

Phe gave him a murderous look.

Bastion twisted her head.

She glimpsed people and horses hustling through the painting—no, portal—they'd just come from. She could make out the pre-dawn sky, the translucent dome's fractures, and Drykz Forest's vines slinking through cracks.

Bastion didn't stop, though, jerking her awkwardly to the side.

Light morning fog swirled along the ground of an empty field, grass peeking through the mist at the edge closest to them. Above and beyond, green mountains scaled into brilliant crystal-blue skies, rising from the fog and drifting into clouds. Out of its foothills, glistening white towers with blue-tiled roofs and silver-pointed tips competed with lower-level archways lined with lush greens—giving Phe the impression they were covered in vegetation, but it was hard to tell with the distance.

The view stole her breath.

Bastion released her. "Welcome to your new home."

"Prison, you mean," Phe said, the instant her muzzle vanished.

Bastion's lips curved upwards slightly, but his gaze was shrewd. "Call it what you want." His scar tightened, lips narrowing to a line. "How did you get the forest to attack?"

She flicked her gaze up and toward the horizon, debating her response. Large birds circled several of the towers. She watched them soar for a second or two, settling her resolve. "I didn't."

"Put her down."

Orc carefully released her, plucking at the vines still encircling her.

"Phe, there is nothing you can hide from me here."

"Who's taken Kyra? Where is she being held?" Phe shook her shackled wrists—hinting they take them off. Orc pulled at an especially long root, but it was entangled with others all along her body. She'd need to cut her way out of this mess. "Why—"

"Genor, you're up."

"Sir!" came Roar's response as icicles pierced into her shoulder and the world melted.

13

A bright, white-walled room morphed around Phe, and an uncanny silence filled the small space. Slowly, she spun, stilling when she met the glowing golden gaze of Ambassador Genor.

A table appeared before him, and he planted his palms on it.

Something rammed into the back of her knees. She toppled backward into a chair, shackles snapped closed around her calves and thighs.

A gasp lodged itself in her throat, sweat dampened her armpits.

Seas.

Phe focused on calming her galloping heart. *Not the first time*, she reminded herself, collecting her bravery and wielding it like a shield. *Won't be the last.* She forced her posture to relax.

"Why was your magic bound?" Ambassador Genor demanded. "Who bound you?"

She gave him an *I-have-no-idea-what-you're-talking-about* look. He wasn't the only one with questions. Had Djall abducted Kyra? Where was she being held? What was the meaning of having magic? Why did someone "bind" her magic? Why hadn't they used magic to protect Kyra? Where were they and how'd they get here? What would happen in Arias? Could she escape?

At her silence, Ambassador Genor impatiently swiped at the table. Phe's eyes widened in shock as it disappeared and he walked through the space where it had stood. Straps cinched on her arms, securing them to armrests that hadn't been there seconds prior.

"In here," one of his hands lifted to take in the room, "I have other ways to get the answers I seek. I suggest you talk. It's less . . . violating."

She tasted the word. *Violating.* Wasn't her life built from one violation after another? Or was it one betrayal after another? The two intertwined.

"Where are we? Where is Kyra?" Phe countered, satisfied her voice sounded strong, calm.

"This," he pointed a finger between them, "doesn't work that way. I ask a question, you answer. What happened in Xafara?"

She slow-blinked. Didn't he already know? Wasn't he part of this magical world?

"Fine. We'll do it the hard way." Ambassador Genor grabbed her head, his touch glacial. His fingers, jagged talons of ice, dug into her temples. Behind the cold, an invasive force slithered on the fringes.

Phe shivered, the fine hair along her body standing up. *What is he doing?*

A slow throb started at the base of her skull. Sweat beaded on her forehead and upper lip as her heat rose, a wave of lava barreling into the sea, holding him off.

It did not deter him.

He adjusted, searching for weak spots and drilling into them.

Phe's flames layered themselves against him, fortifying her walls. Sweat dripped from her forehead, into her eyes, down her nose.

His grip on her changed. A sheet of ice coated her, freezing her sweat, then began a slow, grinding motion on her scalp.

Cripes. Her heart raced. *He's getting in.*

He was crushing her.

You want information? Anger crested in massive white-tipped waves.

She visualized *the room*—the space where her tortured past was created.

The small chamber appeared, its jagged stone walls filthy but not empty. Handcuffs had been embedded into the wall. A chain attached to a collar, with spikes lining the interior of the choker, hung nearby. Hooks dotted the walls, the ceiling. The only entry point was a single wooden door with a small window. Phe pushed the heavy door open, its metal hinges creaking.

Ambassador Genor pushed again.

She dropped her walls, and he stumbled at the sudden give.

She slammed the door shut, sliding the bolt in place.

He twisted, golden eyes narrowed, stance ready.

"You want in my head?" There was a touch of crazy in her voice, and Phe knew it flashed in her eyes and cruel smile. "Have at it." She said as she flooded the room with the three years of memories it held.

She watched him from the window, the one Grum, or one of his friends, had hovered in. The darkness in the corners rushed to the center of the room, swirling around Ambassador Genor's legs.

Slowly, calmly, Ambassador Genor sat, and the darkness enveloped him. Only his glowing golden eyes were visible, latched onto her own.

Her hands trembled. Her insides quivered.

She might be safe from him for now, but those same memories slithered across her skin in a dark caress, threatening to drag her into the darkness alongside him.

14

A hand landed on Phe's shoulder.

She startled, gulping in a breath. Her hand instinctively wrapped around it, preparing to break the arm attached to it...

Then the scent of woodsy smokiness she knew to be Elzac hit her. Phe froze, fingers tense and nails digging into the flesh of his calloused, wrinkled hand.

Elzac coalesced beside her.

A dim light flickered on, chasing the shadows into corners and illuminating his white hair.

"You shouldn't startle me." She brushed his touch off. *How'd he get here? Where am I?*

"I trust you."

She scoffed. "Well, I don't. You don't surprise a feral animal."

"Phe." He peered into the room. "I'd say, if we're using animal analogies, you're cornered, not feral."

With a disagreeing grunt, she swiveled, gazing at his wrinkled face, white-whiskered stubble with matching hair, and those glowing white eyes. No, feral was right. Over the years, she'd had aspects of herself domesticated. She could tolerate social interaction and was no longer selectively mute. Yet there was a fierce, untamed wildness that lived within her. A wildness she harnessed to hone the predator within her with Bastion's training.

"Why didn't you tell me?" The words burst out of her, voice wavering. "And how are you here?"

"It wasn't the right time." Elzac bumped her with his shoulder. "The work we did was to prepare you for this journey, and it has. I couldn't very well give you all the food you would eat for the entirety of your life and ask you to eat it in one sitting, could I?"

"Ah, no?" How was it Elzac always found the most bizarre ways to make a point? No one could eat that much all at once.

"The same applies here. It would've been too much. You wouldn't have been able to absorb everything. And it would've distracted you from what you needed the most: healing."

It was true. When they'd met, Phe had been in what he'd called a dark night of the soul. How could she argue with what Elzac said now?

"Your path led to where we are, and I'm positive there were lessons and experiences you've had that were pivotal in your growth. Let's take Shadow Unit—"

"I'd rather not."

"Your relationship with them—"

She tensed. "Was built from lies."

The left side of Elzac's mouth scrunched, and he said, "Have you told them about your past or your nightmares?"

"No."

"What about your connection to the forest and me?"

"I haven't." Anger heated her cheeks. "But it's not the same thing."

"Why isn't it?"

"Why would they need to know about Grum? Or what features in my nightmares? I thought my time in the forest, you, the village, was a secret? I don't break oaths." A red haze drifted in Phe's sight, her voice raising. "And, it doesn't interfere with my ability to perform."

"And since it doesn't interfere, it's none of their business?"

She chewed her lip, knowing he was setting her up. It *was* none of their business.

"Would you have them break an oath they took?"

"Yes," she hissed, irrationality rearing its ugly head.

"Because?"

"Because magic was used to abduct Kyra." Unwanted tears strained to break free. "I couldn't protect her from magic." Phe's breathing came in choppy gasps, and her pulverized heart throbbed, but she pushed the words out. "And I can't protect myself."

Her lungs seized as the dam on her emotions broke. The flood caused a numbness to creep into her fingers and toes, and her knees weakened.

She couldn't breathe.

With a hand pressed to her chest, she sucked in small sips of air to combat the black dots in her vision.

"Breathe."

Phe shot Elzac a *don't-you-see-I'm-trying-to* glare and leaned into the wall. *Inhale. Exhale.*

Sucking one manually-intensive breath after another, the vise released and the dark smudges in her vision disappeared.

"Better?"

No. "I haven't had one of those in years." She pushed off the wall.

How could she explain her heart was shredded beyond measure? Kyra's abduction ripped out most of the organ, not that she'd had much of one, and the remaining parts fragmented. Then, instead of dying from heartache and a magic rebound, she'd woken to have the remaining pieces crushed into stardust by the few people she had trusted.

She'd trained for the last fourteen years to protect Kyra, and what good was she? Failure wasn't a strong enough word. Incompetent. Useless. And the only thing holding her back from sinking into the abyss of self-pity was knowing Kyra was alive.

Or at least, she hoped.

Who was Djall? What was he doing with Kyra? Why had he taken her? Would he harm her? Kill her? How much time did Phe have to find her? Where should she search? Why did she sense Bastion had withheld information about Djall? Roar too.

Who could she trust?

How could she possibly rescue Kyra with what she knew?

I can't.

The thought stopped her in her tracks. *I. Can't.*

It was a series of words she never used together, especially in connection with Kyra. "I can't" translated into a helpless welling in her chest. "I can't" eroded all possibilities and problem-solving thinking. "I can't" undermined the essence of who she was. It took away her willingness to try, setting her up for defeat.

A wise man once told her, you cannot fail at being yourself, which is exactly what "I can't" thinking tried to make her believe.

The feeling of being sliced from the inside out smashed into her stomach.

What if they held her hostage in Arias? Her heart hammered. Would they lock her in a cell? And what in the seas happened today? Was that all magic? How could she have magic? It wasn't possible. They were wrong. They had to be mistaken.

Phe took a steadying breath, pushing against the heavy weight that settled on her and throatily confessing, "I feel helpless."

"There's a difference between being helpless and uncontrollable situations. Helplessness is an internal process, a belief that no matter what you do, it won't change the outcome. It steals people's power and stops them from doing anything. When they restrained you, did you stop fighting?"

"No."

"When Genor brought you here, did you resign and believe he had the upper hand?"

"I don't think so." She scrubbed a hand across her face. There hadn't been time to think. The only thing she could remember was a spike of defiance once he'd strapped her into the chair. "No."

"Life is uncontrollable except for your inner landscape. Just because these circumstances are well beyond your ability to anticipate, it doesn't mean you are helpless." Elzac tapped his forehead. "It means you're overwhelmed. Scared. Angry. Stuck in this moment. Stuck on the how."

She laughed bitterly. "I'm all those things and some." The heaviness inside her shifted a little.

"I'd be too." The corner of his eyes crinkled, and his mouth softened. "You need to feel those emotions, otherwise the energy can't pass through you."

She stared at the junction of the ceiling and wall, shadows and dirt filled the rough, uneven crevice, loosening her suddenly clenched jaw. There wasn't time, and it wasn't safe. These feelings were big. *Don't snap*, she coached herself. *He's trying to help.*

"I'll keep this in mind," was the best she could answer.

His left eye squinted, one of his endearing tells. "I'm sure you will, while you run around saving the world."

"Seas no!" A laugh burst from her lips, surprising Phe. "The only saving I'm doing is Kyra. Speaking of which, do you know anything about Djall? Where she's being held?"

"Djall has been alive for centuries, but no magic-born knows where he holds hostages. Only *she* knows." Elzac used the word with reverence.

"She? The forest?"

"*She* is many things." Elzac shifted his weight between his feet, a visual balancing scale as he weighed his thoughts. "Do you know where you are?"

"Arias." *Did he just change the subject?*

"Many say it's the best of the five cities." The softness in his face disappeared, gaze serious. "You are going to need to tread very carefully."

"I'll try, but—"

"Do more than try." That was the closest thing to an order she'd ever heard from him. "I know you want information on Djall. If we had more time, I would. But we don't."

Phe schooled her face, frustrated beyond measure. She clenched her fists and released. She wanted to punch things. She had a rescue mission to conduct, and no one would tell her what she needed to know.

"I understand your frustration, and I'm sorry. I need to give you your first magic lesson." Elzac's glowing white gaze settled on her. "You'd asked how I was here, yes?"

She nodded.

"I have the ability to enter people's minds."

"Are we in my mind?" A bolt of adrenaline zipped through her, nerve ends tingling.

"Yes."

"How? Are you—? Is he—?" Her mind reeled. How could they be in her mind?

"Neither of us is harming you," he assured, pride deepening his voice. "You neatly handled Genor on your own."

His compliment bounced off her, not rooting. How could it? She'd be proud if she knew what she was doing, had been working at a skill and achieved it. But this? She'd only done what came naturally to survive.

"I'm going to instruct you on how to erect a basic mental barrier. This will stop those with our abilities from waltzing into your mind." Elzac's eyes flared. "To do so I'll need to touch you and draw you into my mind's eye for a moment. Can I?"

"You'll teach me to protect myself?"

"Of course."

Hope sparked. Shoulders relaxed. "Let's do this."

He grasped her hands lightly, his touch leathery. "Close your eyes." She did, briefly considering how his touch wasn't affecting her.

There was an odd sucking sensation and then a filtered light streamed through a ceiling of intricate branches. Boughs overhead dripped with green vines, their leaves basking in the sunlight. The soft grass underfoot made her want to kick off her shoes and dig her toes in, and the familiar musky scent of the forest engulfed her.

Drykz Forest.

Elzac stood a few feet from her. A stray beam of sunlight shone directly on him, glistening across his age-worn skin, giving him an ethereal appearance. His white aura blurred and shimmered and appeared layered.

"I've never seen an aura like yours." Phe was surprised it hadn't faded.

"That's because it's not my aura. This is what my mental protection barriers look like," Elzac said, watching her. "Touch the outer layer and tell me what you feel."

Phe hesitantly touched the first ring. It let off a soft humming, and a buzz vibrated up her hand and forearm. "It vibrates, and my arm feels tingly."

He smiled, but there was a sadness to his eyes. "For you, this is what you'll feel. For someone else, the outer layer will lock onto them and execute a series of very painful shocks."

"Would something like this have stopped Genor from entering my mind?"

"Genor . . ." Elzac compressed his lips, thinking. "His training and abilities far surpass the majority of mental mages. For the rest, this and all the other barriers we're about to set up should be sufficient."

Phe jumped into his pause. "How do I create this?" *More importantly, how do I use magic?*

Elzac studied her, the corners of his eyes crinkling into crows feet. "This type of magic is imagery based. I will guide you through it. Before we get started, I'd like to link myself into your magic—this way, if someone is powerful enough to breach these barriers or attack you in any form, I can step in."

"You think someone would try that?" Phe shifted her weight from foot to foot, suddenly nervous again.

"Phe," Seriousness veiled his face. "The power you can wield is incredible, beyond what anyone has seen. You are truly a masterpiece, and there are many people in the world who'd seek to control you for their own gains. They could shred your mind completely with a thought if they wanted to."

Gads, that did not sound good. "And you'd be able to help?"

"Yes." A vine dropped onto Elzac's shoulder, snaking around his arm. The leaves arched upward, and Phe watched Elzac pet the underside of several leaves, like one would a cat's chin. "Also, I'd like to have a way of monitoring you, and this would give me access to scan you and make sure you're okay."

"What do you mean, monitor? Would you be able to read my mind?" This set her pacing toward the end of the clearing, she didn't like this idea at all—privacy was paramount for her. The idea of someone having access to her thoughts or feelings unbidden made her shudder.

"For me, monitoring means I would be able to keep a watch out for you if something were to happen, like in the Juncture. Mental magic isn't done on the physical plane, and there's so many different ways to you could be attacked. Thus, having me monitor your safety allows me to step in and stop those."

She stopped at a medium sized rock jutting out of an exposed hillside. A large, oak tree had grown at its side. One of its roots had long ago wrapped around the rock, encircling it. What had once been a tendril, had grown into a thick, strong root the size of Phe's bicep, and it squeezed the rock.

Phe squatted, flattening her palm on its coarse surface. "I didn't hear you say no," she said. With her pointer, she scrapped at the dirt clinging to the rock, uncovering little fissures.

The rock was her. Rough and dirty and with hidden fissures. Wrapped tightly in the arms of life. Squeezed by arms that crushed her. *Gads, how bad was it that she empathized with a rock?*

"Phe." Phe swiveled to Elzac at the solemnity in his voice. "I vow to never read your mind or access your memories." The vines on the tree shook themselves, in a wave of rustling, and focused on her.

She stood, inhaling the forest's musky fragrance. "I consent to your help."

A smile erupted on Elzac's face, rounding his cheeks. "I am honored with your trust. Now, close your eyes and imagine rings forming around you. As many rings as you possibly can."

She did. Heat blossomed in her chest and spread to her limbs.

"Good, good," came his pleased response. "Now imagine . . ." he sucked in an audible breathe, "a spider's web spread across all the layers."

Sweat beaded on her lip, forehead, the back of her neck. She nodded when she was done.

"Now, open your eyes. I'm going to infuse my magic into the layers to give them different defenses. I need you to repeat everything I do. Do you understand?"

"Yes." She fixed her gaze on Elzac.

"The first layer we're going to infuse with a high dose of electricity." Elzac raised his palm to hip level, Phe mimicked him. The air thickened with energy, and her hair lifted to float around her face. "Do you feel the power in the air?"

Phe nodded.

"Pull the power to your hand like you pull your shadows to you."

Phe took a deep steadying breath, willing her racing heart to settle as she tentatively imagined drawing the crackling tension into her palm. She startled when a small, white, fizzling ball formed.

"Good. Keep pulling," Elzac coached. "Get it as big as you can."

Phe flicked a glance over to his palm. A much larger ball of electricity hovered above it. She refocused on hers, and this time, she yanked the surrounding power to her. The small ball in her hand blasted into a two-foot-long sizzling ball of electricity, with wisps flicking outward as if it were licking the air.

"Well done." Phe heard the smile and pride in his voice.

She leaned away from it, giving him a tentative smile back, not shifting her gaze from the ball of electricity. Excitement and apprehension coursed through her.

Seas! She stared at the ball, transfixed, her mind blank. She'd done that, but what had she done? Had she really gathered the electricity in the air? Was this real?

"To infuse this into your barrier, we're going to touch your outer barrier at the same time and place—like a high five." He was already reaching forward, preparing.

Phe, still leaning away from the spitting ball of energy, did as he said. Their palms met and all that spastic electrical energy funneled into the barrier. Instantly, the barrier's clear surface filled with the white, sizzling energy.

High seas! Her mouth slackened and her heart stilled as a sense of wonderment struck her.

"If anyone attacks this barrier, it will give them a shock that should be enough of a warning to stop."

Phe shifted her gaze from their connected palms to meet Elzac's. Worry swept through her. "Did I cover your signature?"

"For our purposes, you have. When combining powers, it's not possible to completely remove someone's signature.

But, someone would have to look specifically for mine, which should be challenging to find because of the amount of power you pushed into the barrier. It's equivalent to trying to hear a whisper in a stadium filled with screaming people." Elzac nodded approvingly, then gestured to the next layer. "Now, let's move on to the next one."

Phe grunted her readiness, feeling a sense of seriousness wash over her. This may be a new world, with magic capable of doing things she couldn't comprehend or anticipate, but doing this now felt good. More than good. Empowering. She may not be able to defend herself outside of this mental barrier, but by the stars, if it meant not allowing anyone to waltz into her head to attack like Ambassador Genor did or worse—try to see her memories or hear her thoughts—she was pacified.

What seemed like an eternity later, Elzac took a step back, scanning her new pulsing and moving barriers. "Good. You've done well." A grimness settled into his chin. "Phe, it's more important now than ever that you keep your oath to me and those of Ligeia. No one can know about us."

"I promise," she pledged.

Weariness crept into his features, forming crescents under his eyes, paling him. "You'll know right away if someone skims your barriers. I'll be notified if they breach the innermost layer."

Phe nodded. It made sense he would want to be alerted only if there was a danger of them succeeding and not at every encounter. "Are you okay?"

"There is always a cost to using magic." The corners of his mouth lifted a little. "Now, let us release Ambassador Genor."

"Ugh." Phe slumped. Releasing the ambassador meant

she'd have to leave Elzac, return to wherever they'd brought her. Face she was a prisoner in a new city, a new world.

The forest faded away, and darkness seeped in, forming the hallway and wooden door. She peered through the window. Genor was exactly as she left him. Cross-legged in the middle of the room. Eyes closed, posture relaxed.

"Do I have to?" she all but whined. "He looks fine."

"Phe." Patience threaded each word. "You know better than anyone else. Looking fine doesn't mean you're okay."

Phe grumpily thumped her head against the wooden door, knowing he was right. "Fine."

"And remember, first impressions aren't always accurate." His voice waned.

She rolled onto her face, smushing her cheek into the window pane, peering around.

Elzac was gone.

Slowly, she dragged her hand up and encircled the cool metal key, fumbling with the lock. Its release echoed in the hallway. She pulled the door open, shuddering when the hinges screamed.

Ambassador Genor's eyes popped open, locking onto her. His face was unreadable.

She had the distinct impression he wasn't looking at her, but beyond her to her shields. A whisper of wind brushed past them. Something sharpened in his predator gaze, and the wind encapsulated her.

She held her breath, waiting for his attack and having no idea how to prepare for it.

His magic pulsed into hers, but instead of ripping down the walls, it melded into them.

What is he doing?

There was something about his eyes that reminded her of one of Sryln Sierras' glacial mountain lakes: its smooth surface, disrupted only by the occasional wind that rippled its vibrant teal expanse and created small lapping waves at its rocky shoreline. Yet if she waded into the lake, powerful undercurrents would wrestle her into the arctic depths, to the underground river rushing through it.

Briefly, she allowed herself to consider what Elzac had said. *"Looking fine doesn't mean you're okay."* Was it true? Her stomach dropped as she realized she too had clear, still water on the surface, yet was engulfed in a turbulent battle of currents within.

She cleared her throat, stopping the train of thought, and leaned on the doorframe. "If I knew how to end this, I would, but I don't. So," she leveled her gaze, pausing for effect. "Are you done?"

One side of Ambassador Genor's mouth quirked up. "For now, yes." He hopped to his feet, the movement quick and hands-free, then tucked his hands in his pockets as he strode past her, out of the room. "But if I were you, I wouldn't be in such a rush to swim with sharks."

15

Phe jack-knifed into a sitting position, ripping free of the arms loosely wrapped around her, and scuttled backwards. She twisted to pierce Orc, the owner of the arms, with a death glare and then swept her gaze across the expansive meadow.

The familiar whisper of a blade releasing from its sheath came from her right.

Orc jumped to his feet, attention over her shoulder, and moved.

Phe shuffled at the sight of a woman appearing at her side, sword out.

Orc positioned himself between them, blocking the woman. "Don't."

Where had she come from?

A small group of people nearby tensed, gazes flickering between her, Orc, and the woman. Phe turned toward them, ready to defend herself.

Finian planted himself in front of Phe, forcing her to bump into Orc's back, as the small group advanced. "Back-off."

"Do. Not. Touch. Her." Bastion's steely voice boomed. Phe's gaze locked onto General Bastion. The scar on the side of his face was taut. His clean-shaven jaw, tight. His piercing stare arched across the field, filleting everyone. "You're all dismissed."

All movement halted for a moment, then the woman and the lingering groups of people—including the one Finian blocked her from—began the long walk toward the towered city.

Ihrone, Roar, Ambassador Genor and Katoa stood next to Bastion, peering at her. Genor's expressionless gaze caught hers. Keen intelligence shone from his eyes. She skimmed Katoa, whose face featured a mixture of wonderment, excitement, and blatant longing—it disgusted her. Her gaze clashed with Bastion's. His brown, soulless eyes drilled into her.

She stalked forward, ignoring Orc and Finian pacing her. When she reached Bastion, she spared Ambassador Genor a small chin tilt, and disregarded Katoa outright. Genor withdrew, but Katoa inched closer.

Too close.

Almost as if he was trying to smell her. Or taste her fist.

Finian squeezed himself between them, brushing against Phe—causing a wave of pain at their contact—as he nudged Katoa aside.

It was Roar who spoke crisply from the other side of Katoa. "Excuse me Ambassadors, we're going to need a moment."

Phe ignored Kirzia and Ihrone as they formed a semicircle around them.

With a steadying breath, she forced out. "Kyra's been missing for hours." Surprisingly, her voice didn't waver or come out treacherously thin, like the almost severed bond barely attached to her. It sounded strong, defiant even. "What's being done? Tell me everything."

Bastion's face was all sharp angles. "The time for the questions." His tone dipped threateningly, "and answers will come. It's *time* for us to see what type of magic you have."

Angry red-hot splotches erupted on her neck. *Kyra's life is at stake and he is refusing to give me information?* She stepped into his space, "You—"

"Sir," Roar interrupted, wedging in between her and Bastion.

Simultaneously, an arm draped around Phe's shoulder and tugged. A burning sensation flared painfully at his touch, tensing hers shoulders. Finian's tone serious, he murmured, "Let's take a walk before things escalate."

Phe swung her aggravation toward Finian, letting him draw her away. He had a point—Bastion would only double down—and, in her current state, she might do something she'd regret. She flicked Finian's arm from her shoulder and sucked in a steadying breath. Clenching and unclenching her hands.

"I know this is a lot to take in." Finian kept them moving. "Kyra. Magic. Arias. Everything in between. I get it. But, you're no longer in Xafara and things work differently here."

"Very differently." Kirzia contributed from Finian's other side. Orc fell into pace on Phe's free side.

"Right now is not the time to go head to head with the General," Finian continued.

Orc cleared his throat, slipping in. "Actually, there will never be a good time."

Finian ignored Orc's interruption. "Because your magic rebounded, and you have a lot of power and you're an adult and your aura's crazy and you ran, which no one knows—"

Kirzia swung in front of her, halting them. "What Fin's trying to tell you right now is it's not the time to be uncooperative. They have no qualms incapacitating you, or worse." Kirzia's gaze hardened over Phe's ear.

Phe roughly scrubbed her face. "Kyra's missing. I don't understand why everyone's in a huff about me and not out there rescuing her." Phe folded her arms across her chest, twisting to glare at Bastion, who was talking with Roar, Ihrone, Ambassador Katoa and Genor.

"Eyes on me." Orc commanded. Kirzia moved out of the way and slightly ahead of them so Phe could see her, and they started walking again. "General Bastion has a team working on trying to locate her, but to him, you are the priority right now. *Think about it.*"

Phe held back a retort. *Nothing made sense.*

Why would they drag me into this city when I should be out there searching for Kyra?

Phe's entire existence in Xafara was solely based on protecting Kyra. It made no sense why Bastion was doing this. None. He didn't care about her. He's tried to get rid of her for years. Yet, here he is. Focusing on her, not Kyra.

"Why is he prioritizing me?"

Orc softened his expression. "It is unheard of to have one's magic bound. Once you learn more about our society, you'll understand why. But someone bound your magic and hid you from the magical community. Which opens a pandora's box of problems and questions, especially when you are so powerful."

Phe swallowed the frog in her throat, her arms loosening. "I'm powerful?"

"Girl," Kirzia's no-sass face tightened the corners of her mouth and eyes. "You have no idea."

"My power isn't going anywhere, and Kyra's in danger. Mortal danger. It doesn't matter—"

"Oh, it matters." Finian's tone fluctuated with each word. "We train from the moment we suckle our mothers how to handle our magic. Everyone masters their magic, and the earlier the better, so we know our place."

"We also know what our capabilities are at birth." Kirzia's attention was on Roar, Ihrone, and Bastion, who were trailing behind them. "Because we're all tested. Which is what you are going to do now. You guys keep going. I want to talk to General Bastion." Kirzia said as she strode to join the others.

Sweeping a brooding gaze across the field, Phe realized it was empty. "Where did . . .?"

"Everyone go?" Orc finished when she didn't. "This," He gestured at the field. "Is our primary entrance to the Arias. It grants us the first level of access into Arias. Then we have two specific jumping stations, one to the city's receiving courtyard and the other to the stables. We're—"

"Oh seas, Edva?" Worry sent rays of guilty spikes through Phe. *How could I have forgotten about Edva?*

Orc slowed. "Phe, I need to explain about the jumps."

But Finian spoke over him, answering her. "She's safe." Finian eased closer. "Ihrone stabled her with ours."

Suspiciously, Phe glanced at Finian. "What's a jumping station?" She asked Orc.

"You're about to find out." Finian's feisty tone and twinkling smile paused her mid-step.

But it was too late.

A suction captured her calf, yanking her forward.

Her leg disappeared up to mid-thigh.

She reared back, fighting the pull, but Finian's big palm

landed at her mid-shoulders, pushing her through. Finian's roaring laughter followed her, as he emerged right behind her.

Phe gritted her teeth. *I'm going to kill him.*

"Fin, not funny." Orc chastised, as he appeared alongside Finian.

White stone archways lined the perimeter of the large courtyard Phe found herself in. It took Phe a moment to realize the archways were gardened walkways hosting trees filled with lush, vibrant leaves, flowers, and overflowing vines. People were lined up in the greenery. Watching.

The receiving circular courtyard, as they'd called it, was huge, and at the center was a massive fountain monument. It portrayed a man in battle, sword held at face height, blocking an attack from a dragon's extended claws as it dived at him. A cut on the side of his face ran from his hairline to mid-cheek. Determination and focus exuded from the grim set of his face. A face she recognized.

Her stomach plummeted. A face she currently despised.

Bastion, the bastard.

Phe swallowed hard. *Bastion had a statue immortalizing him?* Incredulous, she switched her focus to the dragon.

The dragon was enormous, wings outstretched ten or possibly twenty feet past Bastion. Scales glinted with reds and golds, and its lips were curled back in a vicious snarl, showcasing its rows of dagger sharp teeth.

Dragons.

Bastion.

Oh seas, what the stars?

"It's magnificent, isn't it?" Finian swung his arm around her shoulders again, tucking her to his side as they walked, and re-igniting the burning pain.

She tossed his arm off, muttering, "Don't touch me." But she didn't put distance between them, as she normally would.

Unable to articulate anything sensical or appropriate, she studied the clusters of people in the courtyard. Many of them were soldiers she recognized from the field. Yet, there were also women in intricate and vibrant day dresses and other men in sharp suits, some eccentric and matching with companions.

Those weren't what caused her ripple of apprehension.

It was the line of shimmering, black-robed people, wearing pointy black hoods that covered their faces, observing her through slotted holes. It was like they were rows upon rows of grim reapers, here to make sure she finally ascended to the celestial stairway and onwards.

Finian whistled low. "They brought out the big guns for you, baby girl."

Her throat clogged again, and she fought the urge to hide behind Finian. This did not bode well for her.

"Or they think you're dangerous and are readying to put you down," Finian gloated pridefully. "As if we'd—"

"Fin." Roar's patient-yet-strained voice came from behind.

"What?" Finian's tone raised an octave.

Roar ignored Finian and squeezed in between him and Phe. "Phe, General Bastion will accompany you during your testing. We'd go with you if we could, but we're not allowed. You should be safe. Just do as they say, keep quiet—"

"She shouldn't have a problem with that." Finian slipped in.

Phe shot him a scowl, even though he was right.

"We'll find you afterward." Roar talked over Fin.

Before Phe could respond, Bastion strode past them, barking at her. "Phe."

"Go," Roar nudged her shoulder, "and remember, they do this test on babies. You'll be fine."

Phe stalked to Bastion, the bastard who had a fountain consecrated to him. *A fountain.* He was leading her to the row of reapers waiting to tear her soul from her. *You'll be fine, he said. They do it on babies, he said. Ugh.*

Why was Finian the only one not sugarcoating anything? They're here to put you down . . . like a feral animal. That made sense. She was. Feral, that is.

Why am I giving power to what they said? The reminder zapped through her like lightning up her spine. *They betrayed me.*

Yet, hadn't they been protective of her, in a sense? Getting in between her and the other soldiers. Orc's explaining. Caring for Edva. Stepping in between her and Bastion. But they also were the ones who held her down and cuffed her. Carried her into Arias.

She didn't know what to think, and she wished it were black and white. They were either friends or not, helping or not. But it was more complex than that. *Stars, why did this all have to happen at once?* It was too much.

A screech faltered her step. The first ring in her defense system blared an internal alarm. Apprehension coursed through her. She scanned the line of people in front of her, *wondering who was attacking.*

What if I Elzac overestimated my power, and I can't hold them off?

Bastion deigned to glance at her.

The first ring fell.

Her knees weakened, and she knew her hands would visibly shake if she were to hold them up. She hadn't felt this helpless since Grum, not knowing what to do, watching someone rip her defenses to shreds.

Elzac will help. Elzac will help, she repeated, breathing in deeply to calm herself.

Bastion stopped in front of the line.

She halted next to him, sweat rolling slowly down her spine.

Another internal layer demolished.

"We're ready." Bastion announced.

A robed figured glided forward, hand reaching for Phe. "It is unnecessary to accompany her. We will test her and arrange for her accommodations." The inflectionless and genderless voice only amplified her panic.

Phe evaded the grasp. *No one told me reapers needed to touch . . . to better suck my soul out.*

There was no way grim reapers were real; they were myths. Stories. Tales of ethereal beings dressed in all black, head to toe, who came to escort souls in their transition from life to the celestial plane. Then again, that's what she'd been told about magic, too.

"It's non-negotiable." Bastion said nonchalantly brushing aside the reaper's hand.

An uneasy silence descended, broken by the chirping of birds.

"Then so it will be." The figure motioned with two fingers for them to approach. "Let us not waste more time."

Phe watched Bastion clasp hands with the gloved reaper, noticing the way the fabric shimmered in the light. Another one of her defense layers fell. Sweat seeped through her shirt at the armpits, shoulders, under her breasts.

Bastion swiveled and wrapped his calloused hand around Phe's bicep and, for the second time in minutes, everything around her faded. Bastion's touch had transported her, but it was unlike the first jump. There was no suctioning. She was there one minute, and somewhere else the next.

Immediately, the mental attack on her stopped. Leaving a slew of demolished mental barriers around her.

Her eyes hadn't adjusted to the dim orange glow of the room before she was prying herself free from Bastion's searing grasp. Expecting a struggle, she had to adjust her balance at his sudden release.

Sconces lined the wall, covered in inches of dust. Shadows hung in the corners and along the floor. Instinctively, she mentally reached for them, needing their comfort.

Swirls of shadows billowed from the corners, as if caught in a lazy whirlwind, and spiraled across the floor to her.

Her heart leapt to her throat. Phe reared back, and the shadows drifted into nothing. *Did I imagine that?*

"Interesting" Bastion muttered.

Phe ignored him, ignored what just happened, and twisted slowly to take in the room. There were no exits. No windows. Thick dust layered the ground like a blanket of gray snow, undisturbed for years until now, with arched patches matching a drag pattern from those in black robes.

The only furniture in the room, a chair, was placed in the middle of the room. It, too, had inches of dirt covering it. It never boded well to be in a room with a single chair, though at least there wasn't a table of torture tools.

You should be safe. Roar's words reverberated, soothing her for only an instant before she was berating herself. *Gah! Why do I want to believe Roar?*

Four grim reapers surveyed the room. One sauntered to a wall sconce and cleaned it. The orange glow grew stronger.

Another went to the chair, wiping clean one arm rest. "It has been too long since we visited Linaria-Coronaria."

Linaria-Coronaria? Phe scanned the room again, only to rest her gaze, yet again, on the unnerving chair.

"Too long," another black-robed figure echoed as if in agreement and clapped their hands. Dust exploded into the air, then, soundlessly, suctioned out.

What in the . . .? Phe had an elbow to her mouth, coughing. Every single particle of dust was gone except the ones she'd inhaled. Her shoulders drooped and exhaustion hit her with the power of a tsunami. There was so much to know about magic, so much they were capable of.

"Phe, sit in the chair," Bastion directed, interrupting her thoughts.

She eyed the chair and cautiously approached it. There was something more to this chair she didn't see or know about it. How else could it identify her magic? *Infants do this, yeah? And it'll be fine . . .* Phe gulped, Roar's crystal blues swam in her mind's eye, confident she'd be safe. *Why did this not feel fine?*

The chair was a solid, oversized, hand-carved yellow wood with swirling designs of a tree and branches depicted on its surface.

She ran her fingertips along its smooth armrests, feeling a slight buzz everywhere she connected to the seat. The sensation elicited a sense of excitement, a thrumming of something within her, easing her trepidations. She sat.

A warmth immediately seeped into her, easing the tension in her muscles, assuaging her nerves for only a moment, because next, invisible bands locked around her hips, legs, arms.

Her heart hurtled into a sprint and threatened to explode from her chest. The chilled sweat from earlier uncomfortably coated her skin, and every hair follicle stood. *You'll be fine, he said.* The thought simultaneously sarcastic and Phe's attempt to cling to hope.

One of the robed figures bent toward her, reaching.

"Do not touch her," Bastion yet again commanded, striding in between them. "What is it you wish to do?"

The robed figure froze, gaze vacillating between Bastion and Phe. Phe was certain they were trying to work out Bastion's behavior with her. *Me too, Reaper.*

"Remove the amulet, General. Its placement will interfere with Linaria-Coronaria's work," they tonelessly instructed.

What was wrong with their voices?

Bastion immediately gripped the amulet.

Phe wiggled her wrist, attempting to fight off the inevitable. "Bastion, don't. Not the amulet." Her voice wavered. *Don't take the only thing I have left of Kyra. Please,* was what she was really saying, but he ignored her.

Cold air caressed the smooth skin of her bared wrist. Skin that hadn't tasted sunshine in seven years. Her sprinting heart dropped into her belly, its tired, beaten pulses throbbing.

Bastion went to tuck the amulet into a pocket but stopped when one of those black robbed figures said, "We would like to examine it."

Bastion handed it over.

Phe glared, fists clenching and scraping along the edges of the chair.

"You may examine it. But know, this was gifted to her by Kyra Theanora years ago. It has nothing to do with her rebound."

"We shall be the ones to decide this."

Without warning, thick needles slammed into her forearms. Phe hissed, shoulders reaching her ears as she vainly tried to pull free. It *hurt*. It felt as though row upon row of talons had embedded themselves in her.

She dragged in a tightly controlled breath, directing her glare to Bastion. In it, she promised she'd torture him for every single day, every single hour, Kyra was missing.

He was oblivious, staring transfixed at the wall in front of her.

She dismissively glanced at it too, intending to resume her silent death threat, only to blink. Her mind reeled.

The wall shimmered and rippled, to life. What was once a blank expanse of wall now pulsed into what appeared to be a three-dimensional tree.

Bursts of warmth infused the talons. Either her nerve endings were dying brutal deaths or magic was at work again, because her pain ebbed. But she didn't care. She was too focused on the transformation before her.

The tree's bark vividly developed into thick, patchy, reddish-brown pieces. She had the feeling if she could touch it, the surface would be soft yet rough along its plated edges. Six wide branches erupted from its trunk, swirling and curving to cover the entire wall. Each branch glimmered with different colors, shapes, leaves, and flowers. Each one was wildly unique, yet there was a lifelessness to them.

Phe wasn't sure why she thought that. None of the branches drooped, nor were the leaves withered and thirsty.

A dim pink light emanated from under her, capturing her attention. The pink traveled down a tube to the base of the tree, as if the tree was sucking from a straw.

It's sucking my life essence out. The startling realization bizarrely didn't cause panic. Instead, her heart resettled in her chest as a surreal calmness rooted within her.

The base of the tree vibrated with color as it absorbed the pink light, then the middle, and finally its branches. Four of the six branches ignited, each a different color. Red, orange, green, and blue. Muted yellow and brown dimly highlighted the other two, where there had been only reddish-brown before.

On the four branches radiating with energy, the throbbing awakening continued into smaller branches, leaves, and flowers. Red flowers grew, all spikes and edges. Orange whirls glided across its branch, encouraging and nurturing growth. The blue branch bristled, as if an invisible wind rustled the air, and water weighed on its leaves and flower buds. Green oscillated in between shades of colors, no single leaf the same hue. Branches seemed to blossom before her.

A sweet mixture scented the room, too many scents to identify.

Whoa.

Two new offshoots burst from the red and blue branches. The red one exploded into a large, black-lined, pointy-tipped red flower, while the blue limb unfurled more slowly. Heavy rounded petals sprang loose, black and blue; its movement almost seemed as if the blossom was a hand, palm open, stretching toward them.

Bastion broke the entranced silence. His voice a slap. "This exceeds what I expected."

"It appears so."

"We must confer."

What had he expected, and why must they confer? Phe wanted to ask them, but the thought of moving her mouth and forcing words past lips heavy with exhaustion kept her silent. *And they probably would ignore me anyway.*

Just as quickly as the tree swelled with life, its vibrancy

faded. Flowers and leaves curled into themselves, then disappeared into their branches. The colors receded, branches dissolving into the wall, followed by the trunk, until there was only the pink light traveling back to her.

A lightheadedness hit. Her vision blurred. Her strength waned. She barely heard, "Take her . . ." as she listed to the side, the straps no longer securing her in place.

16

Phe sat cross-legged on the crescent-shaped bed, observing the city below her. A city she'd never known existed lay exposed before her. Its labyrinth of streets, parks, and buildings went as far as she could see.

The night sky blanketed the city in soft hues, broken by speckled light from the streets and homes. She could see the rows of rooftops, many showcasing gardens and terraces, multi-level masterpieces, reminding her she was nowhere near home.

The clean clothes she now wore, after showering, smelled of lemon and a fresh outdoor scent, as if they'd been air-dried. They hung loosely on her, the material comfortable. Her long wet hair collected at the base of her neck and along her spine, drenching the tunic.

Phe lifted a palm and pressed it to the window, feeling the hard, cold pane of glass. She was in a tower, possibly hundreds of feet above the city, with no way out. How was she going to escape?

She groaned. "This is bullspit."

Kyra, where are you?

Phe's chest constricted and wetness pooled in her eyes. She closed them, fighting her treasonous tears and taking slow breaths, compelling her lungs to expand. She thought about tugging the shadows around her, to help her feel invisible and safe, but the memory of those same shadows rushing toward her made her hesitate.

She opened her eyes, settling them on a twinkling star, wondering what constellations lived in these skies. A star flickered.

She squinted, narrowing in on it, and the star moved, zigging and zagging across the night's canvas.

It disappeared, blinking out of existence.

She rubbed her forehead, her chilled palm massaging a temple.

She blew a breath out, reaching for her amulet, but finding only the smooth skin of her wrist. The emptiness in her chest widened.

Little wisps of light manifested, hovering right outside the window. She leaned forward, rising to her knees and pressing both palms into the cold glass.

What?

They fluttered, dancing before her. Their orange flames were broken by streaks of iridescent rainbows surrounding a black teardrop. Their movements were playful: chasing one another, hopping over, then sliding under, circling each other.

One flame skidded to a halt at Phe's nose.

Startled, she pushed away from the window.

Its tip twitched as if it was bobbing its head, then another flame slammed into it, merging and doubling the size.

Is this magic? Or am I hallucinating?

They reminded her of little wisps of flame. One of the

smaller wisps drifted through the window, its curiosity palpable as it cautiously wobbled closer.

Phe held her breath, watching its approach in fascination.

The air behind her vibrated, the pulsation a swift caress of awareness, and the flamy wisps dissolved.

Phe pivoted and jumped, her feet sunk into the soft mattress and blankets, ready for anything.

A young woman materialized.

How in the world? This couldn't be another jump station.

She knew there was no "doorway" there because she'd examined every inch of this cell. There had been no way out or in.

The woman had blue eyes and dark skin. She wore tightly-fitted, well-worn brown leather trousers caked in mud. Large bronze buttons lined the seams from her ankles to mid-thigh, and the brown leather varied in shades from reddish to darker brown-gray. Her off-white mud-stained shirt molded to her waist, with thick round buttons stopping at her sternum, the fabric loosening slightly over her chest.

She smelled of sweat, leather, earth, and horses. Her black, tightly curled hair was braided and she had a pink floral bandana wrapped around the hairline of her forehead.

She didn't seem to see Phe, which was odd because Phe was standing over her on the bed. The woman revolved around the small space, then walked toward the washroom. Peering into the washroom, she called, "Hello? Lady Orphne?"

"Here," Phe announced, hopping to the floor.

"Snap, girl." The woman bent, planting her hands on her knees. "You almost scared the magic out of me."

"Sorry," Phe muttered automatically, all the while analyzing her threat level.

Blue eyes fastened onto hers. "Puh-lease, I wouldn't be sorry in your position. But I should warn you, we're a skittish bunch, and you never know how we'll react." On a long and loud exhale, the woman straightened, peering around the room. "I like what you've done to the place."

Phe shrugged, surveying indifferently the remnants of the desk and chair she'd destroyed and scattered haphazardly around the room. "I was testing the strength of the windows."

"Hmmm . . . Bet you figured out quickly those windows are indestructible."

Phe flicked her an unamused glance and met twinkling eyes and a smirk. She resisted the urge to return a rueful grin.

A huge smile erupted on the woman's face. "I'm Zea." Zea slapped her chest, smile dimming a bit. "I've been assigned as your overall Phoenix coach to help orient you to your new life here."

Zea paused, her eyes shining with something altogether different from humor, but Phe couldn't decipher the emotion.

"I am so sorry."

Phe's brow wrinkled. "For what?"

"For this. For you being here, now, against your will. It's easier for our children. They're discovered when they're infants and brought into Arias before they've made memories and connections. But you?" Zea paused, scanning her from head to toe. "You're the first adult to be acquired," Zea's distaste bled into the word, "if you will, in centuries. To me," she stabbed fingers into her chest, "that means they tore you from your life, your loved ones, and the future you foresaw for yourself."

Not if I have anything to say about it. Phe smoothed her face into an expressionless mask, considering Zea. *No one can stop me from rescuing Kyra.*

Zea seemed sincere in her declaration, but some people were innate liars. *Yet she didn't have to apologize,* Phe rationalized. Hope flared, warm and tentative in Phe's belly. Could Zea be an ally?

She smothered the hope. *Knowing Bastion, she's a spy.*

"Okay, I wanted to lead with that because, otherwise, I'd forget, and since now you look like you want to kill me, let's move on. Pretend I said nothing." Zea nodded while she spoke, the pink floral bandana popping with color as it intersected with a stray moonbeam. "So, let's start by acquainting you with your new residence."

"This isn't my room?"

"Nah, this is a holding cell."

Phe bit the inside of her cheek, not thinking about how she'd been imprisoned twice today. "Are you transferring me to another cell?"

"Probably will feel like it, but no." Zea extended her hand. "Come, I'll show you.

Phe flicked an impartial glance at it, not moving.

"Alrighty then . . . " Zea hesitated, then smacked her forehead. "Ah, I was so focused on apologizing for what was done to you, I forgot to ask! See? This is what I'm talking about."

At Phe's bewildered look, Zea continued, "The forgetting important things, such as what you prefer to be called. Is Orphne okay? Cause there's no way I'm calling you Lady Orphne."

Phe silently scrutinized her, eventually responding, "You can call me Phe."

"Nice to meet you, Phe. I'm Zea." Zea's hands fluttered nervously around her. "I know, I've already introduced myself. I bet you didn't know 'Zea' means 'grain,' did you?"

Phe slow-blinked.

"Um, okay." Zea smoothed her pants out, seeming to steady her nerves. "So the only way to leave is to teleport, and I'm not capable of teleporting you without touching you, so . . ."

"Teleport?"

"I'm such an idiot." Zea covered her face, dragging her palms down her cheeks dramatically, then rolled her eyes. "Of course you don't know. I mean, why wouldn't they have told you? Fricken Crystals. Sometimes, I tell you," Zea muttered, paused, then glanced at Phe. "Maybe they called it 'jump'?"

"I walked through a jump station . . . and Bastion, I think, jumped me somewhere."

"Ha! You call General Bastion 'Bastion'?" Before Phe could respond, Zea waved the question off. "I'll get that story from you later.

"Teleportation comes from the magical branch of transportation. This branch includes any magical means of transporting yourself or others. There are *lots* of intricacies, as with all of magic. But," Zea narrowed her eyes, "you've teleported, or jumped, whatever you want to call it right now, so you know. You start at one place and go to another in a," she snapped her fingers, "moment."

Zea stepped forward, as if the explanation was enough.

Phe countered, keeping the distance between them, eyeing Zea's palm warily. Bastion had touched her and bam! she'd been in the tree room. She had no idea how she'd gotten to the tower, but highly suspected it had been Bastion, the bastard, striking again.

"Did those Crystals manhandle you?" Zea's eyes narrowed, hands-on-hips, inflamed. "Did they hurt you?"

Phe considered all the ways she'd been hurt recently. It wasn't the physical stuff that bothered her necessarily. It was the magic. She was having a hard time with all the magic. Being chased, disarmed, and pinned to the ground by *roots* . . . Or torn from Edva's back by a cyclone and landing on her face. She knew it had happened but didn't want to accept it. Because if she accepted how powerless she was to magic, how was she going to rescue Kyra?

Then there was Bastion, a man who had a *fountain* dedicated to him. The very man who'd demanded she devote her life to protecting Kyra, who'd drilled into her that her life's purpose was singularly to ensure her best friend's well-being. And yet, over the last fourteen years of his brutal training, he'd never prepared her for this. Had, in fact, lied to her about the existence of magic and made her question herself and her mind about the things she'd experienced.

And why had none of Kyra's guards used their magic to save her? Or Shadow Unit, for that matter? They'd had no problem using magic to force her to Arias.

It was as if Bastion had cosigned Kyra's abduction.

And he was directly interfering with her mission to rescue Kyra.

She swallowed, shoving those thoughts aside. Zea didn't need to know any of this.

So instead, she stated uncompromisingly, "I don't want to be touched."

"Oh!" Palms up, Zea's shoulders dropped in relief. "It can be clothing, your hair, doesn't matter. If you let me touch the edge of your shirt there," she pointed to Phe's cuff, "we can, you know, leave."

"The sleeve?" Phe suspiciously confirmed, pulling the article in question further from her body.

"Yes, yes. No need to actually *touch* touch you." Zea nodded vigorously.

Phe extended her arm, sleeve swinging, and tracked Zea's protracted movement. Her sky-blue eyes were wide and watching Phe, moving at a snail's pace. It would be funny if the situation was different. Carefully, Zea's fingers pinched the fabric.

This time Phe was ready, kind of.

The tower cell with its crescent bed, curved window, and scattered shards of wooden furniture was instantaneously replaced by a well-lit city street.

Tall, black street lamps illuminated a wide street in both directions, as far as she could see. Giant buildings loomed in the distance.

They were on a gray cobblestone sidewalk that led to a large, white stucco building, its arched entryway grand with four columns overshadowing a circular staircase.

Phe immediately picked up on the circular theme. Circular stairway, arched edifice, oval-shaped windows and door. A part of Phe wanted to make a snarky comment about it, but she held her tongue.

Above the massive door, brass numbers identified the building. IIIIII.

Phe rolled her shoulders, throwing off the disorienting feeling of moving so quickly from one place to another. *It wasn't natural.*

Zea's mouth was hanging ajar.

Maybe Phe hadn't quite pulled off nonchalance. She glared.

Zea blinked and noticed the *I'm-contemplating-killing-you* glare. Hands flying up, she exclaimed, "Don't kill me! It's your aura, it's incredible." She rushed, "I mean, one of a kind. I swear to you, fist to earth, I've never seen, read, or heard of one like yours before."

Zea's eyes went a little askew, and it seemed she was trying to touch Phe's aura. "Has anyone told you this?"

Phe frowned, feeling her eyebrows bunch and wrinkles form on her forehead. Hadn't Finian said something about her aura?

"Well, let me prepare you." Zea's eyes sparkled, and she paused for effect. "People will stop and stare."

Great. Phe grunted. "What do auras and mine being weird have anything to do with Arias?"

Zea flexed her fingers, her smile firming into a solid line. "Grrr, it infuriates me they would take you . . . " The corners of her eyes crinkled. "You were the reason for the disturbance everyone's buzzing about, weren't you?"

How was she supposed to know that answer? Standing around being gawked at was making Phe even more irritated. She knew nothing.

Zea hummed thoughtfully. "Now that I think about it, you must have been. You didn't come willingly, did you?"

Phe scowled at her. *And I plan to get out of here tonight.*

"Ah! This is so awkward. Please stop with the death stare. It's making me so nervous that I'm sweating." Zea fanned herself.

"Can you walk and talk?" Phe wasn't sure if this girl could pull it off.

"Phew, of course." Zea pointed to the circular building near them. "I assume you're having a really bad day, but you don't have to take it out on me." Zea huffed, stalking off with her arms crossed. "I'm here to help you."

Phe inhaled through her nostrils, conceding Zea was right. Swallowing her pride, Phe caught up and apologized.

"Forgiven," Zea announced. "You were at least told you have magic, right?"

"In a roundabout way." *If you count overhearing it.*

Zea grimaced. "Okay, um, to understand the importance of your aura, you need to understand our classes of magic-borns. There are three magical classes. Don't mistake these for our capabilities." Zea stopped at the stairway, pinning her with a gaze to make sure Phe understood.

Phe didn't, but she nodded anyway.

They started up the stairway.

Zea lifted three fingers. "There are three classes of magic-borns. Crystals." A finger dropped. "Wovens." Another went down. "Phoenixes." Zea made a fist. "We can tell what class we fall into several ways. The *primary* way is by our auras."

They made it up the stairs.

Phe tried the door; it was locked.

"I'll show you how to unlock that in a moment. Let me just finish this." Zea leveled Phe with a *this-is-important* look. "Crystals are pure-blooded magic-borns. They like to call themselves the Originals." Zea rolled her eyes. "As much as *I* think that's pure bullspit, it's quite possible. The Elders are all Crystals and they're older than time, which brings me to another need-to-know fact. They don't die, or at least that's what they tell us. I have my doubts."

Zea gave Phe another look that Phe was sure meant something, she just didn't know what. "They are also extremely powerful, and I recommend not attracting their attention. Though I think it's too late for you."

What does that mean?

"Their auras are crystal clear, no blemishes, no blending. Just a single color."

Phe recalled Kyra's cyan aura, Roar's crystal blue.

"Wovens, our next class, originated from the unions of Crystals or Phoenixes and Stills. Their capabilities vary, dependent entirely on their ancestry or pure luck, really. Some have the equivalent power of their Crystal lineage, some not so much. With Phoenix-Woven children, it differs drastically with what capabilities and strengths they have, or if they even have magic. Their auras are a blend of colors that weave into each other."

Jallia. The realization struck Phe. *What happened to Jallia?*

Jallia had helped her escape, and Phe had had a bad feeling about leaving her, but now? With everything that had happened, not only was Phe ashamed to admit she hadn't thought about Jallia once, she had a dreadful feeling that if they dragged her to Arias, cuffed and gagged, they'd have done something similar to Jallia, if not worse.

"Finally, we get to the best class, Phoenixes." Zea spread her arms wide. "That's us, girl, or at least that's me and what they've decided to call you. We are the anomalies of the magic world." She smiled brilliantly.

"We have no magical lineage. Each one of us died at birth, magic-less, and then were reborn with magic. We are extremely rare and are the only ones ripped from the beloved arms of our families and brought here, to Arias, to learn to wield our capabilities and for our protection." If Zea's bitterness and sarcasm were a faucet, it started as a trickle and ended in a powerful stream.

"And, can't forget," Zea wagged a finger at her, "we call everyone without magic Stills." Zea's eyes flashed with some unknown emotion. "Everyone experiences their magic differently, but the majority of us feel our magic within us.

It's vibrant and alive. In the rare cases of those who've been magically castrated, they've reported a stillness where once their magic danced within them." Zea accentuated the word 'danced.' "Which is why those born without magic are Stills because, literally, they're still on the inside. Actually, what are your thoughts? You had your magic bound and now you have it. Does it feel alive? Were you still before?" Zea pinned her with a curious look.

Phe nibbled her bottom lip. Had she been still inside? Her sight and vision and hearing and awareness had changed. When she woke, she'd felt as if she'd been tied to a horse and dragged for miles, battered and bruised and raw and weak.

Zea waited impatiently, fingers thrumming on her leg.

"There're differences," Phe admitted.

"I bet." Zea was smart enough to nod and move on. "Back to auras. Have you noticed my aura?"

"No." Phe squinted at her.

"Don't strain yourself." Zea waved off her attention. "I'll teach you, or someone will. Our auras have a yellowish gold tint with different colors. Not woven, mind you. We have our own unique color configurations. I have been told mine has green and brown spots with, of course, a yellow tint."

Zea steepled her fingers. "*Yours,*" she elongated, "is primarily black—crystal-clear black—but you have a large fissure, the colors of molten lava, halving your aura. Oranges, yellows, reds, like actual flames, *and*, within this, there are strips of rainbows drifting."

"O-kay." Phe sighed. Standing out as special was the last thing she wanted.

"Phew, that was a lot," Zea muttered and pivoted to the door. "Did you catch it all?"

"Think so."

"Great, and we'll review this all ad nauseam during your training too. Now, this is the residence apartments for all Phoenixes in training." Zea pointed toward an indented handprint. "Put your hand in there to unlock the door."

"I had a recent incident with an indentation like this. I'd rather not repeat it." Phe clasped her hands behind her back, emphasizing her point.

Zea furrowed her brow and pressed her lips into a concentrated line.

Phe could see her mind working.

"One day, I hope you tell me your story. I'm dying with curiosity."

Not sure that will ever happen.

Zea walked to the indentation and placed her hand in it, as if to show Phe it was harmless. The door did not open. "The handprint is a way for the building to read your magical impression. When you were assessed for your abilities, they kept the essence of your magical signature for us to use to enter and exit places. They do this with everyone, across all the classes. The indentation will not hurt you."

Stoically, Phe stared at Zea, chewing on this. *They took my magical imprint?* The thought brought a sour taste with it. *What else did they take?*

When the silence continued and Zea did nothing but fidget, Phe strode to the door. *This is fricken bullspit.*

Stomach churning, she forced herself to insert her hand in the slot. The cold wood gave her a slight tingle as it enveloped her palm.

The door clicked open.

Her belly unclenched, tension easing imperceptibly from her shoulders.

Zea pushed the door inwards, beckoning her through,

smart enough not to say anything about how simple that was.

Phe followed, apprehensively tapping an empty thigh sheath. Absentmindedly, she wondered where she was going to find knives. They'd be better to have, but if not, she wouldn't let it stop her from escaping that night.

The entrance was lit, showcasing a grand staircase, its golden wood sparkling and opening to a small, overlooking balcony on the second floor. Opposite the balcony was a wall of windows. The hallways on the first floor, from what Phe could see before darkness claimed them, were wide. Walls glinted with gilded golden frames and green plants.

"I think there is something special within these walls." Zea uncomfortably filled the silence. "Within all of our historical buildings, actually. Can you believe this building is over a millennium old?" When Phe didn't respond, she continued. "Ancient powers resided here.

"There are, of course, other buildings specific to shifters and elementals. Those aren't as steeped in magic because they're newer, built about three hundred years ago."

Phe grunted. The feeling of being watched prickled the back of her neck. Yet there wasn't a person in sight. The walls curved into empty hallways, the grand staircase was semi-circular, and even the railings were circular. They clearly didn't like edges.

"This building is specifically for the mental branch of magic. I'd imagine that must be your most powerful capability."

"Wait, shifters? Elementals?" Phe'd heard of mental magic from Elzac, but these terms were new.

Except that wasn't true. Kyra often read fantasy romance books with "shifters," where people could change into wolves. Had that been truth coated in fiction? "Actually, could you explain all the branches?"

"Oh, sure." Zea took on an excited bounce to her step, hurrying forward. "Shifters are from the mimicry branch and can literally shift between being human to being an animal. They're renowned for their tracking skills, strength, endurance, and enhanced senses. Each magic class has one overseeing Alpha, which we'll get into later, and Crystals and Wovens have several packs. Phoenixes only have one."

Gads. Too many thoughts spiraled at once. Shifters were real. *Kyra would love this. She always swooned over her wolf books. I'll have to be especially careful with my scent trail and—*

"I'll tell you more once I've settled you in your place. It's a lot. This," Zea waved her hands around, "is a lot."

If I must. "Why is it so quiet?"

"Magic. It suppresses noise."

Zea guided Phe down a hallway, sconces and ornate gold frames holding portraits of people sitting rigidly, with half-smiles and distant eyes, hung along the walls. Little plaques hung next to each one.

"Who are these people?" Phe glided a finger across a frame. The woman posing had full lips and deep brown skin, brown eyes gazing into the hallway. Thick black hair was pulled tight on one half, the other comprised of tight, kinky curls. Her hands were clasped lightly in her lap.

"Heroic Phoenixes."

As she brushed her fingertips along the gilded frame, the woman winked exaggeratedly at her.

Phe stopped, heart jumping to her throat. "The picture winked at me."

"No, I'm sure it was just a trick of the light," Zea didn't pause, dismissing her. "These paintings haven't been alive in eons."

Phe grunted. She knew what she saw. Instead of arguing, she rushed to the door Zea had stopped at. It didn't matter if Zea believed her.

What mattered was for Zea to give her as much information as possible and then leave, so Phe could leave too. She'd noticed there were no visible guards along the street they'd been on. It didn't mean they weren't out there, but if they weren't, it made her plans for the night easier.

"Welcome to your new home." Zea was obviously trying for light, but sarcasm underwrote her tone. "You've been assigned unit 240."

The door looked like every other curved door along the hallway, but this one bore a small brass oval that read 240.

"Ohhh, my favorite number," Phe couldn't help biting out.

"Haha!" Zea dramatically swept her hand to the handprint right under the brass 240. "Drum roll, please."

Phe placed her palm on the handprint, and the door clicked open. "What do you mean the paintings haven't been alive?" Phe asked, following Zea in.

Lights activated along the spacious room's domed ceiling. The walls were a light golden hue, with the same rounded appearance of the halls.

The space was larger than she expected. She noticed a small entryway closet and a chalkboard next to the door. Further in, she discovered a kitchen and a small breakfast nook.

"Hmmm." Zea contemplated her. "There was a time when we worked together with Stills. Magic was revered then. But people became greedy. Coveting magic. Doing terrible things to get it for themselves. It came to a point where it was safer for us to withdraw. We erased all traces of our existence and confined ourselves to five magical cities."

Zea released a dramatic sigh. "But life is a balance of energies. By hiding and allowing our more aggressive, dominating energies to lead, slowly, the feminine energies faded. When it faded, our wisps vanished, paintings stilled, fairies stopped visiting. And now, what's left is cold, combative, controlling."

That was a much longer explanation than Phe had expected. Yet, reflecting, she realized Zea had summed up her experience with magic with the last three words. Cold. Combative. Controlling.

The entire back wall of the apartment was glass, overlooking a private stone patio that bled into grass. If Phe was forced to stay here—which she wouldn't be because she was escaping tonight—the patio would be a place she'd spend a lot of time, soaking up the wakening morning and releasing her days into the night.

Phe trailed her fingers along the soft fabric of a sofa facing the lawn. A fluffy white rug covered the wood floor in front of it, and on the wall behind it hung a black canvas. Odd.

"Why is this one black?"

Zea had paused in the kitchen, rummaging through the cabinets, but she perked up immediately and bounced to Phe. "That's a memo-pro. Memory-projection. Think of a happy memory." When Phe stared blankly at her, Zea fluttered her fingers and demanded she close her eyes.

Phe conceded only because it would move Zea along. Conjuring memories of Kyra, she settled on one a short time after they'd become friends.

Kyra was dancing in the water fountain at the entry of House Nereid. Water droplets flew about, mostly from Kyra's dancing and flailing under the rivulets, but some were helped along by her capability, drenching Phe. Kyra's dull blond curls were wet, sticking to her face and shoulders. She was laughing outrageously at Phe's outright refusal to dance in the fountain, her green eyes sparkling.

Phe's chest ached.

"Okay, open your eyes and touch the canvas anywhere," Zea instructed.

Begrudgingly, Phe complied and touched the cool, granular surface of the canvas. Colors morphed under her fingers, and she wrenched her hand away. *What in the seas?*

Before her, hues swirled and coalesced. From one breath to the next, Kyra's image emerged. Her youthful, joyful radiance had been captured in precise detail, including the drops of water suspended in the air.

Phe's lungs seized as a tornado of grief churned within her.

Dragging in a breath, she had to close her eyes and turn away, moving around the couch to collapse into its plush seat.

After a moment of silence, Zea asked hesitantly, "Sister, partner, friend?"

"Sister," Phe choked out. "Sea sister."

"What happened?" Zea cautiously sat on the opposite side of the sofa.

"Djall abducted her." Phe burrowed her face in her hands and leaned her elbows on her thighs.

"She was magic-born?"

"Her name is Kyra Theanora, the last Water Nymph in Xafara. My best friend. Sister. And I failed her." Swallowing, Phe shoved her emotions down and straightened her spine. Saying anything more could give her plan away.

"Ohhh." A sober understanding emanated from the single syllable.

Phe pinned Zea with her gaze. "What do you know

about Djall?" It surprised Phe that Zea didn't shrink into the couch.

Zea pursed her lips, and her left eye narrowed a smidgen. "Djall's a Crystal whose magic became corrupted."

Finally, some answers.

"His only capabilities were on the mental branch of magic, and he is *powerful*." Zea held a finger up. "Not all of us only have one capability; some of us have two, and rarely three." She pointed to herself. "I have two. I have basic teleportation skills, which you've experienced, but my primary branch is elemental magic, specifically earth."

Phe nodded, wanting her to get back to Djall.

"Djall's mental tricks were diversified, but he excelled at possession." Zea squinted.

"Getting into another person's mind and controlling them?" Phe asked, thinking back to stories Jallia had told her. *Fairy tales, my butt.*

"Exactly." Somberly, Zea nodded. "No one realized he'd been corrupted immediately. Apparently, there are signs, but . . ." Zea shrugged. "People went missing, specifically Phoenixes and Wovens. Not because we aren't as powerful as Crystals." She shook her head. "It's because when we relocated into these cities, it became a who-do-you-know game. Wovens had it a tad easier. Their lineage, whether it was a Crystal or Phoenix, protected them. It was the younger Phoenixes who struggled the most, for the obvious reason. We're taken from our families at birth and raised in a communal Phoenix school. Easy pickings." Zea drew a breath. "And he picked."

Phe drafted a picture.

"But he got greedy and started targeting more and more powerful and connected people. Investigations intensified and seers—they are part of the mental magic branch—realized he had somehow blocked their visions. By then, Djall had absconded outside of the city limits. Where? We don't know. I'm not privy to that sort of information, but we've heard rumors."

Phe perked up. Now they were getting somewhere.

"They say he must have lairs all over and constantly moves between them. Always evading the Crystal teams sent to retrieve newborn Phoenixes. Over the years, he's amassed a small army, if the rumors are right, of magic-borns he's possessed."

Phe deflated. Multiple lairs. A small army of possessed. No one had found him in . . . "What's the timeframe?" Zea's face puckered in confusion. "How long have people been searching for Djall?"

"A little over half a century." Zea's eyes drifted over Phe's shoulder as she thought. "Possible sixty years, give or take. You'd have to ask someone in charge of the investigation for the specifics. Us peasants aren't privy to much."

Djall had been able to successfully evade detection with a small, possessed army for longer than Phe'd been alive. The odds were stacked against her.

Zea continued on. "It's said he never comes out himself; instead, he sends his minions. Their whole eyes are black, bottomless orbs that reflect the depth of depravity he's sunken to."

"They are disturbing," Phe agreed, getting to her feet.

"You've seen them?" Curiosity lilted Zea's voice.

"Twice," Phe said, pacing. "They kidnapped Kyra." She nibbled her lip. "Where is Arias situated?"

"We are on the western side of Shalexum in the Xiheria Highlands."

Phe stopped pacing. "The weather's so nice here." The

Xiheria Highlands were infamous for their brutally cold climate.

"Magic."

Phe grunted and continued pacing. "How deep in the highlands?"

"Deep enough. I wouldn't recommend romping around in them." Zea got up and returned to her rummaging in the kitchen.

"Are we close to the southern coastline?" Phe had never traveled this far northwest, but from her studies, she knew the southern coastline held a much more temperate climate. She intended to head southeast through Shalexum and toward Xafara, all the while searching for signs of Djall and his possessed, so they could lead her to Kyra.

"Ah, I was always bad at geography," Zea stuttered, looking uneasy with this line of questioning.

Phe leveled Zea with her *you-must-tell-me* stare.

"I'd guess a hundred miles, and before you ask, we are on the border of Aglizan."

Aglizan was the country southwest of Shalexum. With those two pieces of information, Phe had a very rough estimate of where she was. *Can I survive the highlands?*

She'd survived multiple training missions in the Sryln Sierras, many without proper equipment, thanks to Bastion. They offered, in Bastion's opinion, an arctic climate identical to places such as these highlands and Aglizan's snow-covered countryside.

It was as if he had been preparing Phe for this. She struck the bizarre thought from her mind. *He'd never.*

Maybe I should stay in the highlands as long as possible. They might not suspect I'd take the more dangerous route.

Not wanting to raise Zea's suspicions, Phe switched

tactics. "You mentioned shifters and elemental magic and branches."

Zea finished plating some food and brought the dish to her. "Here." It was a piece of orange-looking fruit and a slice of toast with some sort of spread on it. When Phe would've refused, Zea's gaze steeled. "Eat it. You need it."

Some battles you fight, some you surrender. This was the latter, Phe decided, especially when she hadn't eaten in who knew how long. She started on the toast, the spread immediately sticking to the roof of her mouth, gritty and earthy.

Zea handed her a glass of water, then settled back on the sofa. She watched Phe take a large swallow of water appraisingly. "There are six branches of magic. Mental, Transportation, Mimicry, Elemental, Energy Manipulation, and Physical. Within each of those branches are subcategories of magic. Are you following?"

Phe took another drink. "I think so. There are three classes of magic-borns—Crystals, Wovens, and Phoenixes—and their magic is based off the six branches. Right?"

"Precisely!" Zea trilled. "I am a Phoenix, and my capabilities fall on two of the branches of magi: Elemental, with subcategory Earth, and Transportation, subcategory of Teleportation."

"Do you know what I'm capable of?"

"I wasn't told. I assume mental magic is your primary since they placed you here."

"How would you know?" Phe started pacing again.

"We're told our magical essence will awaken branches on Azora's Tree."

Phe froze. "The tree has a name?"

"Oh yes, you'll find we like naming things here," Zea said lightheartedly. "Wait, did you *see* the tree?"

"Of course I did." *What kind of question is that?*

"Really? None of us have seen it. Or, at least, remember it."

Phe was partially listening, too busy reminiscing about the tree. "The tree woke, four branches seemed to fill with color, all its branches lifted, leaves unfurled, and flowers bloomed. There were two branches that took on muted colors, but nothing else."

Zea collapsed into the couch. "You're telling me you have access to four branches, all their subcategories, and your power level blossomed the tree?"

"Not the entire tree."

Zea puffed her mouth out while exhaling. "Cripes. Girl, I —" she sat up. "I don't know what the muted colors on the other branches mean. Everything I've read said they'd remain dead, not take on colors."

Phe took a bite of the orange fruit and was rewarded by a burst of delicious, sweet juice. She sucked on the fruit, not wanting to miss a drop or make a mess. This was so much better than the dry, sticky-spread toast.

"No wonder everyone is up in arms about you. You are pow-er-FULL." Zea heaved herself from the couch. "I don't know about you, but I am exhausted. I'll explain the branches tomorrow." She walked to the kitchen and grabbed a jar. "You should know this is an Aswagandhia spread. Tastes gritty and earthy, but you'll get used to it. I like to think of it as earth's gift to us. It replenishes our magic and is packed with nutrients for fast recoveries, healing, energy, you name it." Zea pointedly looked at the discarded toast on Phe's plate.

The jar clinked on the counter.

"Let me check your board. See if they have a schedule

for training up yet." Zea called from the foyer. "I'll show you this tomorrow too."

Phe followed, watching her fuss with the chalkboard. She was uncertain how Zea planned to get a schedule from its blank surface when it moved. She inched up closer, amazed to see words and shapes popping up and disappearing with Zea's ministrations.

"Good news or bad news first?"

"Bad."

"General Bastion sent you a message." Zea widened her eyes into a blend of curiosity and warning. When Phe didn't answer, Zea added, "He wants to see you tomorrow."

That Phe had expected, but he'd be mighty surprised to find her absent in the morning. She already felt the thrum of excitement running through her. She needed Zea to leave. "Good?"

"No schedule posted yet." Zea smiled, eyes sparkling for a moment, then dimmed. "I wouldn't try to escape. No one leaves the city without permission. There are wards all along the periphery that no one has ever gotten through. There isn't too much written about the wards, but I've read they get worse closer to the outer shield. *And* the shield is impenetrable."

The look on Phe's face must have made her nervous, because Zea kept going.

"If you trigger a ward, General Bastion, or one of his minions, is notified. They'll come for you. What if he sets Elite teams on you?" Zea visibly shuddered, then opened the door.

There was a certain Elite Team Phe wouldn't mind encountering. "I'll be fine," she assured Zea, waving her out. "I'm going right to bed."

"Sure." The reappearance of Zea's sarcasm was not lost on Phe as she shut the door.

Thank seas she's finally gone.

Phe stood, her ear pressed against the smooth wood grain, straining to hear Zea's movements in the hallway, only to berate herself when she heard nothing. *Not only did Zea probably jump, you banana, she also mentioned the building magically censors noise.* So, even if Zea was there, she wouldn't be able to hear her. *What kind of place does that?*

She thought of General Bastion's fountain. Was she ever going to get over seeing that?

Slowly, Phe crept away from the door, heart fluttering. This was it.

With barely-contained control, Phe walked past the kitchen and sofa and followed the curved wall to the back of the apartment. There, she found a washroom and a bedroom.

Scanning the furnishings disinterestedly, she opened the dresser drawers. All bare. The only thing that greeted her in the closet were swinging clothes hangers, as if they were laughing at her. She shut the closet door with force.

Stalking to the bed, Phe stripped the bedding, taking it all and lugging it into the hallway.

She found the washroom to be a quant affair with a treasure trove of towels. Or rather, two body-sized towels with matching hair and face towels. Grabbing them, she dragged her hoard to the kitchen and continued rummaging.

Conveniently, there was not a single knife stocked in the kitchen. Not even a butter one.

Ridiculous. Phe snorted. *As if that will stop me.*

She did find several pencils, which she slipped into a sheath with a smug smile.

Her nimble fingers quickly created a sack with the bedding blanket, stashing the towels and the jar of Aswa—whatever it was called—within. She also found a glass jar with a lid, which she filled with water and packed, then rolled the whole thing together tightly, trying to make the bundle manageable to carry while running. And that was what Phe was planning to do until she couldn't.

The thick white quilt took a moment to conform, but it was no match for her will. She finagled the bundle to loop around her chest and rest across her back. A little nervous it would unravel, she slung it on, hands testing the knots, the layering.

It's out of my control, Phe reminded herself. *No use in worrying.*

She tread lightly to the glass patio door. Even though she was alone, she didn't quite believe it. Bastion knew her skills, knew it was hard to keep her any place she didn't want to be, so he would be a fool to leave her unsupervised.

Bastion was not a fool.

Night's dark embrace immediately soothed her as she slipped out the door, past the stone patio, and sunk into the lawn. She imagined pulling shadows to her and shivered when she felt a whisper of air cross her neck, remembering with unease how the shadows in the tree room had acted.

An owl hooted nearby, its call loud and ominous in the quiet stillness.

Phe sprinted, sending a prayer to the seas she was heading in the right direction.

She had a vague idea where her building was situated from the hours she'd spent memorizing the city's layout as daylight faded. The cell tower she'd been locked in offered a panoramic view of the city, one she'd drunken in greedily. From her recall, there had been a series of domed roofed and rounded buildings on the outskirt of the city. This expanse of lawn, if she was right, abutted a forest, or more possibly one of Arias' many parks.

Seas, I hope it's a perimeter forest.

The chill air nipped Phe's cheeks, her thighs burned, and her lungs screamed at the grueling pace, pulling her from all thoughts but what she was doing. *One foot in front of the other.* She linked her breath to her stride, eyes on the horizon and cursing the full moon's light. She was too exposed.

There were no signs of pursuit, which only increased her trepidation. From her vast experience with Bastion, nothing was ever this easy.

Cross the field, she coached, visualizing herself entering a woodland. *One obstacle at a time.*

Time was lost in the soft thud of her tread and the light swooshing her tunic made.

This field is unnecessarily massive.

Eventually, looming trees grew on the horizon.

As if it was the finish line to a race, Phe funneled all of her energy into her limbs. Her heart hammered in her chest, matching her brutal pace and threatening to explode. It was only when she slipped into the forest that she eased her pace, forced to maneuver between trees, attend to branches, roots, and undergrowth.

As she swung around a tree, she glimpsed the field.

It was gloriously and suspiciously empty.

She snapped her attention forward, not allowing herself to fall to the harrowing feeling lingering in her gut. A branch slapped her face, its sting reverberating up her cheekbone, and the bundle of supplies caught on a different one.

Untangling herself, Phe ignored her throbbing body. *If only the tingling would subside.*

Silence hung oppressively as she navigated the dark forest. With each step, she tensed more under its weight, senses prickling. Falling prey to one of Bastion's traps was not on her list tonight.

Suddenly, little wisps of light flickered into existence before her. The orange flames hovered haphazardly in the air, moving to and fro unnaturally.

Phe darted to the left; the bobbing flames blocked her. Phe went right, only to come to an abrupt halt as more appeared in front of her.

The ones to her left dashed about, vibrating anxiously. Some crashed into each other, merging.

Phe inched backward, preparing to bolt, when several flames darted around her, warming her cool sweat and stalling her. The rest of the dancing flames formed an arrow, their synchronized movements jabbing in a specific direction.

Her brow furrowed. *Are they trying to help?*

Several of the flares merged and zipped up to her face. It wiggled agitatedly, the top of its flame motioning for her to move.

Phe uncertainly took a step in the pointed direction, and the flames flared, puffing. *O-kay.*

When she didn't move fast enough, the large flame at her face split into three smaller flames that zoomed around her. Warm, soothing heat radiated with their closeness. Then they shoved her, startling her, which was the only reason she stumbled at their surprising strength.

Phe took another tentative step, and the flames enlarged again. She had the distinct feeling they were encouraging her by their wiggling and jumping about.

Eventually, she fell into a fast jog as the wisps took the lead. Several swooped around her legs, guiding her footing. Others hovered at the ground in front of her, lighting the path. The large one stayed at eye-level and was the farthest away, leading.

Phe kept waiting for her internal system to blare a warning. Yell at her for being duped by these little wispy flames she knew nothing about. Yet it didn't, and she really didn't have time to analyze their interaction as they trekked quickly through the wood, pausing only when Phe found branches to use as makeshift staffs.

Spindly trees took the place of aged timbers, and the canopy thinned out. Occasional moonbeams filtered past the canopy cover, illuminating leaves and branches along its path.

The itching feeling intensified.

Most of the wisps disappeared. The remaining wispy flames zigged and zagged like small lightning bursts in front of her nose.

Were they trying to warn her?

Their behaviors heightened Phe's own increasing apprehension. The hairs along her neck rose with every footstep. The tingling she'd assumed was from her run changed to an acerbic sensation, and dread pooled in her gut.

Then the flares vanished, leaving her in daunting darkness.

A cold sweat formed and trickled down her neck. She honed into the faint sound of her breath, steady and strong.

She hiked to the tree line's edge, stopping at the lip of a steep cliff that revealed a rocky barren landscape for as far as she could see.

Moonlight bathed the area. A shimmer captured her attention. Tracing it to the ground, Phe couldn't grasp what it was, but she had a feeling it was the barrier between Arias and the Xiheria Highlands.

Kyra.

Mammoth-sized boulders were sporadically scattered across the rough terrain. Scorch marks with long fissures resembling claws, and other unknown markings, scarred the rocks below. Pockets of wounded earth lay bare, like untreated lacerations.

This was a training field.

Or a killing ground.

Something large arrowed over her.

She ducked, one staff in the air, automatically blocking, and swiveled toward the projectile. It landed on a slab of stone. Its beady eyes locked onto her with cunning intelligence, head tilted.

An owl—the only bird that can silently fly. *Fricken Bullspit,* Phe thought, realizing it was not an owl. *Obviously, Kyra's books are wrong. Shifters aren't just wolves.* She wanted to smack herself for making an assumption based on Kyra's romance novels.

She swapped her improvised staff to her left hand, freeing up her right to tighten the knots of her bundle. It'd be a pity to have come all this way only to lose it, especially with what waited for her past the boundary. When she was done, she gripped both staffs, the rough bark scrapping against her palm.

She met the owl's challenging gaze, as if it were saying to her *what-are-you-going-to-do-now*, and then leapt over the edge of the cliff.

The owl rocketed toward her, talons extended.

Phe heaved a staff upward to block when a rush of bone-chilling air thrust her into the cliff wall. She slammed into the rocky cliffside, digging her heels into the jagged slab.

The ground collapsed under her and she lost sight of the bird as she went head over heels.

The bundle jostled and loosened, strewing contents into the moving earth, burying all traces of her hastily-gathered supplies.

Phe lost the staffs.

Weightless, Phe unraveled. Arms wide to slow her descent, she flipped and curled into herself as the ground met her. Her impact jarred her in too many places to count, but she had control of her roll and used it to catapult to her feet.

She bolted.

A wave of dirt sprayed against her heels and calves. It filled her shoes. Pebbles dug into her heels, her arches. Bursts of pain zapped through her, telling her where bruises and scrapes were actively forming. Blood poured from a cut on her hairline, mixing with the dirt on her neck.

Phe's spidery sense of awareness stirred with warning as people teleported in around her.

Shadows slithered out of burrows and cracks, amassing into a coalescing sea of ankle-high darkness. Its surface rippled, its mass compounding exponentially, like the raging rapids of a river after the breaking of a dam.

Then everything happened all at once.

Darkness descended, and the sky unleashed a deep rumble. Light skittered in splitting waves across the sky.

Someone jumped at her and missed. Another threw some sort of projectile. A viscous fluid punched into her side, knocking Phe off balance for a moment. A third person dug their nails into her bicep, scratching her deeply when she tore free.

Phe recoiled, having glimpsed the disturbingly thin, elongated limb that had grabbed her. *What was* that?

A wolf and a lion sprinted at her from opposite sides. Tentacles of shadows crawled up the wolf's legs.

A ball of light clipped her, searing pain forming a path along the right side of her chest, shoulder, and arm.

Heart pounding, Phe leapt over several smaller rocks and then vaulted off a large boulder. The lion nipped at her, so close she felt his hot breath. Feet and arms pumping, she sailed into the air.

A monstrous body collided with her, wrenching her from the air.

She bit its neck, gnashing her teeth into flesh. She tasted blood.

They slammed into the ground. She smacked her head brutally, her vision blurred, and her limbs weakened. The impact knocked all breath out of her.

Kyra! her inner voice wept, knowing this was it. Bastion had caught her.

An incredible weight pinned her to the ground, and she craned her neck to bite, only to gag on a ball of air. She'd been muzzled. Again.

"Sorry, baby girl."

Oh, she knew that voice. And she *hated* him right now.

"I would've softened our landing," Finian said nonchalantly, pulling an arm of hers free from his unexplainably gigantic form. He didn't let go until cold metal slipped over her wrist and an audible click told her it was secure. "But then you bit me."

Phe blinked rapidly, as if that would change what she was seeing. But it didn't. Finian was enormous. *I hit my head hard,* she realized as a drummer took up residence in her skull, behind her eyes.

Finian shifted enough to roll her. "That wasn't very nice."

She'd show him nice.

She wrapped a leg around his torso and whacked her forehead into his face. The eruption of more pain was worth it. His nose crunched, and warm liquid exploded onto her cheeks. She tried to wriggle free, but he dropped his full weight on her.

Crushing her.

He pressed his mouth to her ear. Spittle landed on her when he talked. She involuntarily shivered, his touch grotesque. "Baby girl, stop."

Gads, she detested when he called her that.

"You did fantastic, actually, but it's over, and it's time to face it."

18

Phe refused to look at or talk to anyone. Which was pretty easy because no one, other than Orc, was paying any attention to her. After her embarrassingly short tussle with Finian—who, now that Orc had healed her concussion, wasn't the size of a giant—they'd used their teleportation capabilities to bring her to a room, seas knew where.

The room was filled with men and women, all weirdly hyped up from her attempted escape. They were talking about how their capabilities hadn't worked correctly and some nonsense about the shadows acting weirdly. Once in a while, Phe heard them throw in something about wards, and their astonishment that she'd gotten through them.

Mostly, she tuned them out.

A part of her knew she should be listening in. Should be absorbing everything, even if none of it made sense now. She would remember every detail later and should be considering how to drill Zea, who had been surprisingly happy to give her information. But she couldn't.

Not when every bone in her body ached with exhaustion.

Orc began to gently massage her scalp. The soothing sensation his touch created trickled into her. She imagined it to be similar to how rainwater seeps into the ground. His touch did that, replenishing the empty spaces within the soil of her being, bubbling up to knit together her injuries. The physical ones, anyway.

She wasn't sure why he bothered.

Right now, she was filled with only dirt and darkness.

Her head still pounded and her body was still broken in too many places. Like her heart.

Bastion was there, but he'd yet to acknowledge her. He was seated at a long, rectangular table, surrounded by the rest of Shadow Unit and a group of people Phe didn't know, talking. Undoubtedly, about her.

About how she'd failed to escape this horrible city, with its unnatural capabilities. They were probably debating on tossing her into a cell and calling it quits. Or heck, maybe they'd put her out of her misery, claim she's feral and dangerous.

Seas, I wish it were that easy.

She dragged in a breath, contradicting the thought immediately.

No, Kyra needs me.

"Talk to me," Orc encouraged again. "I can't even begin to imagine what's going through your mind. Help me help you."

If his touch wasn't literally healing her, she'd have limped away already. She had, in fact, tried, but Roar had gotten in her way.

If only she didn't have whatever they claimed she had. Then she'd be uninteresting and could return to being someone no one paid mind to.

Gads, I wish that were true.

"What you accomplished tonight, no one, since we've established ourselves in Arias, has done." Orc broke the silent standoff.

Phe logged that bit of information to digest later, along with Fin's obvious pride in her earlier. Right now, coherent thinking was outside her grasp.

Finian hopped off the desk he'd perched on and hollered. "Paaaay UP!"

That got an indignant "You bet on me?" out of Phe.

People huffed, groaned, and gathered around Finian.

Orc had the decency to cough and sound ashamed, but unremorseful. "We're an opportunistic bunch, you know that. There was no way we wouldn't bet, especially since we know you so well."

Phe grunted.

"And General Bastion condoned it, of course." Orc solemnly and respectfully added. "He issued a command to not use extreme measures if and when you ran off."

Of course, he did. How benevolent he is.

"We'd all like to know how you got through the wards in the forest."

Well, she'd like to know a lot too. "What's being done to rescue Kyra?"

"General Bastion has a lot of very competent people assigned to rescue her."

"Are they also assigned to rescue all the others he's taken too?" Phe snapped. "Because I'm not feeling too comfortable with their competence." She twisted, glaring into his glowing, mossy green eyes. "Kyra's *life* is at stake here. I should be out there. Finding her."

Orc grimaced, but shook his head. "Not untrained and unaware as you are. Djall has been able to possess people with centuries of lived experiences and protective measures in place. You would be putty in his hands, *and* he had a bead on you before your magic rebound. Which we're still trying to figure out how."

"Why don't you ask Jallia?" Phe rebutted, not able to process his statement. "She didn't seem too surprised." The bitterness she tasted quickly changed to concern. "How is Jallia? Where is Jallia?"

"She'll be fine. She's in Arias."

"I'd like to see her." Phe hauled her arms up and linked them across her chest, one elbow jutting out higher than the other, expecting him to tell her no. No seemed to be a favored word around here.

One side of Phe was covered in what she was told was goo. A viscous liquid produced by magic and shot at her somehow. It was plastered to her side, thick and protruding, causing her to have to rest her arm on its hard, yet sticky surface. The other side featured a strip of burnt fabric across her chest, shoulder, and arm. The skin, prior to Orc's healing, had been peeling off, blistered, and oozing. Now, she had taut, new, bright-red skin covering the injury.

"I'll see if I can arrange it."

"Please." Phe softened momentarily, stiffening again when Finian approached, all smiles and bared muscular chest. *Gads, put a shirt on.*

"I loathe you." Phe pierced Finian with a *you're-dead-to-me* stare.

"It's okay, baby girl." Phe gritted her teeth. "I got enough love for the both of us. And," he thumbed through the wad of money, "enough money to help you get settled."

Her eyes, wide with surprise, shot to his, and a shock pulsed through her lifeless heart.

"And this is just a teeny-weeny portion of the winnings."

Finian's smug smile engulfed his face, his brown eyes twinkling with mirth.

"See, Phe? Opportunistic and loyal to a fault." Phe didn't need to turn around to see Orc's smile; it was woven into his words.

"Uh," Phe stuttered.

"No, please." Finian held up a hand. "Your silence—"

"Fin." Roar threw an arm around him, jostling Fin playfully, but the playfulness didn't reach his gaze as he scanned the money Finian held. "How'd we make out?"

"Like bandits," Finian answered gleefully.

"You gonna organize collecting the rest?"

Finian rolled his eyes. "What kind of question is that?"

"One that apparently provokes your ego," Roar responded glibly before settling his serious blues on Phe. "General Bastion has considerately offered you the choice of where you will sleep tonight. Since you can't be trusted alone—"

"Haha, as if we didn't see that coming a mile away—"

Sometimes she really, really wanted to kill Finian.

"You can sleep in a locked cell, or in my guest room."

"Why yours?" Suspicion shadowed her momentary thrill of relief.

"Well, we all know Finian," whom Roar squeezed in a side hug, "would snore the night away, oblivious to your sneakiness, and I'm not sure you're ready to experience his lair—"

"Hey! I don't snore!"

"—Orc and Ihrone have partners and families. Kirzia has house guests, as you know. Which leaves me, who not only has a spare room you can use, but I'm also oddly attuned to your stealth."

That was all true.

"Wait till you see his veritable rock garden," Fin said, elbowing Roar.

Kirzia and Ihrone meandered to them, joining the huddle. Ihrone plucked the wad of money out of Finian's hand and counted it.

Phe nibbled her lip as she considered which cage she'd choose for the night. The empty cell had an appeal. Primarily because it was empty. She could lick her wounds and wallow in despair alone.

Yet something had lightened when Roar offered her his spare room. She was under no misgivings. Not only was he the only viable option, but with him, there was his steadfast, silent support. He would leave her be, huddled in his spare room, if that's what she wanted. He cared if she was hurt, cared if she was fed, and he always knew whenever she snuck out.

It was annoying.

All of Shadow Unit held special places in her heart. Would she feel bad sneaking away from Finian? No. She'd do it with glee, just to irritate him. But, with the rest, it'd be harder and harder to sneak away for many reasons, but ultimately from some displaced sense of loyalty to them and especially to Roar.

Can I try another escape tonight? Her bone-weary exhaustion answered resolutely. The slabs of stone she now knew as limbs showcased one pain after another and didn't function properly. She dreaded moving.

No, it was better to call this what it was. Defeat. Failure.

She'd regroup in the morning. Strategize. Maybe she'd get lucky again and meet with Zea. Drill her for more information.

"Tough choices." Phe made a sucking air sound through her teeth. "I'll take option two."

"Good choice," Ihrone said and handed Finian the wad of money. "The cell General Bastion had in mind is very uncomfortable. Keep in mind, this is temporary. We don't want you to see us as your prison guards, because we're not. We're your friends." Ihrone's dark gray eyes locked with hers.

Phe's gaze narrowed. Hadn't it been them who had dragged her into Arias? And Finian who had stopped her escape?

"And it's time for you to rest," Ihrone continued, unperturbed. "I, for one, have no idea how you've physically managed to do what you've done since your rebound."

"Well," Kirzia dryly stated. "She hasn't done it alone. She's all but drained Orc."

"I wouldn't go that far," Orc pipped up, standing and offering Phe a hand. He did look pale.

Sighing, she dragged her carcass upright, surveying the unit and looking past them, to the room filled with people.

It dawned on her she could be alone with these others right now, badly injured and unable to defend herself had Orc not been there to heal her.

It could be so much worse.

Things shuffled around in her mind, realigning.

She grasped, for the first time since she woke in this living nightmare, that this group of people standing before her were helping her. It might not be the help she wanted, but nonetheless, they were here.

Making sure she was safe. Giving her choices. Considering her needs in their world.

Elzac's line of questioning from earlier rushed back. She had chosen to never tell them about Grum, or Anala's nightmare. Those were parts of her she kept stored. All they needed to know was she'd had trauma, and they'd concluded, within moments of meeting, this was the case.

Oath-breaking was a different story all together. She'd never considered breaking her oath of silence about Elzac's home, Ligeia. Nor would she break her vow to protect Kyra.

"Did you all pledge to never talk about magic? Outside of your cities?"

"We did." Ihrone's gray eyes shone with understanding, then he gave her a small salute. "Till tomorrow." And he vanished.

Roar released Finian, giving him a slap on the back. "Get some rest, Fin, Kirz, Orc."

"Yes, boss," Finian agreed but winked conspiratorially at Phe before following in Ihrone's footsteps.

"Phe." Roar held his hand out to her.

Her heart sped up, the organ reviving itself from its corner. She slid her palm into Roar's calloused one. The room, once again, shifted, and this time, the tingles racing up her hand were completely different.

Phe freed her hand the moment they arrived in a light blue hallway. At her hip was a long, narrow table with a glazed pottery bowl filled with rocks. Above it was a frame the length of the table, portraying the night sky from a rock extension. *A memo-pro.*

She doubled back to the glazed dish, stilling.

The bowl was filled with tiny stones of all shapes. It would seem impossible, but Phe recognized them. Unbidden, memories of her, over the years, depositing stones into his outstretched palm coursed through her.

Her heartbeat slowed.

Each stone represented a burden she carried, one he accepted the weight of. No stories or explanations needed. No questions asked.

Each stone symbolized support. Patience.

Each stone embodied trust.

"You kept them?"

"I did." Roar smiled ruefully.

Not knowing what to say, she stared at him, mouth dry. Then she shocked herself by saying, "All of them?"

He nodded. "Hence Fin's garden comment. Though I've had to creatively spread them out."

He led her further into his house, and all she could do was stare at the wide expanse of his shoulders. He'd kept all the rocks? All her burdens?

"This is my spare room. My sister's left some of her stuff in the shower, and clothes, I think, too. Feel free to use them."

Phe nodded, briefly registering the bedroom they'd entered, and the washroom.

He closed the door behind her, and she automatically stripped. Prying off the destroyed and filthy clothes and leaving them in a pile, she turned the shower on and stepped under its warm spray.

She couldn't wrap her head around the meaning of the stones.

It was as if a dense fog had lodged itself in her head and she couldn't see around or through it.

It's got to be exhaustion.

She went through the motions of cleaning herself.

It doesn't mean anything.

Water cascaded down her body, mingling with blood and dirt, and rinsing them away. She wished it was just as easy to wash everything away.

What if . . . Her heart beat faster.

The rose scented soap engulfed her, reminding her of the rose garden at House Nereid. Of Kyra. And her erratic heart retreated into its hole, leaving her bereft.

When Phe had dried herself off, she searched for clothes, only to find empty drawers and closets. At least these hangers weren't laughing at her.

With a towel secured around her, she cracked the door open in search of Roar.

Voices.

Roar's and an unknown woman's.

Phe soundlessly plodded across the cold wood floors, intermittently covered in carpet.

It's late.

Her stomach dropped.

Who would visit at such an hour?

She rounded the hall.

Roar stood in the doorway to his apartment with a gorgeous woman. She had brown hair with thick highlights of blond, her bangs reached her chin in wavy curls, the rest pulled loosely into a braid sweeping over her shoulder and down her chest. One of her hands was touching the braid while her other hand rested on Roar's chest. Her brown eyes shone with a powerful emotion, and her nose was cute and dainty, perfectly proportioned to match her heart-shaped face and her sweet smile.

Phe blushed from head to toe. Here she was, with her broodiness, her aversion to touch, her ineptitude—compared to this woman?

Of course, the stones don't mean anything.

A sour taste scoured its way up her throat.

How could they?

She swallowed hard, and her shoulders hunched in on themselves.

Her mental block dislodged, and clarity struck. The

stones embodied everything she was. Hard. Edgy. Smooth. Useless. Covered in grime. A burden.

With one of her steadying breaths, she drew her shoulders back. She would not stand wrapped in a towel, eavesdropping, feeling her heart quake. She cleared her throat.

Roar twisted. The woman's hand fell from his chest.

"Sorry." Phe smiled uncomfortably, her wet chestnut hair sticking to her neck. "I couldn't find clothes."

"Oh, sorry, I thought there was a spare set." He hesitated. "Let me introduce you. Phe, this is Lassandra, a childhood friend. Lassandra, this is Phe."

Phe really wanted to grunt, but dredged up the required etiquette. "Nice to meet you, Lassandra." *Just Phe?*

Lassandra's expression appeared curious, brow soft at first, then hardening. "Is this the nix that arrived today?"

"Lassandra," Roar sharply replied, pivoting to face her. "Why would you say that? Actually," he held his hand up, "leave."

"What?" Lassandra's jaw dropped.

"You heard me."

"Roar, don't be like this." Lassandra pouted, backing into the hallway because he was closing the door on her.

"No, that was completely unacceptable and inexcusable."

"But . . ." Lassandra sputtered.

He closed the door in Lassandra's face.

Roar spun to Phe, features drawn in apology. "I'm sorry about her. I'll grab you a shirt . . ." Tiredly, he rubbed his face. "But I don't think you'll fit into any of my bottoms."

Whoa. Phe's stomach bound upward, giddiness bursting to life. *Roar closed the door in Lassandra's face for me.*

And to confound it all, she fought an even more irrational reaction: the urge to smile at wearing something of Roar's. She'd never be able to tell Kyra about this.

Must be exhaustion.

19

Phe stared at her pale complexion in the mirror. An outline of dark crescents had formed under her eyes. Spare strands of vibrant chestnut hair hung limply to her chin, the rest pulled into a messy knot. She stood gazing into her honey-colored eyes.

Forcing herself to maintain eye contact.

To stare at the person who failed their best friend.

Her slender fingers gripped the edge of the sink so tightly, her knuckles became white with effort.

Today was day two of Kyra's abduction.

A vise tightened around Phe's chest.

Day two of being in the hands of a deranged, power-hungry man who could magically possess people.

Shallow breaths fogged the mirror.

Day two since Phe had peered into her sea sister's terri-fied green eyes.

Day two since Bastion prioritized her over Kyra's rescue.

Day two—

A series of hard knocks sounded, pausing only for, "Wake up, baby girl," before the knocking resumed.

Phe inhaled slowly, praying to the stars and seas for patience. For the strength to not kill Finian.

Splashing cold water on her face, she toweled dry and slowly strode to the shaking bedroom door. She tugged the hem of Roar's shirt self-consciously, ensuring it reached mid-thigh.

"The sun has risen, and so must I," Finian sang belligerently. "To greet—"

Yanking the door open on mid-knock, Phe glared.

"Fin!" Roar called from somewhere in the apartment. "Leave her alone!"

Finian's white-toothed smile dimpled. "The rays of summer days—"

"Stop, please." Phe slinked past him, avoiding any contact, and headed toward the direction of Roar's voice.

"But, baby girl, I bring tidings—"

Phe stopped and swiveled.

Finian almost bumped into her, his smile morphing into mischievous.

"You are," she held her thumb and forefinger a millimeter apart at his nose, "this close to tasting my fist. *Please*, stop talking."

Once the words were out, Phe felt horrible. Deepening her remorse, the twinkle from Finian's eyes faded, his mouth losing its joyful curve.

Jeez, what am I doing?

Threatening someone before breakfast was a new low for her. Actually, threatening anyone was new to her, period.

"Ugh," she blew out. "That was uncalled for. I'm sorry."

Finian narrowed his eyes and leaned in. "Not kind, Phe."

He's right.

"I'm sorry," she reiterated, shoulders sagging. "Could

you, just, lead the way?" Phe pressed herself against the wall, hand gesturing for him to pass. "I need a moment."

"Apparently." Finian strutted by primly, the muscles of his shirtless back tense.

Phe bit her bottom lip, suppressing her unexpected and irrational surge of laughter at Fin's sulking back. Getting her reaction under control, she followed. "What happened to your shirt?"

"I don't know, Phe," he said as they entered the kitchen. "What happened to your kindness?" He threw himself in a seat, crossing his arms and glaring at her.

Roar's kitchen was an open space with a massive skylight and two large windows. A granite counter wrapped around the kitchen and became a nook, with tall stools tucked underneath it.

On the curved side of the counter facing Phe, there was an indentation that held another cluster of stones. Her stones. Two plants grew from within the rock collection. The green stems encircled each other, and their leaves inter-mingled in a canopy that stretched toward the light.

Roar walked past her, holding a mug and a plate with toast covered in a dark spread. A spread Phe was becoming all too familiar with. The rest of the team sat around a wooden kitchen table.

"For you." Roar placed them on the table next to the chair he sat in.

"I'm really sorry, Fin." Phe ignored the rest of the team, halting close to Finian's leg. "This is not an excuse, but with Kyra missing, and being dragged here, I've mostly only felt different shades of anger."

"I'd say I've observed pure, riveted determination, too," Orc supplied helpfully.

"There's a bit of that, too," Phe admitted, connecting with Orc's gaze for a moment before returning to Finian.

"Can you believe she threatened to punch me?" Fin huffed.

"I can," Kirzia said from the opposite side of the table, giving Finian a long look. Fin appeared completely unaware. "And I have." Kirzia met Phe's glance. "He didn't go home last night," Kirzia added for Phe's benefit.

"Collecting winnings?" Guilt now flooded Phe.

Ihrone cleared his throat.

"Among other things." Roar patted the seat next to him. "Phe, sit, eat."

"You know, the only people who threaten me are you guys." One side of Fin's mouth lifted. "As horrible as it sounds, because," he sternly surveyed all of them, "families shouldn't threaten each other or," his gaze narrowed on Kirzia, "act on those threats."

Kirzia sighed. "Do you have a point?"

"It's a sign Phe's going to be inducted!" Finian cackled, the twinkle reappearing, along with a dimple.

"Inducted?" Phe slid into her seat, wrapping her hands around the warm mug and sipping. It tasted of diluted earth. She was getting a double whammy of the Ashwa-something today.

"Into our unit." Finian's tone was heavy with a "duh," evidently forgiving her.

"To become an official member of any Elite team, one has to be inducted into it," Ihrone explained. "The induction is a ceremony unto itself, followed by a celebration banquet afterwards. It's a very big deal."

"But," Orc propped his glazed mug on his chest, "each participant has to undergo a series of public tests the Elders oversee. They ultimately decide if the contestant is qualified."

Finian's elbows slid across the table in slow motion. "I told you I brought good news."

Ihrone nodded. "Yesterday, we formally submitted a request to General Bastion for you to be inducted into our unit. General Bastion accompanied you to your testing to see if you met the criteria—"

"To be considered for an elite unit, you need to have a wide access to three branches of magic." Orc added helpfully.

"Once this was established, General Bastion approved and pushed the request to our Elders. They've given their preliminary approval."

"But—" Something in Roar's tone had Phe swinging her attention to him, and his blue eyes met hers, the corners crinkling. "—Instead of giving you time to train and learn your magic, they've scheduled the test for this morning."

Wait, what? Phe stopped chewing. "You've got to be kidding."

Everyone except Finian, who'd buried his head in his arms on the table, looked apologetic. Yet it was Finian who mumbled, "Nope. But don't worry about it." He limply flicked some fingers in her direction. "The signs have spoken."

Kirzia rolled her eyes.

Phe put the toast down.

This was not how she'd foreseen today going. Not at all. How was she going to escape if they were testing her all day? She'd been ready to demand information, begin strategizing, escape, or, barring that, harass Bastion enough for him to assign her to the team working to rescue Kyra.

"The tests are conducted in a large stadium . . ." Kirzia said, tone grim.

"Which will be packed." Orc said around the rim of his cup.

This hadn't been on the agenda.

Gads, why didn't I make it to the forest?

"Why do you want me on the team?" Mistrust dripped with each word, along with a pang of irritation that no one was asking her what *she* wanted.

Did she want to be inducted into Shadow Unit? She didn't know; her emotions were at war with each other. The simple answer? If officially being part of Shadow Unit interfered with rescuing Kyra, then absolutely not.

Finian made a noise, but Orc spoke over it. "Because you've been with us for the last fourteen years without magic, and your combat and survival skills are unparalleled. Not just anyone can square off with one of us, you know, much less the entire group of us, and still hold their own. That alone speaks volumes. Then we have your mission completion rate at a hundred percent—even we can't boast that—and the list goes on."

Phe's mission completion rates were high because the missions weren't all too challenging. She was an assassin. Yes, sometimes she'd join forces with Shadow Unit for one reason or the other in the field, but when she went out, she went alone. Worked in the shadows. And didn't return until her orders were complete.

"But that's only our rationalization to the Elders." Roar pushed the plate with her discarded food at her. "They wouldn't have considered our request for you to join us if we'd said it was because we care about you."

Ihrone leaned forward. "Phe, I remember when General Bastion first left you with us. You were ten, a little thing cowering in the corner. That was it for me." Ihrone's gaze captured hers. "Because of magic, I couldn't adopt you. So every time we were together, training or on the rare assignment, I made it my objective to care for you the best way I could within the confines of our circumstances.

"We all did this in our own way, with our own reasons, and—" His gaze sharpened, "—it has nothing to do with pity."

A warmth crept across Phe's chest, thawing her cold heart. "I didn't know you felt that way."

She scanned Ihrone's vulnerably calm expression. She'd once told Kyra that Ihrone was the father of the unit. Orc was the honorary uncle, Kirzia the tough-as-nails aunt, Finian the irritating brother, and Roar she'd struggled with labeling, even back then. They'd settled on the boy-next-door friend, the one who eats all their meals with you.

"You are as much a part of us as we are of you. And, with magic no longer acting as a separator, it's not a matter of wanting you on our team, it's a matter of need. You complete our unit."

Phe wet her dry bottom lip.

"O-kay," was all Phe got out, her heartbeat thudding to an odd rhythm—one she wasn't at all ready to examine. Shoving those sensations aside, she refocused. "Tell me about this test."

All their faces scrunched as if they'd bitten into something sour. Roar answered. "The tests are taken between the ages of twelve and fifteen—"

"Unless you're Roar," Finian mumbled.

"After an average of nine years of intensive training to ensure you've mastered your skills in a combat setting," Roar finished, nudging her plate.

"And . . . there's the fact it's held in an arena, jammed

packed with very vocal spectators." Ihrone reiterated Orc and Kirzia's concerns.

After nine years of intensive training. Phe bit into the bread. The ashwa paste immediately glued itself to the roof of her mouth and flicked her gaze between her team. Their worry bled through their expressions. If it was anything like yesterday, it wasn't a stretch in thinking this would be horrible.

After gulping water, she asked. "Is it similar to Fyerir Fighting?"

Fyerir Fighting was a well-known brutal form of entertainment in Shalexum where opponents fought to their deaths in arenas. It was a sport not meant for the faint-hearted. Shalexum, unlike Xafara, enslaved humans. A custom that, over the last few years, was currently in the midst of violent protests to stop.

A Fyerir Fighter was primarily a slave who, if luck was on their side, had received training to cultivate them for a career in the fiery arena's death matches. Phe had been one for only so long as it held Grum's attention.

"No." They all said emphatically.

"I'll heal you in between rounds." Orc assured her.

Phe pushed her plate aside, no longer hungry. "Then I'll survive and be better off than when I fought in those."

Everyone stilled.

Seas, why'd I say that? She'd never told them—anyone— the details of her past with Grum. Orc opened his mouth, and Phe stood quickly, causing the chair legs to screech. Tension tightened her jaw as she flashed them a steely *that-was-not-an-invitation-to-ask-questions-about-my-past* look.

She had no plans to revisit any of her past. Not with Kyra missing and definitely not when she had to brace herself for whatever these "trials" were. Grimly, she crossed her arms over her chest. "Let's get this over with."

20

Dirt crunched under Phe's shoes. A twenty-foot slate stone wall separated the spectators from the arena floor. Seats stretched into the skyline, creating a semi-circle around her that ended at a raised platform. She had to shield her eyes against the rays of the rising morning sun to make out some of the many rows.

Phe swiveled slowly, taking in the already booming sounds of folks mingling and the crackling of energy that rent the stadium air.

Past the stage, thick columns connected to each other in a series of arches, which held another, more intimate seating area above the platform. This one was covered and had a stage extending in a semi-circular shape, mirroring the arena she stood in. She didn't see any doors.

Phe shivered, not because she was cold.

It was the residue of violence in the air, coating her skin.

Roar stood gazing solemnly at her, watching her take in the arena. "I'm really sorry they aren't giving you time to train."

Me too. Phe squared her shoulders, hardening her stance.

"I wish I could tell you what to expect, give you advice." He trailed off, glancing toward the platform. "But none of us have any idea what or how they'll test us."

Why are you acting like I'm walking to my death?

Roar gestured for them to walk toward the platform. "Weapons are over there."

Phe reached for the comfort of her amulet, only to feel the cool, smooth skin of her wrist where it should've been. Clenching her fist instead, she voiced something that had niggled on the periphery of her thoughts.

"Did you ever use magic on me?" Forming the sentence, Phe realized it ranked in importance next to their oaths to not disclose magic. Had they gone into her mind? Bared her secrets?

"Technically, we aren't supposed to use magic outside of the cities." They both jumped onto the platform, stopping at the portion of the wall where weapons hung above a table. "Some of our magic is innate or passive, like Orc's healing. Or our combat skills, so I'd imagine we did there. Ihrone monitored you and intervened when you went undercover during operation sunrise."

Phe almost stumbled. No one spoke about that operation, at least, not with Phe.

Six years ago, when she was eighteen years old, she'd agreed to go undercover into a human trafficking organization because the head of the organization, a man named Seskel Brevil, was so obsessed with her, he collected lookalike Lady Orphne's.

Everything about the operation—which had been named operation sunrise after Oriana, a Lady Orphne lookalike— had been terrible. Starting with her role. She couldn't be Phe, the deadly assassin; she had to be only Lady Orphne, weak and timid and helpless. Many things had come from the operation, most prominently, Edva, her weird and spunky horse.

At her sharp glance, Roar assured. "Ihrone did not read your mind. He monitored any spikes in your brain, and he interceded when needed."

Phlegm coated her throat. She wasn't sure how to feel about this.

"There were other times when you were first assigned to us, the empaths would use their passive magic if you were emitting a lot of distress to help calm you."

Refraining from riffling through memories, Phe admired the weapons table. Laid out, like a gift, were her weapons. Her twins and various collections of knives.

Slowly, she hovered her hand over them. Her heart emitting a soft song of delight at their reunion. One by one, she picked them up. Absorbing their familiar, smooth feel, their reassuring weight, then slid them home.

"So if one of the tests were strictly hand-to-hand fighting or with weapons, I'd be okay?" Phe bit her lip, wondering why she was the one shaking her hastily made defensive barricade.

"Yes." Then Roar grimaced, a ray of light highlighted his deep auburn hair, which Phe distractedly eyed. "But here, none of us just use our combat magic, tapering our assault to only hand-to-hand or weaponry, which is what we did with you. In this test, they're definitely going to use all their capabilities."

Phe sighed. "What you're telling me is you foresee this as disastrous and detrimental to my well-being." Several bricks of confidence toppled.

"We're worried." Roar scrunched his face unhappily.

"You have extremely limited exposure to magic and have not yet been taught how to engage yours, other than your passive abilities."

"Passive?" Hadn't he just mentioned that?

"Yes, it's what we use automatically, without trying, like breathing. It seems you've been accessing your combat skills this way."

Tension tightened the muscles of her shoulders and crisped the lines of her mouth.

If they're concerned, shouldn't I be? Phe tapped into her emotions, riding the flat surface of her acceptance. *I can't afford to be.*

Her mind had other plans, scrolling through the mind-blowing events of yesterday. She'd been defenseless. Just as she'd been defenseless during the first few Fyerir fights with Grum.

In an effort to reassure herself, she said nervously, "How badly are they allowed to hurt me. Will Orc be able to fully heal me in between?" Gosh, could they somehow kill her and bring her back to life? She definitely didn't want to experience that. "They're not going to kill me, and revive me, right?"

"Of course not. This is just a test." Defensiveness crept into his response. "We're not barbaric."

Phe chose to not respond to that.

"About your prior experience." Roar let his sentence hang, gazing intently into the crowd before swinging his full attention to her again. His expression troubled. "You survived Fyerir Fighting before the age of ten?"

Without answering, Phe strode to the edge of the platform and hopped to the dirt ground. *I had to mention that, huh?* She chastised herself. When she was in the middle of the arena, she crouched and dug her fingers into the packed earth.

A part of her wanted to answer. But it would open up too many other questions. Doors to the years with Grum she didn't need to revisit. Details that would only incite pity.

She didn't want pity. Or, what was it Ihrone always talked about? Empathy. Yeah, none of that either.

Phe was not a product of her past. If that were the case, she'd be a greedy, blood-hungry criminal mastermind.

Roar followed quietly, not pressuring her.

She could sense his mind plotting dots into the unknown timeline of her youth. With each pinpoint, he theoretically gained more of an understanding as to why a ten-year-old child had the skills Bastion harnessed.

To distract him, Phe asked, "Will this help me rescue Kyra sooner?" She let grains of dirt fall through her fingers, briefly wondering if Zea, her information-friendly liaison, knew she was here.

"I'm sure it will help once you're trained."

"What if I fail?" The earth under her bricks of confidence quaked. She was no fool. It's why her tactic last night had been to run. She was completely out of her depth and needed to assess the very real possibility she'd not do well.

Would failing be a blessing? Would they see me for what I am? Not special. Maybe they would leave her be then.

Roar's steady gaze washed over her, pulling her into his crystal-clear depths. "The only thing I know is no matter what the Elders decide, we'll be by your side."

The air pulsed with a vibration, a warning before Zea appeared. Her thick black hair was plaited and styled with a fabric band of bright blue that made her flashing blue eyes pop as they locked onto Phe.

She was in similar close-fitted, well-worn leather pants.

These were multi-colored with a triangular, darker brown sweeping up the seams. The buttons were missing, replaced with more straps, sheaths, and buckles lining her upper thighs. An off-white frilly shirt peeked out from under an off-colored brown corset.

Phe appraised Roar's loose fighting shirt and simple pants in comparison. She'd have to ask either Zea or Roar about their distinct styles. She'd never seen Shadow Unit dress like this. Was it only Zea or did all Phoenixes dress similarly?

"Oh my seeds!" Zea all but threw herself at Phe, stopping shy of touching. "What the flipping frogs is going on? Are you okay?"

Phe noticed Zea's green- and brown- dotted aura before it disappeared. Distinctly different from Roar's and Jallia's.

Glancing between the distraught Zea and Roar, she muttered, "I'm okay."

Zea snapped her head in a *I-don't-believe-you* way. "How in the living seas are you okay? You've been through a bloody escape attempt, kidnapped, and now you're being forced to fight?" Zea twisted quickly, spearing Roar with a pointed finger. "What in the earth's crust do you think you're doing? Trying to kill her?"

Roar's expression didn't change, nor did he move. He examined Zea's face intently.

A rush of uncertainty flooded Phe and warmth blotched her neck. Zea was beautiful. What if he—? Phe stopped that thought as quickly as Edva could dismount her on a bad day. Reminding herself she was a rock. Hard, rough, edgy, and dirty.

She didn't even know why she cared. With a gulp, she redirected her errant and erratic thought. *Kyra.* Her name alone stabbed painfully into Phe, centering her.

"I can assure you, hurting Phe is not my or my unit's intention," Roar calmly answered, flicking his gaze to Phe, then back to Zea. "Are you Phe's assigned liaison?"

Zea drew herself up, trying to appear bigger, which didn't work because she was shorter than Phe, crossed her arms, and glowered. "I am Zea."

Roar gave her a slight smile, and amusement touched the corners of his eyes. "Nice to meet you."

Zea huffed disbelievingly. "This is bloody ludicrous. She's had enough happen lately. This should be postponed until she knows even the basics." Zea flung an arm in Phe's direction. "She doesn't even know the branches yet!"

"Zea," Phe interrupted, "this isn't in their hands."

Zea whirled and pierced Phe with blue icicles. "From what I heard, it is entirely their fault. If they'd just kept their greedy mouths shut."

Grooves broke out on Roar's forehead, and his lips curved into the beginnings of a frown.

"Zea," Phe said flatly, swallowing the tsunami of anger flooding her system. Zea didn't get to talk to or about Roar like that. "Walk with me?"

Zea stomped to Phe, gaze narrowed to seething slits. "Why aren't you enraged?"

Phe briskly walked them toward the platform. "When they told me the news this morning, I had so many things go through my mind . . . " She pointedly stared at Zea. "I also know Roar and the unit, and I know they are doing what they think is best to help me, here. This is not how they envisioned this playing out." Phe shrugged.

Zea nodded with understanding.

Phe pivoted to retrace their steps to Roar and caught his gaze. "Now, I'm not saying you can't be angry. That's on you and you can even express it to me." Phe thought guiltily of how she'd treated Zea last night, then she dipped her voice in seriousness. "But don't take it out on Roar or the rest of the unit."

The sea of Roar's gaze embraced her, pulling her further into him. His eyes hooded slightly, radiating warmth and an intimacy Phe couldn't describe. Her heart soared with it. A small smile played on his lips, as if he'd heard her and found her protectiveness endearing.

"Flipping crops, the rumors are true! You actually trained with them as a Still?" It was hard to identify Zea's emotions in that statement: amazement, disbelief, horror, and much more Phe couldn't identify.

"It's true." Phe found herself unable to break away from Roar's gaze, and with each step closer, her heart beat faster and a tingling, giddy heat spread through her. She discovered her lips curling up to match his.

"Why?" Zea prompted. "It makes no sense."

"There were reasons. They seemed logical to me until I learned about magic." They stopped near Roar. "And now I'm even more grateful—"

"Silence." The words felt like a whisper on a wind, slithering past her.

A sudden hush befell the crowd.

"For . . ." she trailed off, both at the silence and Roar's subtle headshake, his gaze widening in warning.

A pin could drop, and it would be heard throughout the stadium. *How is that possible?* She had the distinct feeling everyone was looking at her, as if she shouldn't have been able to speak.

Phe logged this to question later and followed Roar's lead by facing the platform. The seating above was now full. Rows of sheer black robes with pointy hats created a dark splash of foreboding.

The Elders.

They were like rolling dark thunderclouds, looming in the distance and waiting for the right wind to snuff the dim sunrays caressing the stadium.

A figure strode to the edge of their circular balcony. A soft beam of errant sunlight fastened onto them, and their black robes shimmered under its ray.

"Welcome." The whisper wafted by, swirling around Phe. "We are pleased to see so many of you could attend on such short notice." Again Phe was struck by its inflectionless tone.

"We have received and reviewed a petition from General Bastion requesting to induct our newest Phoenix into one of our Elite units. It is an unusual appeal, but the arguments for it are compelling, thus we find ourselves here now."

Nerves hit Phe suddenly, tightening her chest.

"Orphne of Xafara." The weight of hundreds of eyes fell onto her. "You are—"

Zea strode forward, shoulders thrown back, and Phe glimpsed her jaw set. "Excuse me!" Zea interrupted.

The stadium inhaled as one, holding their collective breaths, and the robed figure tilted its head.

"I am here to formally request you allow our newest Phoenix, Orphne, time to train prior to this test." Zea pointed at Phe, as if no one knew whom they were talking about. "She is not only new to our community, but new to her magic." Zea dragged a breath in. "Testing her at this point would be demoralizing for her, but also not provide any indication of the potential she carries once she is properly trained."

"Silence."

Whatever Zea may have intended to add was cut off as

something invisible wrapped around her neck, lifting her off her feet. Zea's hands clutched at the bands, struggling.

Phe scrambled up Zea's body and dug her fingers into the unseen rope. Wrapping her legs around Zea's hips for stability and leverage, she unsheathed one of her thigh knives. She snaked her fingers in between Zea's neck and the rope and carefully sliced into it—wondering if she could even cut a magical, invisible, rope.

The rope withdrew suddenly.

Phe flipped the edge of her knife toward herself to avoid cutting Zea as they both dropped the small distance to the arena floor. Zea crumpled immediately, her legs giving out and taking Phe with her.

The smack of the ground reverberated up Phe's spine and neck. Disentangling herself from Zea, she wondered what kind of terrible place she was in that would treat their citizens this way? This was reminiscent of Shalexum and how masters treated their slaves. How Grum had treated her.

Gads, I need to get out of here.

Phe got to her knees and sheathed her blade, debating if she should help Zea up or let her lie there, sucking in air.

"Are—" Phe started. Roar captured her shoulder, squeezing tightly, warning her to be silent.

"Who are you to question us?" the robed figure asked. "Has it not occurred to you we have considered this? Examined every angle in minute detail? Had our seers scour the possible future ramifications on all the paths?"

Zea hauled herself to her hands and knees, her eyes defiantly flashing. Her mouth moved, but no words came out.

High seas! They can take away your ability to talk?! Phe directed her horrified gaze at Roar.

He wasn't looking at her but gave her shoulder a reassuring squeeze.

She studied Roar's muscular hand, noticing they were calloused and rough. Noticing how they emanated heat. Noticing she hadn't automatically brushed him off. Nor was his touch sending searing pain through her.

Over the years, her body's reaction to his touch had changed.

Uncomfortable, she flicked her gaze to the Elders.

"Leave. We will discuss this behavior with the council." Zea was gone before they'd completed their sentence. "Now, Orphne of Xafara."

Roar's touch disappeared.

Oh seas, oh seas. Sweat formed in her armpits, its tang permeating the air with her fear.

"The rules of this test are as follows," the inflectionless speaker continued. "There will be no dismemberment or killing. Due to the constraints of our candidate, we are allowing for the provision of her submission, which will be done via double taps, either on the ground or on her opponent. At that point, the fight is called. Is this understood, Orphne?"

"Yes." Her firm voice resounded, a complete contrast to her trembling heart. Fighting was not something she feared, but this wasn't fighting. Not the way she knew, anyway. How was she going to fight roots and wind and goo and teleporting and invisible ropes and—

"Orphne of Xafara, your test will commence now."

21

The telltale vibration in the air caused Phe to spin to her left, dirt flying into the air as she leapt to her feet.

A woman materialized.

Her eyes glowed a dark brown, almost black, matching her remarkably short hair, and projected a cold menace as she silently evaluated Phe. An ageless beauty clung to her, in part, Phe thought, because of her smooth dark skin, but also there was something else. The weight of age wrapped around her in the way youth clung to kittens. The lines of her face were taut, including the unimpressed line of her mouth.

The woman's crystal-clear marigold aura pulsed, then faded, marking her a Crystal.

Power oozed from her.

In her hands, the woman held a long, thin sword.

Phe took a deep breath to steady her nerves, fighting the constriction in her chest. She gripped the hilt of one of her twin blades, sliding it free, and gritted her teeth against the fear that slithered over her.

Kyra, she thought, fortifying herself. Kyra was the reason she did everything. Without their friendship, she would have drowned in the turbulent currents that had swept her into a sea of misery. Kyra's name was a lighthouse in a storm, guiding Phe toward her goal.

I will save you, Phe vowed, carefully sending the message into the threadbare connection they shared.

The fear that had taken up residence in her heart recoiled as her determination charged in.

She may not know magic, and after yesterday, she was acutely aware of how quickly she could be overpowered by it.

As much as she hated this place and its magic, a glimmer—that's all she'd give it—of recognition rooted. If all it took was a breeze to stop her, there was no way she'd be able to rescue Kyra.

This is a chance to learn. Before I escape.

The woman smiled, baring teeth, and disappeared.

Bullspit! Senses on high alert, Phe shuffled sideways. *Where is she?*

The air thrummed behind Phe.

Before she'd fully turned, the woman's sword sliced across both her hamstrings. A sharp pain followed as she fell forward, warm liquid gushing.

Phe flipped, blade at the ready, but the woman was gone. She ignored the pooling of blood in the dirt, testing the mobility in her legs. Her left leg was useless.

Flipping seas, the woman immobilized me in one move.

Not hopeful, Phe tested her right. It wouldn't support her.

Cripes, it hurts.

The air stirred to her right.

She threw the blade.

It disappeared into the ether at the same time a blade

slashed across her left side. A heavy throbbing took up residence along the trail it left on her chest.

A thud to her right lifted a plume of dust.

Her twin blade.

It was too far for her to reach, but the coating of blood gave her a boost of satisfaction. This was not a fair fight, but at least she drew blood too.

Hand trembling, Phe unsheathed her other twin blade and waited for the woman to appear again.

Too slow, Phe felt the flesh of her left arm being sheared, but she managed to lunge forward in an attempt to grab the woman's leg. Maybe if they were touching, it would keep the woman in one place. She missed.

The woman vanished and reappeared behind her, carving a Z into her back.

Phe arched, pain searing her, and with it came a disturbing loss of control. She slumped forward, gripping the hilt of her blade tightly, as if it could drain the pain from her. It didn't.

Her vision faded, and her body shook uncontrollably.

Phe hurled her blade at her opponent. Falling to her side from the force of her throw.

The woman rapidly hacked into Phe. Viciously and relentlessly going after her ribs, arms, stomach, cheek.

Phe double-tapped.

Immediately, the woman dematerialized.

Thank the flipping seas.

Phe dropped her head, her vision tunneling, and stared at the granules of bleached dirt. It was the only thing she could see, but she could see each of them with precise detail, their edges crisp and clear.

She lay askew, not having the muscle control to straighten.

Blood, her blood, crept across the arena's floor and, inch by inch, overtook the crystal-clear gravel. Her clothing absorbed it, the added weight pulling at her cuts.

The pain meshed together, pulsating through every nerve that wasn't severed.

Phe angled herself to peer at the sky, the liquid mud mixture smearing onto her face. *Why can't I just die?*

The clouds had darkened into an undulating mass above her.

Because there'd be no one to care about Kyra. But . . . it wasn't only this. Phe knew from experience she wouldn't die. Not from wounds like these.

Orc appeared, kneeling, his bald head obstructing her view. Carefully, his big hands encircled her face. Immediately, a cool, soothing sensation flooded her, healing her.

Phe's heart pumped sluggishly and her lungs struggled to expand. She had expected a challenge—Shadow Unit had told her to expect as much—but this was much more than that.

As she lay there, understanding dawned.

This wasn't about checking the boxes required for their application to induct her. No, there was more to it. She came close to escaping last night. At least, that's how she'd interpreted both Orc's and Fin's statements.

This was punishment.

Meant to show Phe how easy it was for them to subdue her.

They set a cat on a mouse and watched it play.

She could almost hear Bastion. How are you going to save Kyra when you aren't capable of, blah blah blah, things? And he'd be right.

It took all the wind from her sails, the stars from the sky.

This must be Bastion's doing.

He'd see this as a two-for-one. Requiring Phe to go through these motions to see if she was even eligible to be inducted into an Elite unit, which obviously she wasn't. Then to stomp her spirit into dust.

She'd never survive a magical fight.

The only reason she'd survived Djall's attack in Xafara was because of the forest. The forest had saved her.

Seas. Her eyes filled with tears, but she refused to let them fall. She focused on the pain instead, watching the clouds swell as she forced breath into her deflated lungs.

"I got you, Phe," Orc cooed softly.

No, you don't.

Phe closed her eyes, blocking him and the world out. Her heart ached.

The tingling, itchy feeling of her wounds knitting together drew her attention. Her smaller wounds had sealed quickly, but not the wounds on her thighs, arm, and back.

"How many more rounds?" Her voice came out steady and strong, a contrast to the trembles raking through her.

"I don't know."

Flicking her eyes open, she studied the clouds again as the needlelike sensation intensified, her muscles banding together. She wiggled her toes. Flexed her foot. Straightened from the skewed position she'd been in. Then sat up.

"All healed. Ready for the next round?"

Phe turned empty eyes on him.

Orc gave her a small squeeze. His mossy green eyes were heavy, empathy or pity—she couldn't tell which—pouring from them. "Hang in there."

Phe stood slowly and rolled the kinks out of her neck, plucking at her pants and shirt, separating the sticky, blood-soaked fabric from her skin.

Her twin blades were scattered about. With a sense of detachment, she collected them.

It was when she slid the last one into its sheath that the spokesperson announced, "Test two."

Phe hadn't had a chance to even take a breath before a man launched himself off the twenty-foot arena wall, dropping from the crowd into the arena. Her eyes went to the gathering of shadows along the edges of the floor, swirling with the man's disruption.

His loose, tan-colored pants fluttered around him when he walked. Taking a page from Finian's book, he was shirtless, only he also extended that to his feet too. He strutted toward her, a sereneness to his pale face.

"Orphne," he greeted with a hand to his chest as he neared her. "I am Threads. It is my honor to be a participant in your test."

"Don't believe him, baby girl!" she heard Finian holler, the first voice to break through the melding of noise.

Nodding in acknowledgment, Phe surveyed Threads, trying to discern what type of magic he had. *As if I could*, she scoffed.

Then she blinked, not fully understanding what she was seeing.

A replica of Threads stepped out of himself, followed by another, then another. He kept multiplying.

She stared, dumbfounded. *Did I hit my head? Did Orc not heal me?* Her jaw slackened, hanging open a smidgen.

It was only when the crowd of them—yes, crowd—sprinted toward her, with the threat of death beaming from their glowing orange eyes, that Phe reacted. Sliding her twins from their sheaths, she ran into their charge.

This she could do.

She sliced and twisted, aiming for their torsos, and carefully pulling her strikes to not dismember or kill.

It was only after the first three Threads didn't bleed, didn't remain on the ground, or didn't stop their attack that a sense of impending doom scurried up her spine.

She felt resistance as her blades cut through their bodies, felt the impact of their punches and hits, yet . . . she couldn't incapacitate them.

She retreated, or at least tried to, but they had her surrounded. Her right arm was yanked and maneuvered behind her, her twin ripped from her grip.

Hands tore at her hair, then she felt a burst of pain above her hip, and another explosion on her cheek that whipped her head to the side. Her blood sprayed on the Threads in the way. They kicked her legs out from under her.

Once she hit the ground, they restrained her in moments, yanking her limbs, immobilizing her fingers, crushing her with their weight.

Then the real torment began.

The Thread on her belly pummeled her face, while the others kicked or hit anywhere else she was exposed.

She desperately tried to tap out, tried to lift her trapped fingers, but couldn't.

A wave of anger and rage and panic and powerlessness rippled through her, competing with the onslaught of pain.

Thunder bellowed, followed by a cold rush of air.

Then there was blackness.

22

It was the sound that roused Phe, waves of noise cascading over her. Voices melded into a nonsensical uproar, pulling her from the bliss of unconsciousness into the throes of fiery pain. It took her brain a moment to patch things together.

Kyra abducted.

Dragged to Arias.

Botched escape.

Forced magical test.

The coppery tang of blood scented the air and coated Phe's mouth. Her last memory formed. She'd been pinned to the ground and surrounded by a crowd of death-defying doppelgangers intent on killing her with their fists and feet.

Gads, what a bloody awful day.

Orc's thumbs caressed the sides of her cheeks, probably trying to rouse her. He was murmuring something she couldn't make out, her mushy brain unable to pick out the syllables in the chaotic noise.

With much more effort than it should have been, she pried an eye open.

Wetness coated her face and pain throbbed through her

like a steady drumbeat. Each breath was excruciating. It was hard to tell what hurt the worst. Her agonizing headache? Broken fingers and ribs? Heck, body? Bone-deep bruising everywhere?

Stifling a groan, Phe rolled to her side in slow motion and curled into herself. The movement incited a new rush of noxious sensations. Orc's steady touch moved with her. Wetness leaked from her eyes, streaming in rivulets over her face. She fixed her gaze on the shadows along the wall, mentally reaching for them, wishing she could blend in with them.

". . . you did good." She caught the tail end of whatever Orc was rambling about.

Phe cough-whispered through her teeth, her jaw too painful to move. "Liar."

"Not a lie." Orc's fingers splayed along her bruised and fractured face. "You incinerated the illusions and gave Thread a nice wallop of his own."

She made a noise of disbelief.

"Your magic must have reacted when you lost consciousness," Orc continued.

She tuned him out. What he said made no sense, and there wasn't a single part of her that cared for clarity. Not right now, anyway. The day needed to end, and it wasn't even mid-morning.

Can nothing be easy?

This is life, Elzac would say. *It tests before teaching the lesson.*

Phe couldn't help but grumble with the irony of truth his saying had right now.

It is your choice, he'd warn, *to learn the lesson on the first go around or get caught in a loop of your own ego.*

Phe had long ago ascertained egotistical thoughts were

equivalent to a person who'd set their house on fire and was running around screaming and throwing their furniture and belongings at it, trying to extinguish it, not realizing they were fueling it. Not considering leaving. Not even seeing the doors and windows.

That's what her ego did, anyway: filled her with smoke and fire and fear and clouded her judgment so dramatically she forgot about the exits. She forgot she could go outside and seek help. She forgot that sometimes, old structures need to be burnt to the ground, and it was best to let the fire ravage them. Purify. So she could build again.

As her physical wounds knit together, Phe restitched her thoughts, aligning them with her breath, a technique Elzac had taught her. *"You are your thoughts. They either give you power or they make you powerless. You choose."*

I choose to let the house burn. And with one inhale after another, she re-built.

Inhale: *take it one minute at a time.*

Exhale: *I've survived years of this.*

Her heart shuddered.

Inhale: *they won't break me.*

Exhale: *no one can break me.*

Inhale: *I am unbreakable.*

Exhale: *I am unstoppable.*

Inhale: *I AM unstoppable*

Exhale: *Nothing will stop me from rescuing Kyra.*

Each thought and breath steeled her inner resolve. Her heart, which had withdrawn to its shadowed corner, tiptoed out and puffed up.

Phe captured Orc's glowing gaze. "Thank you." One side of her mouth lifted and the corresponding eye narrowed. With her movement, the blood and dirt caking her face pulled at her skin. Sitting up, she brushed Orc's hands away, squaring her shoulders. "Could I have a cloth to clean?" She motioned at her face.

"One sec." Orc's gaze lost focus, then snapped back to her. "After the next round."

Phe tilted her head down and glowered at him.

"Hand up?" His pitch hopeful yet twinged with resignation that she'd give her usual answer: no, thanks.

Phe extended her palm.

Orc smiled, clasping her still-slick-with-blood hand, and helped her up.

"See you in about two minutes," Phe deadpanned.

Orc leaned close. "I'll be here whenever you need me."

"Test three."

Orc vanished as a woman with brilliant reddish-brown hair appeared.

Phe stilled.

Rosea.

How in the world . . .? Of course, Kyra's guards would be magic-borns. They were all under General Bastion's command.

Her chest ignited into a burning mass of pulsating anger as she realized Kyra's guards should've been able to protect Kyra with magic but didn't.

"Lady Orphne," Rosea sang, mimicking Kyra's singsong. "Oh, Lady Orphne, I am so honored to be part of your test." She fluttered her hand at her chest mockingly.

There was a rumbling in the background.

Phe stalked to her twins.

A loud crack of thunder exploded overhead. The storm mimicked her mood.

Rosea's hair was braided, woven with long swaths of black leather that stopped at her hips. Embedded in the leather were spikes. Briefly, Phe wondered how she used them and didn't hurt herself, but discarded the thought, as she was sure to find out.

Rosea's hazel eyes glowed red, contrasting against her light-brown skin. She wore loose yet fitted clothing, and only carried a single throwing knife.

Phe slowly scanned her from head to toe and back again. When she'd finished, she lifted her right brow, giving Rosea a *you-really-don't-scare-me* look. Didn't matter she knew this was going to end badly. There was no way she'd show this woman, her personal bully, fear.

"This is going to be so much fun." Rosea's lilting voice was a bouquet of sarcasm and menace.

Phe answered with a brittle smile, subtly tensing her fingers.

Rosea sauntered toward her, a scornful grin on her face. Then she pouted. "Oh, it must be so tough for you right now, with your precious Kyra gone."

A loud crack reverberated in the arena.

"Must have been quite the shock. Mag-ic." Rosea paused her walk, toying with her braid while peering at Phe through her lashes. "It's boggled my mind how your precious Kyra was too obtuse to realize she had magic."

Everything in Phe seized with Rosea's use of past tense. That simple little word—*was*—eviscerated her, made her want to curl around her stomach to hold her innards in.

Phe straightened against the pain, not allowing it to bend her.

Kyra is not dead.

Defiantly, she transmuted her anguish into anger. Fuel.

"I bet she didn't even survive a day with Djall." Rosea ambled forward, circling Phe. "If you ask me, good riddance," Rosea continued. "She was weak. Useless."

An inferno traveled up Phe's throat, into her eyes. If she

could open her mouth and spew fire on Rosea, she would, but her jaw was clenched so tightly, her teeth might break.

"You know what really surprised me?" Phe moved with Rosea as the woman spoke, mimicking her. "You. You surprised me, and not just with your magic." Rosea fluttered a hand in front of her, indicating Phe. Rosea's posture was relaxed, her movements leisurely. "Who knew?"

The blaze in Phe dropped to her stomach. Her limbs began to tingle.

"Poor, slickly Phe, secretly trained and by one of our Elite units." Rosea was slowly closing in on Phe, and Phe let her. "Yet you failed.

"You taint everything. Shadow Unit. Your precious Kyra." A sly glint sparkled in Rosea's eyes, and her lips curled into a sinister sneer. "Though she'd already been marked. Did you know that?"

Marked?

"Of course you didn't. How silly of me." Rosea tugged her knife free, rotating her wrist with it. "A strategic sacrifice is what we call it."

Strategic sacrifice? Phe forced herself not to frown.

Then Rosea opened her hand, and the blade's tip rose in the air until the knife hung suspended an inch above her open palm, twirling.

The air thickened, and a boom erupted above.

"Even your precious Kyra's family recognized there was more value in offering her than keeping her. Discarding her like—"

Lightning bludgeoned the ground to the right of them, deafeningly powerful, buzzing, and smelling of ozone.

"—the disappointment she is." Rosea dropped her palm, and the knife continued to spin mid-air. "Just. Like. You." The knife flipped and flew at Phe.

Rosea charged.

Phe sprinted the short distance, twisting to avoid the blade, and collided with Rosea.

Feeling, rather than seeing, the knife reverse directions to fly at her, Phe swung Rosea into its trajectory at the last second. It slammed into Rosea's side as Phe pummeled her, kneeing her stomach, crushing her foot, and elbowing the side of her face.

Rows of two-inch spikes struck her repeatedly as Rosea's hair whipped around.

Phe should feel pain, but none came.

Her vision crystalized into minute details: Rosea's dilating pupils, individual drops of sweat beading along her hairline, the pores of her flawless skin, the rapidly-thrumming pulse at her neck.

Unwilling to release her grip, lest Rosea disappear, Phe bashed her forehead into the woman's nose, warm blood splattering across Phe's face.

As Rosea staggered, Phe risked unclenching one hand to batter Rosea's side and back. The hilt of the knife got in the way. It shook with their movements. With a grunt, Phe shoved it in to the hilt.

The knives in Phe's sheaths quivered.

Oh no! Those are mine.

As if the thought alone carried power, they immediately stilled.

Rosea took Phe's legs out, and they both thudded to the ground in a cloud of dirt.

Before she could react, Rosea was on top of her, barraging Phe. The knife in Rosea's side pulled free of its own volition.

The ground quaked.

Phe flipped them and unsheathed her twins in one

movement, then thrust them down with all her rage. She propelled the blades through Rosea's shoulder blades, stopping only when she met solid resistance.

With one hand, she dug her fingers into Rosea's cheek, forcing them to lock gazes. With the other, Phe caught Rosea's incoming knife strike mid-air. The hilt vibrated painfully against the soft flesh of her pinky.

Phe clenched the blade tightly, uncaring that it sheared her to the bone, and dropped her elbow to the base of Rosea's neck.

The knife in Phe's hand wiggled, sawing into her bones. Blood seeped through her fingers. Warm. Thick.

With no other moves left, Rosea's hair slammed into Phe's arm over and over again, trying to get to Phe's face.

"Strategic sacrifice." Spittle flew onto Rosea's face, and a series of lightning bolts pulverized the arena floor. "Explain."

Kyra's family is alive?

If this were true, it was the bastard's doing. Phe knew it. And she would kill him for it. That was the only option. Kill him after she was done pumping information from Rosea. Then she'd set this whole terrible city on fire, starting with that awful statue.

Her fury obliterated everything. Pain. Rational thought. It spiraled her into a funnel of unquenchable vengeance.

What family would sacrifice their child?

Rosea spit. It landed in a heated glob on Phe's cheek.

What type of heinous society would condone this?

Phe leaned heavily into her elbow, digging her fingers into Rosea's cheeks, glaring. "You. Will. Tell. Me."

I'll kill them all.

Rosea smiled, blood coating her teeth. "Eat dirt."

Torrents of rain unleashed, pelting them.

Phe fixated on Rosea's glowing eyes. Her gaze drilled into their depths, threatening an excruciatingly painful death.

Rosea's face lost form, the pebbles digging into Phe's calves disappeared, and the consistent drone from the crowd vanished. The stadium faded.

Darkness funneled the edges of her vision.

She became weightless.

Tendrils of shadows encircled Phe, lacing within her limbs, fingers, hair, anchoring her, then parting to reveal moments caught in time, like the memo-pro Zea had shown her. Only these weren't hers.

Her frenzied rage simmered with confusion.

Where am I?

Only blaring silence answered.

Memory after memory flitted past her as if she was thumbing through a book. She reached out to brush against a frame, but her hand ghosted through it.

Phe held her breath.

Shadow tendrils overlapped and writhed, akin to a nest of snakes, as an image came to the forefront.

A little girl with reddish-brown hair ran into the waiting arms of a woman. The woman's brilliant smile was welcoming, loving, and warm. She swept the girl into her arms, propping her on a hip, and kissed the child's face repeatedly. The kid giggled delightedly.

Rosea.

The child clung to the woman, squirming a little to get comfortable, and lifted a lock of the woman's hair. Eyes wide, smile beaming, she proclaimed proudly, "I hit the target!"

Emotion pulsed into the darkness: joy, pride, excitement, and innocent, child-like exuberance.

A thrilled gasp escaped the woman. "Nice job! Will you show me?"

A sudden heaviness blossomed in Phe's stomach, expanding toward her limbs at the realization of where she was.

In Rosea's mind.

Phe's skin ignited in tingles.

"Yes!" The child wiggled free of the woman's arms, latched onto her hand, and tugged.

A shadowed tendril flailed into the memory, freezing it.

More tendrils slapped onto the frame, causing it to shift precariously to either side, and smoke infused the space as the edges of those tendrils flared into flames.

Fire licked up the memory as quickly as it would a delicate piece of paper. The memory's edges blackened, curling, fading to gray, until the memory was dragged, burning, into darkness.

Horror seized Phe in a vise, tightening painfully around her chest. Bile rose in acidic waves up her throat.

Something was wrong, very wrong.

The selection of framed moments returned, gliding by Phe. This time, a shadow tendril selected a memory.

An adolescent version of Rosea appeared, striding into a kitchen and going straight to a bowl of fruit on the counter. She grabbed an apple and bit into it. Its juices squirted and dripped down the side of her mouth. She leaned against the counter, appreciating the delicious sweetness of the apple, when someone called.

"There you are."

Rosea quirked a brow and pivoted to the doorway. "You knew where I was."

A man walked in. His shoulders sagged as if the weight

of the world had just fallen on them. His eyes featured gray seas of sadness.

Rosea stopped chewing, discarding the half-eaten apple. She forcibly swallowed. "What's wrong?"

"Your mother." The man gripped the counter's edge, his fingers blanching white as he gazed into Rosea's eyes. "She and her team are missing."

"Noooo." Rosea's hand with the apple fell.

"They believe Djall—" A tendril glided up the side of the memory, halting it. The edges frayed, smoldered. Another tendril wiggled into the frame, then another, and another. They dragged its burning fragments into the ethers of darkness.

Into Phe's shadows.

Phe's breathing shortened into small, fast puffs, and her pulse sprinted into action.

This is wrong.

Another memory filled the space.

Rosea lay on the ground, limp and bloody.

A set of feet circled her, each tread loud. Ominous.

"Get up."

Rosea tried, her arms shook uncontrollably, and she collapsed.

"I said, get up." They kicked her.

Rosea lurched upwards, trembling, body curved protectively, waiting for another blow.

"Do you or do you not want to rescue your mother?"

"I do, sir," Rosea grunted, straining to get her legs under her.

"What do you think will happen if you just give up, lay down, in the field?"

"Killed or taken, sir."

"And how will that rescue your mother?"

"It won't, sir." Rosea planted her feet and hauled herself up.

"It won't." The person paced in front of her, a predator about to strike. "You're weak. There is no room for weakness. We beat the weak. We destroy the weak." His icy gaze fastened onto her, and he stepped toe-to-toe, nose-to-nose. "We conquer the weak."

"I understand, sir." Rosea straightened her shoulders, locking her knees to stay upright.

His fist connected with her stomach, and she fell into him as her legs gave out, the breath knocked from her. "Do you?" he whispered as he threw her.

Rosea lay splayed on the ground, fighting to drag in a breath.

"Perhaps," those feet circled her again, "we can spare you. Yes? There are other ways you can be useful."

This time, the shadows encircled the memory, melting the edges. A tendril glided haphazardly down the middle, searing it in two, then engulfing it in flames.

I'm destroying her memories.

Phe had no idea how she was doing this, but she knew, without a doubt, that's what she was witnessing.

Another memory launched.

"No, no, no." Phe whispered in horror, staring past the moving forms to the seething shadows beyond. "Stop."

Nothing happened.

Phe twirled in the space, searching for something, anything or anyone, who could help her.

Her torrid shadows embraced her.

"You must stop!" she shouted into them, only to hear it echo emptily around her.

Phe gulped. Being lost in Rosea's mind was not how she'd foresaw their fight's path. Hands, fists, feet, knees, elbows, blood, bruises, broken bones, yes. That was normal. Knives. Even spiked hair she could deal with.

This?

Unable to control her magic from shredding memory after memory in front of her?

It was wrong on so many levels.

Phe's relationship with her own memories had once been turbulent. Blasphemously—because giving Bastion credit for any inroads in her emotional well-being just felt wrong—he was the first one to talk to her about ways to manage how her past affected her. His reasons may have been self-serving, to obtain the best operational performance from her, but he did plant the first seeds of healing in her mind.

It was Elzac who'd watered those seeds and shown her how to till the garden of her mind. Showed her each planted memory served a purpose, even the carnivorous ones. Helped her learn to handle them. The more she held them, gave space to them, the less they bit, and eventually, she came to accept them.

Phe's memories—the ones she recalled—shaped every element of her.

And her magic was systematically demolishing all of Rosea's.

I'm a monster.

Breaths came faster and faster, yet she couldn't breathe. She didn't know how to stop this.

Phe knew firsthand what it was like to not have memories. Before Grum, there was nothing. Not a scent or color or voice or anything. She had always craved to know her earliest times.

Dizziness swamped her.

Leave! I have to leave.

She swiveled again, seeking a light, a door—only to be met by swirling vines of shadows hiccuping sparks.

What if I'm trapped?

A cough to her left wrenched Phe in that direction, blade out and pointed at the intruder.

Ambassador Genor.

Stepping back, her gaze raked him suspiciously.

Everything about him appeared relaxed. Hands in pockets, shoulders down, hair tucked behind ears, head tilted as he reciprocated her examination.

The stark difference was his backdrop. He wasn't encased in shadow, but in light.

Scenarios skimmed through Phe's mind. He was here to kill her. Imprison her when she had no defenses. Or—it hurt her brain to consider this one—maybe he was here to help?

Please be here to help.

His light flared, burrowing into her shadows.

"Do you know what you're doing?" Ambassador Genor let his gaze drift behind her to another memory her magic was melting.

His light overtook the darkness, halting the disintegrating memory and her magic.

A flood of relief hit her so hard, it weakened her knees. She lowered her knife, sheathing it to cover up her lapse.

"My magic . . . It's destroying her."

He nodded. The slight movement, done without accusation or judgment, pulverized Phe's hope that she was wrong.

She was a monster.

Phe scanned him, looking for more confirmation, but it seemed he was deliberately keeping his expressions neutral or, daresay, even understanding.

"That's correct. Your magic was destroying memories,

but it was also simultaneously sundering her mind. If left unstopped, you would have killed her." His bottom lip extended outward briefly. "All of this you will learn about once you start training. For now, I'm thankful your magic relinquished control without us having to battle."

I am too.

Phe refrained from telling him she'd been relieved the moment he'd stopped her magic. Their relationship hadn't evolved past her preferred grunt and suspiciously track stage. It'd be a miracle if she'd ever trust him.

"Before I can heal her, I need to escort you out." Ambassador Genor offered her his hand. "You need treatment too, and neither one of you can have it until you're disengaged."

Begrudgingly, Phe slid her palm into his dry, rough-yet-soft grasp, as if he worried holding too firmly would cause her to break. His touch was like the brush of a faint wind, barely fluttering, then gone as if she'd imagined it, leaving no trace. And, more notably, no discomfort. The moment their palms met, the stadium reformed.

Noises swooshed around her chaotically, and a surreality fogged her mind. Her gaze fixated on Rosea's brilliant reddish-brown hair and the darker rivulets of blood streaming from her eyes, down her cheeks, pooling around her pale flaccid face.

"Move her," Lear ordered, looking at someone behind Phe.

Hands hooked under Phe's armpits and dragged her off Rosea, giving Phe a better look at Rosea's prone form. Lear aligned Rosea's neck and head, and blood gushed from her ear into the pool surrounding her. Phe's twin blades jutted out of her body.

What have I done?

23

Phe sat at the edge of the stone platform, overlooking the now empty stadium, and diligently studied the remnants of her trials while they waited. What they were waiting for, Phe was certain they'd told her, but it had gone in one ear and out the other.

She surveyed the flecks of blood marring the arena floor, splattered patterns of barbarity. In two spots, blood pooled in different shades, from dark to lighter red. If she wanted to, she could recreate the scenes, dissect their movements into a choreographed dance. But she didn't.

Her skin felt raw and uncomfortable under the pressure of her torn clothes.

Tension rode her shoulders, and her crushing headache had nothing to do with physical injuries. Orc had healed those. Instead, they had everything to do with waves of emotions battering her.

I am a monster.

Lightning had pummeled the ground while Rosea and Phe had clashed. Each strike had charred a tree-like pattern in the dirt. Phe concentrated on tracing those with her eyes.

It was easier than meeting the worried gazes of her team.

The moment she'd regained awareness, she'd found a limp, unresponsive Rosea underneath her. Orc had helped her move, while Roar had pulled her twins from Rosea. Twins she had, somehow, successfully embedded into the earth, pinning Rosea in place. Once Rosea had been freed, she and Ambassador Genor had disappeared.

Technically, Phe had won the last trial, but it didn't feel that way. Not at all. In fact, out of all three trials, this one gutted her the most.

Fighting with hands, feet, and weapons, she could do. Looking an opponent in the eye, feeling every sharp contact, facing them head on—that was the challenge. It pared adversaries and determined skill levels.

What she'd done to Rosea wasn't skill. It was unnatural.

Phe swallowed, risking a quick peek at Shadow Unit.

If I'm a monster, what does that make them?

She slogged through the thought, unable to compute how the group of people lingering around her were monsters. Or how they fit into this terrible society.

Yet they had to be monsters, and not just tiny monster babies. They were full-grown dragons with armored skin, fire breath, razor-sharp talons, spiked tails, and dexterous wings. Hovering horrors.

Phe struggled to envision them this way, except for Finian.

She eyed Finian, contemplating his monster status. He stood shirtless next to Kirzia, beaming.

A proud, vicious dragon, puffing his chest and licking his gleaming teeth.

Finian winked at her, his gaze twinkling, and a dimple appeared.

She averted her eyes, instantly enthralled in the lightning pattern, and hoped he stayed where he was.

Gads, there's only so much I can handle.

It was as if the stars had conspired on what would make life horrible for Phe and then brought every one of their ideas together in succession to see which was worse.

I should've stayed in bed.

Then she'd have undergone the humiliation of Shadow Unit prying her from its blanketed depths, forcing her to face this horrid day.

No, thank you.

Gravel crunched, drawing Phe's attention.

Kirzia, Ihrone, and Finian stood together. Phe caught Ihrone, his tone rising slightly to one of disbelief and incredulousness, saying ". . . all on Areya?" Finian snorted, and Phe tuned out Fin's response.

Orc and Roar sat quietly on either side of her, exuding we're-here-for-you vibes, and listening to Ihrone's conversation.

If Phe could muster the will to speak, she'd ask for clarity on why the Elders had canceled the remaining tests. And how would that affect her plan to rescue Kyra?

She had a lot of follow-up questions, too, centered on the subject of strategic sacrifice. For now, she couldn't focus. Her brain and heart had absconded, squirreled up in some dark, hidden corner, rocking.

"Yess!" Finian yelled, startling Phe, his fists clenched at his waist, showcasing his strong, veiny forearms, eyes and chin dramatically tilted skyward.

Phe gritted her teeth, unlocking her entire body. *Does he have to be so dramatic?*

A smile broke Kirzia's concerned expression, flashing

Phe a glimpse of her striking beauty, before turning to Finian for a double-handed high five.

Finian avidly reciprocated, exclaiming, "Bam!"

Confusion crinkled Phe's forehead and pulled tight at the corners of her mouth as she glanced between them.

"They've decided." Satisfaction smoothed Roar's timber tones and the lines of his features lightened, curving upwards.

At her askew glance, he paused. His blue eyes scanned her, and it felt as if he could see into her shadowy depths.

Warmth crept into her neck, and Phe stared at his left ear.

"General Bastion ordered us to wait here," he explained lightly: Phe got the impression he was repeating himself, "while the Elders decided where it would be best to house you, because even if you weren't a flight risk, the attention the tests gave you would make it unsafe for you to live unsecured."

"The Elders have elected for you to stay with Areya." Genuine warmth infused Roar's tone when he said Areya's name, prompting Phe to glance away from the safety of his ear and connect with his gaze. "Areya is . . . special. Would you all agree?" Roar didn't break eye contact with Phe to see how the others would react to his question. She had the weight of his full attention.

"Yes, sir," Orc and Kirzia responded.

"Totes," Finian gushed.

Kirzia sharply said, "No," in response to Fin's new word.

"Agreed," Ihrone stated.

"Areya has two levels of security—probably the primary reason for this decision—that no one has ever breached. The inner layer is Areya's protective shield. She established a single entry point to her property and monitors who arrives. If it's an unwelcome guest, Areya will return them to Arias.

"A collective of Elders created the outer layer of protection, as she's currently under house arrest. Only approved visitors may enter. You will be safe there."

"Drum roll," Finian called, pounding his thighs excitedly.

"Then there's her property," One corner of Roar's mouth crinkled up. "It is amazing."

"What!" Finian, aghast, stopped his drumming. "You're not going to tell her?"

Roar broke their eye contact then to glance at Finian. "Which is better: describing it or experiencing it?"

Finian grunted, bobbing his head once. "Yes."

Phe's brain crawled back into its designated space and parceled through the information. Areya. Special. Under house arrest. Elders just decided. Then it froze.

How in the seas do they know this?

She had been right here, sitting with them, when it seemed they got the message. But no one had appeared and announced it. They'd just reacted, simultaneously.

She felt the crinkles deepen into grooves, sampling confusion and derision. *Am I that out of it that I missed a messenger arriving?*

"A perk of being in an Elite unit—" Ihrone's cadence was smooth and balanced, the tone he used for teaching, "—is we have the ability to speak mind-to-mind, or telepathically, between ourselves and with General Bastion."

Her brain released the freeze.

A puzzle piece clicked into place.

All those years of synchronized behaviors and speaking

to each other as if they were reading minds. It'd had nothing to do with being a well-versed team. They'd actually been doing just that.

The realization stung. Phe'd tried so hard to merge into their team, attempting to interpret all their cues and respond the same way they did with each other. Yet the whole time it had been unrealistic and unobtainable.

Then there were those missives that Roar would tell her he intercepted on midnight runs.

Intellectually, she'd known there were layer upon layers of lies or omissions they'd steadily fed her over the years, once magic was out of the bag. Rationally knowing this didn't ease the bite of betrayal.

Phe's heart sank into her belly.

She turned to Roar, speaking the first words to them since she'd regained consciousness, unable to hide the quiver of hurt in her voice. "You lied to me." She swept the rest of the unit with a bitter gaze. "You all lied to me."

Roar's hand moved to hover over her thigh.

Phe shifted away from the threat of his touch and stared at the lightning's damage again.

His hand froze, then he slowly withdrew it. "I'm sorry, Phe. We're all sorry."

Finian stepped into her line of sight. "Think of it this way. When you're officially in the unit—" Fin's smile stretched so wide, Phe wondered it if hurt, "—I'll be able to talk to you." Finian was pointing from his head to hers.

Gads, that sounded horrible.

"I wonder," Finian continued, "will you grunt at us telepathically, too?"

Phe slitted her eyes. Not if she had anything to do with it.

"Stop sassing her, Fin," Orc snapped.

"Why is Areya under house arrest?" Phe asked, needing to divert the conversation to one that didn't churn her insides. Thinking of all the ways they'd lied over the years would make her crazy. And there was no way she'd tolerate having people in her mind. What if they read her thoughts? Had access to her secrets?

Nah. No, thank you.

Everyone looked at Roar, so Phe did too.

"It's not my story to tell," Roar simply stated. "Few know the details, as Areya's case was pretty hush-hush. If she wants you to know about it, she'll tell you. Either way, the reason for her house arrest will not affect you. Now, do you all want to accompany us?"

"I'll take her," Finian declared, confidently striding toward her only to halt with the sea of noes. Dumbfoundedly, he exclaimed, "What?!"

"Fin, man, I think it'd be better if Roar took her." Orc wrapped an arm across Fin's shoulders, the other smacking him across his pecs. "You know Areya has a soft spot for him. You're hungry. Phe's exhausted. I'm sure once Roar introduces them, Areya will settle her in, and Phe'll take a nap." Orc's attention fell on Phe.

Phe slowly blinked. Orc wasn't wrong. She was utterly drained. But how could she justify a nap when Kyra was missing?

"How about the rest of us go to Cava's?" Orc asked. Through the years Phe had heard a lot of stories about Cava's. It was a cave that had been converted into a lounge and was the team's favorite hangout.

"I'm in," Kirzia said, two-finger saluting in Phe's direction before vanishing.

"It's like they think I'm a bad influence or something," Fin grumbled, half pouting, half smiling with amusement.

"It's the 'or something,'" Roar dryly stated, clearly exasperated.

"Order me something Fin," Ihrone said as the rest of the team disappeared.

"That was brave." Humor spiced Roar's voice.

Ihrone flashed Roar a knowing smile, then turned to her. "How are you?"

Phe gazed into his solemn gray eyes, debating letting her silence answer for her, but that felt wrong. *Ugh.* She dredged up a single word. "Fine."

There was truth to it; it just wasn't the whole truth. Her body was pain free. All limbs and digits accounted for. She could walk. Talk. See. Hear. It was just everything else.

"You know what I learned today?" Roar lounged on the opposite side of her, one bent leg on the platform, so he could see her. "I learned that fine means: Feelings Inside Not Expressed."

She gave him her best deadpan stare.

Roar held up both hands in a don't-hurt-me gesture. "My sister explained it to me."

"She sure did." Ihrone's glance at Roar was heavy in meaning.

Roar smiled affectionately, tone softened as he indulgently stated, "She is a force to be reckoned with."

Phe'd heard this statement, in some form, over the years. A tiny, itsy-bitsy part of her had been curious to meet Ash, Roar's sister, but right now she didn't care. Nothing mattered except centering herself and then saving Kyra.

"When you're ready to talk, we're here." Ihrone uncrossed his arms, gripped the stone edge, pulled himself heavily to his feet, and vanished.

Roar got to his feet too, offering her a hand. "Shall we?"

Phe gazed at it blankly, then sucked in a deep, audible breath, and shook her head no. She barely tolerated the heavy weight of her soiled clothing or the caked blood.

"Too much." Her voice came out thin, tiptoeing the line of cracking, and she could only force those two words past her lips. Unable to look at Roar, because she considered her aversion to touch a weakness, she fumbled with her shredded sleeve. Ripped a piece free and extended its edge to him.

"It's okay," Roar consoled. His movement was deliberate as he carefully pinched the edge of the fabric.

The arena dissolved.

It was the smell that registered first.

Forest.

Not Drykz Forest, with its green oak scent. Nor was it similar to the pine forest of Sryln Sierras. This forest had a sweetness tinged in its earthy undertones and a mild, indiscernible spice.

The scent wrapped around her in a welcoming hug, and something within Phe eased.

Roar had teleported them onto a well-worn dirt path. The dirt wasn't bleached and dry, like the arena. It was damp, with dark and light browns mingling with earthy shades of red. The vibrant green shrubbery blanketing the sides wrapped around the trunks of the most enormous trees Phe had ever seen.

Phe tracked one of the behemoth trees into the sky. It kept going. She was sure they blurred the line between the sky and the stars. She'd have to wait until nighttime to confirm.

A little of the heaviness in her chest lifted, and a strange feeling of excitement, surprise, and awe trickled into its emptiness. The vise suppressing her voice released.

"What kind of tree is this?"

"Sacredwood."

"It's . . ." Phe found herself gently placing her palms on one. It was spongy, soft, and thick with a deep red-brown bark. An ancient wisdom seemed to radiate from it. "Remarkable."

She retreated to estimate how many people it would take to encircle its base. *Five? Seven?*

"Are they all this big?" She tucked a strand of crusty hair behind an ear and glanced at Roar to find she had his unwavering focus.

It was as if he was soaking in her reactions, memorizing or mesmerized, she couldn't tell which. He'd shoved his hands into his pockets, his shoulders ever-so-slightly rounded, and the smile he'd given her at the stadium before the trials had returned. It was a small, intimate one that warmed her from the inside.

Phe free-fell into his gaze, only to be dragged back by the escape of the clumpy piece of hair that bounced on her cheek. She jerked her gaze to the safety of the tree.

"They're larger, actually. This is the youngest section of the grove."

These are baby trees?

"Wait until you see Areya's house."

"It's more amazing than this?"

"I think it is."

How that was possible, Phe didn't know, but she was eager to find out. She gave the tree one last loving pat and rejoined Roar.

They walked side by side, close enough that Roar's heat prickled her hypersensitive skin.

"Can everyone teleport or jump?"

"Teleportation is part of the transportation branch of magic and not everyone has access to it individually. Over time, they created jumping stations, like the one you walked through yesterday, for those who don't have the ability."

"Do I have the ability?"

"I don't know."

Phe tore her gaze from the passing scenery to Roar. "You don't?"

Roar scrunched his lips into an apologetic smile. "I was told you awoke four branches and all of their flowers and leaves, with two of the branches sprouting a new bloom."

His pace slowed alongside his cadence, emphasizing the importance of his next few words. "It is rare for someone to have access to four branches, and typically if they do, it's at a much lower power level with only a flower or two waking. The new blooms signify new magic and that hasn't happened in a long time. General Bastion believes it has something to do with shadows. We'll see once we start exploring your capabilities. But, to make things even more interesting—"

Because that's not enough, apparently.

"—The remaining two branches were mildly activated, which is unheard of. It implies you have access to magic in those branches. The Elders are researching this, as there is conflicting remembrance of it happening before. If they find a previous occurrence, they'll be able to better assess what it could mean for you."

Roar's stride subsided to a snail's crawl as they approached a curve in the trail. "To answer your question, teleportation magic was one of the branches you mildly activated. We don't know what you're capable of, if anything, on that branch."

Can't I just be normal? Someone who lives under the radar?

They rounded the corner, and Phe's jaw dropped, her feet gluing to the earth.

High seas!

The largest tree Phe had ever seen stood before her. She was a mere insect, buzzing at its base, insignificant to the giant.

An enormous house encircled the base of the tree, and from it, two separate stairways led up to two smaller houses clinging to the tree's side above the main house and on either side. Between the two treehouses appeared to be a rope bridge connecting balcony to balcony.

Another set of stairs were like vines inching upward to a third house that hung directly over the main house. Phe glimpsed the edges of another set of rope bridges off this house's balconies, concluding there was a fifth house on the other side of the tree.

The finale was the last house, set above all the others. This mirrored the main house as it fully wrapped around the tree trunk and showcased a balcony fully encompassing its perimeter.

Wall-to-ceiling windows glinted blindingly in the sun, terraces overflowed with greenery, and the roofs weren't roofs—they were spectacular gardens.

It was straight out of one of Kyra's fairy tales.

"I'm going to immortalize your expression," Roar said, humor lacing his tone with the hint of restrained laughter.

Phe forced her mouth closed.

"It's . . . wow," Phe stuttered, attempting to formulate words. "I'm staying there? Right?" With her luck, she was living in an uninhabitable hole behind it.

"Uh-huh."

"And this Areya." Phe licked her bottom lip nervously, still staring at the treehouses. "She's . . .?" *Not crazy?*

"She's one of the nicest people I know." Roar started toward the house.

Phe chewed on his statement, unsure why Roar's opinion of Areya settled like a brick in her stomach. She sighed dejectedly and trailed behind Roar.

24

The loud babble of a river pulled Phe from the dark depths of sleep. Overhead, twinkling lights draped around unusual and ethereal rock formations, depicting a brilliant night sky, one she recognized immediately.

Phe bolted upright, cool tile on her bare feet, and whipped around, taking in the underground river gurgling past her. The distinct tile walkway. The bookcase.

How'd I get into Kyra's training room?

Phe ran through her last memories. The tree house. Meeting Areya. Drinking tea and being shown her room.

The bond in her chest ached ferociously, deep and unrelenting. Absentmindedly, she rubbed at it as she padded toward the door, realizing it was the first time she'd felt it since Kyra's abduction.

It didn't matter how she'd gotten to Oceanid and into Kyra's training room. Phe's pace quickened. It only mattered she was no longer in Arias. When she got out of here, she'd figure out how to rescue Kyra.

Around the throb, hope tentatively unfurled.

The pain lessened as she got closer to the door, only to

be yanked to a stop with a brutal force that threatened to pull her heart from her chest.

Phe doubled over from the pain, leaning onto the nearby ledge for support.

The agony subsided.

Heaving herself up, she took a step toward the door and the pain returned, but when she leaned onto the ledge again, it eased. She tried it one more time, and the same thing happened. She switched directions, attempting to head to the river, only to experience the same sensation.

Is my pain guiding me?

She swung her feet over the ledge, her bare feet encountering moist, rough rocks.

No pain.

She sidestepped toward the door. The stabbing pain consumed her, forcing her to retreat.

She hesitantly slid a foot across the uneven cavern floor.

No agony.

The tether in her chest pulsed. She took another step, then another.

The lights flickered. Or maybe that was her imagination?

Phe'd never been beyond the marked tile, always sticking to Kyra's side within the training room. The lighting was dimmer as she made her way past various stalagmites, columns, and boulders.

The sensation in her chest transitioned to a feeling of a leash lugging her, its handler uncaring of the obstacles in between her and them. More than once she had to face cleaving pain to walk around a rock, column, or small rivers that emitted evanescent blue lights.

The invisible rope yanked, so powerful it arched Phe's chest, and almost sent her tumbling to her knees.

She caught herself on a slippery stalagmite, her other hand at her chest as if to assure herself it hadn't opened, when she noticed a human form lying curled in the fetal position.

She sidled forward, absorbing the dirty, threadbare slacks and shirt. The garments hung loosely from the person's thin frame. She glimpsed bare feet, tucked together, and a poorly shaved head, face hidden under arms.

Phe dropped to her knees, ignoring the flash of pain that radiated through her legs as she cautiously lay her hand on their shoulder. The person flinched away from her touch.

Heart beating wildly in her throat, she forced out a shaky, "Kyra?"

High seas!?

"Kyra?" Her voice came out stronger, and her hand wrapped around the shoulder, pulling on it.

The person moved with Phe's pressure, twisting to lie on their back, face shuttered. Wide green eyes looked back at her. "Phe?"

"Oh seas! Kyra!" Phe dragged her sea sister half onto her lap and clutched her to her chest. "Are you okay? What did they do to you? How did you get out? Why are we here?"

Kyra leaned into Phe. "Are you real?" Her normal lyrical voice was flat.

Phe snorted. "Yes," she said, searching Kyra for injuries. She hit a few tender spots, but nothing felt broken. "What did they do to you?" Phe's fingers deftly made it up Kyra's neck to her scalp, where tufts of trimmed hair lay interspersed with sections that were bare to the skin.

Multiple scabs peppered Kyra's head, most likely from when they'd sheared her hair. Phe also saw fingerprint-sized bruises sprinkling Kyra's forehead.

"You're not real."

"I am."

"No, you'd never touch me."

"That's not true!"

"It is. You're not real. You're a figment of my imagination."

"Kyra." Phe wanted to shake her. "I'm real!"

Kyra lifted her left hand and shoved her fist against her mouth, tears trickling down her cheeks. Her sleeve drooped with the movement, exposing three blue squiggly lines depicting water and the number 333. The skin was raised and red around the lines.

Phe stilled. Kyra wasn't acting as if she'd escaped, and Phe had no idea how she'd arrived in Kyra's training room. She deliberately slowed her speech. "How did you escape?"

Kyra curled tighter into herself, pressing into Phe. She mumbled around her fist. "I didn't."

"You didn't? Then how are you here?"

"I don't know." Kyra's voice shook. "They—" Kyra faltered. "They threw me in a cage. The only time I've left the cage is when they come and strap me to the table. I didn't escape. You're a figment of my imagination."

"I am not."

"You are."

Phe barely stopped herself from pushing Kyra off her lap and shaking her. "Look at me."

"No."

"Why not?"

"Because you're not real."

"I am!"

"No. Stop messing with my head!" Kyra screamed, her fingers digging into her temples, so hard Phe feared they would leave more bruises.

This time, Phe did dump Kyra from her lap, grabbing

her face and forcing Kyra to look at her. Fear-filled green eyes met hers. "Who's in your head?" she asked, her voice a cord of anger.

"Djall."

Letting Kyra go, Phe gripped her own thighs painfully. She knew what it was like having someone in her mind. It was invasive, and Ambassador Genor hadn't, to her knowledge, tried to possess her. The wave of anger transformed into an even more powerful wave of fear, knocking the breath out of her.

Her brain took that moment to ping her with logic.

If Kyra was locked in a cage and the last thing Phe remembered was being left alone in her treehouse, after she'd had tea with Areya and Roar . . . Hadn't Areya said something about the tea helping her to sleep?

Phe got up and kicked the stalagmite that had caught her fall. The impact shot a ray of pain into her foot. "Seas!" She kicked it again and was going for a third when she heard, "Stop, you're scaring me."

Phe immediately stopped, clenched her fists, and paced. "You're right. The last thing I remember is being in Arias."

"You're in Arias? Where's that?"

Phe paused mid-pace to gaze speculatively at Kyra. "It's a magic city, in Shalexum's Xiheria Highlands, from what I can tell."

Kyra hugged her knees, hiding the lower half of her face in them. "There's a magical city?"

Phe grunted and resumed pacing. "There are five magical cities, to be precise." An involuntary shudder shivered across Phe's shoulders. Bitterly, she added, "Apparently magic exists, and they lied to us about it." Phe's angry gaze latched onto Kyra. "Everyone. Bastion, Jallia, Commander

Elex, Shadow Unit. At this point, I wouldn't be surprised if all of House Nereid's staff was in on it."

Strategic sacrifice.

Phe inhaled deeply, trying to get a handle on her temper. It was not the time to let it rule her. "I think," Phe took another breath, clearing more of her mind, "I think I got into your mind somehow."

"How?" Kyra blinked.

"It's a story, but hey." Phe flung a hand in Kyra's direction, acerbity riding her voice. "You were right! I have magic." Phe nervously rubbed her palms together, then brought her steepled fingers to her mouth.

"You need to tell me everything about what happened from the moment you were abducted. If this is a dream, then no harm. If I'm right and I'm in your mind, anything could be a clue to finding you."

Kyra shook her head, her face still hidden in her knees. "You're not real."

Phe stomped over to Kyra and squatted in front of her. She knew she was onto something here and she would not let Kyra interfere with her own rescue. In a gentler, less frantic tone, she said, "I don't know how to prove to you I am real." Phe stared into Kyra's eyes contemplatively. "Djall has access to all your memories, so it has to be something I haven't shared with you."

Phe considered sharing about the weirdness with Roar lately, but that didn't seem to carry enough significance. It had to be something more. Something only Kyra knew of and had been yearning for details. "Do you want to know a fact about my dream or about my time in Drykz Forest?"

Kyra's head popped from her knees, surprise smoothing the lines of sadness from her face. "Dream."

"It's not me in the dream, it's a child named Anala."

She'd never told anyone the details of her dream, only that it existed.

"That's it?"

"Oh no, but I'm certainly not going to tell you the whole dream now. What if we meet again like this? One fact a dream. Now, it's your turn. Tell me everything."

Kyra swallowed, and it looked painful.

"Are you thirsty?"

"Gads, yes. I haven't had access to water since they took me."

Phe reeled backwards, horrified. Kyra couldn't last more than an hour without doing something with water. "We can fix that right now." Phe grabbed Kyra's arms and hauled her up.

"How?"

"We're in your training room."

Kyra visually brightened and stood taller. "Really?" The word trembled with hopeful inflection.

"Follow me." Phe clasped Kyra's hand and silently navigated them back to the tiled pathway. Once there, Kyra wrenched her hand free of Phe's and ran to the river. A wave formed from its surface and rolled toward Kyra, almost like it was welcoming her again, as she dove into it.

Phe took a seat at the edge of the water and waited. What if withholding water from Kyra was part of weakening her? Phe drummed her fingertips on her leg. Kyra said Djall was in her mind. What did that mean? Was he speaking to her? Was he trying to possess her?

Well, he's definitely not trying to befriend her, Phe chastised herself. She wondered if she should tell Kyra about her family and the strategic sacrifice.

No. The information would do nothing more than demoralize her. *I'll tell her when she's safe.*

Kyra's head popped above the surface of the river.

Phe clenched her jaw as she noticed all over again how gaunt Kyra was, her face pale and her eyes sunken. *This is my fault,* she thought, grief spiraling into her throat. At least a light had returned to Kyra's green eyes.

"Kyra, I don't know how much time we have together, but you have to tell me everything." Pleading crept into Phe's voice.

"It's not much." Kyra gulped a mouthful of water. "One moment I was at the ball and the next I was in a room. Someone was speaking, or chanting, and I didn't have access to my capabilities. I couldn't do anything. They forced me to kneel, and Phe, I thought that was it, I was a goner. But they hacked off my hair, then my dress. They demanded I wear these rags, and when I was done, one of them touched me, and the room I'd been in disappeared. A dark one with small cages lining the walls took its place. In the middle was a table." Kyra's voice shook, and she drank more water.

"They strapped me to the table, and it was then I noticed the cages were full of people. People, Phe." Kyra's green eyes glowed, and horror etched the lines of her face. "In small cages meant for a dog." Kyra closed her eyes. "They stuck a needle with tubing into my arm and left. Just left. I don't know how long they were gone for, but it felt like forever. Eventually, they dragged me off the table and threw me into a cage."

Kyra opened her eyes. The glow had faded along with her light.

Phe could feel how distraught Kyra was, her terror and fear traveling through their tether.

"I'm so sorry." Hating to have to do this, but knowing she needed to, Phe probed. "The first room they took you to. Can you describe it?"

"It had no windows. Tan walls, but they were grimy, and there were foot- and handprints on them. It was dusty, and there were torn clothes and shoes piled in a corner . . . and the hair." Kyra inhaled shakily. "Lots of different colors and types, all over the ground."

"Did you smell anything?"

"The stench of unwashed bodies."

"Anything else?"

Kyra shook her head.

"Did it have a wooden floor? Stone? Dirt?"

Kyra chewed her lip, eyes going distant. "I can't remember. It was covered in hair."

"They took you to this other room. Can you describe that?"

"It's dark and moist. Made of stone slabs. It smells horrible, like a combination of body order, blood, and sewage."

"And the cage you're in?"

"Small. Electricity, I think, is running through the bars, and it zaps me if I brush against it. I have to curl into myself to avoid touching them."

"Have they given you food or a drink since you arrived?"

Again, Kyra shook her head.

Gads, she must be starving.

"Have they fed anyone?"

Another heart-wrenching head-shake.

"What about noises?"

"Sometimes I hear screaming."

"Has anyone spoken to you?"

"No."

"If it's moist, there's water there. Can you call it?"

"I tried. It wouldn't come." This time Kyra's eyes filled with tears, and she slipped under the waves for a moment.

Phe grappled with what to ask next while waiting, her heart galloping in her chest.

When Kyra surfaced, Phe said, "I'm sorry, but I have more questions. Is there a door to this room?"

"Yes."

"Have you been able to see what's beyond it?"

"No." Kyra scrunched her nose. "It's too dark."

"Describe the room."

"The ceiling, floor, walls are all the same gray stone, and there aren't any windows."

"Do you think you're being held underground?"

"I don't know."

"Is there a heaviness to the room?"

"Uh, no?"

"How many cages?"

"I don't know."

Phe gritted her teeth. *How could she not know?*

"Where is the door situated in comparison to you?"

"I'm in the furthest cage to the right of the door."

"Has anyone talked?"

"No."

"You need to talk to them. Find out their names, how long they've been there, and if they know anything: where you're all being held, what type of forces Djall has, anything that can help us rescue you all. If they don't know those details, see if they remember the circumstances of their kidnapping or anything else." Phe needed all the help she could get if she was going to find out where Kyra was being held. The smallest detail could be the key. She only hoped she'd be able to talk to Kyra again and resolved to take her training seriously. Anything that could help her get to her sea sister. "Consider all information important, every detail. Got it?"

Kyra grunted.

Interpreting that as a yes, Phe switched gears. "What is Djall doing in your mind?"

Kyra's face crumpled. "He's talking to me."

"About?"

"You." Her voice wobbled like an infant standing for the first time.

"What does he want to know?"

"Everything."

"What else has he mentioned?"

"He's talked about the bastard and crazy stuff."

"Define his crazy."

"Geez, bossy much?" Kyra sighed heavily. "This has got to be real. You'd be nicer if I was dreaming."

Phe gave her a *don't-get-impatient-with-me-I'm-trying-to-rescue-you* look.

"It's more his mutterings, I guess. He keeps mentioning someone named Tala, I think, and worries about her and needing more magic. Power. He talks about the importance of clan and how I am now part of his. Something about Xafara being his. Oh, he believes I have a family who abandoned me to this fate."

Phe scrubbed her face, obscuring her reaction. *How does Djall know that?*

"He obviously doesn't know my mother died in a blizzard in the Xiheria Highlands when I was six."

Phe needed to protect Kyra from Djall somehow.

Elzac created my protective barriers. "Can I try something?" Phe worried her lip again as soon as the words were out. Elzac had helped her, but she'd hurt Rosea. What if she did the same to Kyra?

"What do you want to try?"

"I learned to shield my mind from invasion. I'm going to

shield you. Maybe it'll stop him?" Her heart double-jabbed her ribs, reminding her she'd almost killed Rosea today by dabbling in mental magic.

Something inside her, which tasted a little like denial, answered her fears. She would never hurt Kyra, and she had to trust that her magic wouldn't either. *I have to do this.*

Kyra sniffed. "Okay."

"Come here, I need to touch you." The water around Kyra surged, bringing her to Phe. "Why don't you lay back, and I'll touch your head?" Phe suggested.

Silently, Kyra let the water settle her onto her back, remaining almost fully submerged.

Phe closed her eyes and began stumbling through what she'd done with Elzac. Kyra couldn't create her own barriers, so Phe made them for her and then began the work of fortifying them. Worry tightened her shoulders and clawed at her chest as she formed the protections.

What if I'm doing this wrong? What if I'm hurting her, like Rosea?

No. There was no way she'd harm Kyra—she was her sea sister—and everything about this was different than what had happened with Rosea. Phe and Kyra were in House Nereid, with sunlight streaming through the windows. They weren't in a dark space, watching memory after memory scroll by. There were no shadows.

As she worked, a blanket of exhaustion coated her, and her magic became sluggish and hard to wield. She forged ahead, drawing on what magic she could, forcing herself to finish. Finally, after what felt like many long, draining hours later, Phe released Kyra and all but collapsed in the water next to her.

"Done," she grumbled, struggling to form the word around the weariness that consumed her.

Kyra rolled in the water to face Phe, her eyes earnest and imploring. "Phe, I'm ordering you not to come after me."

Phe pressed her mouth into a line and slitted her eyes. No way in the seas would she obey that order.

"Don't look at me like that." Kyra countered, firming her chin. "If you try, he'll only take you, too, and I can't live with that." Kyra sighed sadly, and then tacked on, "You've already sacrificed so much of your life for me. Leave me and go fall madly in love with some dashingly handsome warrior."

That quirked one side of Phe's mouth.

"I mean it, Phe." Kyra's eyes glowed. "I love you. You *have* to let me go."

The edges of Phe's vision darkened. How could she consider ever letting her sister go? Especially when she was in the hands of a monster? *Never.* But she didn't tell Kyra that. Instead, as Phe's vision blurred and their connection faded, she simply said, "I love you, too."

25

Sunrays warmed one cheek, the other was pressed into a soft, plush pillow. Phe burrowed into the pillow and cursed the sun, the stars, and all the seas.

She semi-flopped onto her back, releasing the pillow, and squinted before slamming her eyes shut.

Gads, the sun is bright.

She'd caught a glimpse of the wall-to-ceiling windows and, through it, the terrace in its overflowing glory of plants.

How is it I'm in a fairy wonderland and Kyra's in a cage?

A stabbing pain jabbed into her stomach, gutting her. Their roles should've been reversed. Phe dragged her bone-weary limbs into herself, the movement sapping all of her energy, leaving her winded.

How was she even more depleted after her forced nap?

Phe remembered showering before collapsing onto the bed, her skin free of the caked blood from the trials. Her shredded clothing was discarded in a heap on the washroom floor, destined to be burned, and Phe was now outfitted in a loose-fitting tunic set.

She'd been given the treehouse above and to the right of

the main house, and it didn't disappoint. Wall-to-ceiling windows overlooked a semi-circular terrace and the sacred-wood forest. The space had three man-made walls. The fourth wall was the tree itself, its spongy-soft, red-brown bark exposed to the interior.

How the house had been built was beyond Phe's comprehension.

Though it appeared small from the outside, she'd discovered the treehouse had an open living space with a cozy kitchen corner, three bedrooms, and three bathrooms. Phe wasn't even going to attempt to consider the plumbing system. All she knew was it worked because her shower had been glorious.

Every detail, from the construction of the rooms to the furniture, was interwoven with natural elements, creating a sense of serenity Phe had never known was possible. And now that she did, she was forever cursed because no place could compare.

The stars couldn't give without a backhanded jab, huh?

The vaulted ceiling showcased beams of red woods and skylights. Vines encircled the beams, draping themselves into the streaming sunlight. Leaves hung open and greedily fed from the unnaturally brilliant sun.

She couldn't lie in bed all day. She had a rescue to plan and magic to learn.

Phe dug her fingers into the white comforter beneath her and hauled herself up. Even though she'd rested, she was infinitely more exhausted now than she had been before, and it took all her concentration to retrace her steps to the washroom.

After taking care of business, she grasped the sink's edge for support and splashed water on her face. Phe glanced in the mirror and froze.

Her eyes had sunken, and dark crescent shadows encircled them. Hollowed cheeks greeted her, alongside a pale complexion. Very pale. It appeared as if, between the time she'd showered and napped, she'd lost ten pounds.

Her level of exhaustion was incomprehensible.

Using the wall for support, because her legs were wet noodles, she slowly dragged her carcass out of the treehouse and down the set of stairs into Areya's. She entered what she'd named the great room, because it was a tremendous open space of beauty.

Phe didn't gaze around in wonder, as she had when she'd first entered, too focused on staying upright and making it across the space to where Areya and Roar sat in an alcove.

Of course they chose a snug space at the furthest possible distance.

She'd glare at them if she had the energy, but it was taking everything in her to put one foot in front of the other.

Phe stumbled past the thick slab of gleaming red wood that passed as the dinner table. It had been cut vertically from another mammoth trunk and left with its natural curves and bark. It was simple, yet stunning, and could easily accommodate twenty people with its matching bench seating on the wall-to-ceiling window side and the plethora of chairs lining the opposite end.

It was when she got to the largest crescent-shaped, cream-colored sofa she'd ever seen that Roar noticed her.

Thank. The. Seas.

"Phe?" Surprise raised Roar's pitch.

Instead of trying to trek to them, she collapsed into the comfortable clutches of the couch cushions and let her head tilt upwards to stare at the exposed beams above. Vines dangled from them; their leaves angled toward the sun.

"Oh dear," Areya muttered, appearing in front of her.

Phe looked down her nose at Areya because it would take too much energy to lift her head. The first thing she saw was Areya's cool gray A-line dress. She tracked up Areya's form, past her gray-white hair, and finally, connected with crystal-clear blue eyes encased in cool gray. The most unique eyes Phe had yet to encounter.

"It's that bad, huh?" Phe whisper-croaked sarcastically, catching a quick glimpse of Areya's clear gray aura.

Radiating maternal concern, Areya slid onto the sofa next to her, close enough they could touch.

Roar took Areya's place in front of her, his mouth a worried line. "Are you okay?"

Now that's a loaded question.

A stray beam of light decided to reflect off something from one of the side tables and stab Phe in the eye. She flumped her head to the side, sweeping a glance at the enormous fireplace across the room. Two brown-leather bucketed seats and a corresponding loveseat faced the fireside, creating an intimate seating area, with—because Phe had noticed this earlier—a textured rug in its midst with vibrant earth tones of reds, deep yellows, browns, and blacks.

Roar blocked her view again, settling in on that side.

She toggled through a plethora of responses, none of them helpful. Whatever this was, her exhaustion was a symptom. She decided to go with, "I don't know? I slept and woke like this."

"Slept for about twenty minutes."

Phe didn't realized how much effort it took to crinkle one's forehead until she attempted it. She settled for blinking instead, which helped her insanely dry eyes too.

"Did you dream?" Areya asked, her hair popping into Phe's line of sight.

"I did."

"Did your dream have someone in it?" Areya persisted. "Possibly your friend, Miss Theanora?"

Begrudgingly, Phe nodded.

She hadn't planned on sharing her liaison with Kyra. Somewhere between being held captive and the trials, she decided these people did not have the same mission that she did. As such, she would not be forthcoming with information. Not that she had much, but still.

Phe caught Areya's bobbing head in her periphery.

"She's m-de," Areya said to Roar. Turning to Phe, she said, "Think of magic as a well within you. Every time you use your magic, you are using a bucket of water from the well. Does that make sense?"

Phe grunted, flipping her head to gaze at Areya.

"Magic wells are finite. When we use too much of our magic at once, or are continuously using our magic over a span of time, we deplete the well. When the reservoir is empty, magic will turn to the body to fuel itself." Areya paused and seemed to search Phe's face for understanding.

Phe wasn't sure what Areya saw, because it took too much effort to create any kind of expression, yet Areya continued on as if she'd found confirmation Phe understood.

"New magic users don't know the limits of their power or the signs they're close to overextending themselves. For Phoenixes and Wovens, this is a very important lesson to learn immediately, because many are born to live a normal human life cycle, and if they don't stop, rest, and replenish, they could die. It has a slightly different effect on Crystals, as we are close to immortal. We will be depleted, but none have died of magic depletion."

Of course, no one mentioned this.

Phe sighed disdainfully. "Empty?"

"Stands for magically-depleted. M. Dash, D. E."

Phe tasted the abbreviation. *M-de, Mt-e, m-ty. Empty. Why don't they just call it empty?*

"I'll share some of my reserves with you. It will increase your recovery time, and when the general arrives, I shall remind him of the urgency needed to begin your education immediately and start monitoring your magical output."

"Bastion's coming?" Conflicting emotions warred within her. If she could avoid him forever, it would not be enough time apart.

Yet she was furious with him for this entire charade. Inclusive of all the years of pointless training because it was obvious any magic-born would crush a Still in a fight. Not to mention this hostage-holding business. Mostly, though, she was furious with him for deciding Kyra was someone he could strategically sacrifice. That trumped everything. Therefore, Phe was relishing seeing him.

Only, she didn't want to be *empty* when she saw him. She wanted to be at one hundred percent so she could challenge him to a no-magic hand-to-hand fight and annihilate him.

Bullspit stars.

"You're on very familiar terms with him." Areya's pitch lilted upwards into an unasked question.

Roar and Phe spoke at the same time.

"Seas, no." Phe shot Areya an insulted glance.

"I wouldn't call it that . . ." Roar countered, his choice of words careful. "They met many years ago, when Phe was just a young girl in House Nereid."

She scowled at Roar, clarifying. "I refused to go on calling him *General*," even saying the word kneaded revulsion into her stomach, "after a mission."

"Hm . . ." Areya let the sound hover thoughtfully, her gaze scanning Phe.

Phe got the impression Areya was giving the situation more meaning than it had.

Before Phe could muster the energy to contradict Areya's interpretation, Areya said, "For me to share my energy, we must touch skin to skin. I'm aware touch is an issue for you."

Why does it feel like the whole world knows my issues?

"Would you like me to help you?"

Phe glanced at Roar, surveying his quieted expression for a cue. He didn't seem at ease, per se, but his tension had dissipated and the line of his mouth wasn't so severe. His silence spoke for him. He trusted Areya.

"When is Bastion coming?"

"He's walking toward us now." Areya glanced at the path through her window. "He'll arrive in minutes."

Phe wanted to curl her upper lip and grumble, not wanting to be touched at all. Instead, she took one of her steadying breaths and sealed her fate. "Yes." She paused. "Please." She needed energy to deal with Bastion.

Areya carefully splayed her hand across Phe's, fingertips soft.

Phe closed her eyes, wondering why Areya's light touch felt reassuring, then disregarded the thought immediately as energy flushed her system, rushing to all the empty places within her.

"What you did is called *dream-manipulation*, and to get even more specific, *dreamscaping*." Areya slowed her speech. "It's a capability from your mental magic branch. With all magic, there are levels and strengths to each capability, and as we understand yours better, Lear will tailor your training to it. The basics, though, remain the same across all magic-borns. In dream-manipulation, your magic enters others' dreams, where you can communicate and interact with them."

"It was real, then?" Phe hadn't had the energy to consider if it had been real or not. It had felt real. Yet the doubting part of her, the one that still held strongly to the belief magic was a story told to children, even though there'd been plenty of evidence to the contrary, was telling her she'd finally lost her mind.

"Oh, yes, dear. Very much so."

Phe's heart fluttered with hope, and relief surged through her. *Finally, some good news.* She'd confirmed Kyra was alive and had a way of talking to her.

"What you did in the arena to Rosea is completely different. It is part of the mental branch but along a different offshoot called *mental-manipulation*. This stem allows for mental attacks, which is what you did, by mind invasion."

Phe deflated. What she'd done in the arena was grotesque. *I'm an abomination.*

Bastion appeared around the corner of the path, sliding her farther down the disparaging ladder. It was as if he timed his appearance right as she plummeted into self-derision.

How does he do it?

"Who's Lear?" Phe wasn't going to allow herself to wallow. Not now. She needed to learn as much as possible about magic—about her magic—so she could rescue and protect Kyra.

"Lear is my son." A loving warmth infused Areya's voice. "And he has been appointed to teach you about mental capabilities."

Phe relaxed a smidgeon. Areya so far had been nothing but kind and hospitable. Her son would be the same, right?

"You know Lear as Ambassador Genor," Roar said

neutrally as he got up to greet the bastard, crushing Phe's momentary relief.

She mentally shook her fist at the stars, watching Bastion and Roar confer quietly at the door.

"The general is going to question you about your dream," Areya warned.

Phe flicked her gaze to Areya, finding her observing Roar and Bastion too.

Areya refocused on Phe, imploring. "Please don't judge Lear by your first impression. He's an excellent teacher, and I'd hate for you to prolong mastering your capabilities because of how you met."

Phe straightened. Areya's shared energy took the edge off her bone-weary exhaustion. "You know he attacked me, right?" How does one go about forgetting that? Phe most certainly wouldn't.

Areya had the decency to scrunch her mouth and nose distastefully. "I do. You, I imagine, know better than most that orders are orders."

Phe grunted and regarded the now approaching men. She understood orders. She'd killed a lot of people obeying orders.

"Does Ambassador Genor work for Bastion?"

Everything boiled down to this binding agent, trust.

She'd trusted Bastion with her training, surviving one brutality after another, because he always had Kyra's protection as the priority. He broke that trust the moment he didn't go after Kyra's kidnappers himself.

"Lear has many roles, dear. You would have to ask him if General Bastion is overseeing his teaching of you."

Phe huffed. If he was working for Bastion, she wondered how that would affect her training. Could she trust him?

Who can *I trust?*

She wanted to trust Roar and all of Shadow Unit, but they were so closely aligned with Bastion, she wasn't sure she could. There were elements she did trust—Roar's assurance of her safety with Areya, for example. Then suspicion crept in, like an insidious vine inching its way to her neck.

Roar lied to you for years. She couldn't help the thought from surfacing, poking the open wound of his betrayal. *Would Roar lie again if Bastion decreed it?*

"Areya," Bastion acknowledged as he pulled a matching cream-colored seat to the other side of the tea table. His piercing brown gaze locked onto Phe as a predator would its prey.

Roar mimicked Bastion, sitting in a seat diagonal to Phe, which raised her hackles.

"I've seen Djall's possessed look better than you."

Phe gave him her *say-whatever-you-want-you-are-dead-to-me* stare.

"General," Areya chided. Her fingers tightened on Phe's hands, possibly to show support.

Instead, it made Phe want to rip her hands free, energy sharing or not. Phe didn't, though, because Bastion would interpret her movement as a reaction to him.

"That's harsh, don't you think? Especially when it's not Phe's fault she overextended."

"Areya," Bastion placated, breaking their stare-off to glance at the older woman, "Phe can handle it."

Areya puffed up, her voice the essence of a mama bear huffing a stern warning. "Just because someone can *handle it* doesn't mean you treat people this way. Remember, General, you are in my house, with my rules."

They stared at each other for a moment, tension filling the air, until Bastion broke it. "I concede to your house rules." His gaze targeted Phe again, and a muscle twitched in his jaw. "Phe, I apologize. Tell me about your dream."

"No."

Uncharacteristically, Bastion's face wrinkled like a rolled-up piece of paper. "No?"

"You look so shocked." There was only a hint of glee and bitterness in her tone. "What does it feel like when someone has information you want but doesn't share?" Phe knew she was playing with fire, especially because this time Areya rapidly squeezed her palm.

Phe didn't care, though. What was he going to do? Hurt her? Did that this morning. The man needed a taste of his own medicine, and she was angry. Her chest burned with it. Phe would eventually tell him, because there was no doubt he was the wielder of information for Kyra's rescue, but she needed this moment.

"Phe . . ." Roar dragged her name out.

She arched a brow, pressing her lips together into a hard line.

Bastion nodded, reclining in his chair. "So, this is how it's going to be?"

"I think that depends on you. You've withheld a lot of information and outright lied, refused, or ignored me when I've asked before." Phe leaned forward, unable to stop the vehemence in her tone. "Kyra has been missing for two and a half days." Anger smoldered in the back of her throat, and if she could shear Bastion with her eyes, she'd skin him alive.

"Two and a half days," she repeated for good measure. "You've impeded my attempts to rescue her by taking me prisoner. Only for me to find out Kyra was abandoned by her family and had the existence of magic—alongside with proper training—withheld. And the only person I can think of who would be able to do that is you. You used her as bait. And how did that go?"

She answered her own question, not giving him the chance. "Horribly. She's gone. Are you even searching?"

His face had smoothed into his diplomatic expression. The one that told Phe he was listening, but he had no intention of answering her. She clenched her fists, wanting to punch something. Preferably him.

It was Areya who spoke. "Dear, something I learned ages ago is General Bastion makes plans decades in advance and builds toward them progressively with single-minded determination. If we are appraised of his plans, it's because our assistance is required." She patted Phe's hand, half a warning, half endearing touch. "I believe you are feeling more energized. I'm going to withdraw."

With massive effort, Phe reined her tone to sincere. "Areya, thank you."

"Of course, dear."

Phe wouldn't give up or back down. She wanted to know about the charade of her training. The point of the last fourteen years and all those months of separation from Kyra. Nothing made sense anymore, and he was the only one who could provide any sort of clarity.

She held the silence.

Time stretched.

Areya got up and bustled out of sight.

Roar stared blankly at the potted green plant on the table.

The sunlight shifted in the window.

Bastion leaned forward, elbows on thighs, and clasped his hands in front of him. Calculation shone from his brown eyes, their edges wrinkled with intensity. "I see we're at a standstill, and I can't have that. You need to be operational. I also sense," he steepled his fingers, bringing them to his mouth, "you see me as an enemy."

Aren't you?

His eyes narrowed, and he pursed his lips, his scar pulling tight. "Phe, I am not your enemy."

Feels like you are.

"So I will humor your request. To your first question, yes, Kyra was strategically placed, and for many reasons and with years of deliberation. My seers foresaw Kyra would have an important role in the downfall of Djall, but only under certain circumstances. Thus, we created them."

Phe's throat closed. It was true. Her heart beat frantically in her chest, not sure what to do. *How could a society do this to a child? How could Kyra's family do that to her?*

"We've been searching for Djall for fifty-six years and will not stop until we apprehend him. As for the matter of holding you prisoner..." He considered his word choice. "You are a new resident of Arias, and I understand, to you, it would feel like a prison. There is nothing I can do to alleviate this.

"You are an extremely powerful magic-born who doesn't know the first thing about magic. You are not only dangerous to yourself and others until you learn how to control your abilities, but Djall had you in his crosshairs before your rebound. There is no doubt you're a priority target. We know Djall is aware you have combat training now, and when he senses your immense power, he'll be even more enthralled. To save Kyra," Bastion paused for effect, "you need to master your magic. Any type of resistance will only delay Kyra's rescue."

Phe broke through the vise in her throat, forcing words past numb lips. "Why the charade with me?"

"I've considered you a wildcard from the beginning." A

bona fide smile curved the edges of Bastion's mouth. "And you were a wild child."

Phe almost lost control of her jaw, and hoped no one noticed the slight slip. *Bastion smiled at me.* Her stomach punctuated the thought with a repulsive roll.

"When I couldn't get rid of you, I sought guidance from our seers. All of them, combined, could not penetrate the darkness of your future possibilities. Yet they all sensed you would be pivotal in what is coming. From that point onward, they directed your training."

Phe's mouth twisted in disdain, and disgust tinted her tone as she said, "By poisoning a ten-year-old?" *What was wrong with these people?* She didn't bother to mention all the other "training moments." He knew them.

"Their methods can be extreme. The more," he paused, "questionable suggestions, I vetoed."

"They wanted you to do *worse* things to me?"

"They wanted to ensure your survivability, skill, and resiliency."

Phe grunted, at a loss for words.

"Now, tell me about your dreamscape."

Phe chewed her bottom lip for a moment. "Will you give me access to all the information you have on Djall?"

"You will be permitted access, but not right now. Mastering your magic takes precedent."

"That's not good enough." Knowing the bastard, mastering magic would take decades. "You need to give me information daily."

Bastion narrowed his gaze. "You've always needed incentive." He let those words cling to the air.

Phe didn't bother to respond. It was true. Her incentive had always been to be the best fighter she could be to protect Kyra.

"I will concede to disseminating information, but not daily. Now, I will not ask again." Bastion's tone sharpened to its normal edge, and there was no longer any trace his lips had curled.

Was it weird she felt more at ease with his bastard-ness?

Areya returned, carrying a plate with two pieces of toast, the Aswa spread, and a glass of water. "Eat, dear."

Phe took the offering, balancing the plate on her legs, and recounted her dream. When she came to the part about erecting mental shields for Kyra, she stopped. No one knew about Elzac, and since she mimicked what he'd done, she wouldn't risk talking about it.

When she finished, she took her first bite, not minding at all how the spread tasted like earth or stuck to her mouth, and watched Bastion.

Bastion appeared thoughtful.

"Is this the first time anyone's been able to dreamscape with someone Djall took?" Areya asked, holding herself stiffly.

Phe swallowed the first lump of paste with the help of water.

"It is," Bastion answered, and Phe could see his mind churning. "I think the girls bonded."

"How is that possible?" Roar leaned forward, curiosity reshaping the planes of his face.

"It seems with Phe, many things I thought were impossible are possible." Did Phe catch a bit of some sort of pride in Bastion's voice?

No. That was ludicrous.

"Phe's description of the tether. Her ability to dreamscape with Kyra. My inability to separate them. Their ability to sense each others' emotions and life essence." Bastion seemed to check off boxes in his head.

"Fascinating." Areya declared, turning to Phe. "Magical bonding is extremely rare."

"Why is it rare?"

Roar's blue gaze leveled at Phe. "The most prevalent theory is that magic-borns' capabilities resonate with each other in a way that magically connects them to each other. Each union is different, as it depends on their magics, but it typically creates a deep connection between the two where they are capable of sensing each other's emotions, they have an aversion to being separated, and can somehow share their skills in more advanced pairings. What makes this even more intriguing is that your magic shouldn't have been accessible to bond, per say, until after your rebound."

Yes, yes, I'm the unicorn in the room. Phe had the urge to roll her eyes. Briefly she wondered if there *were* unicorns, then shoved the thought aside. "To ensure I understand, because I have this special bond with Kyra, I can communicate with her and gather intel when no one has been able to before?"

"Yes." It always amazed Phe how Bastion could utter a single word, yet laden it with implication.

They need *me.*

"Great job questioning Kyra." Roar smoothed his face to neutral. "My only suggestion would be to ask about her handlers."

All the blood drained from Phe's face.

She wanted to smack herself. *How could I have missed that?* Out of all the things to miss! She knew better than most how important knowledge of the guards and how they behaved was to a mission. Her shoulders slumped.

"It's okay," Roar consoled, tucking his chin a little. "It sounds as though Lady Theanora was tiring with your questioning, and she may not have been able to provide clear details. Next time, you can ask. It is crucial to know if Djall has Stills working for him or magic-borns not under his possession. It may help us narrow our search."

Phe nodded, dredging up two words. "Of course."

What if there were ways she could help Kyra from here? What if erecting the protective shield around Kyra was only the beginning of what she could do?

"Why is Djall taking Kyra's blood?"

"Bloodletting is a forbidden archaic practice. The practice weakens the magic user physically and magically," Roar answered. "Blood carries our power and capabilities in it. When someone drinks a magic user's blood, they gain access to the person's powers."

Djall drinks blood. Phe's stomach rolled.

"Enough." Bastion stood. Impatience thrummed through his movements. "Phe, we need to begin our investigation into your childhood. Come."

"Sir." Roar stood too. "Approval to accompany her?"

Bastion's jaw tightened, scar stretching, as if he didn't want to humor the request. It surprised Phe when he snapped, "Approved."

26

The room was all white, with no windows, a single door, and an ancient wooden chair in the middle of the room. They'd bolted the chair to the floor.

Nothing good ever came from an empty room with a chair anchored in it.

What is it with these people and chairs?

Phe's chest constricted as she eyed it, her jaw hard. "I'm not sitting in that," she announced, crossing her arms defiantly.

"You don't have a choice." Bastion's frosty gaze told her he'd have no problem muscling her into it.

Phe didn't need to do a quick energy check to know she was underpowered. Areya's energy share had taken her from a glass completely empty to a fourth full. The few bites of toast she'd eaten churned in her stomach, its rejuvenating powers all used up. The bastard probably wouldn't even break a sweat with her in this condition.

She nibbled her lower lip, staring at the basic wooden structure.

Roar sighed out of the side of his mouth loudly, drawing

Phe's glance. "This is Tzermel's chair. It's known for its ability to excise the truth from people, which is its primary function, but it also extracts memories."

Phe's hackles rose, and an acidically sick sensation glided over her skin. She fought to control her involuntary shudder. "What do you mean by that?"

Roar's chin jutted out uncomfortably. "Tzermel's magical sentience solely focuses on truth within memories. It has the ability to burrow past barriers and identify any relevant or closely significant memories, and project them for us to see."

"Project?" Her voice came out small and squeaky.

"Did anyone describe to you how a memo-pro works?" Patience oozed from each of Roar's words.

Phe nodded slowly, trying to reel in her reaction. Zea had.

"Similar concept, except Tzermel will put your memories on the wall. We'll see your memories as if they were happening in front of us."

"So . . ." Phe's heart went from zero to Edva's top speed, all effort to control herself lost as it galloped away. She glanced between the two men cautiously. "This is about my childhood, pre—" she licked her bottom lip nervously, "—Grum?"

"I don't know." Bastion's flinty tone skittered along Phe's spine. "Did he help hide your magic?"

Phe harshly chuckled. "I wouldn't give him that much credit." She scrubbed her face. *This is retribution for Rosea.*

Her breath came in small, quick bursts; her back hit the wall. She needed to escape.

Roar strode forward to stand toe-to-toe with her. "Look at me."

Seas, she didn't want to. She closed her eyes, sucking in a

breath, then pried them open to connect with his blues. They were the same color as a never-ending sky, and they held strength.

"We are not going to go through all your memories. It's very specific."

She gulped, admitting to them, "I don't remember anything before Grum." She had come to terms with her past with Grum, though she didn't want to relive it, nor did she want anyone else to see them.

But what came before . . . she had no idea, and she certainly didn't want those memories forced to the surface with witnesses—with Bastion. He'd probably find a way to torture her with them. "Tzermel is known for removing blocks. He'll be able to tell if the blocks were created instinctively, as a protection mechanism, or by someone else." Roar's calmness roped in her anxiety and soothed it. "Aren't you curious?"

She *had* always wanted to know where she came from. If her memories had been blocked by someone else, what did that mean? Would her memories finally give her answers to her past or more questions?

"Time is ticking," Bastion coldly called from his side of the room. Phe wouldn't be surprised if he declared a countdown, condescendingly calling out numbers, extending the tension.

A flash of annoyance tightened the edges of Roar's eyes and, like a quick wind, rippled through his expression, gone before it could take form.

The nano-second of irritation allied Phe to him. Roar wasn't immune to Bastion's treatment of her. She didn't miss how he was walking the line between supporting her and being Bastion's minion.

Phe's breathing steadied with effort, quieting her instinctive response. She ignored Bastion. "I've always been curious."

Roar's lips flattened, yet the corners lifted into rigid angles. Not quite a smile. "Well, then, this is your chance." His eyes shuttered, and he stepped away, wordlessly signaling for her to sit.

There was something he wasn't telling her, but her decision to not be hauled into anything was made.

Phe strode to the chair, heart thumping painfully against her ribs. What if Bastion looked into her other memories? What if the reason she couldn't remember was because these memories were worse than those of Grum?

Gads, I hope that's not true.

She sat on the hard planes of the wood chair, and another set of invisible straps cinched onto her limbs. She tapped into her breath to remind herself of her strength. To quell the new rush of fear.

Breathe in. *They're just memories.*

Breathe out. *I've survived them.*

Breathe in. *They don't define me.*

Breathe out. *I define myself.*

Her body strongly resisted calming.

Breathe in. *I'm safe.*

Breathe out. *Emotions are just energy-in-motion.*

Breathe in. *Emotions only hurt if I hold on.*

Breathe out. *I—*

"Tzermel uses certain measures," Roar interrupted Phe's inner coaching session, "to obtain those memories." Everything, from his posture to his voice, had hardened. He was staring at Bastion, then turned a blank gaze to her.

Pain. He meant lots of pain.

Why hadn't I considered this? Because panic had demolished all thoughts other than sit or be dragged.

He convinced me to sit in a chair that will hurt me. The realization stabbed her, causing an altogether different ache to fester. Roar'd just manipulated her.

The rational part of Phe clashed with these thoughts. His choices had been to enlist her cooperation and have her sit on her own, or help Bastion overpower her, manhandling her into the chair, and destroying any trust she had in him.

At least I'm not the only rock being squeezed by life's roots.

"It's actually for the best you're depleted. Should make this faster," Bastion said. "Tzermel." Magic stirred under her, oozing around her. "Show us any memory she has of who tampered with or bound her magic."

Magic lapped at Phe's skin, encasing her as though she were stepping slowly into a cool pool of water. Once it had fully engulfed her, the magic thrummed as if it were fingers tapping her all over.

The sensation became more intense, the tapping more insistent. In some places, it jabbed her with a blanket of needles. Other places, it was as if large palms painfully kneaded her. Her barrier fractured.

Magic funneled invasively under Phe's skin, widening the hole and filling her.

She shuddered, the feeling worse than insects crawling all over her, because it was *within* her. Teeth gritted, she felt her fingertips grip the armrest so tightly the edges cut into her.

The magic settled.

Her stomach rolled hard. She gagged.

Twinges of pain shot through her, scraping her insides.

Bursts of memories slid past her mind's eye. So quickly,

Phe only caught glimpses of colors and blurry images until it stopped at her first memory.

Grum was perched on his horse, a tyrannical king surveying a beggar who'd disastrously captured his attention. Cunning light brown eyes, olive complexion, and a mob of sandy blond hair scrutinized her. In a single glance, he decided her fate and worth.

Thank the stars the memory isn't projecting.

A sharp pang followed, and the magic burrowed further into her.

Blackness crept around the edges of the memory, and her fear clawed at her throat. Through clenched teeth, Phe said, "Please don't shred my memories."

"Tzermel will leave your memories intact," Bastion said from her side. "What are you seeing?"

"Fir-st," she stuttered past an onslaught of sensation. "Me-mor-yyy. Blac-kn-esss."

"It appears someone interfered with your memories." A solemness laced Bastion's words. "Try to relax into the magic. It'll be less painful."

Try relaxing? Is he insane? Phe glowered. *You try relaxing with a swarm of electric eels wrestling under your skin.*

More of Grum disintegrated.

A pinpoint of light broke the darkness.

A shot of electric energy surged, and her whole body arched away from the chair, the straps digging into her painfully.

Dim light flooded the corner of the darkness. Tall pine trees shimmered into existence on one side of her memory, only to have a swath of darkness and half of Grum's face unveil at the other edge.

It was this half image the chair projected onto the white wall in front of her.

"Ahh, Tzermel's breaking through." A timber of excitement threaded Bastion's pitch, and he strode closer to the wall, murmuring for Roar's benefit. "Grum."

Another surge of electricity stole Phe's breath, and she bowed off the chair. Grum's face melted into blackness.

Wisps of shadows gathered in the corners of the room Phe could see.

The rest of the forest erupted into view, looming overhead. Sniffles and shallow breathing filled the room.

A wave of sadness hit Phe, so powerful it threatened to break her in its wake.

Tight bands of rope wrapped around her, securing her to a large tree. Its rough bark embedded into her back. Hot tears and snot dripped down her face and neck.

She drew her knees up—the movement caused her to gasp as it activated a stabbing pain in her ribs. Vibrant red and orange patterned pants contrasted with the descending dusk. She ignored the pain and tried to wiggle her legs under her to stand, but the rope was too tight. She collapsed and zeroed in on her right hand. It throbbed with pain and was wrapped in a bandage.

A rope encircled her wrists and pulled her arms around the trunk. Blood leaked from the rope burn.

With an audible deep breath, she tugged and strained to slither out of the restraint. After several minutes of this, she switched to the other wrist.

"Shhhh, child," a woman whispered.

The child version of Phe froze, holding her breath.

I take it all back. I don't want to know! Phe shut her eyes, not wanting to see. Her heart thundered. *Who would tie an injured child to a tree?*

The memory continued.

One rope along her belly jerked, followed by the sound of a knife cutting into it.

"MaJaJa?"

"Shhhh, child. Mustn't make a noise."

A sob erupted, expelling the fragments of a broken heart into the silent hum of the surrounding forest.

"Shhhh, I know, child. I know. My heart's broken too. But if you keep it up, they'll come, and there's too many. Shhh."

Younger Phe rubbed her chin on her shoulder, trying to wipe away the tears. She bit her lip until she tasted blood. Her body shook.

One rope fell limp. Another one jiggled, gyrating under the knife's edge.

"You have always been darkness; it is why I call you Orphne. Once you accept your darkness and are remade *from* your shadows, your fire will ignite, and you will shine bright. It is your destiny, written not only in your names, but in the stars."

Orphne only shook harder, gasping for breath.

Another rope dropped, and the woman repeated the motion.

"She didn't bind you for you to die in my care." Grimness radiated from the woman in waves. The rope sagged into Orphne's lap, and the one attached to her wrists moved, wrenching a cry from her. The movement halted, and the woman scuttled to Phe's left hand.

"Oh, child." Sadness gushed from her tone as callused fingers encircled Orphne's arm. With more care, she sawed at the knot, trying to reduce the rope's movement.

"I'd hoped she'd been wrong when she'd set up—" The woman cut herself off.

Orphne's arms collapsed painfully, freed. The woman's

gnarled fingers carefully cradled her left hand, while her other fumbled with unraveling the remaining rope.

Orphne hauled her right hand to her chest, curling into herself.

Gingerly, the woman moved her left arm to rest at her side and squatted in front of her to work the knot on her other wrist. The light had faded into darkness, casting shadows over her features. The memory stilled.

A sizzling bolt of pain paralyzed Phe's lungs as Tzermel's magic gnashed its teeth further into her. Sweat coated her face.

The shadows in the corners grew. Phe glimpsed them agitatedly wiggling up the wall until her memory unfroze.

Weathered eyes bore into Orphne's, and those knobby hands cradled her face, thumbs wiping away tears. "You won't remember this, me, or any other childhood memory, and I'm so sorry it's come to this. I thought I could protect you."

Orphne nestled her clenched fist under her chin, curling her shoulders.

The woman's left hand strayed into Orphne's hair and played with a strand. It was too dark to see the exact coloring but, even with the lighting, the strand gleamed lighter than the rest of her dark hair.

"She said you'd be reborn many times. I didn't know what that meant, but now I have an understanding." The woman paused, rubbing the lighter strip of hair between her fingers. "Everything that came before will be gone, and with it, any identifiable features. For you, it is a new life. A new beginning."

Orphne snaked her hands around her knees, tucking further into herself.

"I love you, Orphne." The woman's eyes filled with unshed tears. "The family loves you, too."

She let those words hang and returned both palms to Orphne's face and squeezed her cheeks. The places her hands touched tingled. A light flashed in her eyes. "Orphne, close your eyes."

Orphne squeezed her swollen eyes shut.

The woman muttered incomprehensibly. From her scalp to her toes, Orphne's skin itched uncomfortably, then burned.

Orphne whimpered.

A tsunami of darkness descended from the edges of Phe's mind. It enclosed around her, creating an immense, impenetrable wall.

The woman stepped back, appraising Orphne. "It is done."

A twig snapped in the distance.

The woman's head swung in that direction, her body stiffening.

"You must learn your darkness. Master it. That is the key," the woman whispered as she hauled Orphne up. A tense urgency suffused the air. "Run, Orphne, run far. I will distract them." The woman pushed her and Orphne ran-stumbled blindly into the forest.

The memory halted, and another bolt of pure sizzling pain blasted through Phe. Then another and another. The projection didn't change.

Consciousness faded in and out, and Phe heard snippets.

"Sir?" Warning laced Roar's question.

"Give Tze . . ." Bastion said. "Break through . . ."

". . . Could kill. . . stop."

Bastion's response was lost in a volley of pain.

The chair's magic suddenly stopped, and its teeth rapidly withdrew.

The bands holding her vanished.

Phe slumped toward the floor. Large hands caught her shoulders.

Why do the stars hate me so much?

"You worry unnecessarily," Bastion's uncaring voice said. "Stop fussing. She'll be fine."

"Sir, with all due respect, she's barely conscious." Roar's carefully neutral voice sounded from Phe's side. Warmth from his touch seeped into her shoulders, thawing the deep chill that had infused into her bones at Tzermel's withdrawal.

Bastion ignored Roar's concern. *Typical.* "What are your thoughts on these shadows?"

"I have some speculations," Roar replied. His answer hovered in the silence that followed. Bastion must have made a gesture giving Roar permission to conjecture. "They've appeared every time Phe's life has been in danger. Her rebound. Her escape attempt in Arias. The trails. Now." He said with more of an edge than the other times. "They've so far only coalesced, appearing agitated. I think they're part of her passive powers, reacting when she is under extreme stress."

"I agree with your assessment. However, they were also present with Linaria Coronaira—which could indicate they react when she encounters magic." Bastion paused, most likely analyzing every time he'd witnessed shadows interact with her. "At the ball, when her magic exploded, it gave me the sense she was being reborn from them." Bastion's tone had lifted, as if even he found the idea incredulous. "It'll be interesting to discover what she can do with those shadows once she taps into her capabilities. What did you see in her memory?"

"Sir, the clothing she was wearing and the reference to *the family* suggests she was part of a gypsy caravan." Roar's hands slid under Phe's arms and gently heaved her upright in the chair. "It's hard to tell their origin. They could be from anywhere."

Phe blinked slowly to bring the room into view and tried to get her body to respond to her.

"It doesn't fit. Gypsies are extremely protective of the family, especially children," Bastion said. "Then there's the matter of that woman having access to magic."

Phe kept trying to get the room into focus and get her muscles to work.

"Maybe it's not the case of having magic, as her eyes didn't glow, but more the case that whoever did this had linked her into the casters' magic. It makes more sense they enabled her to seal the memory trap they'd set. Could the woman be a key?"

Bastion took a moment to respond, as if he was tasting the theory. "Possibly, but they most likely set her role as a one-time lock, and not as a key. Though, if we were to get our hands on her, she'd be a key for us to track Phe's heritage."

The room fuzzily took form. Bastion's bleary silhouette was near the door.

"Tracking her down will be nearly impossible."

Bastion grunted his agreement. "My gut tells me discovering Phe's lineage and why she was bound is pivotal to everything, but I can't fathom how."

Gads, I hate being talked about when I'm right here.

"I suspect Phe's a Crystal," Roar said, his grip on her

loosening. "Her aura may have been affected by being bound at an early age."

"Agreed. She had to have been bound at birth; otherwise, we'd have a record of her." Bastion sounded aggrieved. "What I don't understand is why people hid a magic-born. Especially of her power caliber."

They lapsed into silence. The muscles in Phe's hands began functioning, and she clutched the armrests.

"Sir, have the Elders made any announcements regarding her induction?"

"Not yet, but they will concede. They have no choice." The arrogance in Bastion's voice grated on Phe, and she wished she had the energy to punch him. "She's too powerful to leave without oversight. They know this."

"I heard Katoa requested she be sequestered for research."

"He has, and others have applied to be her keeper." Disgust mingled with Bastion's disdain. "She's been my charge for years. I will not allow her to be left to the whims of the likes of Katoa, uselessly dissected or broken."

Dissected or broken? The words reverberated in her mind.

"Who else applied?"

"It doesn't matter. Other than the Phoenix Council— because the elders imprudently classified her as a Phoenix —none have a valid claim. I've made it clear she's mine, and I will not be refused." Humor lightened Bastion's tone. "They believe we have her welfare in mind."

"For Shadow Unit, sir, that is true."

Phe's hatred for Bastion came back anew. *I am not a possession.*

"Your loyalty is admirable and adds fodder to my plans for her."

"Gads, I despise you." Her thought catapulted the chasm of her mind, bursting into muttered words.

"Hate me all you want. Fight me all you want." Bastion stalked to her and gripped her chin. His fingers dug into the flesh of her jaw and yanked her neck up, their contact sending a wave of discomfort through her. He pierced her with his imperious gaze. "From the moment we met, you've been under my care. Magicless, I've sharpened you to a fine needlepoint. With magic? You'll become *my* indestructible sword."

If Phe could get her limbs to work, she'd kill him. Slowly. She'd rend him limb from limb, all the while watching the pulse of life drain from his cruel eyes.

27

Phe sat alone on the balcony of her treehouse and stared unseeingly into the sacredwoods' mystical depths, contemplating.

One hand loosely gripped a mug of Aswagandhia tea. She sipped it, the lukewarm, earthy tea sending mini-bursts of energy zinging through her.

As much as she wanted to deny it, magic seemed to be an irrefutable fact.

After the trials earlier, it was painfully obvious she couldn't beat them. The logical, tactical decision was to cooperate with training and whatever else they had in store —unless it included chairs. All magical chairs were a nonnegotiable no. If Bastion ever brought her back to Tzermel's, she'd find a way to burn it.

Phe's stomach twisted in agreement, acid erupting to scald her.

She'd throw herself into mastering her capabilities. Lull them into a place of compliance while she studied this unfamiliar terrain and created a new plan. One that ended with Kyra and her back in Oceanid.

Yes, the discovery of magic was a shock. Yet there were plenty of silver linings. Phe was an extremely fast learner, especially in combat training. Hadn't Roar said she may have been drawing from her passive magical ability for this?

Phe tapped the mug with her pointer finger. He had.

Grasping how to engage her magic was the first step, one she needed to ascertain immediately. Not just for Kyra's sake, but for her own as well. Who knew what else the stars had conjured up for her?

Plus, having the ability to dreamscape on command meant she could talk to Kyra. Yet dreamscaping, by its name alone, implied they'd both have to be asleep for them to connect. What if there were other ways she could communicate with Kyra? Or track her?

Instinctively, Phe's hand wrapped around her naked wrist. The smooth skin barely held the indentation of the amulet. The crater of loss in her chest flared, its pain weighing her heart, thinning her lips, and filling her eyes with tears.

She rode the emotion like a boat does a wave, tears cresting with the swell.

Suddenly, learning about the mental branch of magic didn't seem so tedious. Even having Ambassador Genor as her teacher was a bonus. She'd use her dislike of him as a sharpening tool for her focus, honing her blade.

If only I'd made it to Drykz Forest.

It felt like eons ago she'd been riding Edva, hard, toward the forest.

Edva.

Another wave swelled.

She hadn't thought about her wayward horse since she'd been told they had stabled Edva with Shadow Unit's steeds. A bolt of guilt shot through her. She hadn't even considered

Edva when she'd attempted her escape, leaving her here unprotected and in Bastion's cruel domain.

Taking another sip of the chilled tea, Phe swallowed the rising emotion as it broke into a memory.

They'd been riding hard, closing in on Drykz Forest. Balls of magic exploded the earth around them. And scales.

She hadn't had time to do anything other than acknowledge the scales that had replaced Edva's coat before Bastion had appeared on the road and things got crazier. Much crazier.

What did it mean? When she'd rescued Edva years ago, during operation sunrise, from a sinister man who dubbed himself The General, he'd called Edva a monster.

Phe rubbed her callused fingertip along the ridges of the glazed mug. *Who can I ask?*

Shadow Unit.

This time the surge was anger. Three days ago, she would have asked them. If it was related to her magic, she'd ask. Scales on Edva? It was too risky. They might mention it to Bastion. Bastion and Edva saw eye to eye on only one thing: their mutual detestation of each other. There was no way Phe would endanger her by asking them.

Areya was also out of the question.

Areya had done nothing to raise Phe's hackles. In fact, Areya had been nothing but kind the three times Phe had interacted with her. Unfortunately, even the sweetest appearing people had the same capacity for evil as everyone else. Only, their betrayal gouged deeper because they'd lured you into a false sense of safety. At least, that's how it felt for Phe.

Phe needed to get to know Areya better. Trust was earned, and a few hours together was not long enough for that.

If only Jallia were here.

Sadness burned the back of her eyes.

Gads, how many emotions are there, and do I have to feel them all at once? Phe grumbled, blinking to keep her eyes dry.

It had been Jallia who'd cocooned Phe in blankets, cradling her and consoling from her unspeakable nightmares or the aftermath of one of Bastion's trainings. Jallia had been the first adult to nurture her and touch her with kindness.

If she continued listing everything Jallia had done for her over the past fourteen years, it would crack her. Especially since Phe had left Jallia alone, unprotected, in a cell in House Nereid's dungeons so she could escape.

I'm a selfish monster.

The tea in Phe's stomach swished violently.

Gads, is Jallia alive?

When she'd been with Grum in Shalexum, he'd bring her to public punishments for those who'd tried to free slaves or escape slavery. It'd been brutal. This society seemed to share the same aggressive tendencies, from what she'd seen so far.

Would they do that here?

Ignoring her tumultuous stomach, Phe drank the dredges of her tea. It had barely taken the edge off her exhaustion, even though it was her second cup. She knew she shouldn't be relying on something external to refill her; Elzac would chastise her for it if he knew, suggesting she do things like rest or some other time-consuming nonsense. *Not today.*

Phe hauled herself off the seat and strolled to the kitchen to set the kettle to boil.

She'd have asked Elzac about Edva's scales if she'd made

it to Drykz Forest. Then Jallia's sacrifice wouldn't have been for nothing.

She propped a hip against the counter, crossed her arms, and decided to ask Shadow Unit about Jallia. Shadow Unit might be untrustworthy when it came to Edva's well-being because of the bastard, but she was confident they would tell her about Jallia.

The kettle screamed, steam pouring angrily from its spout.

She left it there, because its angry screaming reflected how she felt about Arias and its people and her life, and dragged the Aswa tea canister to her. She insisted on making her own tea because she didn't want Areya to slip her another sleeping tonic. Phe pinched a bunch of ground leaves and roots and tossed them into the cup, not caring if it was unfiltered. When you'd eaten grass, bark, and insects in order to survive, unfiltered tea was a treat.

A treat she'd miss the moment she escaped this city.

Phe plucked the spitting kettle and poured the boiling water. The tea swirled in clumps, steam wafting upwards, bringing with it the scent of earth.

Phe cradled the mug and ambled onto the plush balcony.

Would Zea know?

Phe leaned on the wood banister and brought the steaming cup to her chin, inhaling deeply. Three yellow birds zipped by on the wings of their birdsong and disappeared around the curve of a massive tree.

What Zea had done for her today, standing up to the Elders, had softened Phe's stance toward her. The girl had a set of colossal balls.

Phe felt the corners of her mouth lift in a brittle smile.

Asking Zea about Edva's scales fell to the end of the long list of questions she had. Since Zea had been the only person to give her any information, and Edva was safe, other questions needed to come first.

The conundrum switched to how to get a hold of Zea.

In Oceanid, she'd send a messenger with a note or call for a carriage. At night, she'd slip out on foot, a shadowy sentry patrolling the city. Here, she didn't know if there were carriages, where Edva was stalled, how to jump, or how to send messages. Heck, with all the talk of shields, this forest probably had an impenetrable perimeter.

Shadows in the forest flowed forward. What was mythical and wondrous a moment ago transformed to sinister and menacing.

Phe blinked and gulped her tea. The hot water scalded her mouth like the anger festering in her.

A prison was a prison, no matter its appearance.

Roar seemed to be enthralled with the sacredwoods and, for all Phe knew, was still here talking to Areya. She'd learned there was only one entry point, like a front door, into Areya's property, but one could jump or teleport from wherever they were to leave.

Handy information. Her personal bubble expanded dramatically with it.

Phe muddled through the murky, tumultuous waters of how she felt about Roar. She didn't know what to do. She viewed people as either friend or foe, neatly placing them in a black or white spectrum and never playing in the messy gray. Until this all began, Roar was one of the few people in her friend category. All of Shadow Unit had been in the friend category, only her relationship with Roar had been deeper. One he'd earned by silently supporting her through years of following her midnight nightmare runs and taking her burdens.

Burdens he then kept.

He convinced me to sit in that chair. Echoes of electric pulses ghosted through her.

No, Roar had given her a choice. Her two choices were bad and worse, but they were choices, and he'd let her decide. Plus, no one had so directly interfered with Bastion's treatment of her before, primarily because Bastion never showed the depth of his true colors around them. He'd buffer his treatment of Phe until they were alone, sinking her into his depths of brutality then.

She wanted to shove Roar, and all of Shadow Unit, into dark enemy seas. They'd betrayed her, hadn't they? Brought her here. Stopped her escape. Were blatant minions of Bastion's. Roar had lied to her for years about messengers and who knew what else.

Ugh.

He'd led the chase in Oceanid and, she was pretty sure, had stopped whoever was throwing those exploding balls of light. He'd had Shadow Unit surround her protectively during the chaos of the forest attack. He'd announced she was one of them. Hadn't he accepted a challenge from another soldier when they'd captured her in Oceanid?

She was pretty positive, when she'd regained consciousness after Ambassador Genor's attack, that he and Ihrone had been petitioning to have her inducted into Shadow Unit. And she couldn't forget he'd offered her his guest room last night, when he could have let her stay in a prison cell.

It would be so much easier if she didn't care. Even better if she understood her body's odd reactions to him and this weird draw she'd recently developed.

Phe swallowed another sip of tea, carefully tapping the tip of the iceberg in her mind. *He witnessed my memory.*

Having any of her memories forced from her was bad; a magically blocked memory? Violating.

She waffled between horror that Roar'd witnessed her memory and gotten a glimpse into how Bastion really treated her and gratitude he'd been there.

Gads, there were too many conflicting currents in gray waters. Each one latched on and tore her in a direction.

Her fingers lost feeling.

Dragging in a steadying breath, she forcibly relaxed her grip.

The memory.

Unable to dance around it any longer, she faced it head on, shuttering her emotions and approaching the memory with logic.

It hadn't escaped her she'd worn clothes from her nightmare. Nor had MaJaJa's name gone unnoticed.

This was a puzzle piece. She just didn't know how it fit.

Anala had a streak of white hair and had an adopted mother, father, and four siblings. For the past seventeen years, Phe had plucked the strings of Anala's belonging from her dream. Siblings clung to her. Parents relied on her. She was in the web of gypsy life and would stay there, encapsulated from what Phe'd learned. Families in gypsy caravans meant everything and, unless they married into another family, they stayed in their family units, no matter what.

Why would anyone tie a young child to a tree?

What happened within gypsy families was a little less clear, as they were a secretive bunch. Was it possible they punished people by doing this? Including children?

The fear Phe felt with the memory wasn't merely punishment. It was devastatingly life-threatening. Why else would the woman distract whoever was coming and tell her to run? This contradicted how families reportedly cherished their children.

How dangerous could a child be? What would warrant this extreme reaction?

Movement on the path tossed aside her ruminations. She spotted black-plaited hair with a band of bright blue fabric. Zea.

One problem semi-solved.

Phe gulped the rest of her tea and ignored the flash of heat from her mouth to her stomach. She deposited the mug on a nearby table, a zing of excitement coursing through her. *It's question-and-answer time.* With as much speed as she could muster, which wasn't a lot, she descended to the great room to discover Zea and Roar talking heatedly.

Areya strode to Phe. "How are you, dear?"

Phe barely stifled her grunted response, reminding herself she needed to wield more finesse. *I'm a polite monster guest.* "I'm better, thank you."

Roar and Zea turned to her. Roar's expression was carefully controlled except for his blue eyes; those blazed fiercely. Zea had her arms crossed, gaze narrowed, and the edges of her mouth were tight.

With the two of them standing side by side, Phe couldn't help but catalogue their differences. Zea's black hair seemed to be woven from the darkest night sky compared to Roar's, whose hair seemed to be of burnt sunsets with its deeper auburn in contrast. Zea's darker complexion was paired with a fragile feminine beauty. Her cheeks were flushed.

Roar's skin tone, in comparison, was pale, and his features portrayed strength and power—pure masculinity, which his slightly crooked nose enhanced. Even their blue eyes showcased differences. Zea's were a righteous sky blue, while Roar's were stormy at the moment.

Zea's side glare bounced off Roar, whose sole focus was Phe. "I'm here to escort you to meet with the Phoenix Council. A-lone," she emphasized.

"You don't have to go—"

"Oh my earth!" Zea exclaimed, eyes rolling to the ceiling. "She's a Phoenix." Zea flung a hand up, fingers flexed in consternation. "Which means she's ruled by the Phoenix Council. Not you. Not General Bastion." Zea twisted to face Roar, her neck flushed.

Phe darted her gaze to Roar, waiting for his response, and absently wrapping her hand around her amulet-free wrist. Roar's jaw was tight.

"Phe, it's up to you. If you don't want to go, I'll contact General Bastion."

"What would happen if I don't go?"

"Anarchy." Zea crossed her arms and turned her slitted gaze on Phe, widening her eyes as if to say, what are you doing? "Crystals do not tell the Phoenix Council what they can and can't do with us. The Phoenix Council rules us as the Elders rule them."

"The Elders don't rule over us?" Phe's brow wrinkled. Then why she had been forced into the trials? Where had the council been then?

"Not quite," Areya answered. "The Elders oversee all the magical classes broadly, governing them to ensure we are all compliant. Phoenixes and Wovens have appointed councils to regulate their respective magic classes." Areya delicately cleared her throat. "Anarchy seems an extreme choice of words; however, she's not wrong in a sense. You would set off a chain reaction of sorts."

Phe toggled her gaze between Roar and Zea. Roar was

willing to trigger a power fight between Phoenixes and Crystals, all to give her a choice. Warmth surged into the emptiness it had just vacated, roots sinking into her chest cavity.

This was the second time today Roar gave her a choice, and it felt good. Really good. She wanted to relax into the sensation, but Zea's posture had stiffened.

Bullspit cause and effect. Something bad would undoubtedly result from her refusal. *Why else would I be given a choice?*

So the stars can find another way to crush my soul.

She sighed, the fleeting image of the rock entangled in life's roots rising in her mind. Either choice she made, the root would constrict. How much compression she could endure?

Zea had said not going would cause anarchy. Phe wondered if that meant the Phoenixes would start some sort of war with the Crystals. From what she'd seen so far in this despicable place, people would die. Was saying no because she wanted to be selfish worth risking lives? No. Life was precious.

Phe's shoulders drooped. "I'll go."

A smile overturned Zea's salty expression.

"Phe is under General Bastion's protection." Roar kept his eyes on Phe. "She is not to go anywhere but the council meeting and then back again, understood?"

Zea lifted one shoulder and slyly gazed at him, her smile pulled into the slightest smirk. "Excuse us, majesty." Zea dramatically pressed a palm to her chest. "How does it feel to be overruled? And by a nix." She clucked, extending an arm to Phe. "Come, princess, your escort awaits."

"That was rude," Phe growled, seething. *Hadn't I just talked to her about this?* Phe unsheathed a thigh knife and raised it to shoulder height, aiming its gleaming tip at Zea.

Zea stilled, gaze frozen on the blade.

"You can touch this," Phe said, her voice preloaded with her nonnegotiable stance.

Zea's eyes widened, pupils constricting. Zea extended her right pointer finger and, as if moving through sludge, tapped the underside of the blade.

Immediately heat from a huge fire caressed Phe's cheeks.

Keeping her blade at her side, Phe scanned the circular room they now stood in.

The walls featured windows from hip height to ceiling and provided a panoramic view, broken only by a stone fireplace that rivaled Areya's. Orange flames licked the air and came to Phe's mid-thigh, the fire crackling. The rock chimney was almost double the size of Phe.

A single rounded door, the top portion glass, summoned her.

Zea scuttled from her instantly, her mouth puckered. "That was uncalled for."

Phe pierced Zea with her gaze, tired of power plays. "Don't be rude to Roar." She turned back to the glass window, scouring the mountainous winter landscape.

They had built the single-roomed cabin on the highest peak in this section of the Xiheria Highlands, offering a bird's-eye view of the glistening snow-packed ridges. One ridge featured a shear drop, while the peak the cabin was on had been flattened. Past the flattened portion was a ring of wind-ravaged, snow-covered pine trees. A plume of smoke from the fireplace whorled in an air current before blending into the clouds.

Zea huffed.

To Phe, it sounded halfhearted, but she was barely paying attention. Her heart clobbered her throat as she neared the door. *Could it be that easy?*

"Sorry," Zea continued. "I got carried away. It's hard for me to, um, calm down once I'm angry."

Phe tried the door handle, but it didn't budge. She sheathed her knife and gripped the knob with both hands, trying to force it to turn under her unrelenting grip.

"It's locked." Zea stated the obvious; Phe flicked Zea an unimpressed brow raise. "Not just locked, magically locked." Zea shuddered and her shoulders caved. "Geez, I forgot how scary you are."

Phe resisted punching the windows. Hope, which she hadn't realized surged, now profusely seeped from her. "Same type of windows as the tower?"

"Yes."

Phe stifled the rush of anger taking its place and catalogued the center of the room. A brown leather love seat faced six ornate matching chairs, a circular rug separating them.

With one of Phe's steadying breaths, she half-apologized. "I don't mean to scare you."

"What in the flipping crusts do you think pointing a knife at me says?" Zea crossed her arms defensively. "It certainly isn't screaming, 'hey friend!'"

Phe bit her inner lip, keeping the line of her mouth straight even though the corners wanted to go renegade and curl at that. She considered Zea's perspective, and her stomach plummeted. She'd acted like the bastard, a complete schmuck, a monster. "I'm sorry."

"Girl." Zea flung herself into the love seat. "If you hadn't been demolished at the trials, I'd make you work for it a bit. But, snap, that was bad. What happened after they cleared the stadium?"

Nothing that was any of her business. "What does 'nix' mean?"

"Ah, redirection. What a great tactic." Zea exclaimed with false enthusiasm while fiddling with her braid. "It's a term used to refer to us Phoenixes. Phoenix was shortened to 'nix.' Within our class, it's used across a wide spectrum based on context. When other classes use it, it's mainly derogatory."

Phe grunted at that. *Is it a requirement for every society to do that?* She considered the countries she'd been exposed to. Shalexum had terms that fit this description. *Or is it just the horrible ones?*

She tossed aside the forming snowball thought and studied the view. There were no other buildings or signs of civilization except a few plumes of smoke further down the mountain where there was a speckling of rooftops.

"What town is that?"

Zea squirmed on the couch, making herself more comfortable. "Yeabrus, but don't get any escape ideas into your pretty head." A sternness filtered Zea's words.

Phe ignored the warning, switching topics. "Where's the council?"

"They'll be here any moment."

"Do you know why the council wants to meet me?"

"You are the new, shiny, or," Zea paused for effect, "shadowy Phoenix. I also think since you've come to us as an adult, the normal ways they'd meet you no longer apply. It's not like they're going to send you to school with the babies, now is it?" Zea frowned. "Can't see you in a class of youngsters sitting through a Meet the Phoenix Council day."

Phe blinked, not having considered what her education would look like. *Seas, let it not be that.*

Zea continued on, unfazed. "They've petitioned the Elders, from what I heard. Many believe you shouldn't be inducted so quickly into Shadow Unit because there's only one track on that path. They—now I could be wrong—want you to have options and not be locked into something Crystals want because they want to harness your—" Zea's hands swept up and outlined Phe's body and dropped her tone, "power."

Does it have to always be about power? The telltale vibration in the air had her unsheathing her twins while she spun to the seated area.

"Wowa! Calm your horses," Zea hollered from the couch.

Six people suddenly lounged in the empty chairs, as if they'd been waiting for Zea and Phe to arrive and not the reverse. They wore clothing similar to Zea, all buckles and ties and asymmetry. The hair on Phe's nape raised. Gripping the hilts of her knives until the blood leeched from her hands, she lowered them but didn't sheath them.

Zea stood, smoothed her pants unnecessarily, and walked to the chair closest to the fire. "Let me introduce you to our Phoenix Council." Zea's voice had taken on a deeper, steadier, more reverent tone. "Council Member Misha."

Misha sat ramrod straight. Her glowing brown gaze was intense and set in a heart-shaped face. Her skin, also brown, seemed to glisten in the fire's light. There was a delicateness to her. She was thin, too thin in Phe's opinion, which seemed exaggerated because of the tight corset and fitted pants. Her brown hair was textured and wild, which Phe liked.

Misha's head bobbed. A grim smile fluttered across her lips. Phe returned the gesture.

Zea moved to the next chair. "Council Member Seff."

Seff was a tremendous specimen of a man, with broad shoulders and a barrel chest that exuded power. If he stood, he'd tower over Phe. Black dreads reached his shoulders, and he had a matching, scruffy beard with hints of white in it. Freckles scattered along his cheekbones and serious, almost black eyes tracked her. Tattoos swirled up his arms, trailing from underneath the black leather covering he wore on his wrists and disappearing under his shirt.

He inclined his head regally, as a king would to a servant.

Zea continued her shuffle to the next chair. "Council Member Treva."

Treva's bearing was solid, with thick, strong limbs and a wide ribcage. Her feet dangled from the chair, not reaching the floor. Wavy, multicolored hair hung in free wisps around her face, ranging from honey-blond to darker mahogany brown with a streak of brilliant red. It matched the red gaze Treva directed at her.

Her chin dipped, a genuine smile plumped her cheeks, and her eyes glittered.

Zea strode to the next member. "Council Member Firo."

Firo had slate-colored eyes beneath bushy black-and-gray brows. His complexion was pale underneath his olive skin tone. A musing gaze connected with Phe's, and intelligence radiated from his depths. His shoulders curved around his chest, leaving Phe with the impression the hunch came from sitting bent over a desk reading for hours.

Firo's bushy brows arched in acknowledgment.

Zea stepped to the next chair. "Council Member Adriata."

Adriata emanated youthful vitality. She had an oval-shaped face with unblemished porcelain-pale skin. A corset emphasized her curvy feminine features. A secretive smile played at the corners of her mouth as her hazel eyes scanned Phe. Her hands gripped the armrests, the color slowly draining from them, betraying her otherwise relaxed stance.

Adriata nodded, her lavender hair fluttering around her with the movement.

Zea pranced the last few steps. "Council Member Liri."

As Liri's brown gaze scanned Phe, one of her immaculately pruned brows quirked and her mouth pursed, as if in thought. She had a square jawline, which could be why there was a strong masculine sense to Liri even though she was the only one in a skirt. Mahogany curls cascaded down her back.

Keeping her arm firmly on the armrest, Liri raised her right pointer and middle fingers to acknowledge her.

"Orphne," Treva's calm voice washed over the tense silence. "We understand you've had a challenging day, so we'll overlook the insult of your weapons being drawn. Today. This will not be tolerated at any other time."

Phe's grip on her twins tightened. These people may appear harmless, but they weren't. Phe's skin prickled during the introductions, her senses hyperaware of every movement and sound.

"We'll keep this short," Firo's slower drawl replaced Treva's, "as I can sense your deep exhaustion. They should know better than to m-de you." He shook his head, his chin wrinkling glumly. "Having been classified as a Phoenix, it is our responsibility to oversee your training and prepare you to live within Arias or any of the other four cities. Since you've garnered so much attention from your unusual circumstances, we know this will not be the case."

"That has not," Misha cut in, "stopped us from trying to help you. We've petitioned for guardianship, if you will, without hope of being appointed. Our brief glimpse into your future shows a different path."

Firo, Treva, and Seff nodded. Liri was rolling the edge of her skirt between her thumb and middle finger, keenly assessing her. Adriata hadn't loosened her death grip on the chair.

Phe's entire body clenched at Seff's deep voice. It was filled with power and dominance, engulfing her and threatening to force her to her knees and drop her eyes. *Seas, no. Not going to happen.*

"Unlike all the other applicants, we, your Phoenix Council, are in a unique position of advocating for you. You are one of us, and we protect our own."

Phe leveled him with her gaze, her jaw locking. It didn't matter what crazy magic this was, she would *never* get on her knees for anyone.

"The fact you present to us today, two days into your stay in Arias, m-de, bodes poorly and confirms our decision." He paused, his gaze probing, inspecting her. Probably waiting for her to throw herself at his feet. "In order for us to advocate for you, we will arrange weekly meetings for updates."

"I will not go anywhere without my weapons." Assertion punctuated every word.

"That is a wise choice," Liri stated, her voice a deep baritone. "As long as your weapons are sheathed, they'll be allowed."

Treva sighed deeply and hopped to her feet. Phe immediately estimated her height at four and a half feet, and that was being generous. She pinned Zea, who'd been trying to blend in with the wall, with her eerie red gaze. "Zea, return her please, and don't yammer with her. She needs her rest to recharge."

Those eyes landed on Phe. Treva's short stature didn't

take away from the power she exuded. "Orphne, you must rest and care for yourself. Otherwise, you won't be able to handle what is coming."

Anger swelled in her belly, melding with exhaustion and grim determination. Whatever was coming, she would survive it.

28

Phe gasped and bolted upright in bed. Her heart was stampeding like a herd of frightened buffalo pulverizing the terrain. Only the terrain in this case was Phe's ribcage.

What the seas?

She shoved wet, clingy strands of hair off her cheeks and rocked, face in her hands.

A nightmare.

An avalanche of feelings crushed her, too overwhelming to decipher, other than the impending doom and a knowing she was being hunted.

Run.

Phe slid from her bed fully clothed, with her weapons still strapped to her, and made her way onto the balcony, stopping at its threshold to inhale. The scent of sweetness tinged in earthy undertones engulfed her but did nothing to soothe her.

She sprinted across the balcony and vaulted over the banister, spreading her arms wide as she plummeted the countless distance. She landed in a roll, head tucked. The jolt of the impact was painful, especially with her twins digging into her back and shoulders. She catapulted to her feet and ran.

The cushioned mossy-green lawn transitioned into low-level brush, forcing Phe to dash to the entryway path or trip and face-plant. Her limbs pumped, feet barely brushing the dirt path as she flew down it.

Her lungs burned.

Low-hanging branches with snake-like vines reached for her. Fear tightened its grip on her throat, strangling her already shallow breaths. Her legs blazed, the fiery release burning some of the residue of the nightmare.

One foot landed on the dirt path, the other landed on a wood floor, the forest vanishing around her in between breaths.

Reflexively, Phe twisted, barely avoiding hitting a piece of furniture, and slammed into a brick wall.

Hard.

She bounced off it and froze to scan the room.

Where the stars am I?

A fireplace.

L-shaped couch.

Coffee table.

There was a wall with floor-to-ceiling windows, heavy gray drapes at each end.

A noise came from her right.

She swiveled, knife flying. Blue walls. Deep auburn hair.

Roar dodged the knife.

With a thud, it embedded into the wall next to his head.

"Seas! Sorry!" Phe exclaimed, palms up.

"What was that?" came an alarmed feminine cry from somewhere in his house.

"Phe?" Surprise echoed in Roar's pitch.

Phe exhaled. Roar's hair was wet and his shirt clung to

him in spots on his chest. The fresh, clean scent of sandalwood. The feminine scream. Embarrassment flooded her, and a blush spread up her neck like a nasty rash.

How in the stars did I get here?

"So sorry," she murmured. *Get the knife, leave.*

She strode toward Roar, keeping her gaze fixated on her knife's hilt, yanking it free. She was briefly grateful this side of the room wasn't brick. The knife could have ricocheted off it and hurt Roar. She sheathed the blade. "I didn't mean to . . . I'm leaving."

Roar blocked the hallway. "Are you okay?"

"Roar?" the woman's voice wavered.

"Don't worry about me." Phe attempted to slide past him, continuing to avoid his gaze. Anger and fear and shame and confusion at how she'd gotten here flared uncontrollably within her. And that voice. Something about it set her on edge.

Roar mirrored her movements, impeding her escape.

Phe leaned in, all seething, unrepressed anger. "If you don't move, I'll break your bloody window."

An emotion flickered in his piercing blue gaze. "You're not going anywhere."

"Roar, what was that? Are you—" Lassandra appeared around the bend, the rest of her question lost as her jaw hit the ground at the sight of Phe.

Phe met Lassandra's furious eyes.

"La-Sa," he said, his gaze never leaving Phe, "Go home."

"Roar." Something akin to jealousy irrationally smoldered in Phe at the nickname. La-Sa sounded intimate, and for whatever unfathomable reason, that stoked her already out-of-control fire. Phe fumed, her angry cadence slowing to punch out each word. "I'm obviously interrupting. Let. Me. Pass."

"Absolutely not," he said firmly.

"Are you serious?" Lassandra half-whined, half-yelled. "How did she get in?"

Phe swiveled, strode to the fireplace, and snatched a fire poker.

"Phe," Roar warned, stepping in between her and the window.

"I'm not kidding, Roar." Her voice took on an unhinged pitch as images from her dream flashed in her mind's eye. Cages. Bloodied bandages. She tightened her grip and visualized shattering the glass.

"La-Sa, please," Roar requested, tone harder, tracking Phe.

"No, Roar." Hands on hips, Lassandra stepped into the room, glaring. She wore a silky dress that emphasized her curves and left a lot of skin uncovered. Phe's grip tightened even more, her knuckles turning white with effort. "I want to know how she got in here."

"How do you thi—" Roar said. Phe bolted for the hallway. Roar slammed her into the wall, setting all her nerve endings on fire. "—nk?"

Both hands clenching the fire poker, Phe shoved the bar against his chest. "You need to let me go."

"Lassandra," Roar said, his tone deepened with irritation. Phe could practically hear the impatience in his voice this time. He released her, planting his hands on either side of her and caging her in as he ignored the poker she banded across his chest. His blue eyes scalded her.

Her breathing fluttered.

"I don't see why I'm the one who has to leave." Lassandra's anger was palpable, her voice ringing with offense, as if she'd been wronged somehow.

Roar turned to Lassandra. "Because I'm telling you to leave."

Phe ducked under his arm. His body collided with hers, knocking her back into the wall. Heat seared into her.

She hissed.

He eased the pressure, but not his contact.

"Agh! Fine, but your mother's going to hear about this," Lassandra growled, disappearing with a telltale vibration.

Roar pinned Phe with his gaze. "Drop the fire poker."

"You're worried about the poker?" An edge of hysteria crept into her voice. He should be worried about her losing the thread of control that's kept her from attacking him.

"No, I'm worried about you. I just don't want you to suddenly decide to use it on me."

"I don't intend to hurt you," Phe said, the words taking all the fight from her. She sagged against the wall.

"Likewise." He gave her an inch. "What happened?"

She huffed. She didn't want to talk about it.

"I've never seen you like this. You look . . . hunted."

She didn't respond.

Roar sighed, retreating a foot, and thrust his fingers into his wet disheveled hair. "Phe."

She propped the poker against the wall, defiantly crossing her arms.

"You were running, weren't you?"

Phe quirked a brow in response.

"I'll get my shoes on."

She noticed a world map hanging above the L-shaped couch over his shoulder.

"If you flee, I'll be on you in a second," he said over his shoulder, jogging from the room.

She grunted and propelled herself off the wall, stalking right up to and then onto the couch. *Map.*

She flattened her palms on either side of the world map of Aethra. Sighting Shalexum, she located the swath of Xiheria Highlands and searched along the Aglizan border for Arias.

Excitement bubbled when she found it. Her estimation of Arias's location had been relatively accurate. She switched to searching for Yeabrus, but the map didn't show any small villages, only the countries' capitals and several other cities. The marked cities caught her attention.

Roar padded back into the room, his shoulders relaxing at seeing her on the couch. He sat on the shortened portion of the L.

"I've never heard of Galvenor." It was on the southwestern tip of Aglizan, the country to the west of Xafara.

"Heads up." He tossed something at her.

Phe swiped the familiar braided leather amulet out of the air. "You got my amulet back?" She stretched the band out, inspecting it. No damage had been done.

A barrage of emotions surged into her already tight throat, rendering her speechless. How could she explain that having the amulet returned to her felt like someone had reattached an amputated limb? Phe swallowed repeatedly to loosen the boulder of emotions strangling her. She mustered a wobbly, "Thank you."

A small smile replaced the compressed line of Roar's mouth. "It was a team effort. We know it's important to you."

Her heart thudded as she laid it on her bare arm and clasped it to her. It affixed like a second layer of skin, and, with it, a sense of ease settled in her bones.

"And to answer your question, Galvenor is one of ours."

Phe perked up, shoved her emotions aside, and scoured the map, free hand toying with the speck of suspended water. "Magical cities, you mean?" There were more.

Vaetela, a country to Xafara's northeast, had two magical cities, Ezura and Xybell. Hadn't someone said there were five?

"Yes."

Phe jabbed her finger at the fifth, a city off the northern coastline of Piopina, frowning in confusion. "Is Nen in the water?"

Roar propped himself on his elbows, watching her. "It is."

"Huh." *Wonder what that would be like?* She hopped off the couch. On his coffee table was a rectangular bowl filled with rocks. She grabbed one, rolling it on the palm of her hand. Embarrassed, Phe peered at him through her lashes, an apologetic grimace curling her upper lip. "I'm sorry. I didn't mean to interrupt you."

"You didn't interrupt," Roar assured her. "What's wrong?"

She closed her eyes, rubbing the coarse rock's surface, but not feeling it. Instead, she felt the pliable sweetness of baby Jayden in her arms. Visceral pain stole her breath as her rib cage caved in. Electric shocks zinged her from the cage bars.

Phe swallowed, finding her throat clogged, and opened her eyes, tossing the stone onto the pile. It clacked as it hit.

Petrified green eyes stared at her.

"Phe, talk to me," Roar urged, drawing her attention back to him.

Bleakness strained at the lines of his eyes and mouth when she didn't respond, then he stood. "Let's run."

Phe was on his heels until they were outside. Stone sidewalks blurred under her feet. Narrow alleys with dim lighting flew by in swaths of colors. There was a gradual incline, eclipsing from a stair here and there to flights with small plateaus between houses. The further they climbed, the darker the streets became. At one point, Phe glimpsed trees painting the landscape ahead.

The burn in her legs and lungs was electrifying. Sweat soaked her shirt. Other than their labored breathing and synchronized footfalls, the streets were quiet.

She scanned Roar. His deep auburn hair was in a tight bun at his nape. Sweat seeped through his shirt too. Here he was, in the middle of the night, quietly running with her after she'd interrupted his evening with Lassandra.

Should I tell him about the dream?

Her nightmare, the same one she'd had for the past seventeen years, had never altered before. Until now. *Could magic have done that?*

Who was she kidding? People teleported from place to place, and she'd dreamscaped into Kyra's mind. Who knew what magic could do?

Phe spit, gathered her bravery into a ball in her chest, and forced her lips to move. "My nightmare was different tonight, and I'm not sure if magic was involved."

They entered the forest. The cool canopy was chilly, and its woodsy scent refreshing. The path was well worn and wide.

"The first part of my nightmare was normal," she huffed through burning lungs, deliberately not telling Roar about Anala and MaJaJa and everyone else. "Instead of waking like I have since I was seven, I woke up in a different dream.

"My injuries from the previous dream stayed with me. I couldn't move, and it hurt. I mean, hurt as if it was real. There was music and laughter, and after a moment, I could make out Kyra's voice, but I was too far away to hear what they're saying because, for some reason, I was in the woods."

Her words came out halted. *High seas, it's hard to talk and run uphill.*

"I was able to get an arm under me and glimpse snippets of what was happening. Dancing." She huffed. "People were milling about, chatting, basking in the sun. Then an ominous darkness drifted into the gathering, but no one seemed to notice."

Her lungs constricted with the memory, and she had to focus on dragging air in.

"I screamed for Kyra, for anyone, to warn them." She puffed. They entered a clearing with a stone bench, and Roar stopped. Hands on her hips, Phe walked in small circles, practically gulping air. She couldn't look at him, so she kept her gaze down. "No one heard me, and no one seemed to notice the tendrils of darkness."

Phe wanted to skip the part where Velimir appeared and beat her unconscious, his eyes black orbs and his voice not his, but she didn't. That was truly when her nightmare twisted. "I'm positive it was Djall speaking through him, repeating, over and over, 'You're meant for me. You're mine.'" A chill ran along her spine, and she reiterated. "He just kept saying. 'You're mine. You're mine.'"

"Everything went dark. Then I came to in a cage next to Kyra. Someone was strapped to the table in the center, just like Kyra described. It took some *finagling*." That was Phe's code for ignoring the electric current that had continuously zapped her as she'd reached through two sets of cage bars to wake Kyra. "I was able to rouse Kyra, who begged me to give up on her." *As if that would ever happen.* "She was terrified Djall would wake. At the end, he did wake, and . . ." And Elzac stepped into Kyra and blasted Phe from the dream. "Kyra did something to wake me."

There, that was concise, and she'd censured the details

Roar didn't need to know. She glanced up and realized Roar had brought her to a lookout point.

A huge portion of Arias lay exposed before them. Building upon building sloped downward and narrow cobblestone streets backed the hillside, interconnected by flights of stairs. Beyond the city limits was an endless night sky, twinkling with stars.

She stared into the celestial abyss.

"This lookout reminds me of you." Roar sauntered to the bench, sitting. "Every time I come here, I imagine you sitting right here," he patted the empty space next to him, "and gazing into the vastness of this city, loving it."

Phe froze, hanging on his words. *He imagined me here, with him?*

He gazed at her. "We need to talk about your ability to jump directly into my home. Do you recall our conversation at Areya's?"

Seas, which one?

"We talked about how no one can jump into other people's homes, unless, of course, given permission and access."

Oh, that one.

"If I'd been alone, what you did wouldn't be an issue. With Lassandra there, I can assure you that, not only do my mother and sister know, but half of Arias is aware you have access to my house." Roar paused, considering. "The problem is, we can't just tell people you accidentally did this. Crystals' homes have wards to only allow entry to those given permission. No one overrides the wards. The moment people know your abilities can override their protections, consider your death sentence signed.

"This leaves us with only one viable option. We tell people I've allowed you access."

"Okay?" Phe said, not yet fully understanding the problem. "Could we use the excuse of my situation? Or being part of your team?"

"We probably will." A wry smile twisted Roar's lips. "But you know, Fin will make a scene and demand access too."

Phe laughed. "He will." Then she sobered. "Wait, you're not telling the rest of the unit?"

Roar looked at the sky. "I don't think it'd be wise to."

"Bastion." A chill set in, no doubt from her cooling sweat, and her legs were suddenly tired from standing. "Are you going to tell *him*?"

"No." Roar grimly stated. "It's safer this way for you." He dropped both elbows to his thighs and propped his chin on his fists. "Whatever explanation we give, people will assume we're in a relationship." His jaw clenched.

"Lassandra."

"She and I are not in a relationship." Roar's features hardened. "Never have been. La-Sa and I grew up together —which is rare . . . Crystals don't have many kids. Anyway, our families are closely aligned. La-Sa has this belief that we'll end up together, and the last few days, it's been really awkward."

I bet. Phe rolled one of the amulet's braided cords in between her fingers.

The crickets chirped softly around them, filling the silence.

Roar shifted uncomfortably. "She has the uncanny ability to stir up drama. Which she will do, and you're going to be featured in it. I'm not especially worried about her, though.

"There's a small group of people who believe Phoenixes and Crystals shouldn't have relationships. In fact, they see Crystals as this pure race and Phoenixes as only a tool to make them more powerful. There was a brief time in our history where Crystals enslaved Phoenixes and, because shifters were often enslaved, they refer to Phoenixes derogatorily as pets."

In that moment, Phe felt so world-weary What is so hard about looking another person in the eyes and intrinsically seeing their value as another being? Why was greed so rampant?

Her knees wobbled with the weight of life's injustices. She slid into the empty space next to Roar.

"They're a small minority, but they are vocal and have caused troubles. I'm telling you this so you're not blindsided by them. They know you are vulnerable and can be particularly nasty. Once you're inducted into the unit, we won't have to be so worried, but who knows what one of them might try before that?"

Maybe they are why I'm sequestered right now. "Are there any drawbacks to you?" Phe asked.

Roar reclined, stretching his arm along the bench, grazing her back. "I'll get some backlash . . ." He shrugged, his arm brushing into her and sending tingles of awareness along her spine. "Nothing I can't handle."

Phe fussed with her amulet and fought the urge to lean into his arm. "Either way, it doesn't seem we have a choice."

"I'll adjust my wards when I get back." Roar smiled, and Phe noticed he was close. Real close. So close, a wiggle would bring their thighs to touch. If she were to move her arm, she'd graze his chest. And if they were to lock gazes, she'd see all the beautiful imperfections of his blue eyes.

She swallowed the giddy panic rising in her. *Be normal.*

"Are your dreams always this intense?"

Phe shrugged nonchalantly, shoving her giddiness aside.

He nodded, as if expecting her answer. "I'm inclined to

think what you experienced was dream-fare, I just don't know how Djall could do it. My understanding is, mental magic can only be done after there is physical contact with the person, but apparently I may be wrong."

"Dream-fare?"

"It's warfare in the dream realm."

That didn't seem . . . right. Dream-fare was akin to sneaking into a house to kill a defenseless, fragile, half-blind, half-deaf, ninety-year-old woman while she's sleeping. There's no honor in that type of killing.

Roar shifted sideways to face her, and Phe's heart leapt into her throat. All thoughts were waylaid, replaced by the sensation of their thighs touching, casual as it was.

"We'll have to consult with Lear when we return to Areya's." A hint of mischievousness lit his blue eyes. "You should know, he's not a morning person."

Tingles rumbled up Phe's thigh and spread to other parts of her, and it was too much. She adjusted, wiggling into the corner of the bench, bringing a leg up. "In dream-fare, do you feel real pain?"

"Yes—again, from what I've been told. I haven't experienced it. Ihrone's primary magic is mental, and he established protective measures with everyone in the unit. He'll do the same for you once you're inducted."

"Why are we asking Ambassador Genor then?"

"He's the only one technically supposed to be working with you on this branch since he was assigned your mentor. It's expected of us to defer to him with any concerns or questions." Roar mimicked her posture. The only difference in their positions was Phe's leg was up and bent, a barrier between him and her, whereas his leg lay perpendicular across the bench, his calf touching her shoe. "And," he flashed a sly smile, "because he hates being woken."

Phe shook her head, returning a smaller, shyer smile. She had no idea why Shadow Unit delighted in playing small pranks on each other. Any opportunity to deliberately irritate someone was like an afternoon snack to them.

Roar sobered. "The first part was your reoccurring nightmare, right?"

The tingles faded, and her crazy body was yearning for more. *What is wrong with me?* To him, she nodded.

"Have you considered it's not a dream?"

"Yes." Her thoughts went to her memory with MaJaJa. If MaJaJa was real, then the dream must be too. "But wouldn't it have come up in the chair?" The one she'd refuse to name out of pure spite.

"Does it have anything to do with suppressing your magic?"

"No."

"There's your answer," Roar simply stated. "You didn't tell me about that part of the dream."

"I didn't," she said, sealing her lips.

"Were any of Djall's possessed in it?"

She let her gaze roam the night sky. Something about the dream compelled her to hold it close. She'd always viewed it as someone else's. It was Anala's story to tell, not hers. Yet this detail was important. It connected points, like constellations in the night's sky.

"Yes, they were there. Attacking."

"That could have been how Djall knew about you and got your magical essence. Tracked you." Seriousness now glinted in Roar's blue depths and lines sprouted at the edges of his eyes.

"Please don't tell Bastion," Phe blurted, realizing if Bastion knew, he'd try all his ghastly ways to extract the dream. She couldn't have this nightmare magically ripped from her.

Roar was silent for so long, dread curdled her stomach. "I'm walking a dangerous line with you." He exhaled out a long, stressed breath.

"Let's try to keep these omissions to the minimum, yeah?"

Her whole body relaxed, and she could breathe again. "It would help if you didn't ask me direct questions about them."

"Point received. What about the next part of your dream? What's your interpretation of it?"

All Phe had wanted to do was run the slimy remnants of horror and helplessness out of her. Then she had to open her mouth. "I'm worried about Kyra."

"Dig deeper."

She scoffed. *No one but you can make sense of your life.* Elzac's favorite saying. She glared at the sparkling night sky.

Another star flashed.

Afraid it was those wispy things from the night before, Phe glowered at a tree instead. "Kyra's out of my reach in the dream, and I can't help her." Like she is now, prisoner to some blood-drinking magic-corrupted madman.

"What does Velimir represent?"

"Djall." She cleared her throat. "I detest Velimir, so it makes sense he appeared through him."

Roar tilted his head. "What was he repeating?"

"'You're mine.'" Disgusted, Phe dropped her chin and pinched the corners of her mouth.

"Well, he's definitely the possessive type." One corner of Roar's mouth quirked up.

A laugh unexpectedly burst from her, lightening the weight of the moment.

"It's those cages that have me the most concerned." He dropped his half-smile.

"Could Djall have trapped me in the dream?"

Roar's jaw flexed. "A possibility."

"What if—" this was feeling right, "—he had me, but he couldn't hold onto me?" Phe paused, processing it. "Then Kyra intervened."

Seas. She'd been so close to being trapped and had had no idea. "He's hunting me." Technically, this wasn't news to her. Bastion had said it earlier today, but this was the first time it landed. And it landed hard.

"He is."

"Ambassador Genor will stop him, right?" Fear slithered down Phe's spine. *And I will learn all the magic I need to protect myself.*

"He should be able to, and Ihrone will too." Roar rubbed his chin on his knee.

Phe followed his movement. His chin was scruffy, lips slightly parted. She had the bizarre urge to run her fingers along his jawline.

"I don't think we'll know, but now I'm definitely waking Lear up. He's going to need to set up protection until the induction."

Why hadn't the shields Elzac created worked?

"Did Kyra talk to you?"

"Yes. Barely. She wanted me to desist from rescuing her and to have warrior babies in the woods," Phe said dryly.

"Ha, she said that?"

Phe smirked. "Sure did." Only to have her expression fall to the last memory she had of Kyra. Terrified green eyes, now sunken into pale skin and gaunt cheeks, begging her to save herself when she shouldn't even be there. This was all Phe's fault.

"Hey." Roar gently touched her cheek. The pads of his fingers sparked an electric sensation.

She froze, eyes shooting to his blues.

"You did not fail Kyra. You performed as we trained you to, against forces you had no clue about. In fact, if it hadn't been for you and your magical immunity to the spellcaster, we'd all be in Djall's dungeons right now." His fingers trailed down her chin, icy-hot tingles racing through her, then pulled away.

Phe bit her bottom lip, drawing it in slightly, unable to compute what was misfiring in her body.

Roar's eyes tracked her movement, and they burned with an emotion unknown to Phe.

"Immunity?" Her voice came out husky.

"You were unaffected by the mage's magic—meaning you have some sort of magical immunity—whereas the rest of us were eating floorboards."

Great, as if she wasn't sparkly enough.

Roar blinked, clearing his gaze, stood, and stretched.

Phe scanned the city, ignoring Roar because her heart was thumping off beat and he was the cause. The sight truly was breathtaking.

"What happened with the Phoenix Council?"

"They introduced themselves to me. Did you know they have meet-the-council days in their school?" The concept seemed so foreign to Phe. Why would the ruling council do that? In Xafara, there was both the parliament and the royal family, neither of which spent any time going to schools and or getting to know their constituents.

"I'd heard that. Phoenixes have a smaller population and, because they're taken as infants, one of their primary goals is to create a tight familial community. Anything else?"

"Other than they want to meet with me in weekly meetings, no," Phe said.

"Hm." Roar held out a hand to her. "I'll jump us to
Areya's."

Phe slipped her hand into his palm. His large hand
closed around her smaller one and tugged her to his side.
"We're not going to run back?"

"No," he said dryly, gazing down at her. "I'm tired."

"What?" Phe gave him her best shocked expression, and
their gazes connected.

He gave her a lazy smile, and the world shifted. Literally.

29

Phe stared blankly at the gargantuan building blocking the early morning sun. There was a stillness to the air, the same subdued silence she'd experienced while walking through building IIIIII when Zea had shown her the Phoenix residence she'd been assigned to.

Finian bounded before her and gave her a sideways half-bow. Gesturing to an overbearing building, he said enthusiastically, "I formally welcome you to the Klulora Center. Named after the Klulora family themselves."

Phe slid her apprehensive gaze to Finian. He'd arrived with the sunrise all gleeful and chipper, testing her already shortened temper.

When the sun broke through the night's darkness, it officially made it day number three that Kyra was being held hostage, and what had Phe been able to do to rescue her? Nothing. Her attempt to escape, squashed. The only information she'd gotten about Djall so far was from Zea, and Bastion planned to distribute the rest like treats to a dog when she behaved.

To add to her grumpiness, she hadn't been able to sleep

once Roar and Ambassador Genor had left. She'd been too nervous Djall would somehow get through Ambassador Genor's protective measures. She'd spent a considerable length of time trying to summon Elzac, closing her eyes and repeating his name over and over again.

Nothing happened.

The rest of the night she fluctuated between thinking about the dream and Kyra, then rehashing her conversation with Roar and how her body had reacted to him. How *she'd* reacted to him. There'd been this yearning tension she'd never experienced. Is *this what Kyra is always going on about?*

Whatever it was, it was a distraction, pure and simple, and she couldn't be distracted while Kyra starved to death in an electric cage somewhere. Phe's solution? To avoid Roar as much as she could.

Yet when Finian had shown up, bright and early and cheerful and with a shirt on, and not Roar, a sinkhole had formed in her stomach. What was wrong with her?

Then there was the matter of what the stars had planned for her today. With Finian's presence, Phe was dubious there wouldn't be a repeat of yesterday.

Which is why she stared nervously at the windowless building before her. The only door she could see was a glass door. No other exit or entry points. The building itself was huge, consuming at least five city blocks, with a bulbous dome that overshadowed its neighbors. It was ugly.

"Don't be fooled by the outside." Finian's eyes twinkled, hustling her through glass doors that slid open on their own. *Some sort of magic.* "This building is the best training center in all of our cities. She's been built to withstand the most powerful Crystals, and has a self-containment capability if anything were to go awry."

"I'm sorry I don't share your enthusiasm," Phe quipped,

toying with her amulet as she entered a sterile white marble hallway. "I know several teams are trying to track Kyra, but aren't they the same teams who've been trying to track Djall for how many decades?"

"I checked in with them last night," Finian assured her, his cheerfulness sobering a smidgen, "and they're doing their best to trace her."

Of course they were, but their best was not Phe's best. "That's not reassuring. Do they have any leads?"

"They didn't give me any details."

Phe grunted unhappily. Once past the entryway, wall-to-ceiling windows allowed them to gaze into rooms on either side of the corridor. To their right, there was a small group of children practicing roundhouse kicks as their instructors held kick pads.

The first room to their left was empty, the one after wasn't. An inferno of fire blazed from a woman's hands. Halfway through its deadly arc, ice met it from the hands of a man opposite her. Sparks and shards of ice and water exploded everywhere at their collision.

"Can't window shop today," Finian interrupted Phe's interested trance. "We have to keep on moving."

Phe grunted. *How can they do that?*

In another room, a group of three people fought. Weapons hung suspended in the air, engaged in their own battles, while below them the three opponents also fought each other. A staff was wrenched out of one of the fighters' hands. Without missing a beat, they reached their open palm into the midst of the battling weapons and the hilt of a sword flew into it.

Finian crowded her to keep her moving, but she stopped as soon as she saw what was in the next room.

A real-life dragon.

Phe's chest seized, and blood drained from her face. *High seas!* Her hands gripped the handles of her sheathed thigh knives. Would they do any good? It'd be like coming to a fight with toothpicks.

The dragon's scales rippled a wave of deep crimson. Golden orbs tracked her. It opened its muzzle, displaying razor white teeth caging a person sitting cross-legged on its split tongue. Its nostrils emitted plumes of smoke.

"She's gorgeous, isn't she?" Finian asked, swaggering to the glass. "Chinga, we should meet up soon. It's been too long."

Does he not see the person in its mouth?

Those golden orbs locked onto Finian, and the madman winked at it. *At the dragon.*

Phe shuffled ahead, her grip on the cool hilts of her knives not as reassuring as it once was, glad the dragon's laser focus was on Finian and not tracking her. In the next room, a man stood in the center, lightly jumping on his toes, punching the surrounding space.

The moment he noticed Phe, his body exploded. Clothes shredded, muscles bunched and grew, neck thickened. Eyes glowing red-brown fixated on them, square jaw protruding with yellow teeth, and he stomp-ran toward them, roaring.

Phe hissed, unsheathing her twins.

Finian sauntered casually between her and the monster, as if he didn't notice the beast pounding the glass. "Nothing to worry about, Phe," he said through a puckered smirk, then knocked on the glass with a single knuckle, completely unperturbed. "Hey! Fido, knock it off, man. Can't you recognize my baby girl?" Finian was only a quarter of its size.

The beast's glare stayed fixated on Phe, threatening to rip her apart.

Finian's playfulness hardened. "Don't make me go in there."

Those red-brown disks scowled at Finian, huffing.

"I know. She's a cutie," Finian continued, nonplussed, and apparently not seeing the blatant death threat Fido's piercing gaze promised Phe. "I'll introduce you. Fido, this is Phe, *my baby girl.*"

Fido grunted, and specks of green mucus hit the window in globs.

Finian wrapped an arm around Phe's shoulders, sending waves of uneasiness along her spine.

Phe controlled the instinctive urge to move away from his touch, choosing the lesser of the evils to contend with because the alternative was to be attacked by a beast.

"Phe," he gave her shoulders a squeeze, "Meet my pal, Fido."

Phe smiled around her gritted teeth, which undoubtable had to appear as a mix between a grimace and a warning.

The beast squatted, ripping the last threads of the pants he wore, and pierced Phe with a scrutinizing gaze. He pressed his fingertips, which were each the size of a large apple, on the glass pane and leaned into it to peer at her.

After a moment, Fido nodded as if he'd concluded killing her would be more problematic than leaving her be, and gave her an askew smile, displaying his yellowed teeth.

"Good. Glad we're clear on that." Finian removed his arm, and Phe side-stepped away from him, still clutching her twins. "We're off to her first day of training!" Finian moved with her to messily ruffle the top of Phe's head, as if she were an adorable young child.

Jerking out of his reach, Phe gave him a slitted glare.

Finian snapped his fingers, returning his attention to

Fido. "We're going to have to postpone tonight, have you heard?"

A palm twice the size of Phe's head landed on the glass. Fido whined, shaking his head, then heaved his huge nude body up.

"No? My baby girl's being inducted today." The twinkle in Finian's eye returned.

Fido tilted his chin to look at Fin through his lashes. If Phe had to guess, it was an *are-we-sure-this-is-good-news* look.

"Right?" Fin's voice pitched higher. "That means we get to celebrate later."

Fido's grunt was decidedly happy sounding.

"I'll look for you," Fin said, walking away.

Phe followed, sheathing her twins and keeping her gaze ahead. She was fine not knowing what was happening in any of the other rooms.

"I'm being inducted?"

"Yesss." The happiness radiating from Finian bombarded her and did nothing for her mood. *Isn't anyone going to ask me what I want?* "The ceremony will start right at mid-day, then it'll be followed with the celebration banquet."

Phe grunted glumly. Had anyone explained what this induction ceremony was? She didn't think so. They'd talked about it, but not what it meant. And now there was a celebration banquet after?

They passed another room, and Phe caught glimpses of movement.

"Interesting, isn't it?"

Phe schooled her expression to neutral. "You could say that." She was glad her voice matched the cool shell she'd donned.

His smirk reappeared. "Don't worry, they won't be able to stop themselves from falling in love with your sweetness."

She narrowed her gaze.

Finian winked and picked up his pace. "Stop dragging your feet, the team's waiting."

Nervously twisting the braided leather at her wrist, Phe let him get a few feet in front of her, contemplating if she should end it for him now. Before she could decide, he stepped into a room.

In it, Ihrone and Kirzia appeared to be in the midst of a push-up challenge. Quick, sharp inhales punched their movements as they pumped up and down, side by side.

Finian slapped the glass window and instantaneously the glass darkened and Phe couldn't see out of it. "We're here!" Finian unnecessarily announced, sitting on Ihrone's back.

Ihrone kept moving as if Finian's weight were inconsequential, which Phe knew from recent experience was not the case.

"One hundred fifty-six," Kirzia proclaimed proudly, jumping to her feet. Wisps of her raven black hair stuck to her forehead and the sides of her face, the rest knotted in a severe knot at the base of her neck.

Ihrone hopped his feet to his hands and launched Finian off, then he stood and brushed his hands together. "One hundred eighty-four."

Kirzia grumbled and pulled out a small wad of money, ruffling through until she pulled out a note. Ihrone took the note, keeping his ever-calm composure.

"I did as was suggested and walked us through," Finian said, vaulting to his feet and ignoring the exchange. "I didn't think I'd ever see Phe pale." He tapped a temple with an index finger. "It was priceless. She was white as a ghost when she spotted Chinga." The smile plumping his face made Phe want to strangle him. "You guys were right. Showing is much better than telling."

"Fin," Phe gritted out threateningly.

"Make sure to memo-gram it for us," Ihrone said, "Kirzia and I made a bet on how quickly she'd pull her weapons. No offense, Phe."

What was it I ever saw in them?

"What's a memo-gram?" Phe asked.

"Has anyone explained what a memo-pro is?" Ihrone's tone settled into his smooth teaching voice?

Phe nodded.

"So you know, memo-pro's take a single memory, a captured moment, and transfer that to a canvas. Memo-gram's are similar, except they will take the entire memory and transfer that onto a canvas so, in this instance, we can watch Finian's memory of you starting once you entered the Klulora Center until you joined us." Ihrone gaze scrutinized her reaction. "Does that make sense?"

Phe grunted yes. Her shoulders sagged under the weight of how much she didn't know and needed to learn—from memo-grams to everything magic to the ins and outs of this new society.

"Phe." Kirzia brushed the sweat into her hairline. "You look tired. Did you sleep at all after all the excitement?"

"No."

"Before we get started," Ihrone strode purposefully to her, "I want to check over Lear's work. Can I touch you?"

She didn't want to be touched. To delay the inevitable, she gazed into Ihrone's dark gray eyes, noticing that he too had drops of sweat along his hairline, and counted to ten. "Yes."

"Back to monosyllable words?" Finian asked.

Phe responded with a hooded glare and, in defiance to Fin, asked Ihrone, "Why aren't you my mentor?"

A smile lighted Ihrone's gray eyes. "Lear Genor's primary specialty is mental magic. His capabilities span the width of the branch and his training and experience is extensive enough to warrant his position as a mentor with the Elders. That is no small feat. I, on the other hand, am a warrior and have been trained as such since I was a toddler. The difference between our two levels is drastic. If we were artists, my bold abstract streaks would seem unrefined compared to his fine, detailed brush strokes."

That makes sense.

Ihrone placed the pads of both middle and pointer fingers to her temple. His touch was feather light, and his eyes glowed. Ihrone's magic was like his touch, a gently flowing breeze.

"Heard Lear was pis-syy last night," Finian said, humor lacing his voice.

Phe hummed her response. Ambassador Genor had been less than thrilled to be awoken. "Where's Orc and Roar?"

"Roar is following through on a challenge he'd accepted, and Orc is there for his healing touch," Ihrone said. His warm breath heated her cheek and smelled of coffee.

Phe's abdomen clenched. She was sure she already knew the answer, but still she asked, "What's a challenge?" Was Roar in danger?

"A challenge is a fight. The goal is to win what they're arguing over."

Dread gurgled in the sinkhole of her belly. "Um, does this have to do with me?" *Please say no.* "And why aren't you all there?"

"Has everything to do with you, but," Finian replied, "baby girl, there's nothing *we* wouldn't do for you."

"And it's nothing he can't handle. In fact, it's better this way. Roar will deal with them and remind them why it's unwise to challenge an Elite soldier." Kirzia sounded disgusted someone had. "Orc's there cause he's a mother hen and refused to let Roar go alone. You'll learn he takes his role as healer very seriously."

"As for us," Ihrone said, "we're here to teach you how to create a shield."

"Our plan is," Kirzia added, "you're not leaving here until you can."

"Ambassador Genor is meeting me back at Areya's for a lesson soon," Phe mumbled, suddenly nervous about this training session.

Ihrone seemed satisfied with whatever he saw and stepped away. "I'll be more at ease once you've been inducted and I can double up your protections with my own."

"Won't be long now," Finian butted in.

"The mental barriers you and Lear set up look good, except you have to fix the ones that fell. I'm surprised Lear left you like this."

"He left her vulnerable?" The playfulness vanished from Finian's tone, which was now hard with the threat of violence.

Phe peered at Fin, surprised with the vehemence of his reaction, to discover he'd gotten incrementally bigger. His shirt was stretched to the point of tearing, and veins popped along his skin.

Phe blinked. Hadn't Finian's behemoth size been an aftereffect of her concussion?

"Calm yourself," Kirzia commanded, not surprised by Finian's new size.

"Ambassador Genor said he'd show me how to fix it this morning." Phe cleared her throat, uncomfortably glancing between Ihrone and Kirzia, and ignoring the urge to stare at Fin. "He wasn't in a teaching mood last night."

"I'll kill him." The sound of tearing fabric followed.

"Keep your pants on, Fin!" Kirzia ordered in a stern voice. The tearing stopped.

"I'm sure he didn't expect you to leave Areya's for a jaunt to the Klulora Center," Ihrone said in an understandable tone. "No harm was done, Fin. Only a few of her barriers fell with more than enough still in place, and he'll remedy the problem once we get her back. For now, not only are the remaining protections she has in place more than adequate, she's with me. She'll be fine. Kirzia, you're up."

Phe peeked at Finian. His torso was double the size, his shirt reduced to a puddle at his feet. His lower half had grown to look like stuffed, muscular sausages in his barely intact pants.

"Eyes on mine," Kirzia demanded, motioning to her eyes with two fingers.

Phe snapped her eyes to Kirzia.

"Don't mind Fin. We've discovered he's got a fierce protective streak." Kirzia smiled a little witchily. "Who'd have known?"

Fin grumbled.

"You and I are going to work on shielding." Kirzia rubbed her hands together, gaze intense. "Technically, it's called force field generation, but no one calls it that, and it's from the Energy Manipulation branch. What it does is protect you from attacks."

"Couldn't you have taught me this yesterday morning?" *Before the trials?*

"We weren't allowed to. The Elders wanted to see your innate capabilities." Kirzia had the decency to look disgruntled with the statement. "I'm going to erect mine, so you have a starting point on what it feels like."

Nothing happened.

Phe glanced around, bewildered.

"Raise your hand and step forward."

Phe did, and her hand met a sluggish resistance that she pushed through.

"Huh," Kirzia muttered.

"Did she just walk through your shield?" Incredibility suffused Finian's voice.

Kirzia ignored him. "What did you feel?"

"Some kind of resistance I pushed through."

"Good. Can you stand in the resistance?"

Phe backed up a step, but the feeling didn't return. "No, it's not there anymore."

"Would one of you check the shield? I feel it's in place, but . . ." Kirzia requested, never taking her gaze off Phe.

Ihrone stepped forward, laid his hands on an invisible barrier, and pushed it, his arms straining. "It's there."

Kirzia crinkled her nose. "Let's try this a different way. Where do you feel your magic?"

"Um . . . I don't?"

"What about when you woke up from your rebound?" Ihrone prodded.

"Everything hurt," Phe told them dryly.

"Imagine a protective bubble around you," Kirzia tried again.

Phe closed her eyes, and images of protective bubbles flaring around Swaney, Jezzie, LaLora, and Jayden flashed so quickly it set her nerves tingling. With a deep breath, she cleared her mind and imagined a similar bubble around her.

After a minute or two, she peeked at her teammates. "Is it working?"

"No." Kirzia was tapping her thigh thoughtfully. "We know your combat skills are passive, so why don't we spar? This way you can get a feel for what your magic feels like when it becomes active."

"If it's passive, how will it be activated?" Phe asked.

"Because we're about to rain terror on you," Kirzia said, the look in her eyes reinforcing her promise.

"Oh." Phe drew her twins as her skin prickled uneasily. "That sounds delightful."

Ihrone calmly rolled up his sleeve. "And that's one of the things I appreciate about you. You always find the silver lining."

Not so sure that's true.

Then they attacked in unison, and it all blurred. Time became inconsequential from one breath to the next. Drops of sweat sprinkled the space like a dusting of rain. Arms, legs, and weapons collided until they'd pummeled her to the ground, only to repeat over and over again when her magic didn't spontaneously appear.

Phe stayed where she'd fallen, staring at the ceiling. Pain radiated from spots all over her, and she could probably wring sweat from her clothes. With a pull-two-weeds-with-one-yank motive to delay them from dragging her up for another round and to hopefully satisfy a sudden curiosity, she rolled her head to the side and asked. "How old are you guys?"

Fin lay on the ground next to her. Sweat covered him. Phe watched his chest rise and fall.

Kirzia plunged first. "I'm three hundred twenty-seven."

Phe bit her lip to hold her jaw in place.

"Grateful to be six hundred forty-two," Ihrone shared. "Orc is five hundred and ninety-eight—"

Flipping stars . . .

"Roar's twenty-eight, only four years older than you." Finian interrupted, no doubt, reading through her attempt to be stoic and winking at her. How he had energy she did not know. "And I'm one hundred sixty-nine."

Phe blinked at Fin. *How was it Roar, at twenty-eight, was the commander of this geriatric unit?* "What's the life range of a Crystal?"

The twinkle in Fin's eyes brightened and a full smile eclipsed his features. "Infinite. My mother's working on her second millennia right now."

Seas. How do they not go crazy? "Why is Roar your commander?"

"Roar demonstrated exceptional—"

"Because he's a prodigy." Finian interrupted.

"—leadership capabilities and overall control of his immense magic at a very early age. We typically rotate the commander position every few decades. When it was time to re-assign the role, Roar was appointed." Kirzia explained.

"You wait baby girl, you're up next." Phe could hear Finian's smirk.

Not going to happen. "Can you tell me what's happened to Jallia? Is she all right?"

"She's all right in the sense that she's alive. A little banged up, but alive," Kirzia said from Phe's other side. Phe flopped her head over to look at her. "Last I heard, they were deciding her punishment and consulting with seers."

"Does that mean they won't kill her?"

"They weren't considering that level of punishment for her crime."

Thank the seas.

"I thought training the youngins was the easiest job ever," Fin whined. "Hanging out with all the cute kiddos, teaching them, you know, stuff. But this is hard; not even your shadows made an appearance."

Phe spun her head to glare at him. What was he complaining about? It was three against one, and she'd hit the floor every single time.

"I think it's because she trusts us," Ihrone said from his place at Phe's head. "And she was never in true danger."

"You're wondering if her magic activates in life-or-death situations?" Kirzia clarified.

"I am."

Phe peered at the ceiling and asked, "Have you been going easy on me all these years?"

"By not trying to kill you in training?" When Kirzia put it like that, it made it sound bad.

"No, we've always catered our training together to levels —albeit a challenge—you could handle," Ihrone answered, standing and looming over her. "Did today seem like we were harder on you?"

"Yes." Phe hauled herself into a sitting position.

"You're exhausted, and I wonder if you're still partially m-de," Kirzia said, sitting cross-legged on the floor.

"You mean empty," Phe prompted, because m-de was for the birds, and mopped at the sweat on her face and neck.

Kirzia half-smiled, but kept going. "Once we figure out how to engage your magic, it'll be easy."

What if my magic is broken? What if I can't get it to work and Kyra dies? She reached for her amulet, her fingers digging into the leather.

"After the induction, our magic will be merged and some of the restraints we have will be gone. It'll definitely be easier," Ihrone assured them. "For now, we're going to have to call it quits. Maybe Lear will have better luck with you."

"I'll take you back, baby girl. Lear's in a mood, and I don't want him taking it out on you," Finian said, jumping to his feet effortlessly.

"How do you know? And why?" Phe asked.

"The last two rounds, he's been telepathically yelling at us." Kirzia smiled delightedly. "Meh, it might be because we haven't left him much time with you."

30

Piercing golden eyes bore into Phe's, their cunning intelligence working to strip her barriers and delve into her secrets. Phe returned the spirit of the gaze, matching Ambassador Genor's intensity.

They were in Areya's great room, sitting across from each other at the mammoth dining table, Phe's back to the forest. Flecks of sunlight drifted over her shoulder, highlighting Ambassador Genor's sun-bleached, wavy hair, which was parted to the right and swept across his forehead. He'd mostly tucked the unruly strands behind his ears. Days-old brown stubble covered his cheeks, jaw, and upper lip. Even though he'd been woken in the middle of the night, there wasn't a hint of dark circles under his eyes.

If only Phe were so lucky. She didn't need a mirror to know dark crescents marred her pale skin and exhaustion etched into the lines of her face alongside the sweat from her session at the Klulora Center.

Finian had escorted her back, and after some private words with Ambassador Genor, where Fin's veins popped, he left, ruffling Phe's hair again on the way out.

Ambassador Genor broke the silence. "Orphne, especially because we met under less than desirable circumstances and because of your inexperience with the way mentoring works, I want to start with going over some basics with you."

Resting his elbows on the table, he clasped his hands and leaned forward a bit. "Normally, a Phoenix would never be assigned a Crystal mentor, which makes our relationship something unusual. Typically, each magic class trains their own.

"Crystal mentors are highly sought after and are appointed by the Elders to ensure those in genuine need are given support. Since there are only a handful of us qualified to be mentors, and because of the thoroughness of our work, we only take on one mentee at a time. For me to work with you, I was relieved of my previous mentee."

He paused to let that sink in.

Phe kept her expression porcelain smooth. She heard what she thought he wasn't saying. Having a Crystal mentor was an elitist privilege, one she obviously didn't qualify for. Not only had the Elders appointed him her mentor—which seemed to be insulting enough—but in doing so, they'd forced Ambassador Genor to end his last mentee relationship, and he was not happy about it.

"Mentor relationships, specifically within the mental branch of magic, develop close bonds because we work within each other's," he unclasped a hand to tap his temple, "minds."

Definitely not happy.

"The level of work we'll be doing together requires trust. A lot of trust." They still hadn't broken their stare-off, but he tilted his chin and peered through his lashes. "Which circles me back to the brief history we share. I attacked you. Will this be a problem?"

Phe drew in a deep breath. She couldn't tell if this was his way of trying to finagle out of mentoring her or if he was trying to establish the first building blocks of trust.

"I think that depends on who you work for."

"The mentor-mentee relationship is exclusive. It would not work if there were outside influences interfering, and what we do is confidential, which means everything stays between us."

"So . . . if Bastion were to ask you for updates on my progress or details about what you've seen in my head, you wouldn't tell him?"

"Correct. Though in your case, I'd recommend the three of us meet to review your progress. I believe I heard General Bastion will disseminate information to you about Djall depending on your growth." He paused again, giving her space to confirm or refute this. When she didn't, he continued.

"If we exclude him, this would be reason enough for him to continue to withhold information from you. We don't have to have meetings if that's not the case. If it is, we'd decide what to disclose prior to those meetings, so you are never blindsided."

Phe grunted, surprised at how clear and fair he was being. He was offering her an out, so there had to be a catch. *The stars wouldn't be so kind.* "If I were to decline you, who else would be appointed?"

"There are several options who live in other cities. The Elders would decide who they thought best."

She contemplated this, her gaze unfocusing in the golden sphere of his eyes.

Ambassador Genor was Areya's son. Not that that was a

reference. Yet it eased the disquiet until an errant image of her stomping her foot and threatening to tell Areya on him fluttered past.

Phe almost snort-laughed. *Who does that?* She still couldn't quite wrap her mind around the fact that Lassandra, a grown woman, had.

Clearing her mind from *that*, Phe assessed what she knew of Ambassador Genor. He'd attacked her. Elzac implied Ambassador Genor was affected by her memories and hadn't been concerned about him, even though he'd invaded her mind. Areya was his mother. She'd discarded her initial impression of him being a hawk and changed it to a golden eagle perched at the top of a tree, surveying its territory.

Essentially, Phe knew nothing about him.

Hmm. She tapped her fingers on the table.

Shadow Unit's reaction to his appointment as her mentor had been of acceptance. They'd forewarned her of how bad the trials would be. They'd protected her when she'd been caught in Xafara. Yet they seemed at ease with Ambassador Genor being her mentor, other than a few digs at him. This was a huge, albeit silent, reference.

Can I trust someone who's attacked me?

Historically, she had, repeatedly. The rules with Bastion had been simple until three days ago. Survive. Protect Kyra. Be the best you can be. Practice.

The greatest lessons Bastion taught her stemmed from his cruel treatment of her. They surpassed the skill development and wilderness survival because she found her value despite him.

"Will you attack me again?"

Ambassador Genor gave a slight head shake. "As your mentor, my goal is unilaterally to build, strengthen, and educate you. When you graduate to a level where you can defend attacks against me, I will test your skills. Testing will appear in a variety of different ways, attacks being one of them. My intention with the use of attacking is to ensure your skill, knowledge, and utilization, not in harming you."

"Hmm." The more he talked, the more reasonable he sounded. *What are the stars planning?* There had to be a catch. "Have you told anyone about what you've already seen in my head?"

"No," Ambassador Genor stated firmly.

"Did Bastion ask?"

"I've had several inquiries about our encounter. I felt it prudent to maintain your confidence."

"Why?"

"I have my reasons." Ones that Phe was obviously not privy to when he didn't further elaborate.

Phe toyed with the braids on her amulet. Ambassador Genor was the only one who knew the depths of her experiences with Grum and, if this mentoring business was as in-depth as he made it seem, switching to another mentor could mean two people would know. It would also release the ambassador from his discretion.

"I accept you as my mentor."

The first smile she'd seen on him since Princess Attiva's ball lifted the edges of his lips, but didn't quite make it to his eyes. "It will be my pleasure to assist you in mastering your mental capabilities. Please call me Lear. What would you prefer I call you?"

"You can call me either Orphne or Phe. I have no preference."

"All right, Orphne, since your team wasted our training time this morning—" a not-so-subtle jab at Shadow Unit,

"—we do not have time for what I'd had planned, so we'll focus on your protective barriers."

A prickling sense of unease slithered through her.

Lear tilted his head. "I know Elzac erected your barriers." His words doused Phe in a cold bath. Her heart stopped.

Seas, how did he know? She steeled her face, hoping Lear's unwavering gaze missed the momentary crack of shock in her defenses.

"In fact, we'll defer the subject of Elzac, for now, and focus on what I am sure he didn't have time to teach you: protective barriers.

"As mental mages, we are in the unique position to both protect and attack. Our skill set, in my opinion, is the most advantageous. We can kill from distances while our enemies are completely unaware of our presence, and we can also help to heal the mind, and thus the body and spirit. Our powers are a balance between life and death."

Revulsion coated the back of Phe's throat. What he thought was valuable, she thought was monstrous.

"The protective barriers Elzac established are a front line to ensure another mental practitioner doesn't waltz in uninvited. They should've been enough to keep Djall out last night, which means he came in through a different route. We'll go over what I did to protect you in another lesson.

"As all things in life, once we build something, we have to continue to maintain it. Thus, the moment the attack on your protective barriers ended, you should've repaired and re-erected those that had fallen. This is what we are going to do together now."

Phe understood and appreciated Lear's approach. She

couldn't be the best at a skill if she learned it and stopped practicing. That was why she trained daily.

"Close your eyes and center yourself in the space in the middle of your forehead. Think of it as an open balcony. I will meet you there."

Hesitantly obedient, Phe did as he said. Rather than pure darkness, she found herself in a foggy blend of light and dark. Lear appeared a moment later and with him, a crisp clarity.

They stood on the rocky shores of her favorite glacial lake in the Sryln Sierras. Around them, majestic snow-capped peaks encircled the teal waters. Lear stood near her, gazing toward the peaks.

"This is beautiful. Where is it?"

"Xafara." Phe was deliberately vague. This treasure was not on any map she'd seen and, to her knowledge, no one else knew it existed. It was inaccessible during the winter months, buried under feet of snow, and only melted into existence in the brief thaws of summer. Yet it was hers. One she'd discovered on one of Bastion's intensive wilderness trainings.

Lear turned to her then, golden gaze landing on her. "Call your barriers by imagining them around you."

What if I can't? What if I'm inept?

Whether she'd broadcasted the thoughts, or Lear sensed the doubt still gripping her from her failed shield training with Shadow Unit, he said, "Don't fear the magic you have. It is an irrevocable part of you. Because this world disconnected you from it, your innate connection was severed, which only means there still exists a gap between your awakened magic and you harnessing it. The only way to fix the gap is to reach for it, to build the canals."

Shuttering her uncertainty, Phe stared across the water's

smooth surface, imagining the barriers appearing around her.

"Good." Lear's voice was reassuring. "See the ones that have been damaged?"

Phe grunted. How could she not? It was as if a horde of teething puppies had descended, demolishing everything in a fit of frenzied, rapscallion-spawned tug-of-war.

"Great. Now repair them."

Phe balked. The other barriers revolved around her dangerously. How was she to get to the outer layers without hurting herself?

"Your barriers will never harm you. Reach through them physically if you need to. Or, alternatively, you can imagine the barriers repairing and healing."

She glared at the barriers, irritated that Lear seemed to know what she was thinking. She strained to imagine them rising and stitching themselves together. Frustration chewed at her when nothing happened. How had this been easy with Elzac and now felt insurmountable?

He let her struggle go on for a while until, with a disgruntled exhale, he broke the silence. "If time were not an issue, we'd be here until you figured it out on your own. But, thanks to your team, it is an issue." He kicked a rock the size of a fist into the lake, the water splashing as it hit. "So, we'll go about this a different way."

An image of Kyra formed from the mist of the lake, crystallizing at the edge of the last fallen barrier. Even though Phe knew this was mist, it looked just like Kyra. Her heart faltered painfully.

More wisps of mist formed into darkening masses above the lake.

"What if those fallen barriers are the ones between life and death for *her*?"

Oh seas, Phe knew what he was doing, yet it didn't stop the panic. It was as if a snake had wrapped itself around her chest and constricted, crushing her lungs.

With desperation-tinged vigor, she visualized the shredded pieces of the first barrier pulling in toward each other, all the while those dark masses slunk threateningly toward Kyra.

Fighting for breath, Phe prioritized the first boundary. Patching and sealing the walls and erecting them just as the masses hit them. They held. Barely.

She envisioned energy inflating the wall, strengthening and smoothing it from the inside. A soft buzz broke the tense silence, and the barrier lit up. The dark masses scattered.

Relief eased the pressure on her chest, and she set to work doing the same thing to the other barriers, one by one. When she was done, sweat trickled down her neck and waves of exhaustion threatened to buckle her knees.

"You did well," Lear said, hands in his pockets. The hair he'd tucked behind his ears had escaped to frame his face. "And I now know your motivation is based on a need to protect. I can work with that."

Casually, he walked up to the first barrier and laid a palm on it. He didn't jump when it zapped him. The only sign he'd felt something was the clenching of his jaw and the tightening skin around his eyes.

"I'm going to reinforce the barriers with my magic. This way, anyone who tests your boundaries will see my magical signature, which will act as a deterrent and a promise of severe retribution for anyone idiotic enough to attack you."

His magic seeped from his hand, creating a spiderweb around her barrier. "I'd like to infuse this web into every layer. May I?"

"Why?"

"Because I want to ensure the only magical essences anyone can identify are yours and mine. I can sense Elzac's, though faint." Those golden orbs latched onto hers. Lear smiled, baring his teeth ominously. "We wouldn't want anyone to know about Elzac, now would we?"

"No," she breathed, worry crushing her vocal cords. She couldn't be the reason another person close to her was targeted.

31

Power pulsed against her skin in a way Phe'd never felt before, and every part of her was reacting to it. Gooseflesh covered her limbs under the black satin shirt and pants she wore. The hairs at the back of her neck prickled, her stomach clenched, and her limbs felt light and restless.

The entire crater below was packed, unnervingly so. This didn't feel like a simple induction. The weight of thousands of stares landed on her, and she contemplated retreating into the windowless chamber at her back.

Roar cleared his throat behind her, prompting her to move.

Taking a deep breath to steady her nerves, Phe unlocked her fingers from the doorframe and took the first step onto a thin stone path that switchbacked through the throngs of people and ended in the basin of the crater, where large stone pillars had been erected in a circular formation. She took another step, then a third. Her gaze was rooted to the stone path as she descended into the bowl of the crater, her heightened senses aware of every move, every noise around her.

Immediately, the protective barriers she'd repaired moments before this pinged with the force of a swarm of angry wasps. Each time the barriers activated, shocking someone, a jolt of panic zinged through her.

Featherlight touches brushed invasively against the exposed skin of her face, neck. More forceful touches tapped her torso. One went as far as shoving her.

Phe hid her fists in her sleeves and forced her tense shoulders away from her ears. She would not show any weakness.

Dread clogged her lungs. *Why are there so many people here?*

She slowed as she finally neared the stone circle. Raw power pulsated from the pillars, thrumming against her skin. They were more than double her height, and in the middle of each of them was a vertical line of symbols.

As she walked through the perimeter of rocks, a light sensation traced over her and the attacks stopped abruptly.

Within the stone circle were six large pillows on which Kirzia, Orc, Ihrone, and Finian sat. Two more pillows closed the circle. She sat next to Finian, who winked at her.

Dragging in a deep breath to steady her nerves, Phe peered around.

Seas, why did I assume it'd be a private formality?

Her stomach churned with the realization she hadn't questioned the induction at all.

She'd assumed it was an official gathering with the team and maybe an Elder to declare her inducted into the unit. Her mistake glared at her from all sides.

Hadn't Ihrone said something about magic merging this morning?

He had, and she'd been too distracted by her insecurities to question him. Seas.

Phe stiffened and swept a glance around the team. They lounged comfortably on their cushions, expressions and postures calm. Whatever this was, they didn't seem concerned.

Yet it didn't make sense a simple induction—a controversial one at that—would have thousands of attendees. These monsters wouldn't come out unless they scented blood or something about this ceremony piqued their interests. Namely, her.

Phe cleared her throat. "What's happening?" Her voice was sharper than she'd intended.

"Baby girl," Finian crowed, his tone oddly gentle, as if he sensed her mounting alarm. "You're being inducted."

Leave it to Fin to state the obvious. She gripped her thigh tightly, angry with herself for waiting until now to ask for details. "I thought that was paperwork and some sort of small, official ceremony."

"No one told you about this?" Orc asked, his expression morphing from horror to a grimace. He shot a glance at Roar.

"No." Her heart rate accelerated. *Why would Orc be horrified?*

"We didn't get to it," Roar said. His face flashed through several emotions, all ease gone. "I thought this morning you guys would have gone over it with her."

This isn't good. Phe flicked her eyes from one to the other, dread mounting in the pit of her stomach. "What didn't you tell me?"

The telltale vibration in the center of the circle skittered over her, and she barely controlled her flinch. Phe bit the inside of her mouth, hard, and sealed her lips.

Bastion appeared. He was wearing a similar matching satin shirt and pant set to hers, only his was blood red.

"Ihrone," he acknowledged reverently, then turned to Finian. "Finian," he said in the same tone. When his eyes landed on Phe, his reverence drained to scorn, and his eyes slitted. "Gag and restrain her."

What?! She broke out in a cold sweat and her heart ratcheted up, trying to drill through her rib cage. *I didn't do anything.*

An invisible gag forced its way into her mouth and bands slid around her torso, locking her in place.

Rage-infused helplessness seared through her.

A brittle smile took form on Bastion's clean-shaven face. "We don't have time for one of your tantrums. This is happening, whether you like it or not." Dismissing her, he continued on with his solemn greetings.

Phe strained against the bands, stabbing each of her supposed teammates with her glare. Their faces transformed, shuttered to stoic. They sat stiffly impassive as one of them restrained her. Why had she been a fool to lower her guard?

Every single one of them met her gaze, each wordlessly communicating.

Kirzia's silent message seemed to be: *Girl, calm down and get it together.*

Orc's was: *I'm so sorry.*

Ihrone's said: *I didn't realize you didn't know. I'm sorry this is happening to you.*

Finian's was: *Baby Girl, it's gonna be okay. Relax.*

Roar seemed to say: *I'm sorry for the colossal mess up and . . . we'll tell you everything after.*

Phe closed her eyes, swallowing her bitter disgust around the gag. Gads, she despised them. All of them.

"Welcome," Bastion called to the crowd, arms spread in greeting. "Let me introduce you to my Shadow Maiden,

Orphne. I have known her since she was ten years old." From Phe's angle, it looked like he was skewering the crowd with his gaze. "As a Still, she completed extensive training and trials of survival, guided by our seers and under my tutelage.

"You can imagine my shock at discovering she's a powerful magic-born who was bound at birth and discarded." Bastion shook his head, disdain edged his cadence. "Not only was she sentenced to a childhood filled with hardship, but her formative years to master her capabilities were wasted. I plan to personally investigate why this has happened because, over the years, I have come to view her as a daughter."

Phe's stomach cinched harder and bile burst into her throat. *Bastion is appalling.*

The bastard drew in a breath. "It is with great honor that I induct her into Shadow Unit, who has assisted me with honing her skills over the past fourteen years."

Phe closed her eyes against the blast of grief and rage.

"*Astro Atas*," Bastion boomed. Power vibrated with his words, then he quieted his voice to command. "Phe, open your eyes."

Phe kept them shut, unwilling for anyone to see them glistening from the power of her emotions.

Then invisible tendrils pried her eyes open to meet Bastion's. The brittle smile was gone; even his steadfast cold gaze had melted, replaced by a triumphant warmth.

Rending him limb from limb no longer would suffice.

A kaleidoscope of rays erupted from the center of the circle. It spiraled around a blue shield encasing Bastion, then cascaded down, pooling at the ground. The colors were stunning.

It was beautiful.

The wave of colors gushed around them, quickly flooding the space.

When the magic swirled up around her chest, panic clawed Phe's throat. She struggled against the invisible straps, tilting her chin up and clamping her mouth shut. Were they going to drown her in magic?

It was when the magic lapped at the corners of her mouth, the tips of her earlobes, that Bastion ordered, "Release her binds."

The bands and gag immediately vanished as magic engulfed her. She reached for the surface, only to be weighted down by the magic. Her lungs burned with her need for air, and black dots entered her vision.

"Baby girl." Finian's concerned voice warbled in the swell, sounding like he was underwater. Phe connected with his brown gaze, a worried look marring his usual over-the-top confidence. "Breathe. It won't hurt you." He was hovering over the cushion, sitting cross-legged, his hair crazy. Then he added, "I won't let anything hurt you. Breathe."

But you already have.

She fought the burn, the darkness, until her body took over and sucked in a glorious magic-filled breath. Instantly, her heart leveled and the burning disappeared.

Bastion chanted nonsensical words. *"Om sha lum, grata concav."*

The magic tingled, and unlike Tzermel's chair, it was blissful. Soothing. Euphoric. Her limbs felt light, her body relaxed in a way she'd never experienced before.

"That's it, baby girl," came Fin's stifled encouragement, and when their gazes connected again, his face had softened with shades of vulnerability. "You're doing great."

His words, his kindness, came too late and gnashed into

the sucking wound in her chest. She tore her gaze from his and scanned the area.

All of Shadow Unit hovered an inch above their pillows, their expressions varied. Everyone's auras shimmered around them, at first appearing as translucent mirages that then solidified. Bastion stood in a sphere of blue magic, separated from them. He was slowly turning within the circle, elbows at his side and palms open.

Her own aura mesmerized her with its crystal-clear blackness, as Zea had described, and the jagged line of raging fire severing it into halves. Oddly, Phe noticed it represented how she felt, dark, filled with life's dirt and cleaved together by flames of rage. It thrummed as if it was purring.

Tendrils of power extended from each of Shadow Unit's auras, intertwining together.

"*Maagikija*," Bastion thundered. Their magic paused. "*Rato denar comp vestio.*"

Her black tendrils vibrated so strongly, they shook Phe, then burst into a brilliant rainbow color show. The light hold it had on the others' auras became a fierce grasp, and their wisps bulged under the constriction.

Magic welled within her chest, soothing the fractured fragments of her heart.

"*Greoto frenzia mata allo.*"

Her vicious grip on the tendrils eased, though it coated them with her darkness.

The well of magic in Phe's chest bubbled with joy, and tingles of happiness shot all the way to her fingers and toes. The source bubbled over, and her magic playfully reached out and nudged the others' tendrils.

A few of her own wispy-tendrils swirled at the bottom of

her well, clearing some of the debris to expose a slab covering.

"*Zion daskio ukaleska.*"

Her magic scraped at the bottom of her well, its claws catching on the rough, uneven slab, and heaved. It slid an inch.

Those wisps slithered into the crack and disappeared beneath it.

"*Yejito.*"

A wave of panic pummeled her as her magic savagely sunk teeth into the others and dragged them to the pit of her well. It swirled around them, tasting their essences.

What's my magic doing?

Her magic wove the others' tethers around themselves, and then it attacked the slab covering. Phe's breathing shallowed. Their tendrils strained, some threatening to tear. Finally, the cover popped and was thrust to the side as a vast flood of magic gushed from its depths.

"*Umm shevah tenito.*"

Phe's magic released the others, but they didn't let go. Instead, as one, they speared into her magic. Her magic reared back, thrashing in its attempt to shed them.

A ball had wedged itself in Phe's throat, and her stomach recoiled.

When her magic couldn't dislodge them, it traced their individual lines and rammed into each of their magical centers. As her magic smashed in their wells, more anchors appeared and hauled Phe's magic into them.

"*Benuw.*"

Their magical ties throbbed. One, two, three times, then the boundaries of their ties merged. Another swell of euphoria scoured over her, but it did not obliterate the nausea, the sweat trickling down the ladder of her spine, and the electricity bristling every hair on her body.

What have they done?

Eyes squeezed so tightly she saw her own little color show, Phe focused on her breath. She counted to five and opened her eyes. Where there had been a kaleidoscope of colors, there was now a sea of crystal-clear black.

Her magic.

At the surface of the darkness, waves rocked into the stone barrier, their tips golden flames.

"Benuw."

A drain opened around the shield Bastion stood in, and the magic coiled into the earth's depths. The lid at the bottom of her well fell, sealing the abyss of Phe's magic, as the last drops of the earth's magic siphoned away and the channel closed.

It's over, baby girl. Finian's voice brushed past her, and her mind grappled with how she heard him, because his lips hadn't moved.

A tsunami of awareness slammed into her.

Phe hissed, pressing her palms against her eyes and temples, and forced herself to breathe through the pain.

The water separated into individual drops, pinpoints of activity. She identified Shadow Unit, Bastion, Lear, Areya, Commander Elex, Rosea, and a few more of Kyra's guards within the spectators. Each mind omitted a unique signature, and there were thousands. Thousands of minds.

A drummer took position right behind her eyes.

I can sense people's minds. Her nausea curdled.

The musician launched into a set, the rhythm of his drumming vibrating through her skull. She lugged her hands down her face, squinting into the now piercing brightness.

Instinctively, her gaze connected with Roar's.

Seas, it hurts.

His blue eyes captured hers, where concern and resignation and something else wrestled. *Are you okay?* Worry flavored his voice, yet his lips hadn't moved.

His lips hadn't *moved.*

Phe's stomach erupted. Acidity spurted up the back of her throat, and she clamped her lips closed, refusing to vomit, to show weakness in front of these monstrous dragons. She shook her head, as if it could flick Roar from her mind.

Gads, this isn't happening.

The drummer increased his tempo.

Bastion's shield dropped, and his glowing gaze swept the crowd. "Let us now celebrate our newest Elite soldier. Orphne, my Shadow Maiden."

32

Phe stared at herself in the mirror. The dark circles under her eyes were hidden under a layer of foundation. Black charcoal had been applied thickly to her eyelids and extended in a line to her temple, curling inward there, and a deep red lip gloss accentuated her mouth, yet none of that held her eye.

She tilted her head to the left, catching the light in a way that highlighted the silver streak that had appeared in her hair after the induction. That silver streak, off center to her left side, when it had first been pointed out, had frozen her to the depths of her soul, and she'd yet to thaw.

Anala.

The bludgeoning racket in her head had quieted once Roar had jumped her to Areya's, disconnecting her from all the minds that had thrummed painfully into her awareness. Thank the seas a maid had appeared and whisked her into her treehouse and away from Roar, because rage simmered under her skin, and she wasn't certain she could've controlled it.

They're in my head.

The repetitive, intrusive thought wormed its way past the numbness her hair caused and licked across her skin to flare in the hole of her stomach. The restraints, their passivity, and the magical violation of the induction had catapulted Shadow Unit into the churning dark waters of foe.

How could they?

Just as quickly, Phe's anger drained, and numbness returned as she contemplated the silver streak. She'd belonged once. And been loved.

Shadow Unit's tethers tingled in her chest, causing a shudder to rake her. It was invasive. In fact, it was the worst thing she'd experienced since coming to Arias.

Areya's maid, who'd introduced herself as Birin, finished braiding Phe's hair, and she swung in between Phe and the mirror to analyze her work. Birin's light brown gaze was intent, her mouth slightly puckered, as she carefully pulled and tucked hair where she wanted it. The brief moments Birin's fingertips touched, Phe's scalp burned.

"There." Birin sounded satisfied. "Does it aggravate your headache?"

Phe shook her head.

Birin's nimble fingers latched onto Phe's amulet.

Phe yanked her wrist to her chest, cradling it and glaring daggers at Birin. She'd have to pry her cold, dead fingers from it first.

"Okay," Birin said, hands up, and retreated a few steps. "We'll leave it. Come step into the dress."

Still cradling the amulet, Phe stood. Acquiescing was the only way this night would go by any faster. With everything that had happened, she'd forgotten Shadow Unit's alliance was to Bastion and Bastion only.

The induction had been a brutal reminder.

Her throat tightened, remembering how they'd done

nothing—only stared at her—while one of them restrained her.

She'd trusted them. *Ugh.*

Birin had arranged the dress into a puddle on the floor, and Phe stepped into its center. Removing the silk robe around her, Phe drew the dress up.

The top of the dress was a leather corset with hard, crisp lines across the bodice, and leather sweeping over the left shoulder, keeping the right bare. Phe snaked her arm into the left sleeve, admiring the asymmetry of the corset as the right side swept past her waist, encased her right hip, ended in a point mid-thigh that exposed her right leg. The material of the skirt was a black shimmering silk, ending at her ankles.

It reminded her of Jallia. How Phe wished she could speak with her.

"Adjust your breasts," Birin instructed from behind her. Phe did while Birin tugged the corset around until it hugged every curve. "Gosh, this dress is something."

Phe grimly nodded.

Roar's mind popped into existence at the barrier of Areya's property, forewarning her of his arrival. With his entrance, the drummer behind her eyes began another solo set.

Once the induction had ended, she'd been pulverized with an overwhelming awareness of people's minds, alongside with their location. She needed to talk to Lear about this, to find a way to manage the pounding headache it caused.

"Your lady's maid must be ranked as a master tailor, with a specialty in dressmaking," Birin continued as she walked to collect something from a table. "The magic in this corset is remarkable."

"My lady's maid?" Phe propelled the words past the heavy blocks of her lips, twisting to see Birin returning to her. "Magic corset?"

Birin smiled encouragingly. "Yes, I believe her name is Jallia. Isn't she your lady's maid?"

Phe shook her head again. Jallia was officially Kyra's maid, nanny, dressmaker. Jallia had taken it upon herself to include Phe.

"Oh, my apologies." Birin seemed perplexed. "She made this dress, and she enhanced the corset with some sort of protective magic. Here." Birin held an ornate black knife and sheath. "For your right leg."

"Do you know what's happened to her?" Phe asked, bending over to strap the sheath on when a knock sounded at the door. *How did Roar get here so fast?* She inwardly grumbled, yet she knew. Her new awareness had tracked his progress. He'd jogged.

"I have to answer that," Birin said, hustling out. Phe heard Birin greet him.

Phe closed her eyes, hurt rumbling through her body like a rogue wave. She collected her emotions into a package in her heart and crammed them into a dark space, then opened her eyes and straightened.

Roar, dressed in a tuxedo that fit him perfectly, entered the room. He'd slicked his hair back, which darkened the hue of his red. He gave her a cautious smile. His blue eyes scanned her from head to toe, then up again, and even though she was upset with him, a warmth blossomed in her chest.

Birin said something to him and bustled by him to get to Phe's side, blocking his view. "Could you turn for me? One last look before you go."

Phe's toes twirled slowly on the soft rug, resigning

herself to a night of misery. Another full day with no progress toward rescuing Kyra. After the induction ceremony and the new tethers forged in her magic, she was seriously contemplating taking her chances trying to escape again.

Part of her frozen soul wondered if they'd kill her this time, feeling resigned to dying if that's what it took. Another part of her railed against the thought and reminded her there was no one competent to save Kyra. She couldn't give up. Kyra needed her now and afterwards, as her sea sister recovered from her ordeal.

"Shoes!" Birin snapped her fingers and ran into the closet, coming out with sparkling high-heeled death traps.

Phe crossed her arms, pressing her lips into a straight line, and shook her head.

It wasn't that she couldn't wear high heels. It was more of a protective measure. She wasn't sure if she'd be able to stop herself from ripping them off and stabbing Shadow Unit with them. She wasn't sure she'd be able to manage the knife on her thigh, either, but its weight was reassuring and the heels were a nuisance.

"I'd suggest looking for boots," Roar offered while he strode closer to Phe and ducked his head to catch her gaze. *How are you?* he asked in her mind, then said, "You look like you're going to war."

The anger she'd packaged dodged her constraints and burned the back of her throat. Enunciating each word, Phe said, "Get out of my mind."

Roar's face tensed.

"How about these?" Birin called from the closet doorway, shaking a pair of dressy black booties at them.

Phe nodded and walked to Birin to put distance between her and Roar.

"Let's not forget your gloves."

"Thank you." Moments later, fully situated, Phe turned to Roar. "Let's get this night over with." She tapped the glove where her amulet was as she stalked toward him. "You can touch that," she extended her arm, "to jump us."

"As you wish."

Roar jumped them into a private balcony overlooking an astonishingly opulent hallway. An enormous chandelier, made from the vast roots of a tree, dripped sparkling gold crystals and tiny white lights. Its mere presence defied logic.

A mob of minds pummeled into her temple. Her breath caught with the force of it, and she hoped Roar thought she was reacting to the scenery and not the bombardment of pain it caused.

"Phe." Roar had immediately stepped aside. "We're sorry about the miscommunication."

Turning her back to him, Phe gripped the balcony railing tightly and waited for the rush of rage to subside.

"We feel how upset you are. We know you are in pain."

Her lungs seized. It had been terrible enough to have them in her head, speaking to her, but now they felt her emotions too? Her pain? In between the shattering of her heart, fury flared. How could they've done this?

"Sharing this type of connection with a team is . . ." Roar hesitated, and Phe got the impression he was reconsidering his words. ". . . intimate. It literally welds us together, which is why it is only done with our Elite teams. Ihrone and Orc are chomping at the bit to help you."

Phe locked her jaw. Why couldn't they have given her more than three days of being in this forsaken city to induct her? Why hadn't they gotten her consent and explained what the stars they were doing and what the repercussions of it were?

"I don't want help from any of you," Phe whisper-seethed. "Who restrained me?"

He drew in a breath. "I did."

Phe twisted to glare at him and swallowed the bitterness glazing her mouth. *I trusted you.*

Roar flinched.

Phe felt her eyes widen and quickly spun to face the entryway, blocking his view of her.

He heard me.

The realization plummeted the outrage in her belly, and it felt like someone had throat-punched her. Were her thoughts even safe? Had they overheard and felt everything since the induction?

Silence stretched between them as she grappled with her emotions. When they were settled enough for her to trust her voice, she asked in a steely tone, "What's expected tonight?"

"We're expected to mingle, eat a formal dinner, and afterwards, dancing and the real celebrating begins."

"When can I return to Areya's?" She needed an outline for the night, a timetable to help her get through it. Whether it was the discovery of the levels of her mental invasion or the sudden surge in new arrivals, each mind in the area hammered into her awareness, and the tempo of her headache picked up. Her eyes throbbed with the pressure.

"After dinner at the earliest."

"Let's get this over with." Unclenching her fingers, she swiveled to Roar, nodding at him to lead the way.

"One of us needs to be with you at all times." Roar scoured the intimate lines of her face, her eyes, searching pointlessly for emotion. Emotions he wouldn't find because she'd reined them all into the endless pit of darkness within and sealed them.

Phe had a lifetime of practice suppressing emotions. This was old stale cake for her, and she wouldn't allow her emotions to obscure her goal to rescue Kyra.

The stars kept putting one horrible situation after another together to test her, and she would not fail. She'd find a way around it. She had to.

Roar grimly navigated through the third-floor labyrinth, descending them to the lower main levels. Elegant dresses of all colors glided by. Some with billowing skirts extending two to three feet from the person. Others wore tight-fitting dresses that left no curve hidden, and then there were those somewhere in between.

"Pet," someone hissed.

Phe ignored the barb, but noticed Roar's eyes snapped in their direction. His shuttered gaze was gone, supplanted with deadly perception and menacing calculation.

They walked through pockets of flowery perfumed scents with underlining sandalwood musks while Phe examined the links in her magic. Her magic had already tried to remove them when it happened and had failed.

She concentrated on where they connected, how they felt, and pondered if she could somehow smother their connections enough that they wouldn't be able to sense anything from her.

Sounds of raucous laughter and chatter surrounded them, but Phe only felt the tense silence between them as Roar buffered her through the crowd, careful to not touch her.

"Shadow Baby!" Finian hollered from up ahead. "Everyone, get out of my way." The crowd immediately parted, as though he were a king walking through his subjects.

Finian jogged to her in his tuxedo and lifted her off her feet, squeezing. Discomfort erupted at every point their skin connected. In her ear, his breath hot and moist, he said, "Baby girl, I'm so sorry." Just as quickly as he picked her up, he released her.

"Fin," Roar growled.

Phe leaned close to Finian, letting her lips brush his ear, her voice steady and blisteringly crisp. "Do not touch me."

Finian paused and searched her face, and whatever he saw caused his jaw to tighten and his eyes to shutter.

"Don't growl at me." Finian tore his gaze from Phe to spear Roar with it. "You've got incoming, and I think you've only upset her more, so . . . it's my turn with our girl." A wicked smile erupted on his face as Lassandra slipped her arm around Roar's waist and plastered herself to his side.

Fin leaned close to Phe and stage-whispered, "Let's leave these two lovebirds," followed by an exaggerated wink directed at Roar. When he noticed the crowd had surged around them, Finian strong-armed the throng and threateningly glowered a path through it, ensuring no one touched her.

"Shadow Baby, you're killing me," Finian muttered. *What can I do?*

"Severe the connection." Phe watched Finian actively survey the sea of people around them.

"That's never going to happen, baby. It's too . . ." His face scrunched sourly. Phe followed his gaze. A woman with dazzling green eyes, lush blond hair, and features too similar to Kyra arrowed toward them. "Cripes."

Phe's stomach revolted. Was this woman Kyra's mother? The woman who agreed to Bastion's plan and allow her daughter to grow up alone, believing she was dead. "Is that who I think it is?"

"Yes." Finian attempted to dodge the woman. She matched his moves, decreeing, "Finian. Introduce us."

Phe wrapped her hand around the hilt of the knife at her thigh. *This woman willingly abandoned Kyra.*

Finian angled his body in front of Phe's. "Not the time, Thetis."

Phe unsheathed the knife. *This woman sacrificed Kyra.*

Thetis's eyebrows reached for her hairline as she spit back, "Not the time? I've been waiting."

Don't stab her, Finian mind-spoke, then said firmly to Thetis, "You'll just have to wait longer."

Ihrone separated from the crowd and stepped into Thetis's space, head dipped to her ear, lips moving.

"Maybe I should stab you?" Phe asked Fin, fingering the smooth hilt while Finian expertly maneuvered them away from that woman.

"If that'd help you feel better. Go ahead."

She slid the knife into its sheath. She had no intention of helping to relieve him of his guilt.

Lear's and Areya's minds popped into the mix of the throng, and she sensed Commander Elex too. If she could, she'd abscond into the crowd and track Lear. She wouldn't, though. Finian, when he applied himself, never lost a target. Then there was Roar's and Ihrone's lingering presences behind them, with Kirzia and Orc up ahead, if her newfound awareness was right.

It'd be wasted energy, and Phe would not be predictable.

When they reached Kirzia and Orc, Finian announced, rubbing his face, "We're dead to her."

"Phe." Orc's imploring glance skimmed her. Concern radiated off him in waves. "May I help with your headache?"

She scowled a no at Orc.

Of course they knew her head was pounding. They were

in it. It seemed petty to refuse the relief he could give, yet she would accept none of their help.

Let them feel the anguish and pain they caused.

Kirzia's gaze was more calculating and matched the cold deep blue of her ball gown.

"There is no excuse, we know," Ihrone said, coming up. "Retrospectively, we should've told you about the induction process before your trials. Laid it all out for you then. We're so sorry."

Phe let the grim line of her mouth answer for her. Unfortunately, their actions overshadowed their words.

"Phe." Kirzia's tone was icy. "You need to get over this. It's something we've all been through. Our futures were chosen for us when we were toddlers and showed potential, and none of us had a choice in the matter."

Phe straightened, returning a piercing glare, her anger flaring into blue flame. Had Kirzia told her to get over being magically violated?

"Ah, Kirz." Finian's tone tempered a warning within his confusion. "What are you doing?"

"We need to stop sugarcoating things for her." Kirzia crossed her arms, hard angles forming on her face. "None of us had a choice, and this is a privilege."

Phe stared shrewdly at Kirzia. Once the spike in her anger was contained, Phe wondered why this reaction was so common. The "get over it and move on" and "I had to endure it" and the allowance for repetitive, cyclic abuse—because that's what it was. Kirzia had played a part in violating her, and now Kirzia was justifying it.

How would it change the world if, instead of this reaction, there was compassion? Or they ensured no one else went through the same thing?

Phe halted her thoughts. This society was horrid, filled

with all types of ruthless, blood-hungry monsters. It was like wishing for peace.

"Kirz." Ihrone's tone alone sealed Kirzia's next words. "There's a difference. An enormous difference."

"We might never have had a choice in the matter, but we grew up knowing it was our future." Orc's tone was serious. "We all knew what to expect, and we all wanted it."

"La-Sa, I need to talk to my team privately," Roar said from behind Phe, sending shivers of irritation racing down her spine.

Another wave of new arrivals to the celebration sent the drummer behind her left eye off. The intensity of his musical set had Phe blinking at the involuntary wetness it caused.

Stars, I need Lear.

"Kirz, don't make this about you," Roar said, and Kirzia slitted her gaze. "And do you really want to act like your mother?"

Kirzia recoiled as if she'd been slapped. "That's not what I'm doing."

A tether pulsed with undiluted rage, marinated in hurt. *Is this how they feel my emotions?*

Finian coughed. "Isn't it, though?"

"Kirzia, why don't we take a walk?" Ihrone said in his calm way. "There's too much heightened emotion right now."

The anger shifting in the pane of Kirzia's face smoothed over; the transition from rage to outward calm was impressive and scary. "You're right, Ihrone." Kirzia's tone was stiff. "I wouldn't want to risk alienating a team member because of my lack of restraint." She paused. "Or rather, should I say because I *restrained*? Now, if you'll excuse me." Kirzia glided away, the skirt of her blue ball gown fluttering behind her.

Phe blinked. Had Kirzia jabbed at Roar for restraining her?

Finian whistled. "Phe and I are—" he thumbed over his shoulder, "—going to do a quick round." He waved her forward, and they stepped into the throng.

"Can we find Lear?" Phe asked, hoping she sounded nonchalant.

"He's making his way to us," Finian said, his uneasiness deepening. "We," he cleared his throat and rubbed the back of his neck, "heard you wanted to talk to him about your, ah, new capability."

Phe hoped no one noticed how her whole body tensed.

"Until he gets to us, I figured I'd introduce you to a few friends." Finian gave her the saddest smile she'd seen on him yet. "A bunch of them are busting at the seams—literally—to meet you."

"Are you sure that's a good idea?" Orc said from behind them, following closely.

"What?" Finian's pitch was jokingly edgy, yet carried a hint of strain. "They've been warned. They all know I'll kill them if they even think of trying anything with my shadow baby."

"If you say so." Orc didn't seem as confident.

Finian huffed, as if stung, then thundered, "Caath! Man, you look good. Let me introduce my baby girl." The man, Caath, moved as if to kiss Phe's cheek. Finian's hand thudded hard into Caath's chest, and Caath's gaze flicked to Finian's. "Nah, man, you know my rules. Absolutely no touching." All lightness gone, replaced by deadly menace.

"My apologies," Caath said, looking more wary than apologetic. "I forgot. Won't happen again. Orphne, I've been looking forward to meeting you."

Phe pasted on a small smile, one that wouldn't fatigue

her face too much as the night went on, and politely responded, "Nice to meet you, Caath."

Thus began the barrage of introductions that, surprisingly, were light and playful. While Phe mentally tracked Lear's snail's-pace progress to her, she discovered Finian's friends were interesting and varied widely.

It was after Chinga, who was not only a dragon but also a cute, super petite, delicate woman with hooded eyes and straight black hair, introduced herself and began badgering Finian that Phe realized she was grateful to be with Fin.

The conversations were filled with mirth and jokes and laughter and, even though they didn't touch the frozen block of her heart, this was so much better than stilted, over polite conversation.

How badly had her world flipped for her to be glad she was with Finian?

The rest of Shadow Unit had drifted closer to them, creating a loose semi-circle at their backs. Lassandra hovered near Roar, looking like a sexy panther stalking her dinner.

All the while, Phe examined the invasive magical tethers. They reminded her of tree roots, thick and stiff. The image reinforced her resolve. Roots could be dug out. For now, she gathered her magic and created a weight she gently draped across them. She'd apply it slowly, hopefully crushing the tethers without alerting them.

Phe perked up when Commander Elex parted from the crowd, clasping hands with both Finian and Orc, before his curiously heavy hazel gaze landed on Phe. "Lady Orphne, congratulations."

"Commander Elex, please call me Phe." A real curve lifted her lips, and anticipation fluttered her heart at the chance to get information. "It's a pleasure to see you, and I hope you bring news from Oceanid."

He smiled, but it didn't reach his eyes. "It is not very celebratory news."

Orc cleared his throat. "We can tell you about it tomorrow."

"I'd rather hear it from Commander Elex." She gave Orc a crisp smile. "Please, I need to know how the royal family is. Was anyone else taken? Hurt?"

Commander Elex's gaze shot to Orc's, as if silently seeking his approval to tell her. Phe caught Orc's slight head nod in her periphery. "The royal family came out unscathed from the event," Elex said. "There were others hurt, but none were taken. There were two fatalities caused by the crowd stampeding for the exit."

"Who?" Phe hoped she didn't know them.

"Dorisann Cassyon and Sigeric Bilberry."

"I knew Sigeric." Phe nodded solemnly. "May their souls be at peace." She paused, letting the weight of her condolences set. "What was the reaction to Kyra's abduction? To magic?"

Commander Elex's gaze swung to Orc again. "Many people didn't see her abduction."

"General Bastion, the royal family, and Parliament agreed to not release information about her abduction, though rumors are flying around with the intensity of the flu," Orc answered instead.

"Oceanid is up in arms about you, about Drykz Forest moving closer overnight, about Kyra's supposed seclusion and the attack at the ball," Commander Elex listed.

"Drykz Forest moved?" Incredulity raised Phe's voice an octave.

"The night of the ball," Commander Elex confirmed.

"There was so much going on the night we brought you to Arias, I'm not sure if you knew the forest attacked." Phe didn't respond to Orc's unasked question. "Because the forest's magic is contained within it, to attack, the forest had to grow around us. We're unsure why it attacked. It's never grown, if you will, since it became corrupted, let alone executed an attack. The consensus is it went after your magic."

Oh seas, people must be petrified. "Are people able to cross it?"

If Drykz Forest became impassable, then Xafarians would be trapped. The only port in all of Xafara was Oceanid. The rest of the island's edges were sheer insurmountable cliffs.

"It's traversable." Commander Elex shrugged. "But people are leery."

"I would be," Phe said. "Have you heard if the royal family has released an opinion of," she swallowed, suddenly nervous, "me?"

Commander Elex's face softened. "Yes. They are claiming you saved Princess Attiva." The hand that had reached into her chest and vise-gripped her heart released. Relief weakened her knees. She hadn't realized how much their support meant to her.

"Velimir is a problem." Commander Elex scanned the crowd, his eyes catching on someone. "The rumors he's spreading about you are rancid." Commander Elex's eyes lighted and a genuine smile curved his features, then he turned back to Phe, his grin dimming. "You know how many already view you."

A man stepped out of the crowd, exclaiming, "Elex!" He embraced him in a huge hug, heartily slapping his back. "What a surprise."

"Slatar, give me one moment." Commander Elex stated and leaned around the man. "Lady Orphne, again, congratulations on your induction and, please, when we meet again, call me Elex." With those words, both men melded into the crowd.

Phe twisted to Orc. "Why didn't you want him to tell me?"

Orc calmly met her gaze. "It wasn't that I didn't want him to tell you. It's because you've had three days packed with information and are already really upset, I wasn't sure if hearing news of Oceanid would upset you more."

Phe took a steadying breath in. "Don't withhold information from me because you think I can't handle it or are trying to buffer my reactions. I am the only one who can judge that. Is there any more news?"

"It won't happen again." Contriteness settled in Orc's eyes.

A woman with fiery red hair sidled up to Orc, distracting him. Her blue eyes twinkled, and she gave him an impish smile, which only highlighted her delicate features, button nose, and freckles—like constellations in the night sky— dotting her cheeks.

Finian shouldered Orc to the side and swept her into a hug, lifting her off the ground, and shaking her like a rag doll, while saying, "Asssshhhhhh."

"Fin," Ash whined, even though she looked a combination of delighted and unimpressed. "Put me down, you beast. Mother's around, and I don't want to get her started."

Finian dropped her. "No one wants that."

"Plus," Ash swiveled to stare at Phe, a mischievous smile alighting her lips. "I need to meet my new best friend."

Finian slung his arm around Ash's shoulders. "You will not corrupt my baby girl."

"Oh, hush." Ash waved Finian off. "I'd do no such thing." Yet the giddiness in her voice and the sparkle in her eye seemed to contradict her words.

"Ash." Warmth infused Orc's tone, and he bent forward to peck her cheek with a chaste kiss.

"Where's Rus?" Ash mumbled into his cheek.

"He's around somewhere." Rus, Phe knew, was Orc's long-time partner. She'd never met him, though. "Phe, this is Roar's sister, Ash. Ash, this is Phe. As I'm sure you'll find out soon enough, when this girl sets her mind on something, she is unstoppable, so we'll finish what we were talking about tomorrow."

"I'm fascinated by you and enraptured with getting to know you." Ash steepled her fingers and covered her mouth, exuding unrestrained joy. "I've heard so much about you."

Lassandra inched to Ash's side.

The smile Phe barely held wilted. What had they told her?

Ash dimmed her beam. "All good stories," she assured.

Phe mustered a wan smile. "I've heard stories about you, too."

Ash planted her hands on her hips, her golden gown fluttering with her movements. "Did they tell you about the *wand* incident?" Her eyes flared red for a moment, and accusation hugged each word.

"The wand incident?" Lassandra repeated, confused.

"They did." Phe cracked a slight smile because the story had been ridiculously ludicrous.

"That—" Ash's voice rose, "—was supposed to be a secret!" Crossing her arms, she glared around Phe at each team member, her glare staying a tad longer on Roar.

"Ash, calm your flame," Roar lightly said from over Phe's shoulder. "Your secret's safe."

"Yeah, until you announced it," Kirzia added. "Now everyone is curious to know."

Ash speared Kirzia with a look. "And you won't tell them because you all took oaths. Only the team and Rus know."

Ihrone rationally explained, "Phe's part of the team."

"And she hasn't told a soul about it. Right, Phe?" Finian asked.

Phe compressed her lips and made the motions of locking and throwing away a key.

Ash humphed at them and refocused on Phe, letting her fake irritation go. "It wasn't one of my finer moments. But it's hilarious, isn't it?"

"Yes."

"Ash? What are you talking about?" Lassandra questioned.

"La-Sa, it's one you don't know. *Thankfully,*" Ash loudly proclaimed.

"Ash." Lassandra's voice was low. "Aren't you upset he gave her access to his place and not you?"

A smirk swept hold of Ash's mouth. "Oh no. Are you kidding me? He'd never give me access." Mischievousness twinkled in Ash's eyes. "I'm elated he's given Phe access. Do you know what this means?"

"No," La-Sa grumpily stated.

Ash'll want me to get her into Roar's place.

"He *trusts* her." Ash sucked in her breath dramatically, as if the idea was outlandish.

Lassandra blinked, her face scrunching sourly.

Lear's mind was within feet of Phe. Even though a part of her was morbidly curious about what else Ash would do —the team hadn't exaggerated in their description of her— Phe wrenched her gaze from Ash to devour the crowd. She needed Lear more.

Their gazes connected first, then he separated from the throng, murmuring to the sensuous dark-skinned beauty at his side without breaking eye contact with Phe. The woman smiled, a mix of intimacy and confidence and ease, and her gaze skimmed over Phe as she walked away.

"Phe?" Ash's voice had lilted, and Phe got the impression Ash had asked her something she hadn't heard.

Phe flicked her gaze to Ash. "I'm sorry, what did you ask?"

Before Ash could respond, Lear stepped up to them. "Ash, I'm sorry, your question will have to wait. My mentee and I need to talk." Lear stuffed his hands in his pockets.

"Hm." Ash smushed her lips together, fixating Lear in a scorching gaze. "Nice to see you too, Lear. It's been a long time, but please don't let me or proper manners get in the way of your work." Ash turned, wiping her irritated expression from her face. "It's okay Phe, I'll look for you after dinner."

Lear and Phe both watched Ash retreat and link arms with another man, cozying up to his side. With a sigh, Lear asked. "Do we need privacy?"

"They already know," Phe said glumly.

"Hm." Lear's eyes narrowed a smidge. "Why don't we find our seats and talk?" He then mind-spoke, *"Is that okay?"*

"Can the team hear us?" she responded telepathically, outwardly nodding.

"No. I won't let them eavesdrop."

"That's how they learned I wanted to speak to you. They're in my mind." Phe paced Lear and dove right in.

"I imagine you're more likely broadcasting your thoughts and emotions to them. It's common for us telepaths to do, and since you've bonded with the unit, it makes sense you don't know the boundaries."

Phe side-eyed him. Her vision blurred slightly from her headache, not at all happy with his answer. *"How do I stop?"*

"You need to create boundaries."

Why did this conversation suddenly remind her of Elzac? He'd often harped about boundaries. *"How do I create boundaries? They feel my emotions, hear my thoughts."*

"I have no direct experience with this. I'd suggest asking your team. But, you can try imagining a specific set of barriers around their tethers."

She instantly encased each connection and then infused her magic into the barrier to keep them out of her mind. It was hard to not notice how quickly she'd done what he'd suggested, which only confirmed what he and the others had said. Her need to protect motivated and activated her magic. If this had been anything other than protecting her inner thoughts and feelings and past, she'd likely still be struggling. *"Hopefully that will work."*

"We'll see, and if not, Ihrone I'm sure can easily guide you." Phe felt Lear's gaze curiously brush her. *"Why haven't you asked them?"*

Her suddenly dry mouth had her switch topics. *"I can sense every mind in this room, in the building, and those who are lingering outside. My head is pounding and gets worse every time someone new arrives. Can you help?"*

"I'll see what I can do. Would you hold my hand?" He offered her his open palm. *"The contact will allow me to assess what's going on and hopefully to funnel the pressure out."*

Phe slipped her gloved hand into Lear's, and they continued walking as if this was nothing. Yet it wasn't. Besides the lack of discomfort, which she attributed to the raging headache threatening to level her head, this was the first time she'd walked hand-in-hand with someone other than Kyra, causing her heart to ache. Gads, she missed her sea sister.

"I'm astonished you're standing and coherent," Lear stated grimly. *"I'm going to join with your capability and release this build up."* Phe didn't care what he did as long as there was relief.

The only sensation she felt was akin to light pokes to what seemed like her pocket of built-up magic, which left her imagining her magic was like an angry pus-filled cyst Lear had pierced, releasing the pressure inside her as his magic latched onto the opening and sucked. When he was satisfied with its drainage, he flushed the cyst with his magic.

The relief was bliss.

They entered a massive room filled with round tables. The centerpieces were glazed pottery bowls filled with small rocks and emitted orange-red flames that flickered a foot into the air.

"I have an immense pain tolerance, I'm told."

"I'd concur." He squeezed her hand, his mind-speak voice becoming serious. *"Next time, tell me it's urgent. I took my time getting to you because I thought it was only to talk about a new capability."*

"I don't know how to mind-speak to you."

"We'll fix that tomorrow morning. If your brain didn't need time to heal, I'd show you now. I plan to be at Areya's early for our lesson." Phe peeked at him. Lear didn't notice, too intent on moving around the crowd and tables. *"With your new awareness, do you recognize any minds in the crowd? Or do you only pick up on the minds?"*

"I can sense people I know. I felt you and Areya and a few others, and I tracked your progress through the crowd to me."

The awareness hadn't dissolved. It lingered, pain-free, in her mental periphery.

Lear guided her up the stairs to a platform, where a single long rectangular table overlooked the room. Bastion stood at the opposite end of the table, a hand on a seat.

"Which implies you could have sought me out. Why didn't you?"

"Shadow Unit's being really," she searched for an innocuous word, *"protective."* Phe stopped at the end seat, releasing Lear's hand to pull the seat out. She'd sit as far from the bastard as possible.

"Sorry, Phe, that's my seat," Kirzia interjected with her kindest tone from behind. "You're next to General Bastion."

Phe's gaze swept over Kirzia and then the rest of the unit, who were waiting either on or at the bottom of the steps. Roar gave Phe a quick chin dip, Finian gave her an encouraging smile, Orc's left eye twitched, and Ihrone's solemn gray eyes met hers.

Flipping bullspit stars. Drawing in one of her steadying I-can-survive-anything breaths, Phe unfurled her fingers.

"You don't like the general?" Lear asked, startled, and continued on with her to Bastion's side.

Phe grunted noncommittally, eyeing the said monster, who was laughing.

Lear pulled the chair out for her, then said out loud, "I'd suggest you retire after dinner to rest." Lear's gaze locked on to someone over her shoulder. "We're training early in the morning."

Phe slid into the seat and gazed across the spectacular ballroom. Roar sat in the chair to her right and Ihrone next to him. She refused to look at them. She shook out her napkin and watched the crowd take their seats as if on cue.

Bastion ended his discussion and pivoted to face all the

upturned faces staring at them. Phe felt his gaze settle on her, and she found the silverware extremely intriguing.

When she didn't acknowledge him, he leaned forward and lifted a flute filled with a bubbly golden beverage. The room mimicked him. "Let us eat and celebrate with our newest Elite soldier, my Shadow Maiden."

Phe fingered the hilt of the knife and watched the room salute her. She met the sea of gazes, defiantly not lifting her own flute.

Bastion leaned over her shoulder and tapped the flute she'd refused to lift. "Seems someone's in a mood."

Would stabbing him make me feel better?

Servers immediately entered the room with ladened trays, drawing her focus. She knew Bastion didn't feel an ounce of remorse for what he'd done.

She ducked to the side to let the server place a plate in front of her. What really stayed her hand was Grum. He had used violence excessively. She detested using violence for anything other than a singular purpose, like protecting Kyra. She would not stoop to Grum's level.

"I've heard you are not adjusting to the induction well," Bastion mentioned, pulling his napkin across his lap, completely unaware of how close he was to having a knife protruding from his thigh.

She stared at the plate in front of her. A single black, circular, rice-looking thing with orange sauce zigzagging through the middle was dead center. She selected a fork, deciding her best option was to ignore the bastard.

"I also heard about your new ability," Bastion continued with his one-sided dialogue. "It's a phenomenal tactical and offensive capability, and I'm very pleased with your range."

She raised a small forkful and sniffed, smelling only a

spicy sauce. She cautiously nibbled, and it dissolved in a delicious blend of spicy garlic, rice, and . . . fish.

Commander Elex's mind spiked. Phe flicked her gaze to him and watched him jog toward them.

"Interesting," Bastion murmured, delicately dabbing the corner of his mouth with his napkin. "You can sense emotional spikes too."

Commander Elex dipped close to Bastion's ear and rapidly whispered, "Djall's attacked Oceanid. House Nereid is calling for assistance."

His words ricocheted in Phe's mind. *House Nereid is under attack.* Phe stared at Bastion wide-eyed. Their gazes locked, his full of predatory calculation. His jaw flexed, pulling taut his scar.

What is he going to do?

He broke eye contact and placed his napkin on the table, the scraping of his chair too loud as he stood.

"Soldiers, gear up," Bastion announced. "We're going to battle. Prepare your steeds. All commanders in my office now." With that, he disappeared.

Phe gazed at the space Bastion had occupied. Relief winnowed through her. Oceanid was not capable of fighting magic-borns. They needed General Bastion's magic-born army.

Stars, what about the royals? Her heart thundered in her constricting chest. Gads, would they even let her fight?

Roar stood. "Ihrone, take Phe, ensure she's prepared, just in case."

33

The scent of peppery leather infused with green filled Phe's senses, followed by a chorus of neighing. The stables had barely materialized when Ihrone released her arm and strode from her toward the line of horses. Horses she recognized.

Edva—her steadfast, feisty mare—stood fully tacked and waiting for her next to Niall, Roar's stallion, and the rest of Shadow Unit's rides. Phe glanced down the line of horses and soldiers, mounted and waiting for orders, before hustling toward Edva.

Her anger had simmered down, replaced by anxiety. It thrummed so intensely through her veins, it caused pangs in her fingertips.

Worry for the royals—and for Oceanid—was at the fore-front of her thoughts. Were they safe? Was Djall hunting them? Had he taken them already? Were they too late? At the back of her mind was how close she'd be to Drykz Forest and Elzac—if she was allowed to fight.

"Edva," Phe called, burying her nose into Edva's neck and inhaling her musky-sweetness.

Edva whined and leaned into Phe.

"Hey, baby. I missed you," Phe muttered into Edva's side.

Edva snorted a *hello-I-maybe-sorta-missed-you-too*.

Phe withheld her smile at Edva's attitude and straightened to check her tacking. "Oceanid is under attack." She skimmed the blanket and checked the girth and then the breastplate, continuing on. "I don't know if they'll send us. Bastion's being a bastard."

Edva huffed, as if to say, *when is he not?* Then she twisted and bit into Phe's silky gown.

"I *know*," Phe said ruefully, moving to Edva's head to gaze into her eyes. "Ihrone jumped us to his place . . . but none of my stuff was there." Phe shrugged. At this point, it wouldn't matter to her if she was dressed in this gown and weaponless, as long as she went.

Edva nuzzled her.

Phe trailed her fingers along Edva's neck, briefly recalling her scales before clamping the thought down. It didn't matter that ever since she'd applied the pressure to the team's tethers she hadn't heard from them. She didn't know if she was somehow broadcasting all her thoughts to them still.

Anger bubbled in the pit of her stomach at the reminder of what they'd done.

"Phe!" Ihrone called.

Swiveling toward his voice, she spotted Ihrone—weapons covered every available space on his black-clothed body—and Birin with a bulging backpack. The hilts of her twins jutted out of it. More of her chest opened with hope as she jogged over.

"Birin, thank you!" The moment the pack was in her hands, she ripped into it.

"You're welcome," Birin said and vanished.

Phe's weapons were jammed on top. She rummaged past them until she felt a bundle of fabric at the bottom. Depositing the bag on the ground, she shook out the wad to discover black pants. Uncaring who watched, she toed off her shoes and slid the pants on.

"You're changing here?" Incredibility hung on Ihrone's words.

Unabashedly, Phe met his gaze and grunted yes. She wasn't going to waste time finding a private changing room. Who knew when the others would arrive? What if their orders were to leave her? There was no way she would risk them leaving without having to look in her eyes.

She looked at Ihrone. "Does this mean I'm going?"

"I don't know." Ihrone leveled a warning stare at the soldiers near them, who quickly averted their eyes and snapped back to getting ready.

Phe dumped the contents of the bag on the ground, searching through her knives for a shirt and a bandeau. No other bundles of fabric appeared. Her stomach sank. Birin hadn't packed her a shirt, bandeau, or combat boots.

She exhaled her frustration. *At least I have pants and weapons.* Phe slid her booties back on, grateful to have worn them. Then she plucked the closest blade—a thigh knife—unsheathed it and hacked into the dress at the seam of the corset.

"What are you doing?" Ihrone asked, snapping his gaze to her.

Phe met his gaze. "There's no shirt."

"Can you breathe in that?"

"Jallia makes these corsets breathable somehow." Phe returned her attention to the gown, twisting to get the back.

With a sigh, Ihrone strode over. "I'll get it." Phe refrained from telling him she could do it, opting to hold herself still as he sliced the remainder of the gown off.

"Thank you." She set about strapping her weapons to her. As she slipped her twins over her shoulders, Orc, Kirzia, Finian, and Roar appeared. They, too, were dressed for war. They all stopped and stared at her.

Uncomfortable, Phe scowled.

"Phe," Kirzia's no-sass, all-business voice whipped. "What're you wearing?"

"I had Areya's servant pack Phe's bag," Ihrone answered over Phe's grunt. "Birin forgot a few items."

Explosive laughter erupted from Finian, bending him at the waist.

Phe did *not* appreciate it.

Orc slapped Finian's curved spine. "Stop, it's not funny."

"Sir," Kirzia addressed Roar, not bothering to look at him, "look at her. This is just another reason she shouldn't come."

"I'll be—" Phe startled as Lear, mounted on a horse, materialized. Her heart catapulted into her mouth, not expecting that to appear out of thin air. "—Seas, Lear!"

"Sorry, Phe." At least he had the decency not to comment on her outfit.

"Kirzia, you heard the General's orders," Roar stated, walking toward his horse.

Tension gathered. "We heard the general," Orc said, checking his tacking, "but I don't like it either. It's like dangling candy in front of Djall. This is too much of a risk."

"I'm not worried about that," Kirzia said with derision. "She's going to try to escape."

"You heard General Bastion. It is our responsibility to make sure she doesn't escape," Roar said, his voice muffled as he bent to check his tacking.

Bastion's allowing me to go!

Phe's heart broke out into a full-out spastic dance but settled as she realized the implications of her plans: Shadow Unit would be punished. Gratefully, she noted how Roar didn't ask her if she would attempt to escape, probably to not put her in a position of having to lie to them. Phe preferred not to lie, but she would if it meant a shot at rescuing Kyra.

"Oh, baby girl," Finian, said through his laughter. "Your outfit alone will slay everyone." He wiped at his face, obviously not attending the conversation. Was he laughing so hard, he was *crying*?

I'm going to kill him.

"Fin . . ." Kirzia warned, unimpressed.

"Mount up," Roar said, getting on Niall. "Portal's open, and General Bastion wants us at the front of the second wave. Phe, you're with me. Your orders are to find the royal family. General Bastion assured us you are intimately familiar with the royal palace and its grounds and believes with your new ability, you'll be able to lead this rescue mission."

"He wants me to *lead*?" Surprise and uncertainty ejected her irritation. She didn't want the responsibility of leading Shadow Unit for so many reasons. Top most was that commanders wouldn't abandon their soldiers, nor would they put them at risk unnecessarily—which is what her plan would do.

Yet, simultaneously, it brought relief. No matter what, she had planned to ensure the royal family was safe, and this way—with her new capability and her intimate knowledge of the grounds—she could do it faster.

She gritted her teeth in frustration, feeling the squeeze of life and comparing herself to that bullspit rock again.

"Technically, no," Roar said, adjusting in his saddle. "*Lead* in the sense that you will guide us through the fastest, safest route to the royal family, just like you've practiced in training with us."

"And I am here to help you," Lear added from behind. *How's your head?*

"Afterwards, you and Lear will accompany the royal family to Arias and help settle them," Roar finished.

Manageable. "If we're returning, what are the rest of you doing?" Phe asked as she quickly untethered and mounted Edva.

"We'll be assigned a new set of orders once the royals are in Arias." Roar turned to stare at her, then he glared accusingly at Lear. "Whatever you did to block us, undo it. We need to be able to telepathically communicate."

Phe bit her lip. Roar just confirmed she'd muted their connections, gifting her a rush of excitement. There *was* a way to keep them out of her head. She must have taken too long to respond because Roar leaned closer to her and said in his steely commander's voice, "Open your telepathic lines of communication."

Phe's hand tightened around Edva's reins. Gads, she didn't want them in her head, but was she willing to risk their lives because of it?

Begrudgingly, Phe dropped the weights that covered their tethers. She wouldn't let her dislike of them invading her mind compromise their well-being. *"Better?"*

"Much. Thank you." Roar re-positioned himself and urged Niall into a trot.

Matching his pace, Phe was surprised when they turned a corner. This road was double or triple the size of where they'd come from, and it was filled with soldiers and horses moving in units. Within seconds, soldiers halted—on both sides—to let them in.

Roar nodded solemnly to the soldiers who'd stopped as they passed. He led their unit onto a massive field where the air vibrated. Phe counted five mammoth portals, each larger than the size of a house, breaking the sky.

Fire ringed the outer layer of the portals, their inner circles showcasing a smooth surface that displayed a night sky broken by bolts of lightning and rolling clouds. The surface of the portal shimmered as a battalion of soldiers galloped through.

High seas.

They fell into line, trotting quickly toward the pulsating fissure.

"We're coming in under pressure," Roar said, *"Orc, shield us. Lear, hide our signatures."*

A duo of "dones" responded.

Phe's heart raced in her throat.

The air thrummed, pushing against her skin. She couldn't see past the lines of soldiers ahead of them.

They broke into a gallop.

Edva kept pace with Niall, unperturbed by the magical, pulsing door that had ripped the sky open. Hooves pounded the field.

Right before Phe plunged through the suctioning wash of magic that would send her from Arias into Oceanid, her heart steadied itself, and a wave of calm precision flowed. The anticipation of fighting—of tapping into the untamed wildness within her that called on her shadows—smothered her fears and sharpened her senses. In that moment, her mysterious past was forgotten. All that mattered was what came after—the fighting, the training, the surviving. She had been born—or rather, reborn—to do this.

Salty sea air greeted her.

Oceanid.

The battalion in front of them broke into two, surrounding a group of Djall's men directly ahead and engaging them. Immediately, tainted minds pressed against her mind's eye. She could sense groups of them clustered throughout the property, the largest at the portal.

It took Phe a moment to grasp where they were on the palace grounds, but once she knew, she veered her team to the right. Hard. She stretched her senses, scouting for the royal family. They were in the palace. A group of Djall's possessed split from the fight with the battalion to pursue them.

"I'm taking us to the servants' entrance on the south wing," Phe told them, reveling in the wind in her face and her braid thrashing into her.

"Incoming, rear," Finian stated.

"I count twenty, Phe?" Lear said.

"Same," Phe replied, considering their options. They were on a massive stretch of lawn, which they could take all the way to the palace, but it would allow whoever was chasing them to follow on their heels, taking away the opportunity to enter the palace undetected.

The only other option was to go through the palace's garden labyrinth. Its hedges were twenty feet high and would obscure them. The problem with it was the sharp turns, the narrow passages—they'd have to slow down dramatically, and they'd still have these people at their heels.

"Labyrinth," Roar interrupted her thought.

"It'd put us at more risk," Phe countered.

Something hit their shield, rippling it.

"Labyrinth," Roar commanded. *"Let me worry about that."*

Phe redirected Edva, hoping Roar realized how close their pursuers were.

"*Yeah, baby girl!*" Finian hollered. "*Lead us through the maze!*"

Phe reined in Edva and took the sharp turn through the maze entrance, forcing the other horses to bunch up behind her. This was such a bad idea.

"*Any possessed in here?*" Roar asked.

"*None.*"

Once Roar was in the maze, he sent out, "*Orc, enter the maze last. Let me know when you do and drop the shield around Phe and I. Got it?*"

"*Yes, sir.*"

Phe took another swift turn. This aisle of the labyrinth was as long as a hallway, allowing her to pick up speed. It was short lived, though; she turned and maneuvered them down another, shorter section.

"*Sir, I'm in. I've dropped the shield around you.*"

The next second, the ground shook.

Hedges burst in all directions, expanding around them, blocking the path behind them, covering them in a murky twilight of towering hedges.

"*Seas, was that one of you?*" Phe asked.

"*Prodigy boy,*" Finian responded.

"*Orc, shield us. Phe, get us out of here,*" Roar commanded. "*Djall will not ignore what I just did.*"

The tainted minds following them all stopped. "*What did you just do?*" Phe asked.

"*Sealed all the entrances, trapped those following us, and blocked our ariel view,*" Roar replied.

They lapsed into silence as Phe led them, turn after turn, through the maze. When they neared the exit, she said. "*Our exit is ahead. It's clear. Roar will you open it?*"

The hedges writhed around her, and up head, they split apart.

"Djall has a small group of people running the length of the maze. They'll see us when we head to the palace." Phe and Roar burst onto the lawn.

Roar settled at her side. Niall shook his mane, and Edva edged closer to him—she had a soft spot for Niall; Phe lightly brushed against Roar's leg. Behind them, the rest of Shadow unit was surging out of the maze. Roar's shuttered gaze softened a smidgen, just enough to warm the glacial pools of his eyes. *"You're doing well,"* he said and then reined Niall in to drop behind her.

Warmth crept into her chest. She didn't need his approval, but it was nice to receive. Especially considering the circumstances. Though she'd been in countless solo fights through the years as an assassin, in her training with Bastion and Shadow Unit, and with Fyerir Fighting, she'd never been in a full-scale battle—much less a magical one.

"Sir," Ihrone said, as he and the team caught up to them. *"If you open up several new entryways along their route, it could distract them."*

"Orc, drop the shield." Roar ordered.

"Dropped, sir."

She heard hedges wrench themselves apart and signalled Edva to gallop.

"Shield up." Roar commanded as Niall took his place behind Edva. *"Let's go,"*

The palace wasn't far, and its looming presence shadowed them as their steeds raced alongside it. Phe leaned into Edva's sweating neck, her mane sticking to Phe's cheek. Hard scales had replaced her softness and covered her musky-sweet smell. It changed the feel of Edva's muscles rippling under Phe's touch. "Be safe, Edva."

To the team, she said. *I'm going to jump.* Without waiting for a response, she leaned forward, released her reins and feet from the stirrups, gripped her saddle as she flung her leg over it, and vaulted. The moment her feet hit the ground, she bolted through a rain of dirt—as Edva shot off without her—to the palace.

Behind her, she heard the others hit the ground.

Her senses stretched past the imposing walls of the palace, resolve settling like a weight around her shoulders as she searched for the familiar minds of the royal family. Easily finding them, she mentally zinged through the many routes they could take to get them, dismissing each quickly as she factored in the location of the tainted minds, until it was clear there was only one path.

Her lungs burned as she sprinted with steadfast focus. She called out to Roar, knowing he'd hear her. "I have a plan."

34

Phe flattened herself into the hard outer wall of the royal palace. The leather sheaths of her twins sheltered some of her exposed back from the rough wood. Where their protection ended, the wall dug into her.

Bullspit corset dresses.

Phe wrapped her hand around a cool metal doorknob. Her gaze swept from the end line of Shadow Unit to Lear, landing on Roar, who was at her shoulder. She waited for his cue to open the door.

"How many possessed on the other side?" Roar asked, leaning close to her.

"None." Her awareness canvased the empty hallway. The only sign servants were nearby, hiding, were the panicked minds Phe sensed. It hurt her to abandon them as if they were not worth saving.

"Go."

Phe slid the door open. Moving on silent feet, she ushered Shadow Unit and Lear into a linen closet four doors down. Immediately, she began searching the shelving wall for the hidden latch that would open the secret passageways, while the rest of the team crammed into the space.

"Phe, I'm going to connect with your ability to see minds now. I need to sense and see what you do," Lear said, creeping in between her and Roar.

Phe swiveled from her search of the shelving to face him. *"Touch?"*

"Yes. And I have to warn you. If I need to draw on your magic, it will hurt."

She nodded, and offered a hand.

Instead of clasping her hand, as they had before, Lear cupped her face, sending shards of discomfort through her. His golden eyes glowed inches from hers. This time, she felt him glide into her mind and merge into wisps of her magic.

"Remember," Kirzia said, intruding in their moment, *"your orders are to recover the royals, and then both of you will escort them to Arias."*

"We haven't forgotten," Lear coolly replied, dropping his hands. *"We're good."*

Phe returned her attention to fiddling with the shelving. She missed the deceptive latch on her first two searches and narrowed her attention to the feel of her fingers skimming the porous surface. Finding the latch, she pressed it and tugged the hidden door open, and the musky, stale, cold air of the palace's passageways hit her.

She stepped aside. *"Go in. I have to close it a certain way."*

While everyone filed past, Phe stretched her awareness beyond the servants' minds, locking onto the familiar minds of the royal family again. *"Princess Attiva and Prince Fynn are in the south wing passages with us. If we rush, we'll quickly intercept them before they get to the underground tunnels."*

Then to Lear, Phe added. *"The minds Djall possesses feel tainted, or dark. Is that normal?"*

"*Yes,*" came Lear's smooth response.

"*What about the king and queen?*" Ihrone probed.

"*They are in the east wing, second floor, in a safe room off the blue library. They have a lot of Djall's minions around them.*"

"*Why isn't it connected to the passages?*" Finian rhetorically asked.

Why is the sky blue? Phe thought, not bothering to answer him, and took the lead with Roar at her back. "*Ready?*"

"*Phe, I'm going to resuppress our magical signatures, pay attention.*" Lear said. He gathered their collective magic and created a thick blanket, which he then settled around them. The brightness of their minds faded under its weight. Phe couldn't help noticing the similarity in what he did with what she instinctively did with her imaginary cloak.

Phe tucked that knowledge away.

"*Lead,*" Roar commanded.

She jogged, guiding them through the hidden labyrinth throughout the palace. Her strategy was to get to the underground tunnel entrance first, where they would secure it. Then, she would convince the royal siblings to join them in rescuing their parents and going to Arias.

Once they were past the servants' section, she could sense more tainted minds traveling the palace's open hallways. Each time they neared a group, Phe slowed, and as they got closer and closer to the tunnel entrances, there were more and more tainted minds.

A cluster of Djall's minions were wandering in the room next to them, raising Phe's hackles.

The hidden passageways had converged ahead and, because they'd had to slow down, the royal party was in front of them. "*It may be best for you to all hang back a little while I talk to them,*" Phe mind-spoke as she crept forward.

"We have," she double checked her counting, *"fifteen minds in the room next to us. If I approach the royals alone, they may not attack and tip off Djall. Plus, with my relationship with them, they're more likely to listen."*

"Why not mind-speak to them?" Lear asked.

"Stills wouldn't react well to someone popping into their head." Ihrone said.

"You can say that again," Finian mind-muttered.

"We'll give you a little space," Roar conceded.

"I think you'll lose them the moment they see what you're wearing." Humor laced Finian's telepathic voice.

Phe rolled her eyes and quickened her pace.

When she was several feet ahead of them, she walked through a mushy resistance.

Alarm spiked in Orc's mind. *"Phe just walked through my shield."*

"Phe, stop," Roar commanded.

"Just a little more space." She increased her pace.

"Phe." Roar's voice hardened.

She didn't respond, knowing full well she was disobeying her commander. This was why she worked alone: there was no one to interfere with what she knew she had to do. Especially with the only people who hadn't betrayed her in the last three days. Unlike her team.

"She walked through mine this morning, too," Kirzia stated grumpily. *"I told you, we shouldn't have brought her."*

"Disobeying the general is not an option," Ihrone countered.

Phe ignored them, speeding up. She got close to the royals' rear guard before breaking the silence with a whisper. "Prince Fynn, Princess Attiva, it's Phe."

Instantaneously, the rear guard swiveled, sword jabbing toward her.

Phe shuffled backwards and continued to whisper, "Stop.

I mean you no harm, but on the other side of this wall are fifteen people who do." Palms open in surrender, she motioned to keep quiet.

"Phe?" Princess Attiva's voice wavered and was shushed by someone.

One of the mindless minions tapped on the wall by Phe's shoulder, as if testing to see if the wall was hollow.

"Shhh." Phe put a finger to her mouth and slowly pivoted to the wall, the hair on her nape standing up.

"I've found you," Djall's minion breathed through the wall. The air filled with crackling tension.

"Incoming!"

"Phe, shield!"

The wall blasted inward.

Phe's magic spiraled out of her and wrapped protectively around the royal party. She'd barely covered her face with her forearms when she was pelted in a shower of wood shards, plaster, and nails. The exposed skin of her shoulders and arms became a graveyard of embedded shrapnel.

Phe hissed past her clenched teeth and flicked her hands toward her twins. Before her hands had connected with them, she was grabbed and dragged through the hole.

Darkness skittered over her.

The wall to her left exploded as a beast launched through it and savagely attacked the person holding Phe. The beast was a hideous mixture of claws, bulging, scaly muscles, and a half-formed muzzle of razor-sharp teeth. From one moment to the next, it had shredded the person holding her.

Phe stumbled backwards, unsheathed her twins, and prepared herself to be the next victim. The beast twisted and lunged toward another minion.

A volley of fireballs and icicles flew, slamming into

several targets, missing others completely. Where the fire hit a wall or floor or curtain, it extinguished. When it hit a person, they caught on fire. Kirzia, Ihrone, Roar, and Orc chased the explosion of flames and ice, bursting into the fray.

Shadows filled the room, their wispy darkness thick and rolling.

A man to her far right turned into a wolf and charged Phe. She bolted to meet him, twins at the ready.

Several things happened at once.

Tendrils of shadow shackled the animal's torso, smashing the wolf to the ground.

Her magic latched onto Djall's dark, polluted magic, encased the wolf, and, like a leech, sucked. Hard.

Without warning, Lear's magic taloned through hers and wrenched her magic from her. The all-engulfing pain dropped her to her knees. Then he sent their magic billowing out around Djall's minions, beamed into their minds, and stabbed at the pulsing activity center of their brains.

Phe dropped to her hands and vomited. Gads, when he said it would hurt, he hadn't been kidding.

"Get the royals," Roar commanded, landing in front of Phe, blue eyes scanning her injuries.

Appearing over Roar's shoulder, Orc pushed him aside. *"I'm healing you."* Not waiting for her permission, he carefully touched her biceps, and immediately, his soothing energy flushed into her.

"Did you have to draw so hard from her?" Roar accused, staring behind her, presumably at Lear.

"I did. She'll be fine in a moment."

"We don't have a moment," Kirzia hissed.

At the same time, Princess Attiva said, "Seas! Phe, are you all right?"

"I made us a moment," Lear said confidently. *"I didn't just level Djall's minions in this room. I killed every single one of them in this wing."*

"What?" Finian exclaimed out loud, swiveling to look at Lear as he toed a prone form dressed in bloody and torn rags.

Lear squatted next to her and tucked a stray hair behind her ear, careful to not touch her. "We could have gone further but I didn't want to chance draining her. She's that powerful," he said out loud to the group, then mind-spoke to Phe, *"I'm sorry I hurt you. Are you all right?"*

Phe met his concerned gaze and nodded, fighting the urge to put a few more inches between them.

"I'll check on Ihrone and Prince Fynn," Roar said, striding toward the hole in the wall.

With Orc's infusion of healing, Phe hauled herself to sit on her knees. Shakily, Phe lifted her arms and surveyed the forest of splinters and nails. Her right arm had a shard about two inches wide lodged in her, with the remaining three inches of it sticking out.

"I'll get you patched up in no time," Orc said, his glowing eyes pulling her away from her injuries. *"When this is over, I'll fully heal you."*

"Phe, you need to drop your shield, your friends are safe, and I will protect them now." Kirzia mind-spoke from wherever she was in the hidden passageway. *"One way I drop my shields is I imagine drawing my magic into me."*

"Thanks," Phe said out loud to both Orc and Kirzia, doing as Kirzia instructed. Then she responded to the princess, "Princess, I'm fine."

Princess Attiva skidded to a stop next to her. She was

wearing riding pants, a shirt, and boots. Phe thanked the seas Princess Attiva wasn't in a constricting dress with heels.

"You don't look fine," Princess Attiva pointed out. The large shard fell from Phe's arm, while Princess Attiva watched with gruesome fascination. "Ew." More splinters and several nails followed.

"Where's your brother? Have you agreed to come with us?" The last of the wood shavings fell out of her. With it came a burst of recharging energy. "Orc, I'm good now," Phe said while she broke his hold on her and jumped to her feet. "We've got to get going."

More minds were converging into their wing at an alarming pace, and the ones around the king and queen were dangerously close to them.

"Why are you in a corset?" Princess Attiva asked. It was obvious from her tone she found it ridiculously out of place.

"Clothing mishap. Come." Phe corralled the princess with her to join the huddle around the prince. Roar made room for her to slip in between him and Prince Fynn, whose wild curls were slicked into submission.

"Phe," Prince Fynn said, his serious gaze scrutinizing her. "How are you not hurt?"

"Oh," Princess Attiva linked her arm with her brother's, pressing close to him as if for comfort. "She was, and I watched her heal. It was disturbing and amazing at the same time."

"Prince Fynn." Phe dove right in. "I'm sure Commander Maverick and Ihrone told you General Bastion sent us to find you and your parents and bring you to safety."

Phe really hoped portaling them to safety in Arias was actually safe for them, unlike her. "Your parents are in the safe room off the blue library. We need to get to them."

"What if we refuse your assistance?"

Phe flicked her gaze to Roar, not knowing the answer, and offered, "The way I see it, you have two options with three possible outcomes. You can refuse and will either be caught and taken prisoner or killed by Djall, or you can come with us."

"We'd rather have you come willingly." What Roar didn't say, yet everyone heard, was they were coming with them, willing or not.

Those tainted minds were almost through the south wing. "I'd love for you to have time to debate this, but we have to go. They're almost on us," Lear said from behind her.

Phe nibbled her bottom lip as she considered the fastest, safest route, her gaze fastening on an entryway for the servants' stairs.

The secret passageways were empty, yet they would take the most time to maneuver and the likelihood they'd be found again weighed heavily. Right now most of Djall's minions were in public areas, with some in the servants' sections. The majority of them were on the first and second floors. On the third floor, there were five.

"I think the fastest way would be to use the servants' stairway and run to the third floor. I only sense five people there." Or rather five tainted minds. "We'll cross relatively undisturbed and then fight our way through the throng when we descend to the second floor."

"Works for me," Roar said, then telepathically. *"Phe, you disobeyed a command, which resulted in your injury and Orc using his energy to heal you. Can I trust you not to do it again?"*

Phe's gaze caught on Roar's. They were standing shoulder to shoulder, almost touching. His chin dipped slightly, so he wasn't looking down his nose at her. She couldn't tell by his tone or expression if he cared she'd been hurt, or if he only cared about his wasted manpower to heal her. Then again, why did it matter if he cared?

What he needed in this moment was for her to act as the perfect soldier and follow his commands. This was her only set of orders, but it wasn't theirs, and they needed all their reserves.

Phe pivoted and jogged to the doorway, hearing the others fall in line behind her. *"I will obey you until our orders are complete,"* was the best response she could give. She wouldn't promise anything past that.

"Ready?" She peeked over her shoulder. Roar was behind her, Lear after him. Finian turned to the princess, said something, and picked her up, cradling her to his chest. Prince Fynn was behind them, and two of their guards lined up next to the prince and princess to run parallel. Past them were Kirzia, Orc, and the rest of the guards. Ihrone brought up the rear.

"Kirzia, shield," Roar directed. *"Go."*

Phe's bloody hand twisted the handle, and she sprinted up the stairs. The staircase echoed with the pounding of their footsteps, eclipsing the sound of quick breathing and rustling clothing.

Phe's heartbeat synchronized to their hammering footfalls, and sweat beaded along her hairline. They shot onto the stairway to the third level when the first of Djall's minions hit the second floor stairwell. "Incoming, stairwell." Moments later, the doorway blasted open, dinging off the shield.

Gads, should I stop? Were the prince and princess hurt?

"Keep going, Phe, the shield will hold," Roar answered her thought.

"The five minds are moving real fast," Phe mentally gasped. Her thighs and lungs burned. Not entirely knowing what

Roar meant, she pushed her magic into Kirzia's shield and almost lost a step when she felt the impacts of the attacks.

Fierce determination and her anger spiked, and she slammed all the fire in her veins into Kirzia's shield. The outer-layer burst into flames and extinguished just as quickly.

"Cripes!"

"What the?"

Phe wrenched open the door and bolted into the third-floor hallway.

"Phe, slow down!" Roar grabbed her with one hand and yanked her into his chest and out of the jaws of a waiting hyena. For a moment, their bodies collided and feet tangled, and Phe pitched forward. Roar twisted around her, his shoulder hitting the barrier, his other hand sweeping around her waist and pulling her closer as they tumbled within the protective shield.

Phe blinked into the face of the hyena, inches from her own, its lips drawn back and quivering, mouth wide open and scraping its teeth along the shield, trying to rip into it.

High seas! Phe retreated further into Roar's chest while grabbing her thigh knife.

"No need," Roar said, his lips brushing her earlobe. "Shield will keep it out. Up." Roar stood, taking her with him, keeping the shield to his back.

The rest of the unit cleared the stairwell, and a tremendous boom shook the wood floor under her. The team paused. Some of the royal guards paced in small circles, breathing deeply, while clutching their weapons and staring at the hyena.

"What was that?" Phe asked, peering into a plume of dust erupting from the stairwell.

"Ihrone demolished the steps." Roar answered, they

were so close, their chests almost touched. "I lead, you direct."

Phe broke into a jog.

He paced her. *"Did you feel the shield?"*

"No." Phe passed Princess Attiva, who Finian had put down, and whose gaze vacillated between raptly watching them and the hyena. She looked pale and frightened. Phe wished she could reassure her. Lear's golden gaze caught hers, silently asking if she was all right. She nodded.

"Did you feel Orc's?"

"It felt mushy as I passed through it."

"Huh," Roar said, and Phe wasn't certain if it was to her comment or directed at the hyena that stalked alongside them. Its beady black eyes tracked her. *"Straight?"*

"Yes." There weren't other alternatives unless they wanted to go into a room. Some rooms were dead ends, others had connections to the one next to them, though those were often locked. Unless . . .

"Could you make a hole we could jump through in the floor?" she asked the team at large, leaning into the ease of their telepathic connection. She'd grudgingly admit mind-speaking did have its merits.

"Yes," Roar answered.

"What about the shield? If we were to drop into the room below, would the shield be able to cover both rooms?" Another two hyenas had joined the first.

"That's a little more complicated. We'd have to drop our shield and someone would have to go through the hole, secure the room, and shield. How many people are in the room?"

Phe recounted. *"Seven."* Her gut shifted.

"Lear, what about doing that thing you did?" Kirzia asked.

"Phe's magic hasn't fully recovered. Plus, I'm not sure what a second pull would do to her," Lear answered.

"I'll clear the room," Finian volunteered.

"How many people between us and the library if we take the stairs?" Ihrone asked.

Lear responded, *"I'd say about twenty-five right now."*

There was a bit of silence as they contemplated.

"I'll go with Fin," Orc declared.

"Okay, so Fin, myself, and Orc will clear the room. Kirz will keep the shield, and everyone will wait until we've secured it," Roar recapped.

"Great, five doors down on your left," Phe said, and they herded into it.

"Everyone, stand at the edge of the room," Roar ordered out loud and took position in the middle. He raised his hands, palms flexed and directed at the floor. A burst of light shot from his hands and blasted the floor away.

"High seas!" Princess Attiva screamed, clutching her brother's side.

"Kirzia, drop the shield on three. Ihrone, Phe, keep the hyenas out of here."

Phe shooed those clustered near the doorway away. Ihrone had closed the door already, and it alternated between quick shaking—as if the hyenas were trying to dig their way through—and loud, hard bangs as they threw their bodies at it. These weren't regular hyenas. They were hyenas on steroids.

Phe leaned her weight into the door, shaking with the movements of it. Ihrone drew his sword.

"One, Two, Three." Roar jumped. The door slammed into Phe hard, thrusting her backwards, and a hyena wedged its head into the slim opening. Phe fought to keep the door closed.

Ihrone sliced down, and the hyena's head dropped with a thunk and rolled into the center of the room, blood splattering everywhere until it, too, went through the hole. Phe got the door shut.

"Phe, the shield's up," Ihrone told her. "It'll keep the door stable."

The sound of grunts and furniture breaking sent Phe to the edge. With her heart throbbing in her throat, she peeked below. They were all fighting. Finian had transformed into another hideous shape and had three attackers on him. He sported a long deep cut down the length of his ribs. Furniture and fire flew around Roar. There was too much movement for Phe to see if he was injured.

"I can't get my shield up!" Orc exclaimed.

Phe watched Orc's opponent get a lucky strike in. Orc stumbled, and his opponent went to stab Orc in the gut. Roar swiveled and beheaded the man as Orc blocked.

"It's a trap." Realization chased the dread in Lear's voice, as tainted minds popped into existence and a mass of minds poured through the doorway, overrunning Finian. Finian's tether convulsed in her chest.

Phe jumped through the hole. Her twins were out and slicing through an opponent's neck before her feet hit the ground.

Shadows coalesced into a writhing mass on the floor, caressing her ankles.

"Fin!" Her heart stopped, but her body didn't. She plunged into the line of black-eyed men and women, blades and blood flying, trying to plow her way to him. Hands and feet and claws came at her from all angles.

Tendrils of shadows seized the tainted magic and sucked.

An outbreak of pain seared through Finian's tether, and her magic screamed in rage and fear. Fire burst over the sea of shadows and billowed up the possessed, her shadows wrenched bodies aside, and mini-explosions shook the wood floor.

"Flipping cripes," Orc blurted.

Phe slid to Finian's side, scanning him with both hands and eyes. Her heart was galloping hard in her chest; her breaths were quick and shallow.

Oh stars! Oh stars!

He was unconscious and partly back to his normal shape. The cut at his side had stretched and torn. She could see his intestines bulging. He was covered in gouges and blood, and one of his eyes was black. But it was the touch of tainted magic seeping into his mind and blood that rocked her to her heels.

Orc was at her side instantaneously, stilling alongside her. Orc's fear and grief harpooned into her. "Nooo!"

She would not, could not, let Djall take him. She would *not* kill him. Her magic writhed frantically within her, smoldering with a need to consume. To heal.

Phe planted her hands onto Fin's chest, and her magic poured into him.

"Phe, don't touch him." Orc tried to pull her off, and her magic zapped him.

She lost sight of everything but Fin's slack, bruised face. The all-consuming need to devour the rancid darkness—to save Fin—drove her magic, and it wouldn't be stopped. The two powers clashed. Tainted darkness stabbed into her, and her magic let it. Let it burrow and fix its nasty claws in, when suddenly her magic hurled every ounce of power into swallowing the taint whole, ripping its grasp from Finian.

Then the sensation of her magic shifted, and a flood of new, softer magic flowed into Fin.

Phe watched, transfixed, as Finian's skin shimmered with light. His cuts knit together. His bruises faded. It wasn't until his eyes blinked opened that she could breathe and see again and her magic withdrew.

Finian tensed under her fingers and jumped to his feet, scanning the room for danger.

"Fin, you okay?" Orc's wide gaze flitted between Finian to Phe before settling intensely on Finian's eyes.

Finian shook out his arms, as if shedding excess energy, and a smile blossomed across his face. His dimple emerged. "Amazing."

Orc's focus jumped to her. "How do you feel, Phe?"

She felt light. She felt energized, and her magic felt giddy.

"Fine," she muttered. How could she explain that her magic ate Djall's and wanted more? It seemed her magic had recharged itself and her, and she had no idea what to think or feel about it. There was no way she'd open that barrel of snakes with anyone.

A deafening explosion had Phe ducking into a crouch, her twins up.

There was a tremendous hole in the exterior wall of the palace.

Phe scanned the rest of the room. The queen, king, prince, and princess were huddled together, their guards encircling them. Someone must have gotten them from the safe room while Phe'd been preoccupied. Lear stood next to the guards, eyes on her.

Orc jogged toward the missing wall where Kirzia, Ihrone, and Roar were studying the terrain.

Phe re-sheathed her twins, watching her team strategize the best way to secure the grounds and open a portal.

Finian wrapped a heavy, slick arm across her shoulders and tugged her close. Shards of discomfort skimmed her skin, and she leaned into the pain, grateful he was unpossessed and alive. He dipped his forehead to rest on the side of her head and whispered, "thank you."

Emotions welled in Phe so thickly she had to clear her throat. Living in a world without Finian's teasing—even though she wanted to kill him all the time—was incomprehensible.

"Fin!" Roar called, his blue gaze catching them over his shoulder. "Stop fondling Phe and get over here. We're not done yet."

35

Phe rolled her neck and peered through the hole in the wall, then back up at the hyenas trying to burrow their way through Orc's shield on the third floor. Their black beady eyes and tainted magic tracked her as she stretched her arms and wrists.

Possessed hyenas were creepy.

She returned her gaze to the happenings below and slowly replaced the boundaries around the team's magical tethers. Ihrone signaled for her to jump.

She did, landing in a crouch, then sprang to her feet and moved aside for Orc. Kirzia was opening a portal, its bright circular light widening. Lear and the royals stood together near the edge of it.

Queen Oltha reached a hand toward Phe, silently beckoning her.

The thud behind her as she went to the queen told her Orc had landed.

"Dear." Queen Oltha's hand hovered for a moment, as if she was unsure if she wanted to wrap Phe in a side hug or insist they hold hands. Then she curled her fingers and dropped her arm. She studied Phe quietly, her face drawn and pale, her eyes big and white with fear.

"You'll be okay. Lear will help you get settled in Arias." Phe flicked her gaze to the portal, then to her team members. The hyenas were now perched in the spot she'd been a moment ago. Swallowing hard, she took a small step back.

There would be no finessing this.

Her heart rate kicked up in anticipation. "They'll keep you safe."

Another step back.

She scanned the team one more time and locked eyes with Roar.

He knew.

Lear twisted, lunging for her as Phe broke into a run, sprinting through the shield and into the elaborate gardens. Shouts rang behind her and the magical tethers in her chest were yanked hard. She kept going and whistled, hoping Edva was in hearing distance and could come.

There were tainted minds spread sporadically throughout the gardens and fields, which she wasn't too worried about. It was the hyenas that had her concerned.

Phe smashed her fear aside and focused on the burn in her lungs, the ache in her legs, how her arms pumped and her feet barely touched the ground. She'd take this risk for Kyra.

It had taken seconds for Roar and Finian to give chase, precious seconds she used to put as much distance between them as possible and head for the palace's labyrinth. She could see it.

The hyenas passed Roar and Finian.

Four more tainted minds were sprinting toward her on her left, their pace too fast. Animal fast.

Her heart catapulted into her throat and threatened to burst.

Phe could see the thick green foliage of the labyrinth wall. She pushed herself to get there. Just get there.

The hair at the back of her neck stood on end as the hyenas got closer.

Gads.

And closer.

Sweat flowed down the ridges of her spine.

I'm not going to make it.

One of them leapt.

She unsheathed her twins, twirled, and surged to meet them, her blades barely sliced across the hyena's spotted muzzle.

The other went for her leg, snatching her out of the air and pummeling her to the ground. Searing pain raged up her leg as it pulverized her bones. Then it shook its head, tearing tendons and muscles and digging its teeth deeper and deeper.

She kicked the hyena in the face with her free foot.

The other hyena pranced around her, eyeing her.

She slashed at it with her blades.

The hyena gnawing on her leg savagely shook her again.

Brown roots shot from the earth, cinching around the hyenas, and crushed them to the ground.

Roar and Finian reached her right before the other tainted minds did.

"Incoming, left," Phe yelled, her voice heavy with pain.

More roots shot from the earth, big and thick and close together, forming a wall around them as the four new hyenas leapt, slamming into it.

Phe's magic funneled down her leg and barreled into the mouth of the hyena, latching on. A wave of piercing hunger, so strong her bones ached, pulsed through her and drank Djall's tainted venom in.

Finian killed the hyena to her side, its enraged pack cackling with laughter and trying to force their way past the wall.

The hyena attacking her went slack, and she crab-crawled backwards, dragging her damaged leg. The hyena transformed into a gaunt, naked woman.

"What were you thinking?" Roar said as he hauled her up.

Phe closed her eyes, her chest and stomaching sinking to her feet. It wasn't the pain shooting up her leg that had her battling a flood of tears. It was the last threads of hope she had. Now she would never get away from that terrible city and save Kyra. This had been the perfect opportunity to get to Drykz Forest and Elzac, and she'd failed—again.

She imagined her shadows encasing her protectively. Reassuringly.

Alarm spiked in Roar's mind, and then he and Finian's minds were gone, along with the hand bracing her.

Phe fell, landing in soft moss.

The green scent of Drykz Forest speared her senses. The sounds of birds singing, insects buzzing, and rustling leaves hit her before her eyes opened.

How'd I get here?

She sat and reached for her twins. Dread curdled her stomach when she realized she'd left them on the ground with Roar and Finian.

"Elzac?" Phe tried, thought-beaming, afraid to speak and upset the forest.

Vines slithered around her, as if she'd landed in a nest of snakes.

Her heart pounded. The acidic feeling of fear and adrenaline scoured her insides.

"Elzac?" She tried again, thinking louder and reminding herself, *I want to be here.* She held her breath and cranked her face to the side as a leaf fluttered at her neck.

Slowly, she pulled her non-injured leg under her, her fingers sinking into the cool, spongy moss. Cautiously, she straightened, not wanting to upset any of the vines or leaves.

Blue lightning struck to her right, leaving the scent of ozone to wash over her.

Phe flinched.

Shadow Unit's tethers pulsed in her chest, creating a bizarre sucking sensation so strong her chest concaved.

Then, one after another, bolts of blue lightning speared the earth around her, until one hit her. A rush of exhilaration engulfed her, and she floated into oblivion.

36

"What did you do?" Bastion's cold, accusing voice pierced through Phe and rattled her weary bones. She didn't need to look at him to know he was standing next to her, grim-faced and hard, overbearing angles.

She was trying to patch together how she could be responsible for what looked to be a makeshift emergency shelter filled with white blanketed cots, each holding an occupant.

Did I hurt these people with my magic?

Phe'd regained consciousness what felt like only moments ago, enough for her to do her bodily business, brush her teeth, and wash her face before Bastion and this crowd—Roar, Orc, and Lear—had descended on her.

She'd had enough time in the washroom to see how haggard and gaunt she looked. Her cheeks had hollowed and her skin felt translucent, showcasing spiderwebs of blue veins. Exhaustion chased each of her movements, not willing to release its bone-clenching grip on her.

The numbness that accompanied her exhaustion drowned out feelings she knew lurked. How could they not?

Phe'd failed, yet again, to get away from these monsters and this horrid magical city. And to compound matters, she'd been unconscious for two days because she'd been magically depleted. Her failure meant Kyra had been in Djall's clutches for five days.

Five whole days.

Her stomach knotted at that.

Focus, Phe. What was the last thing she remembered? *What did I do?*

Djall attacked Oceanid. They saved the royal family. "What happened to Xafara?" Phe asked, her flat tone subtly rising a level with alarm. Had Djall won? "How are the royals?"

Roar's arm brushed hers, sending juicy tingles along her nerve endings, and her heart took a quick, excited sprint around her rib cage. Gads, what was her heart doing? She clenched her fist, fighting the sensation.

"Shortly after you disappeared . . ." Roar's pitch was carefully neutral, and he surveyed the auditorium.

Phe peeked at his profile. His chin was scruffy, with possibly two days' growth, and his hair had a bit of a greasy sheen to it. The skin under his eyes looked slightly swollen with a bluish tint, which she knew happened when he didn't sleep.

". . . An energy blast swept through Oceanid, and in its wake we discovered the blast eradicated Djall's connection to those he possessed. Freeing them. Oceanid is safe, and the royals have returned."

Phe plucked the important details. Xafara was safe, and the royals returned. A blast freed people from Djall. Yet that did not explain the row upon row of cots in front of her, Bastion's accusation, and the oppressive silence hanging in between hushed whispers and muffled sobs.

"And then I hurt them?" Her tone dulled. Did it have anything to do with her magic's all-consuming hunger? A vise tightened around her chest, restricting her breathing.

"No." This time it was Lear, who stood on the other side of Bastion. "Your magical signature was embedded in the blast. You helped free them. We need to know what you did."

Phe was obviously missing something. "Then why are these people here?"

"Being possessed is a scarring mental violation, and they were possessed for decades. They are here because they have agreed to work with healers," Lear explained. "We have another, much smaller location set up for those who have refused healing."

"People refused?" Why would someone reject healing?

"Healing is always a choice," Orc contributed from Roar's other side. "If you want, I'll ask you the same question next time you refuse to let me heal you."

Phe scowled at him and toyed with her amulet. His point hit its mark.

"You haven't answered my question," Bastion edgily reminded her.

"My memories are fuzzy," Phe admitted and decided to take everyone down memory lane with her. "I have been unconscious for two days and Kyra's been missing for five." She loaded a punch into the five. "We'd completed our orders. The hyenas chased me." Her leg itched, as if to remind her she may have healed, but her body clung to the memory of bone-crushing jaws snapping her leg like a twig.

"You ran," Orc stated.

Phe glared at him. She'd skimmed over her attempt to escape for a reason. She hadn't planned to remind Bastion because she didn't want him to dole out a punishment.

Continuing as if Orc hadn't botched her plan, she said, "Roar and Finian helped me and then . . ." There was darkness. "You said I disappeared, but how?"

"We don't really know. If you'd teleported, I should have gone with you since I was holding you." Roar shrugged, his arm brushing her again, sending those tingles into a warm tizzy that spread. "All I know is one moment I was holding you—" a muscle in his jaw twitched, "—the next you were gone."

Phe clunked around the haziness, finding it extremely weird they didn't know how she disappeared. Yet she was with them. "I disappeared, right? Then how am I with you?"

Roar made eye contact with her for the first time. His eyes were devoid of any emotion.

A heaviness settled in her chest. She was ragingly angry at Roar, yet she hadn't been prepared for his withdrawal. For the void consuming their friendship. An aching sadness speared her.

"The induction's primary focus is to merge our magic together. However, there are times it gifts teams with new capabilities."

"Like telepathy," she said.

"Close, but you already had access to telepathy. It gifted us with a capability no one had, Teleportation Manipulation, which means, in this case, we can jump others to us. That's how I was able to bring you back."

Another wave of heartache washed over Phe, the anguish in her chest surging with it. He was the reason she was back in Arias with the monsters.

Whatever Roar saw in her gaze had him breaking contact. "We've dabbled with the capability since we discovered it, and so far, I am the only one who has the ability, and it's limited to the team."

Phe shoved the hurt aside. What had she done, where had she gone, to have helped all these people? Hope surged so fast and hard, everything in her stiffened and her heart stopped. "Was Kyra rescued?"

Bastion huffed, somehow making it sound condescending.

"No," Roar simply stated.

How could a single syllable have the effect of a hangman's rope? It plummeted her fast and viciously from hope to despondency.

"We rescued one hundred and eleven people," Orc offered. Phe met his compassionate gaze, almost forgiving him for reminding Bastion of her escape.

A residue of bone-chilling fear froze her insides. "Drykz Forest," she blurted. It was the only place her fear response was that heightened. She clarified, "I'd been in Drykz Forest."

"Were you alone?" Bastion said impatiently.

Phe leaned into the darkness of her memory. "I don't know. All I remember is blue lightning."

"Blue lightning," Bastion repeated, unimpressed.

"Blue lightning," she confirmed, swiveling her head to see the bastard. "Don't even consider taking me to that chair again."

"He did," Lear said, his tone carefully concealing his thoughts, "while you were unconscious."

What?! Her mouth fell open. Mushy emotions bubbled within her murky, heavy waters. *He's despicable.*

"Tzermel could not assist you with remembering," Roar offered, then mind-spoke to her. *"Because you set it on fire."*

Phe snapped her mouth closed, compressing her lips into a tightrope even a novice acrobatic could perform on.

Gads, she wished she'd been conscious to see Bastion's face when it burst into flames.

"You saved Finian," Bastion stated, blatantly disregarding his atrocious actions. "How did you accomplish that?"

Phe exhaled slowly. What would happen if she told them her magic ate Djall's? That it clawed through her to latch on like a ravenous leech? Eating someone's magic had to be bad, Djall-level dangerous. Add to the fact her magic got a boost from it? It felt wrong even to her. They'd kill her if they knew.

She let the silence stretch.

"Sir, I don't think Phe can answer that question," Roar said after a moment. "We know her magic is protection-based. Right now, sir, we need to focus on training her."

"I agree with Commander Maverick." Lear stepped forward, diplomacy chilling his tone. "I'm sure Phe doesn't clearly understand what she did, nor has the ability to articulate it. Speaking of training, it appears we are at an impasse." Lear gestured for Phe to join him. "Thus, I will begin training on mental magic healing, per your request, General."

Lear paused long enough to give Bastion space to respond. When he didn't, Lear's gaze slid to Phe. "Phe, would you come with me, please?"

Phe didn't hesitate, needing to be as far away from the loathsome bastard as possible. Who puts an unconscious person in a chair to force memories out of them? There were so many levels of wrongness in what he'd done.

Lear led them into the belly of the auditorium.

Phe let her gaze wander the room only to eye Lear's strong shoulders. She was grateful he'd told her Bastion had taken her to Tzermel's chair. He hadn't had to, especially when she wasn't sure any of Shadow Unit would have. He'd not only told her, but he'd told her in front of the bastard and Shadow Unit, clearly ensuring they all knew she knew, and he'd done it casually, not concerned with Bastion's reaction.

Part of Phe wondered if Roar had been about to tell her, too. She stopped the thought because she'd never know. She didn't want herself caught in a cycle of deluding herself because she wanted to return to the ease of their trusting relationship before magic shattered the illusion.

"Thank you for telling me about Tzermel's chair."

Lear shrugged. "You are my mentee; therefore, any information I believe is pertinent to you, you will know. I probably should add, now that we're away from the general, that you destroyed Tzermel's chair, so it's a bit of a sore topic right now."

Phe's appreciation deepened. "I thought Bastion wasn't in charge of our training?"

"He's not, but his point was valid," Lear said, slowing as they neared an empty cot. "Mental healing is an art that takes practice and time. I cannot teach it once and expect for you to be competent. Plus, we have an overwhelming need for this particular skill right now."

"I'm a killer," Phe confessed; the whole idea of healing others had her skin crawling. "Not a healer."

Lear was not fazed by her proclamation, though. "You are many things, Phe, and not a single one defines you. Your potential as a healer is just as limitless as everything else you apply yourself to."

Why does Lear sound so similar to Elzac at times? Phe sighed with frustration, dredging up the reasons she'd be unfit. "I prefer to grunt or be silent than to talk. I'm not good with emotion, and I am sure I will hurt them."

"I hear you're uncomfortable, and I understand. I do. But what if your friend Kyra was in one of these beds? Would you want to heal her?"

"Absolutely." *With every molecule of my being.*

"Though I'd never recommend healing friends and family, I want you to consider each and every person in here to be Kyra. They all deserve the same fierce dedication you've shown for your friend."

Phe glowered at him. When Kyra was rescued, Kyra would need the help. Phe knew herself well enough to know she'd want to be extremely versed in whatever techniques they were offering to heal Kyra, so she could help . . . and yes, maybe even do some of the healing herself. Phe's shoulders slowly dropped from her ears. She'd do this for Kyra.

"Let me also distinguish mental healing magic from counseling, because I think it will help you. Counseling in Arias involves talking, processing events, thoughts, etc. This does not involve magic." He paused and his gaze flickered over her shoulder, tracking a person who'd appeared in the auditorium. "When Orc heals you with his magic, what happens?"

"His magic fills me, and then my body heals."

Those golden orbs landed on her again. "Same applies to our magic. Only our magic fills the wounds in the other's mental injuries, were Orc's focuses on healing physical ones."

That eased her tension briefly. *What if my magic tries to eat the others?* Her stomach rolled at the thought and her shoulders resumed their place near her ears. *Gads, that'd be horrible.* "I'm not convinced I wouldn't hurt someone."

"I will observe you until I have deemed you competent. You will not be alone until you're ready to be."

Phe pushed the queasy feeling aside, as it seemed she

didn't have a choice. She'd learn this for Kyra. "All right." Hesitation colored her tone.

"Before we start, I need for you to be able to reach me whenever you need me." Lear patted the disheveled mattress next to him, suggesting she sit.

Phe scrunched her nose.

"When you tried to reach me at the ball, what were you doing?"

Phe cleared her throat and looked at his feet, feeling silly. "I tried beaming your name from my head."

"Ah." An endearing smile formed on Lear's face, and his gaze softened. "I'll explain that capability on another day. Close your eyes, and I will walk you through the process. It's quite simple."

Phe did, rolling one of the braids of Kyra's amulet nervously between her fingers, and rocking from her heels to her toes.

"Imagine me."

Phe visualized Lear's eyes, chin length hair tucked behind his ears, and the casual, relaxed way he always seemed to hold himself.

"Now, mind-speak to me."

"Hello?"

"Whenever you are telepathically communicating with someone, envisioning them creates the link to them. There are several caveats to this. You need to have met the person and often, a telepathic link is established after physical contact, such as a handshake," Lear explained patiently. *"Now, you should be able to reach me whenever and wherever you are. Distance shouldn't interfere."*

"This is helpful," Phe said aloud, opening her eyes. The process was so simple, she wondered why he'd not told her at the celebration banquet. The thought was quickly overshadowed by another. Maybe she could talk to Elzac?

"Also, whatever we see inside someone's mind must be kept confidential. Do you understand?" His features hardened with seriousness.

Her face pulled into a mask of solemnity. She viscerally understood. "Yes." Her response was an oath. She'd hold their secrets as tightly as she guarded her own.

The right edge of Lear's mouth lifted into a half smile at the vehemence of her reaction. "Generally, physical healing is something we all naturally do. A broken bone, for example, will heal to the best of its capabilities, right?"

"Yes."

"Are there times when the body will physically heal and yet cause further damage?"

"Of course." Phe realized Lear was someone who, in his teachings, started from the basic, foundational building blocks and built upwards, slowly and meticulously. From learned experience, rushing someone like him would only extend the lesson. Since she wasn't in a rush to start the lesson, she slowly answered, "If we don't set the broken bone, the bone will heal misaligned and cause other problems. Like a limp and chronic pain."

"Great example. Another example is an infection. The wound itself may heal, but if it hasn't been cleaned properly prior, it will seal an infection within the body."

Phe nodded, conveying her understanding.

"When we experience traumatic events, it can create wounds in our minds." Lear's gaze dripped with intensity, watching every facial nuance she made. "And using the same metaphor, similar to our physical bodies, fractures and infections can set within those wounds, only those wounds aren't visible. Does that make sense?"

Phe tasted what Lear was saying. Did she believe it? Could mental wounds become infected? Misaligned? Had hers?

The resounding answer was yes.

During the Drykz Forest incident when she'd been sixteen, her mental infection had been so severe it had almost taken her life. She'd survived years of physical abuse from Grum and torturous trainings with Bastion, and all those physical wounds had healed. Yet, their underlining, invisible wounds—the mental wounds—had been left untouched.

"Yes, this makes sense."

"People with our skill set have the capability of seeing the wound, which means we can assist in healing these types of injuries." Lear paused and a touch of gravity entered his tone. "I want to be clear. You are not healing them, per se, even though the name implies it. You are a support tool only. Your magic can only help them heal what *they* are ready to heal."

Phe shifted her weight between her feet. Lear was drawing up a set of boundaries and expectations for her. It was like learning how to properly grip your weapon and get into a fighting stance. Again, she nodded.

Lear rested his elbows on his knees. "Now that we've covered those pieces, let's move onto the magic lesson. For the foreseeable future, we'll merge our magic and you'll observe." Lear gestured for her to sit next to him.

Phe took a steadying breath and sat. She did not want to do this.

Lear's hand hovered at her cheeks. "Touch?"

Did she have a choice? "Yes."

Again he softly cupped her chin. His thumbs rested on her jawbone and fingertips grazed her cheeks. The light touches created sparks of pain. His magic swirled into hers and merged even quicker than before.

"First, we always get their consent." Lear moved to the bed across from them, his weight dipping the mattress. He leaned close to murmur to the person huddled under the blanket and exchanged a few words before turning back to Phe.

"Otis has agreed." Then Lear switched to mind-speaking. *"Close your eyes and watch."*

Phe did as instructed, and as quickly as if they'd jumped, she was standing next to Lear in near darkness. She watched Lear glance around for a moment, then he strode into the blackness.

Phe lunged to snatch the back of his shirt before he disappeared into the darkness. She had no desire to be lost in someone's mind.

There was only silence and darkness until they stepped into a dimly lit space. Phe stepped to his side, wiggling her fingers from the weirdness of having to hold onto his shirt.

Frames with frozen images glided past them, distinctly different from Rosea's. Each image was covered with a thick black tint. Phe's stomach nose-dived. Otis had seen everything through those blackened eyes of his.

The sickening reality that he'd been a prisoner in his mind, forced to watch as Djall controlled his body, hit. *What has this man endured?*

"This is a terrible idea, I'm not equipped to do this." Phe mind-spoke to Lear, her voice pitched higher.

"I'm sorry, Phe. Learning to heal others is even more powerful than harming them," Lear smoothly responded. *"Once we're done, we'll talk about what is coming up for you."*

Does he know who he's talking to? Phe didn't talk, or at

least not to virtual strangers. She talked to Kyra and Jallia and Elzac and Roar and her trusted horse, Edva.

She bit back her response to him when Otis's skeletal form emerged from the shadows. His arms were tightly crossed, shoulders hunched, and eyes downcast.

"Otis, this is Phe. She is the one who is training with me." Lear's voice was as smooth as softened butter. A soothing calmness emanated from him and Phe inched closer to him.

Otis's gaze swung to her feet, then to her knees. In a grainy, low, unused voice, he said, "You're the one."

"She is," Lear acknowledged to her confusion. "Are you ready?"

I'm the what?

Otis peeked through his lashes at Lear, and flicked a quick, what appeared to be curious, glance at Phe. Through clenched teeth, he muttered. "Yes."

"Please pick a memory you'd like to work on."

"I'm the one? What does that mean?" Phe telepathed, uneasiness spreading through her.

Silently, Otis touched the next frame, and the image enlarged.

"He recognizes your magic from when you helped save them," Lear explained, watching Otis.

Phe sucked in a breath. The thought of people thinking of her as their savior felt untrue and reprehensible. Especially when her magic seemed to have an appetite for others. Plus, she wasn't so sure she had saved them. She'd remember something like that, wouldn't she?

"Can you see the fractures in the projection?" Lear asked, pulling her from her thoughts.

Phe narrowed her attention onto the image, and at first all she saw was the black tint. It obscured the clarity of the image. Underneath it, the entire image was broken by tiny fissures.

"How do we heal that?" Phe wondered what her own memories looked like. Were they fragmented or whole? Had she successfully healed them or only convinced herself she had?

"Our magic has the capability of binding the fractures together to the extent the person we are healing is able to heal."

"What do you mean, to the extent the person is able to?"

"Mental magic is based entirely on the person's recovery readiness. Sometimes, all our magic can do is fill the spaces until the person is ready to move to the next step. As I said, we aren't saviors. We are tools. A person always heals at their own pace, whether they understand the timing or not."

Phe flicked her gaze to Lear's profile. She wondered at the amount of patience he must have to bear witness to the same horrific memory someone harbored, over and over, with no apparent progress.

She swallowed uncomfortably. Did she have that level of patience? Of compassion?

"Watch my magic," Lear instructed.

The light of his magic seeped into the room, wisps of it encircling Otis and his memory projection.

Otis jogged on the edge of a dirt road, gnarly alpine trees lining its perimeter like guards, other people alongside him. Phe could feel his hunger was an ever-present ache in his bones, and his mouth and throat were desert dry. They passed a road crossing, and Phe barely caught the two names, Dreuzer's Way and Shuxeey Pass, as they barreled by.

Up ahead was a horse-drawn wagon. The unlucky travelers, a middle-aged man and woman, nervously shifted in their seating. A child sat in between them.

Djall's voice boomed, echoing in Otis's mind, "Bring them to me."

The black tint lightened a barely noticeable shade as Lear's magic infused into Otis's memory.

The group increased their stride, unnaturally propelled forward by the command. As one, they threw themselves onto the horse, crawled up the wagon sides, and dragged their screaming occupants apart. A mound of people converged on the man, pounding him into submission.

Otis ripped the young boy from his mother as another group threw her off the back of the wagon. Her screams catapulted into a higher pitch, one filled with panic and pain and terror. Otis didn't need to see what they were doing; he knew.

Phe focused on the broken fragments of the image. Lear's magic had filled them, the hue changing from white light to that of Lear's golden eyes. Instead of pulling the fragments together, like puzzle pieces to hide the brokenness, Lear's magic suffused into the cracks.

The young boy valiantly fought Otis's unrelenting grip as he screamed for his mother, spittle flying and eyes white with fear.

"Taste him," Djall commanded.

Otis slammed the boy down, the movement fast and violent and unexpected. The back of the boy's head hit something. His scream cut off mid-wail and vacant eyes stared over Otis's shoulder.

The memory froze.

Lear's magic withdrew.

In between the fissures, golden streams ran, melding the shattered image together. The black tint remained, although lighter than when they'd started, with hints of color.

The image was magnificent. A portrait of fragments held

strong by golden glue. There was a strength and character and resiliency to the memory, which only increased its allure.

Her heart lodged in her throat, Phe dragged in a breath she hadn't known she'd held.

"For me, this is a privilege." Lear's solemn voice resounded in her mind. *"I get to witness the miracle of someone reconnect the pieces of themselves. It may be my magic that salved the wounds, but it is their willingness and openness to let my magic flow and fill their spaces. Without this, our magic waits on the sidelines and cannot do anything."*

There was an unmistakable marvel in what Phe'd witnessed. The memory was heavy with powerlessness, shame, horror, and disgust. Yet the overwhelming sensation had been one of surrender.

The weight of Lear's golden gaze landed on her, and she glanced at him. His golden hue had darkened, and it felt to Phe that Lear allowed her, in that look, to see into the depths of his soul. *"Have you ever noticed the beauty in the cracks of life?"*

She hadn't, not until this very moment. She'd only ever noticed how her cracks had been filled with dirt and life, and she'd never considered it beautiful.

"Yes," she whispered through their connection, while awe rippled in ever-widening circles throughout her.

Then, like a bucket of cold water was dumped on her, Phe became enraged with Djall. How could someone do this to others? See them as nothing but another notch of power they could add to their collection? Hold them prisoners in their own bodies and force them to do their heinous biddings?

She wrapped her hands around the pommels of her

thigh knives, the metal cool and firm and grounding. *Djall needs to be stopped.*

There were silver linings to learning to heal and to witnessing Djall's inhumanity.

He'd just replaced Bastion as the most vile creature in Phe's mind. She vowed to hunt him to the ends of the earth and make sure he never hurt another soul again.

After, of course, she'd rescued Kyra.

And she now had a new obsession with maps.

37

Lear's golden gaze scanned Phe again. "Are you sure you're okay?" He'd been asking her this question continually since they started mental healing training.

"I'm fine," she replied, knowing he didn't believe her response.

She knew why. She'd forfeited sleep for over a month now. Its ravaging effects were blatantly obvious. What she looked like didn't bother her, as long as her exhaustion didn't fog her mind. Only when her mental sharpness dulled, or her body's need for sleep overwhelmed her willpower, did she allow herself to succumb to it.

She had her reasons for this.

"You're managing your power level?"

"I'm not *empty*," Phe assured him, understanding his concern. She'd been magically depleted twice in the forty-seven days since Kyra's abduction and Phe's arrival in Arias. The second one had left her unconscious for two days and had taken her over a week to fully recover from. It was not an experience she wished to repeat.

"How's your sleep?"

"It's fine." When she slept, she fell into the black void of oblivion, too tired for the disruptions plaguing her to penetrate.

"Nightmares?" he probed.

"None," Phe replied, fidgeting with the water drop on her amulet. She blinked, the movement a momentary relief to her dry eyes, and images of the countless maps she'd studied nonstop arose.

She cleared her thoughts, in case an errant one went to Lear or Shadow Unit.

The main reason for her recent bout of self-imposed insomnia was simple. Kyra.

From the first memory she'd witnessed while healing to the one Lear and Phe had just finished, she collected data. Roads and cities and towns and all the places Djall forced those he possessed to go. At night, after training with Shadow Unit, Phe poured over the maps Zea provided. She scavenged them for the slightest hints of geography and tiny, sometimes unnamed, roads.

What she'd found were the routes Djall used. From there, she'd assessed and deduced where he'd established several bases.

There were other reasons for her continued sleep deprivation.

Memories filled with vivid colors and echoes of laughter and giggling children had jolted her awake, as if they had electrocuted her. Vestiges of Anala's life surfacing.

She had a perverse interest in those memories. The need to dissect each one rivaled that of her mission. When it became clear to Phe they interfered with her focus, she'd adjusted, as nothing would obstruct her goal.

The last reason to avoid sleep had been nightmares featuring Djall. They were eerily similar to Djall's dream-

fare attempt, where she'd barely escaped. This she had told
Lear about, having needed him to check that the protection
he'd put into place was intact. After the third request, she'd
insisted he teach her how to protect herself from dream-fare
and how to check them on her own.

"I'm meeting with the Phoenix Council," Phe reminded
Lear, as she often stayed with him until a member of
Shadow Unit, usually Finian, collected her. Then she'd
spend her evenings learning to engage her magic in a
combat setting. This past week had been big. She'd been
learning all about shielding and was finally able to engage
and erect her own shield. "Zea should be here any minute to
take me."

The weekly check-in meetings with the council were an
awkward affair, mainly comprising of them interrogating
Phe on her week and Phe giving them one-worded answers.

Phe didn't mind it, though, because visiting the Phoenix
Council cabin got her out of Arias and away from everything else. Chiefly, Shadow Unit training.

Lear sighed, as if put out. "I remember. Their insistence
on weekly meetings is unnecessary. I'll talk to General
Bastion again and see if we can reduce it."

Phe gave him a tired smile, not caring one way or the
other, and plucked an apple from a nearby fruit bowl. The
bowls had appeared on her second day of training with Lear
in the auditorium, spaced every other bed, and always filled
with fresh, succulent fruit. She rubbed the apple on her
shirt till it shined, then bit into its juicy goodness.

His eyes scanned her again, worry creating crows' feet at
their corners. "How did the session with your team go?"

Phe shrugged, breaking his gaze and browsing the silent
auditorium. He knew there was a powerful undercurrent in
her relationship with the team. "Meh."

"If you ever need to talk—" Lear's gaze focused over her shoulder, where Phe knew from her prickling awareness, Ash had appeared, "—I'm here."

Phe pivoted to watch Ash approach, taking another bite. It wasn't that she refused to talk. It was more the case of not having access to the people she trusted to talk to.

Jallia, she'd been told, was still serving her punishment, and Phe hadn't been allowed to see her. She'd tried to connect with Elzac multiple times, but he never responded, and at this point she'd stopped trying. She wasn't sure if it was her, the distance, or some block created by those pesky stars to keep them apart. Even her access to Edva had been limited.

A smile swept the contours of Ash's face, transforming it from pure determination to a genuine, friendly greeting. Phe wasn't fooled. Ash's blue eyes glimmered with her well-known tenacity. She was on a mission, and it included Phe.

Ash planted herself in front of Phe. "Lear," she spared him a glance, "Phe, so nice to see you." Ash honed in on the apple in Phe's hand as Phe took another bite. "Phe, please have lunch with me?"

Phe chewed and swallowed, contorting her mouth into an apologetic line, as this was not the first time Ash had asked. Ash had been coming weekly to invite her, sometimes twice a week. "I can't—"

Ash dropped to her knees, slapped her hands into a plea position at her heart, and gave Phe the best puppy eyes Phe had ever seen. "Please come with me," Ash begged. "How can we be best friends if we don't hang out?"

Lear cough-laughed behind Phe. "Ash . . ."

"Hush, you." Ash glared past Phe to Lear. "You hog her all the time."

Phe compressed her lips, ruler straight except for the

edges. She softened those into a curl and explained, "I can't. I have to attend my weekly Phoenix Council meeting."

"What about tonight? Dinner?" Ash stayed firmly rooted in place, hands now clasped to beseech, apparently unwilling to be told no. "We *need* to talk to you about a certain grumpy someone."

Phe sighed. "You know I don't control my schedule. I'd love to have dinner with you, but you have to ask Shadow Unit."

"Snap, girl, get on your feet," Zea sauced, appearing next to Ash with a surge of vibrating air.

Ash shot Zea a glance, one that appeared to be simultaneously mischievous and irritated, and got to her feet, Phe's answer seeming to appease her. "I'll hunt them down and demand it. I've already told them I think they're training you too hard." Ash smoothed out invisible lines on her shirt.

Zea made a long, hissing sound. Her eyes roamed Phe critically. "Girl, you look like my doormat."

Ash gasped, her features widened with affront. "That was rude."

Phe hid her smirk behind her apple, used to Zea's uncensored ways.

"I tell it as I see it." Zea shrugged unrepentantly. "We need to go."

This, Phe completely agreed with. Her chest tightened with anticipation as she lifted her pack. "Lear, see you tomorrow. Ash, hopefully we'll have dinner tonight."

Phe checked the team's tethers again, ensuring they were completely cut off from her, and slid her backpack on.

Zea touched her pack. The auditorium blinked out of existence, replaced with streaming sunlight and the scent of smoke from the ever-burning fireplace of the Phoenix Council cabin.

Phe's heartbeat quickened as she speared the room with a glance. *Thank the stars the room was empty.*

She reassessed her plan as she strode to the chimney. From everything she'd learned, shields and protective barriers kept everything within them *in*, as well as everything out *out*. Which meant there was no protective barrier on the fireplace and chimney; otherwise, all the drifting smoke would be caught inside, suffocating them.

Phe gripped the stone mantle, grateful her pack protected her long braid.

Without hesitation, she swung her feet through the raging flames, and planted them up the chimney. Her body flowed with the motion, her hold released. She curled inwards and snapped open, planting her hands on the opposite wall of the chimney. It was awkward, and the only reason she didn't fall was because she funneled all her strength into her hands and feet, her body a tense string suspended above the flames.

Sweat burst from every pore in her body.

She ignored Zea's shout, ignored the searing pain of incinerator-hot stones. She moved.

Halfway up the narrowing chimney, Phe slid.

Her heart leapt into her throat as she caught herself mid-way down.

Adriata stepped into the flames, and Phe scurried up the chimney faster, barely evading Adriata as the woman's magic reached for her.

The moment she felt the frigid wind lash her face, she hurled herself from the chimney. Heat chased her, and she had no doubt flames were flickering into the sky behind her.

She slid down the icy, snow-lined roof and landed hard. Old magic, she'd learned from Zea, kept the consistent, stinging wind on the top of the mountain, ensuring it stripped the ground of any powder and left only a hard icy layer of snow.

Phe thrust herself to her hands and knees, the freezing surface soothing to the wounds on her hands, and launched herself downward. Her sheaths dug painfully into her thighs, and she tucked into a ball. The bone-chilling air froze the hairs in her nose and her sweat-drenched clothing.

She didn't know how long she had until the Phoenix Council stripped the cabin of its ancient protective shield. She knew they would, and she knew they'd come after her. It was only a matter of time. Time she hoped she had on her side.

"Turn around now." Bastion commanded in her mind.

"Phe, what are you doing?" Panic pulsed in Finian's mind-speak voice. What she'd done at the celebratory ball, blocking total communication from her team, had been a fluke. One she hadn't yet been able to replicate. She learned she could close the tethers from them, ensuring they didn't hear or feel her, but when they wanted to mind-speak, they could. *"Baby girl?"* Finian packed too much emotion into her nickname for Phe to decipher, nor did she have the capacity to.

Spindly trees were rapidly approaching.

She unraveled from her spinning sphere enough to yank a thigh knife free, plunging it into the ice. The momentum carried her into the forest line and slammed her into a tree, knocking the breath from her.

"Phe, please come back." Orc's voice was seasoned with a pinch of soothing and cajoling. *"It's too dangerous."*

The barrier dropped, and instantly Firo skewered through the first ten layers of her mental shields.

She sucked air into frozen lungs.

"Phe, what's happening?" Lear's telepathic voice sharp. *"Why is Firo attacking?"*

The ground shook. The mid-afternoon sun cast viny shadows across the ground.

A huge dark-gray wolf barreled toward her, the sheet of ice she'd slid on gone.

The lashes of wind sharpened. Roots burst to the surface, angrily flinging themselves toward at her.

Seas!

Phe rolled, hauled herself to her feet. *"Can't. Talk,"* she huffed and bolted into the forest, sheathing her knife while she ran. *"Escaping."*

Bitter air burned her lungs as she ran-slid down the slope, her body slamming against gnarly trees along the way. Each one gifted her with spikes of bone-bruising pain.

"Phe." Lear stretched her name into disappointment and worry. *"You're nowhere close to ready. It's too dangerous."*

She didn't bother responding. Instead, she grappled with her mental magic and wrapped it around her, replicating what Lear had taught her in the palace and cloaking her magical signature.

The hair on the back of her neck rose. She peeked over her shoulder as she rebounded off another tree.

The wolf was gaining on her.

"Shield!" Ihrone exclaimed, as if he could see how close the wolf was, or how the unnatural-moving trees seemed to exact stabbing pain as they and their roots tried to latch onto her.

The wolf lunged.

She tried to thrust her shield into place, but nothing happened.

Stars, not *this time.*

Shadow tendrils spiraled up Phe's legs and arms and engulfed her in darkness.

One foot to the next, the glacial cold disappeared and her lungs filled with warmer pine-scented air. The ground transformed from icy-snow to a rough, rocky road.

She tripped, smearing herself across sharp stone edges as she flew downward with the tilt of the ground. Her hands latched onto a medium-sized rock, her face smashing into it as her body careened around and semi-plunged over an edge.

High seas! Phe's heart galloped wildly in her chest.

Inch by pain-filled inch, she lugged her bruised and bleeding carcass onto solid ground. She clambered a safe distance before collapsing and taking in the narrow ledge she sensed was a farce of a road.

The tops of pine trees peppered the view off the ledge, looking more like stubs of grass, and gave her an unobstructed panorama of the mountain valley she was in. Crisp blue skies outlined green-colored peaks. The absence of snow and the warmth was concerning. At the bare minimum, it meant she was somewhere in the lower levels of Xiheria Highlands, and closer to the more temperate eastern side.

"Phe," Roar's shuttered voice interrupted her gulping breaths, his tone suggesting he wasn't talking privately to her. *"The general will order me to teleport you back."*

What he didn't say was that he didn't want to jump her back. She knew from their team discussions since the induction that none of them wanted to do anything to her against her will. Yet orders were orders. These nonnegotiable—tyrannical, in her opinion—directives, they made clear they would follow.

An irrational ache seized her heart.

She'd tried to deaden her reaction to Roar, remind herself he'd restrained her without hesitation. That he was Bastion's minion. Yet the broken pieces of her refused to cooperate. They'd whisper with memories of rocks and laughter and hard trainings and years of friendship based on hard-earned trust.

Phe wiped the blood streaming into her eyes away and gasped in agonizing breaths while taking inventory.

Everything hurt.

The wound on her face, though the bloodiest, wasn't the worst. A few broken branches had stabbed into her torso and legs. Her hands were blistered and swollen. It was painful to breathe, so she had likely fractured her ribs, but she disregarded the pain since she could walk. That was all she needed to do right now.

"Commander, teleport her back," Bastion ordered, including her, to let her know her game was over.

The now familiar sucking sensation hollowed her chest.

Phe's vision flickered and the all-too-familiar chest-vise clamped onto her ribcage, extracting pain like one would squeeze an orange for juice.

She burrowed her fingers into the rocky terrain under her. She knew it wouldn't stop him, but decided if Roar was going to teleport her back, he'd have to drag half the road with him too.

Shadows emerged from their shady hidey-holes. Their wispy tendrils slithered around her like a mass of snakes.

Phe lost the wavering sight she had.

She didn't dare to breathe.

Her shadows drained, revealing the crisp blue valley skyline, with fluffy white clouds drifting along the horizon.

"Sir," Roar's voice remained solid and emotionless. *"The teleportation was blocked."*

"Commander, you will keep trying," Bastion ordered. *"Phe. Listen closely."* The promise of impending pain oozed in Bastion's connection with her. *"If you think any of the punishments you've experienced with me before were bad, just wait. You have no idea what I'm capable of."*

She didn't doubt that, and maybe a perverse part of her welcomed his challenge. Bastion had publicly flogged her, then left her hanging by her thumbs for hours for her attempted escape in Oceanid and for disobeying direct orders from her commander. There were no amount of threats or monsters out there that would stop her from rescuing Kyra.

"Baby girl, please be careful," Finian said, his pitch ladened with defeated acceptance. *"Reach out if you need help. We can rescue you from just about anything but Djall, so don't let him catch you."* He paused, then tacked on. *"And try not to kill yourself, 'cause that was a close call."*

"Girl," Kirzia mind-spoke, *"you need to work on shielding while in action. That was close."*

Her stomach sank. *"How would you know?"*

"Oh," Finian's voice perked up, and an image of him winking at her popped in her mind. *"We have our ways."*

That's bullspit! Phe clenched her fist, only to freeze with a hiss of pain.

"Are you telling me you can see me?" Paranoia prickled each word. *Do they know where I am?* Her heart catapulted into her throat, wary they'd appear out of nowhere.

Phe's thoughts skidded to a stop, and her brain advised her there were limits to teleportation. No one could jump to a place they'd never been to before, except, apparently, for her.

"Right now, no. We could see everything on the council's peak," Finian shared, and Phe believed him.

A tremor began in her chest, then moved with the velocity of an earthquake throughout her. She may have incredible pain tolerance, but even she was not immune to shock.

Slowly, Phe fumbled her pack open and took out the canteen of Aswa tea. It wouldn't help with her injuries; those would heal with time. But it would help with refreshing her magic, thus speeding her recovery.

"Phe." This time it was Lear, and he used his ultra-soothing magical healing voice. *"Be careful."*

Instead of answering Lear with words, she sent a burst of appreciation to him.

Phe zoned the rest of what anyone said out, focusing on the magnificent view, and carefully inhaled the feeling of success.

Step one—escape Arias—complete.

Now to step two.

Figure out where she is then find and rescue Kyra.

38

Phe dove into the frigid depths of a clear, indigo-blue mountain lake. Gooseflesh sprouted with the shock of it, and all her pesky nervousness vanished. She swam until her lungs burned, then burst through the calm surface in an eruption of bubbles.

Teeth chattering, she treaded water.

There was a serenity to mountain lakes. A peacefulness Phe found at their quietly-lapping shores that went beyond gratitude for a water source. This one, like the ones before it, gave her a sense of solace and offered a cleansing.

Not just of her body, which the stars knew she needed, but of her mind and spirit.

This lake was tucked into a valley between mammoth mountains. Pine trees acted as sentries to its shores, obscuring its presence amongst the giants. The majestic panorama humbled her with its never-ending sky, jagged peaks, and wild wilderness.

It whispered to Phe.

It told her that her spark of life did not differ from the fish in the water, insects in the soil, and roaming animals. It explained she was part of the intricate web of life, where all life carried equal value, no matter their appearance. It evoked the impression of how precious life was as she passed through its seasons, and how her life, though important to her, was only a speck of dust in the earth's existence.

Phe clung to the last part. Being a speck of dust in the existence of time. It meant if she failed tonight, she could return to being a building block for other life and climb the celestial staircase.

A little rogue wave smacked her face, and Phe couldn't help but think it was Kyra, upset with her train of thoughts.

She wouldn't fail. At least, she wouldn't fail Kyra. The knowing in her bones that she'd rescue her sea sister was heavy and fierce. It was the part about her fate that left an unsettled sensation in her gut.

Nerves were normal, she told herself. Especially when she faced a deranged, magically-enhanced man who had access to a small army of possessed minds, all capable of magic she probably knew nothing of and would have no defense against.

When her shivering lessened and her body was all but numb, Phe returned to the rocky shoreline. She lingered long enough to run fingers through her dirty hair in an attempt to detangle it and scrub at the dirt covering her.

Over the last sixteen days, Phe hadn't bothered with anything other than quick wipe-offs. She'd used small streams and waterfalls she'd found along the way for those, too driven with identifying and following the landmarks and clues she'd mind-mapped.

It wasn't until she had breached Djall's compound that Kyra's tether snapped taut.

Clenching her jaw to keep her teeth from quivering, Phe emerged from the water. Her body was covered in the subtle hues of fading yellow and green. In some places, her skin puckered from where she'd had scabs.

She'd realized several things as she'd dragged her carcass from one ridge to another, through one unexpected jump to the next. The first was that, even though her body healed abnormally fast, without Orc, her recovery took time. The second was that she needed to learn to control her jumps, instead of going from one place to another unexpectedly and slamming into trees or rocks or bramble bushes or whatever obstacle waited to confront her.

Phe'd hustled into her underwear and shirt when the hollowness hit. Dropping to her knees, she gripped the stones under her and imagined them as anchors, while shadows coalesced around her. She wasn't sure what she was doing, only that whatever it was, it'd so far stopped her from being teleported to Arias.

The fast-paced *lub-dub, lub-dub* of her heartbeat was the only sound within the encasing blackness. It didn't matter to her that she'd successfully evaded being jumped since her escape; every time Roar tried, her heart pounded with trepidation.

I'm so close to Kyra. What if this time he succeeds?

She wedged her fingers deeper in between the rocks, not allowing herself to let those thoughts run wild. All she could do was take it one step at a time and consider all possibilities.

Phe'd debated, ever since finding the base Djall was holding Kyra in, if she should tell Shadow Unit she'd found her target. Would Roar stop trying to teleport her, or would his efforts increase?

Bastion would lose his mind, she was sure of it. He'd bombard her with incessant threats and distract her. As it was, the bastard connected with her daily to refreshen her memory on what he would do to her.

Her chest concaved with the suction. She gasped for breath, fighting the sudden deflation in her lungs. Then the sensation flipped. The emptiness became a tangible, prickling energy that engulfed her ribs and heart and arched her chest until it exploded out of her.

Her magic bounded from her, wrapping itself around the magical signature bursting through her, instinctively cloaking them.

Someone stumbled on the rocky footing, the sound sharp and intrusive.

She snatched the closest knife and scuttled backwards until she was ankle deep in icy water.

Her shadows evaporated.

Roar stood five paces from her, palms out, shoulders tense, his blue eyes trained on her. A backpack peeked over his shoulders, and he had sheaths strapped to his legs.

Phe slitted her eyes and barely refrained from hissing. Every muscle in her body tightened with tension. If he thought he was dragging her back to Arias, he had another think coming. She'd knock him unconscious and stuff his body into the hollow tree trunk she'd passed close to here.

Roar's weighted gaze traveled down her wet shirt to her bare legs. Phe knew there wasn't a detail he missed, from her injuries to the lake's shimmering water and the distant peaks.

She couldn't feel her hands or fingers or feet, and even though moments earlier her swim had been soothing, now she regretted it.

"Steady," Roar said, as if speaking to a feral animal, his shoulders loosening. "I'm not going to hurt you."

The edges of Phe's lips plunged toward her chin, and she

tightened her grip on the knife. "I'm *not* going to Arias with you." Her voice wavered from disuse and the cold.

"It's a good thing we can't teleport back, then." Roar retreated to firmer ground, shrugged the pack off, and squatted. Even though he looked about to riffle through his pack, Phe knew he lowered himself to give her the power deferential. "Can you cloak my presence?"

"Already done," Phe snapped. She inched out of the water, her feet searching for steady footing. "What are you doing here?"

"Would you believe me if I said I decided to join you?" Roar stilled, his posture appearing semi-relaxed.

Phe huffed, and suspicion etched the sound. "The old, 'can't beat 'em, join 'em' mentality?" Her tone told him she didn't believe it. She crept to hover over her belongings.

"Not exactly." Roar's bottom lip stuck out a little, and his gaze stayed unwaveringly on her face. "Your lips are blue."

She arched a brow. If it weren't for him, she'd be dressed with her hair wrung out, braided, and on her way to Djall's base. She'd have warmed up by now.

A shrill bird call filled the silence.

"Please, finish dressing. I promise not to do anything." Roar pivoted on his toes, giving her his back.

"What are your orders?" Phe hauled her pants on and crammed her feet into socks, then shoes. She fumbled with her sheaths. Her numb fingers weren't working properly, and she had to leave them half-buckled.

"Until a moment ago, it was to teleport you to Arias. If I had to guess, the general would order I restrain you while Kirzia opens a portal for us," Roar said.

"If you had to guess?" Phe didn't miss the specificity of his conjecture, nor that Kirzia could create portals while being in a different location. "Does that mean you can't hear him?"

Roar's head bobbed. "Yes, that's exactly what it means."

"How did you block him?" That was a skill she needed to know.

"I didn't. Lear did. You decent?"

Phe grunted, feeling slighted. Why hadn't Lear shown her how to block Bastion? "Why?"

"Lear understands I can't ignore an order." Roar took that as his cue to swivel and face her again. "If I can't hear the order, then there's nothing that can be done."

"What about Shadow Unit relaying orders to you?"

Roar grimaced. "We have a few hours, at most. They've made themselves inaccessible for the moment, and Lear worked his magic with them too. They're standing by to help if needed."

Phe gathered her soaking hair, squeezed it out, and quickly braided it, hiding where she could the silver strand to avoid moonlight reflecting off it, and then covering the rest with a black bandana. The back of her shirt was a cold, wet mess, which she slipped her stinky sweater over and then slid her pack on. "I meant, if you're not here on Bastion's orders, why *are* you here?"

Roar's fingertips pressed into the earth to balance his weight. His jaw set. "I'm here because someone I care about is on a suicide mission, and I won't let her do it alone."

"This is not a suicide mission." Phe's eyebrows formed a wrinkled V on her forehead, and her lips puckered as if she'd tasted something sour. The uneasy sensation skittering in her gut tightened with her lie.

Roar's lips compressed until they were a slim line.

If I'd gone in last night . . . This wouldn't have be an issue.

She'd have rescued Kyra already, and they'd be on their way to Xafara.

Phe countered her thought; it would have been unrealistic. The last four nights she'd been scouting the base, observing their security, and moving within the shadows to figure out where Djall kept everyone. It was only last night she'd figured out what building held the entrance to the underground system Djall imprisoned his captives in.

Phe stood. It didn't matter if he considered this a suicide mission or not. She was rescuing Kyra, and she was doing it tonight. "Is that the only reason?" Phe tensed and relaxed her cold-swollen hands, and rocked from her heels to her toes, trying to warm up.

"No." Roar watched her fists.

Phe gave him a pointed glare to continue.

"Want my help warming up?" Roar offered his palms.

"I want you to answer my questions," Phe retorted, eyeing those warm palms of his. The aching, broken place in her heart yearned for her to slide her palms into his and feel the tingly sensations his touch elicited. Her mind skewered the ache with the harsh reality her heart wanted to forget.

She couldn't trust him.

Roar dropped his hands. "My second reason is to tell General Bastion where the base is."

Phe toyed with her amulet and kept her stare vacant. She'd planned to rescue Kyra alone due to everything that had happened. Kyra was not Bastion's priority, and she wouldn't give him any room to interfere with her mission. Thus, she hadn't planned to tell anyone anything. A huge risk, considering the likelihood of things going wrong.

Maybe it was the cleansing from the lake, reducing her to a speck of dust. Or the fact Roar was willing to risk his life to ensure Bastion and the others knew where the base was that dismantled her faulty thinking.

Stars. Phe lowered her head and gaze, swallowing the disgusting taste of shame. *Kyra isn't the only prisoner in there.*

She knew, from her work with Lear, the damage of being in Djall's possession. She knew the depravity and the neglect and the horror of their helplessness. She *knew*, and she'd put it to the side, her sole focus Kyra.

Gads, what type of monster does that?

Hammering the derision in, Phe knew there were fifty-six tainted minds at this base, and she'd only considered the one she came for. *How inexcusably selfish and Bastion-like.*

"Was I wrong?" Roar asked, and Phe resurfaced from her thoughts.

"No." The truth tasted vile, yet the single word freed her from ingesting a revolting lie that would eat her innards.

Roar gave her a sad half-smile. "I understand why you've kept your silence. We shattered your trust." And that right there was why her heart throbbed over their friendship. Her "no" may have been a single utterance, but it was loaded with vulnerability and authenticity and contempt and judgment.

She was the monster here, not him and not Bastion. Yet instead of condemnation, he'd gathered her unsaid emotions, like wildflowers in a field, the thorny and ugly alongside the petals and blooms, into an untamed bouquet that he delicately preserved.

Phe peeked at Roar through her lashes and fell into the soothing depths of his eyes. She'd missed these moments, the ones where he seemed to touch her soul.

She shuttered her gaze and returned to the question at hand. *Can I trust him?* Gads, she wanted to. Her heart desperately craved to.

He'd jumped to her.

The team collectively blocked Bastion from communicating to not have to act on his orders, to delay the inevitable.

Roar wanted to join her on her suicide mission to save Kyra, knowing more than Phe did what their chances were.

He kept offering her pieces to rebuild their demolished house of trust. She was the one who kept refusing to take them. What if she took this piece?

Roar rummaged in his pack, not rushing her.

On a sigh, Phe buckled. "You have impeccable timing. My plan is to go in tonight."

"You look like you're starving." Roar pulled something from his pack and tossed it at her.

Instinctively, she caught it. It was some sort of jerky stick. Her stomach rumbled. A small, appreciative smile snuck past her defenses, urged on by her traitorous belly and heart.

Biting into the dry, chewy, earthy-tasting stick, she realized it was made of Aswa. Five bites later, it was gone, and she was gulping from her canteen of water. "Djall's base is about an hour's walk from here." The evening light was dimming, and she shoved the rest of her scattered belongings into her pack. "I was planning to get there by dusk."

Roar stood and heaved his pack on.

Phe followed suit and walked toward the treeline. As she passed Roar, she pinned him with an *I'm-trusting-you-don't-mess-it-up-and-force-me-to-hurt-you* look.

He lifted his palms in a placating motion. "I promise. I'm here to help."

Phe intensified her glare. In it, she reiterated her threat and added a jab at him for reading her so well.

Roar was not affected by her at all. In fact, an oddly attractive half-smirk emerged in response to her last look.

While they walked, Phe told him about the other location she'd deduced from mind-mapping and what she'd discovered in her surveillance of this compound, the layout of the buildings, and that there were Stills in Djall's camp.

As they neared the encampment, she wiped her sweaty palms on her pants. Her heart rate quickened, and the returning sense that something was going to go wrong gnawed at her.

Roar's presence both calmed her and bothered her. Phe knew she was willing to risk her life for Kyra's because she was the only family Phe had. The only person who had been willing to see Phe, not as a ten-year-old violent, traumatized street urchin, but as a friend and a person with value.

Phe turned to Roar, who stood close enough she could bend her arm and touch his chest. "Bastion's going to punish you," she said, tilting her face to his.

"Definitely."

She crinkled a brow, confused. "Why are you here?" She knew Roar's drive and motivation. Knew how much his career meant and how hard he'd been working. Knew that any punishment from Bastion was direly unpleasant and that he was risking everything he'd worked for.

"What if I'm doing this so we have a future?"

The crinkle spread to both brows. "We have futures." They were at a juncture in their current path where one future was eternal possession by a crazed maniac, while the other path lead to Kyra's rescue followed by severe punishment. Neither was pleasant. "Though they're a little dim-looking right now, and you didn't answer my question."

"Why are you rescuing Kyra?"

Phe gave him a *why-are-you-answering-my-question-with-a-question* look. He knew why she was doing this. "She's my sea sister, and I gave my word I would protect her."

"Because you care about her?"

"Yes." Phe glowered at him. "Why aren't you answering my question?"

"What if I am doing this because I care about you?"

"You do?" The idea was startling. Roar cared enough to risk everything?

"Yes."

A warmth blossomed in her chest and spread to her neck.

Phe's mouth suddenly dried as her errant mind took the reins. Did he mean he cared for her like his sister, Ash? Like a teammate? And that he would do this for anyone in Shadow Unit? Then she answered her own questions. Roar was a deeply loyal friend and protector. He would do this for any of them.

Unbidden, the rocks in his entryway came to mind. The sleepless, silent nights they spent on the stone slab in Spirit-vale, or whatever overlook Phe found in the other places they'd been. The burdens he took and cherished.

The intertwining plants in his kitchen stone garden.

Roar had shifted closer, their chests almost touching.

Step away or stay? Phe's body made the choice for her, rooting her feet to the spot.

"Are you ready?"

Why did it feel like there was a double meaning to his question? "Yes," she whispered. *No.*

"In case it all goes wrong." His eyes ensnared hers, and she found herself unable to look away from their blue depths. A tendril of air, soft and tantalizing, stroked upwards on her neck, leaving a trail of wanting in its wake.

Phe's mouth parted, and she sucked in a breath, the sensation sending tingles of warmth into other corners of her body. It felt good. Better than good.

Roar's lips touched hers at the same time his fingertips grazed her cheek. Magnificent sparks of pleasure zinged through her, awakening a part of her that was dormant. His soft lips firmly glided over hers, and then they were gone, taking the zings with them. She almost swayed toward him as he drew back an inch, blue gaze diving into her. "Remember, we stay together no matter what."

He kissed me.

Phe retreated a step. Then another. *My first kiss.* Right before a suicide mission.

He doesn't think we'll make it.

She drew in one of her steadying breaths, internally shaking herself. *"We'll make it,"* she assured him, her telepathic voice strong and confident. Even though what she really meant was 'he and Kyra will make it'. She'd had sixteen days to grapple with and accept the likelihood she wouldn't.

Without waiting for an answer, Phe turned and stealthily weaved her way into Djall's encampment, wrapping her comforting shadows around them. Once she'd breached its perimeter, she telepathically linked with Bastion to initiate their plan. *"Connecting to Bastion now."*

To Bastion, she arrowed into his mind the estimated location they were at, what she was doing, the general location of the other base, and everything else they'd decided was crucial information for Bastion to have. Then she cut the connection, directing the bastard to Roar. *"Done."*

They emerged from the forest under the cover of night and shadows, passing the outer layer of ramshackle buildings. Their roofs were weary and sagging, moss ate at their sidings, and their windows and doors were broken or hung askew.

Phe believed this had been done on purpose, to give the appearance of an abandoned settlement, lost to the ravages of nature. A message that there was nothing to see here, and explore at your own cost, to anyone who, by horrible happenstance, stumbled upon it.

Djall's taint was everywhere, yet Phe didn't feel his mental presence. She wasn't convinced this meant he wasn't here. She'd only been able to sense everyone's presence once she breached his perimeter, and she acknowledged Djall'd probably kept his own signature cloaked separately from the base.

As they passed the dilapidated structures, most of them empty, Roar marked them with a simple touch.

The buildings improved in construction and care as they got closer. In these buildings, there was a combination of Still minds, with only a half-dozen possessed magic-borns scattered amongst them. Presumably, Djall's defense. Though Phe had more reason to believe they were there to ensure anyone who stumbled in never made it out.

"Two buildings to the right, one MB," Phe told Roar; MB was her new abbreviation for magic-born. *"Third hut to the left, another one."*

"And Stills?"

Phe knew Roar was relaying this to Bastion. *"Twenty-five, an average of two per shack."* She paused at the last building and stared at the side of the mountain. A castle was nestled into an opening in the cliff side and inside it was the only entry point to what lay underground.

What would they find? Her stomach churned. This was too easy. Djall might be maniacal, but he was also paranoid and brilliant.

Kyra's leash urged her onward, unaware of the obstacles between them.

Phe's instincts screamed this was a trap, one she planned to walk into no matter what. Yet with Roar at her back, his life now in the balance, apprehension clogged her lungs with a heavy fog.

She'd recklessly endanger her life for Kyra. The last two months proved this repetitively. Could she risk Roar's?

The sinking hole in her stomach told her no. She might not know what to think about his kiss and their tattered friendship—those thoughts were for after this mess was over—but she valued his life. Which made walking into this trap worse.

"Why don't you go back?" Phe mind-spoke in a last-ditch effort. *"You can coordinate with Bastion."*

"We're staying together." Roar's response was the same non-negotiable answer he'd given her when they'd talked about her plan.

"What if I disappear on you? Leave you completely defenseless?" Phe voiced one of her rising concerns. Whatever she was doing to teleport around the mountains, she had no control over.

"I'm willing to take that risk. You are not going in alone."

Phe swallowed, her mouth dry. She should've knocked him out and bound him, left him for Bastion. Why had she let him talk her into this?

Unable to do anything other than proceed with their plan, Phe bolted around the side of the castle. Last night, she'd checked the windows and found one easy to pry open.

Once they were both inside, her heartbeat competed with one of Edva's high-speed gallops and fear-infused sweat dampened her armpits. This was the part where her plan became reckless. She knew where people were in relation to her, but hadn't discovered the exact location of the doorway.

"Wait." Roar sounded distracted.

Phe glanced over her shoulder at him. His blue eyes glowed in the semi-darkness. *"Make it fast. We have three people coming toward us."*

His hand hovered over the small of her back. *"I have a sense of where the doorway is. Can we go left?"*

"How?" Phe took the left, grateful he hadn't suggested the other direction.

"My prime capability is elemental magic, which means I can connect with all the elements. This castle was carved from the earth. I can tap into the land and get a sense. Can we take the next right?"

"No." The three possessed minds had somehow gotten into that room and were heading toward them. *"Back up, fast. We've got incoming."* Phe's heart lurched.

They shuffle-retreated, retracing their steps.

When she realized they wouldn't make it to cover in time, Phe yanked Roar into the only other door in the hallway, a closet, and shoved herself in after. Her back pressed into his solid chest, and his head was bent over her left shoulder to fit underneath the shelving. His warm breath tickled her neck and sent the few stray hairs there swinging.

Phe gripped her thigh knives, the cold pommels reassuringly firm, and fought the wash of panic enclosed spaces gave her. She contemplated asking about his other capabilities, or the teams, but decided it was irrelevant. If she survived this, she'd ask.

They waited for what felt like an eternity until the minds had moved on.

"We should be safe." Phe slid the door open, able to

breathe once she escaped the closest. She took the right Roar had indicated.

"Through this room, and it should be on the left in the next hallway," Roar said, then added. *"I never realized you don't like tight spaces."*

"It never came up," Phe dismissed, even though it had, many, many times.

They passed through a tremendous dining room, its table double the size of Areya's. An enormous portrait hung on the wall at the head of the table. Its gold frame was thick with an ornate design.

"Hm," Roar mind-muttered, not fooled.

Phe slowed to absorb the man featured in the painting. He was stunning. His face was angularly cut with a short, trimmed dark beard and thick, shapely eyebrows. His light brown eyes gazed over the expanse of the table with an intensity that was unnatural for a painting, and his bottom lip was slightly fuller than his top.

"Is that him?" No one had shown her what Djall looked like.

"Yes."

There was something about the portrait that raised Phe's hackles, and she scanned over her cloaking of them. Nothing was out of place. It didn't ease the feeling, so she rushed them into the adjoining hallway. This hallway was wider, with arched ceilings. Phe slowed at the first door on their left.

"Third door down."

Following Roar's instructions, she cracked opened the door and a blast of cool, putrid air slapped her senses. *Gads.* Breathing through her mouth, she inched down a slick, barely-lit stone stairway.

Kyra's tether started pulsing.

The carved stone in this portion of the castle was edgy and porous. The only sound she heard was the rhythmic *drip-drip-drip* of water. Djall's taint stained the air with a viscous energy that Phe had never quiet experienced before. The only reference she had was when she'd assisted Bastion with halting a sex trafficking ring.

The moment she'd stepped into the dungeon system where people were being held, there'd been a heaviness—as if all the pain and torture and fear and helplessness and evilness had congealed into the air and permeated into the ground. It had felt as if the land had been scarred.

This was worse. Much worse.

Phe's magic lurched hungrily, wantonly, in her chest. Djall's sullied magic settled on them.

They descended the first level of the spiral steps, leaving what little light they had behind. At the second landing, Kyra's leash yanked, pulling her into pitch-black darkness. Phe's skin prickled with the feeling they were crawling into the belly of a dragon.

"Bastion is readying to deploy. We only have a few more minutes."

"We're close." Phe's heart sprinted with nerves and anticipation. She stopped and blindly groped the moist surface, searching for a door handle. *"Kyra's on the other side of this wall. Help me find the door?"*

Precious seconds passed as they scoured the wall. *"Got it,"* Roar announced. *"Bastion's incoming."*

Sweat burst on her forehead, even though it was cold. Phe linked into Kirzia and asked, *"Are you ready?"*

"Girl, ready when you are," Kirzia replied, including Roar in her response. Phe inched closer to Roar until she felt his warmth, only able to make out the barest of outlines in the darkness.

"Opening," Roar stated, and the moment the door cracked opened, he flew backwards. A loud thud reverberated in the hall.

"Shield!" Roar commanded.

Phe threw her shield up, something they'd agreed to only do once their presence was announced, and the ground shook with a series of blasts. Each building Roar marked detonated in one continuous rolling explosion, shaking the foundation. Dirt trickled from the ceiling, and the hallway filled with the sound of grating rocks.

Phe shuffled in Roar's direction. *"You okay?"*

"Fine," he mind-grunted.

Good enough for her. *"My turn."* She pivoted and kicked open the door, only to be tossed backwards by a jolt of power. Instead of hitting the stone wall, powerful arms snatched her mid-air, and then they both sprinted into the room together.

"Kirzia, now," Roar mind-boomed.

The door slammed shut behind them.

A wave of Djall's power swept through the room, and following it, eighteen pairs of tinted glowing eyes broke the darkness at mid-thigh height.

Gads, this guy does creepy well.

Djall's poisonous magic caressed her shield, its filthy tendrils wrapping around it, and she had the distinct, disturbing impression it was tasting her magic.

"Phe, you've come to me," Kyra's flat, monotone voice broke the fetid silence. It might have been Kyra's voice, but it was Djall talking. Movement in a cage at the back of the room—six cages down, if Phe correctly made out the cages in the dark—drew her. Its occupant clutched the bars, and a pair of achingly familiar, black-tinted, emerald glowing eyes stared at her.

Phe's heart stilled. *Djall has possession of Kyra.* Phe's magic recoiled in her chest, anger igniting like brushfires in her veins. Her attempt to protect Kyra while dreamscaping had failed.

The air vibrated just outside of Phe's shield next to Roar, and a pinprick of light broke the darkness. Kirzia's portal.

"I'm going to kill you," Phe vowed to Djall, staring into the void of her friend's gaze. "Let them go," Phe said, even though she knew it was impossible to rationalize with someone as power hungry as Djall.

Kyra burst into eerie laughter, setting off a domino effect of laughter from all corners of the room. Possessed minds in other rooms began moving toward them, and the collective sensation was disconcerting.

"Don't engage him," Roar curtly commanded.

"Djall is mobilizing the others," she told him. Her magic clawed at her chest.

"Bastion is here," Roar said, pushing on her shield. *"Can you expand this?"*

Phe envisioned her shield pulsing, and with each beat, expanding until her force-field pressed against the room's stone walls. She engulfed Kirzia's portal, which was now the size of a toddler and was still enlarging. Its bright light illuminated the dirt and sewage in the room.

Unable to help herself, she reached out and touched Kyra's hand, a zing of electricity shooting painfully into her. Kyra twisted her wrist, grabbing Phe and pulling her arm so that Phe's face slammed into the bars. Kyra's other hand throttled her neck and squeezed.

Staring into the blackened eyes of her best friend, Phe gritted her teeth as electricity seared into her. Kyra's nails bit into her cheeks.

Tendrils of Djall's magic slithered around her neck,

crept into her ears, her hairline, and down her shirt. Bile burned her throat as his magic explored her breasts and traveled the planes of her stomach. She could feel its vile darkness lapping at her relentlessly, and she shuddered in revulsion.

Like a volcano erupting, Phe's magic flooded the room and latched onto Djall's caged eighteen. Its grip yanked their hunched postures straight and crushed them into the tops of their cages.

The zapping buzz of electricity ricocheted in the room.

Phe's magic burrowed into the prisoners' skins and, like the parasitic leech she was, sank its teeth into the corrupted magic and sucked.

"What are you doing?" Roar asked.

The door was wrenched from its hinges and thrown at Phe's shield. The impact caused a burst of sharp pain, which heightened to agony as bodies pummeled it. Djall's filthy magic bombarded her, awakening the pesky drummer behind her eyes.

"Fighting Djall's magic," she said, simplifying the truth, keeping her secret. The prisoners in the cages were writhing silently, and the ones at the door pounded her shield.

Kyra crumpled to the floor, releasing Phe—who also tumbled to the floor. Phe's magic zinged with a surge of energy, which she funneled into her shield. The others dropped one by one, each time boosting Phe as she took Djall's magic for her own.

"Mine won," she announced, unwilling to attend to her heart's cringe at how she'd won. *"You're up."*

Roar's magic collided with hers, and for a moment, fear choked her. Would her magic try to eat his too? Instead of feverishly clamping onto him, their magics intertwined and danced, and then Roar's magic was tearing the cages apart.

Her heart stuttered with relief, only to be crushed under the weight of a mountain as the stone ceiling collapsed into her shield.

"Get Kyra . . ." She gasped around the pain, unsure of how long she could hold her shield in place, and watched Roar gather Kyra in his arms and carry her to the portal. A wave of relief so powerful, it threatened to overwhelm her swept through her at knowing Kyra was safe. *". . . others, portal. Hold."*

On hands and knees, Phe twisted to the doorway in time to witness the entire rock wall explode.

If her elbows hadn't been locked, the blast would've buckled her.

Seconds later, Djall's possessed lined the hallway in lieu of the wall and hacked at her defenses.

Warm liquid trickled from her ears.

"You're mine," Djall said. The disturbing proclamation was announced, uncannily, from those he possessed as they rammed her shield. Fire and ice, fists and feet, rocks and debris, anything and everything he could use to stab her. "You don't belong with them; you're meant for me."

Seas. It hurt everywhere. She wouldn't be able to hold much longer.

Fractures splintered her force-field.

Spots appeared in her vision, and the solo drummer went wild.

Phe squinted at Roar, confused by his sudden dark hair, before realizing it was Finian. He must have stepped through the gateway and was helping Roar scoop up people and pass them through the portal.

Shadows coalesced on the floor, writhing in furious spools around her ankles and wrists.

A cord of Djall's magic squeezed into a fracture on her shield and arrowed toward her.

A shadow vine intercepted it mid-air, blue fire erupted to encase their collision, and their magics grappled.

More fissures broke the surface of her shield.

"Last one," Roar said, the sound another jab of pain. Phe glimpsed him hurriedly handing the limp person off to Finian and turning toward her.

Djall's magic rode each break, squirmed into the barest openings, and rended them open. Then, like the release of a thundercloud, Djall poured his power into her shield.

Magic tore from Phe's chest in response, crashing into Djall's, but her magic wasn't enough.

Befouled lines cinched around Roar and her, just missing Finian as he stepped through the portal.

Phe watched in horror as noxious ropes wove around Roar and toppled him to his knees.

Her stomach bottomed out. *No!*

Roar's grim blue gaze locked onto hers. His jaw clenched.

Rancid strands banded around her neck and tightened, hauling her onto her knees and cutting off her breath. She couldn't look away from the black tendrils that lashed onto Roar, sprouting tiny roots that burrowed into him.

Fighting for air, Phe sank her nails into the bands at her neck and tried to ignore the disgusting sensation of bugs clawing into her.

Blackness shimmered across Roar's eyes.

Roar, nooo! Her throbbing, oxygen-deprived heart thudded painfully against her rib cage. Something inside Phe fractured.

Within her next gasping breath, blue lightning struck Roar.

Terror rippled along the stairway of her spine as his body seized.

Blue light radiated from under Roar's skin, then it pulsed within him.

The black veins entrapping him tensed.

Another wave of blue light rocked Roar, and Djall's black magic combusted, shards of black exploding from his body. Blue light followed immediately, bursting out in rays of exquisite light, until both black and blue were gone.

Roar sank to his hands, barely holding himself up.

Thank the seas.

Djall's magic merged around her. The air vibrated.

The well of magic in Phe's chest emptied, draining into the ground unhelpfully. Her muscles burned with the strain of supporting her magic. She clawed at the bands around her throat, desperately trying to suck in air. The drummer in her mind increased his pounding tempo.

Phe envisioned anchoring herself to the stone ground and gathered the shadows tight, fighting the weightless pull of the impending jump.

The air crackled with power. Hers. Djall's. Roar's.

A column of effulgent light surrounded her.

Her kneecaps dug into uneven rock as the weightlessness retracted, the burst of relief so strong that, if Djall's magic weren't strangling her, she'd have face-planted.

Bolts of blue lightning hit, filling the air with ozone and green oak. The blue light adhered to her shield and filled the cracks to the quickened rhythm of her heartbeat. The first beam illuminated all the threads of battling magic. The second outburst clamped onto the corrupted magic. And the third flare . . . white light infused Djall's tendrils, creating a stark visual of lightning skittering across the blue light, and then it disintegrated with a pulse of electricity that zapped Phe where Djall's vines clutched her.

She collapsed, gasping for breath, and stared through the mass of shadows. Sparks of light lit the thrashing shadows around her, and for the briefest moment, Phe thought she saw rainbows floating in their depths. It must have been the pressure building in her head, or the lack of oxygen, because it was gone the next moment.

It was weird to feel your muscles be consumed, your bones sucked cleaned, your heartbeat whither, but that was exactly what she felt. And there was nothing she could do about it. Her magic had turned on her as a fuel source, and she couldn't let go yet.

Phe wasn't holding onto her shield and magic for just Roar. It was for those achingly gaunt prisoners of Djall's tearing at her shields. Those souls she knew she couldn't leave without fighting for.

"Cripes, Phe." Roar clambered to her side, gathered her to his chest, and snaked his arms under her.

Flames flared at the surface of her shadows and intertwined with the blue light, drawing entwined shadow light into a tidal wave of shadowfire that crashed into and through her shield, pulverizing Djall's possessed.

Roar stumbled to his feet shakily with her, his arms trembling so much she shook.

"No," Phe mind-whispered, entranced with the battlefield of magic. *"Can't . . . leave . . . them."* Her vision funneled into tiny spheres of light.

"Sorry, Phe," Roar gritted, but he was obviously not sorry at all because he kept staggering to the portal.

"They'll . . ." The pain lightened as a blast of energy rebounded into her magic. *". . . die."*

"You're dying."

Phe's shadows clenched around the fallen and another bolt of blue lightning sizzled into the shadow midst.

The drummer in her head abandoned his set in rage, took hold of his drums, and bashed them against walls of her mind. Words were harder and harder to form, so when she tried to tell Roar the possessed were free, it was a bunch of nonsensical sounds.

A deep rumbling shook the castle foundation.

The portal loomed in front of them, emitting a blinding light that drove spikes of pain into Phe's head.

She fixed her sights on her shadows, watching them wriggle over bodies beyond her reach. Obscuring them. From one second to the next, her shadows dissolved, and a stillness settled into the gaping darkness.

Roar stepped through the portal right as a blast threw them into Arias and the portal vanished in a spiral of light.

"Orc!" Roar called, his chin lightly touched the top of her head.

She was jolted when Roar's knees buckled.

"Got her." Another set of arms wrapped around her. "Sir, you can let go."

"I don't think I can," Phe heard Roar mutter as sparks of light burst in the crowding darkness of her mind.

Hadn't the lake whispered to her, from life to dust, and from dust, life is created? Surrendering never felt so good, knowing as she left, her speck of dirt would birth new life. *May theirs be easier than mine,* Phe wished for them.

Her gaze glided to the majestic celestial stairway in front of her and she drifted toward the glittering stars.

39

"It's time to wake up." Elzac broke the endless, blissful silence of the void.

Phe shifted, and the embracing darkness snuggling her like a weighted blanket moved with her. She didn't want to wake. She didn't want to do anything other than float in this peaceful oasis, where her worries were gone.

"Phe, it's time."

Phe mentally swatted at him, rolled her featherlight body, and sank into nothingness.

Elzac cleared his throat, the sound grating. *"You've been drifting for seven days."*

Drifting? Is that what he called this? She'd ascended the stairway. Added her spark of light next to the others in the great cosmos.

Apparently, Elzac hadn't gotten the message, because he continued to hound her. *"Phe, there are consequences to drifting for too long. You have to wake up."*

Grr, no.

A lightness had settled over her achy bones and extreme lethargy. Her pain had vanished and, along with it, the incessant worry she carried for Kyra. A squirrelly suspicion chittered in the recesses of her mind, and irritation bloomed.

Where was he when I'd called for him? Sparks of anger flared halfheartedly in her gut. *When I'd needed him?*

Elzac's tone was his overly patient, wise-man one. *"There are roads that must be traveled alone. And life has a way of ensuring that is the case."*

The vexing deduction he'd answered her thought was superseded with frustration. Why couldn't the people in her life just answer her questions? *"That is not an answer."*

"The protections established in Arias," Elzac conceded in explaining, *"make it nearly impossible for you to connect to me."*

"But you talked to me in Arias." Phe didn't bother to disguise the whine in her voice.

"My skill level is much more advanced than yours."

She humphed.

"Which is something you need to work on." Elzac's voice slid into his *I'm-concerned-for-your-well-being-child-and-you-need-to-listen* tone. *"Most magic-borns never experience a single episode of magic depletion, let alone three in three months. It's taking a toll on you."*

How does one go about telling someone else they've died? Phe wondered, realizing Elzac considered her one of the living. *Should I coach him to let me go?*

"Over the span of my long life—" He switched tactics, probably because he heard her thought, *again.* *"—I've come to believe there is an alignment of one's soul with their life's purposes. It's only when the two have converged, their tasks complete and their souls ready, that they traverse the celestial stairway."*

Phe perked up, alarm scurrying along her arms. *"Are you

telling me my life's purposes—as in plural—have not been completed?"

Grim silence answered her.

How the seas is that possible? Phe only had one life purpose, and that was to protect Kyra. She'd rescued Kyra, thus she'd fulfilled her purpose and she could rest now.

"Our purposes come in different shapes and sizes. Some we clearly know about, and others remain a mystery, at least until we ascend. How do you feel about Djall?"

The question derailed her momentarily. The spice of guilt stung her throat. *"He's a monster." And I vowed to stop him.* That stilled her beating heart. *Oh stars!* What had she done? Had she volunteered for this purpose when she'd made her vow?

Phe's mind fired off one thing after the next. Was she supposed to stop Djall? Was she responsible for more than Kyra's welfare? Did she have to work with the bastard? Go through the tedious duty of learning about magic? And, even more challenging, learning to use hers? What would the beasts in Arias do if they learned her magic ate Djall's?

If Elzac was right in his belief—whether she believed it or not—and she hadn't, in his insinuation, completed her life tasks, it meant . . .

"Are you telling me I am not *dead?"* A vise squeezed her chest. *Oh, seas.* The weighted blanket slipped. The unceasing worry she'd escaped while drifting knotted her stomach, tightened her shoulders, and invaded her thoughts. *Kyra? Roar?*

"Your friend, Kyra, has returned with her mother, Thetis, to Oceanid and she is . . . struggling." Elzac tone was carefully neutral. Phe knew he felt her friendship with Kyra was unhealthy. Enmeshed, he'd called it, and it probably pained him to tell her this. "As for your commander, I have no doubt he'll survive his punishments."

Reality speared her, raking her with the unforgiving truth of what this meant. If she wasn't dead . . .

She was alive.

Mother-flipping seas.

She pried an eye open, intending to skewer Elzac with it. Light stabbed her eye, and when her vision cleared enough, it was Bastion's piercing brown gaze that flayed her.

An unrecognizable emotion flickered, candle-flame quick, to be replaced by his ever-present, brutally-cold stare. Crescent-shaped bags clung to the underside of his eyes, and deep wrinkles engraved his face.

She slammed her blurry, crusty eye closed. *Stars, please be a hallucination.*

The effort to reopen her eyes was unnatural, resulting in her brows crawling up her forehead and the feeling of her eyes over-stretching at their corners.

"Phe." Bastion's voice boomed, and her head instantly throbbed to the rhythm of her pounding heart. A slow, sinister smile broke the planes of his face, baring his teeth.

Seas, why do the stars hate me?

EPILOGUE

The woodsy scents of dirt and pine wrapped around her. Cold emanated from the hard, rough rock she sat on, her feet swinging in empty air. Before her, an endless night sky painted the horizon. Inhaling the chill air, she scoured the sleeping city landscape, finding the large oval where the four major roads of Xafara connected in Spiritvale.

She retraced her memories, trying to figure out how she'd gotten here. Elzac had woken her, thrusting her from the void she'd been in directly into Bastion's hands—where he'd immediately begun the series of punishments he'd promised her while she'd been rescuing Kyra.

On the rock, Phe swallowed and held up her hands, rubbing her fingers together, grateful for her skin and lack of pain. She must be dreaming. Bastion's latest punishment wouldn't have healed this quickly.

A twig snapped, and she swung her gaze toward the narrow entrance. Tense.

"One day I am going to clear a path so wide—" Roar grunted, repeating his usual threat, "—I will tiptoe through here in total silence."

She huffed.

He sauntered toward her. He'd pulled his deep auburn hair into a tight little bun. She could just make out the strong lines of his face. Even though she couldn't see his blue eyes, she felt them trained on her.

Phe straightened her spine as he sat next to her and scooted close, her heart fluttering. Roar dropped his feet over the ledge, his thigh pressed against hers—infusing warmth into her—and their shoulders gently collided. Surprisingly, her skin didn't react.

"What are you brooding over?" Roar teasingly asked.

Phe rolled her eyes and returned her attention to the city. "Are we dreamscaping?"

"Definitely."

Phe sighed, toying with her amulet. "Are you okay?" She hadn't seen him since she'd woken.

"I'm fine," Roar said. There was an edge to his voice.

"You know," Phe bit her bottom lip to keep from smirking, "I learned recently that FINE means Feelings Inside Not Expressed."

Roar laughed and nudged her shoulder. "To me," he said, "the more important question is, how are you?"

"Did Bastion skin you?" Phe asked, ignoring his question and luxuriating in the pain-free experience of their touch.

"No." Roar shifted tensely. "Is that your punishment?"

Phe inwardly cringed and avoided his question. "I'm wondering what Bastion has in store for the finale of my punishments."

Roar inhaled deeply, as if trying to control a rush of emotion.

"Why are you here and not Kyra?" she asked, redirecting them. She shouldn't have mentioned the skinning, and honestly she didn't want to know what else Bastion had planned.

"I don't know," Roar said, and she felt his shrug. "It's your dreamscape. Were you thinking about me?"

"Maybe?" Her tone pitched higher with the question. Phe rolled one of the braids on her amulet between her fingers and ignore the heat creeping up her neck. She'd thought about him often, wondering what type of punishments he was going through, and sometimes she'd let herself think about their kiss—but she'd never tell him that. "I've been trying to dreamscape with Kyra since I woke, and it hasn't worked. Do you know how she's doing?"

"Lear knows more about how she's really doing, as he's been meeting with her weekly for healing sessions—though he probably wouldn't tell you anything unless Kyra gave him permission."

Something akin to a clamp eased in her chest at knowing Lear was helping Kyra. After working side by side with him in the healing tent, she trusted him with Kyra.

"Commander Elex has been keeping in touch though, and from him we've heard that Velimir moved in, and the staff is not happy about it. He's been boldly hinting he'd like to move into your room because Her Grace prefers to sleep in it. Alone—from what the servants are reporting."

Phe's heart throbbed. There had been a time in Phe's life, a little after Kyra and she had become friends, that Phe would sneak into Kyra's room and sleep on the floor to be closer to her. She'd done it partially because she had this fierce need to protect Kyra, and partially because she felt safer when she was near her. *Is that why Kyra's doing it now?*

"Kyra's mother, Thetis—I know she tried to introduce herself to you at the celebration banquet—she's moved into House Nereid."

Phe snorted angrily, interrupting. "She's no mother. She should never have abandoned her."

"She is trying to help Kyra and is trying to repair their relationship."

Tension stiffened Phe's jaw, and it was her turn to breathe through a flood of emotions. Phe may be angry with Thetis and not want anything to do with her, but the woman was Kyra's mother. Kyra had loved her mother. When Phe was able to look around her mistrust, she realized having Thetis there could be exactly what Kyra needed. Not only because it had been one of Kyra's deepest desires growing up, or because Thetis may offer a nurturing, healing rela-tionship, but because Thetis might be able to buffer Velimir's manipulation. "How are they getting along?"

"It's been rocky. Her Grace is struggling."

Gads. The ache in her chest increased. "Why did Bastion send her to Xafara?"

"From what I heard, Xafarians demanded her return. There's also, of course, her oath. She needs to be there to truly manage the waterways."

Phe squinted into the night sky, not bothering to ask why Thetis wasn't taking over—Roar wouldn't know. She needed to find a way to talk or dreamscape with Kyra. "What about the royal family? How are they? How are they taking Thetis's reappearance?"

"The royals seem to be fine. When they were briefly in Arias, after Djall's attack, they were re-acquainted with Thetis—whom I'm sure you know was good friends with Queen Oltha. Their friendship is tenuous, as Queen Oltha was very upset at Thetis for what she did to Her Grace." Roar shifted next to her, brushing against her. "They've been working with members of the parliament, General Bastion, and a small retinue of magic-borns to settle the unrest caused by Djall's attack and repair the damage he'd caused."

"Is Bastion allowing magic to be used outside of the cities?" Phe asked, wondering what the role of the advising magic-borns was.

"Only in Xafara."

Phe straightened and snapped her gaze to Roar. "Are they controlling them?"

Roar shook his head no. "Some of the advisers are seers. They're looking through all the possible paths forward and providing everyone with what appear to be the best methods for integrating magic-borns into Xafara—as the Elders have foreseen this as an unavoidable outcome. Others, like Lear, are taking the edge off people's fear. As you know, fear can muddle how people think, and it elevates emotions. By providing a sense of calmness, angers aren't flaring, and they're having productive conversations."

Phe relaxed. That made sense. Fear was often counterproductive to progress. Her mind veered to Lear. "Did Lear get in trouble for helping?"

"General Bastion gave him a proverbial slap on the wrist, which surprised even him." Roar admitted. "We think it was a combination of Areya calling in some favors—because she's an extremely protective mother—and Lear's own legacy. Plus, what he did ended up helping the cause."

Phe huffed. Of course it all boiled down to who you knew in Arias. This made Phe wonder what Areya's crime was to be under house arrest at all if she was so well connected. She held off on that line of questioning because Roar had made it clear it wasn't his story to tell. She switched to asking about the love of her life. "How is Edva?"

"Causing her normal array of trouble. Nothing worrisome."

She smiled, and the effects of it drifted through her—Edva was something.

The feeling didn't last long as she forced herself to ask her last question. "How is Shadow Unit?" *Do they hate me?* Hung, unspoken, in the air between them.

Roar smiled gently. "They're all good. General Bastion didn't attempt to communicate with the team while their mental blocks were in place. In fact, it seems he didn't know about them at all, so none of them were punished. They are worried about you and—forewarning—may plan something for when you're released."

Tension zinged through her. "Plan something?" Were they going to make her survive their own set of punishments?

"Nothing big. We're tossing around ideas about showing you the city or something fun to welcome you home."

"Oh." The apprehension drained from her. If they wanted to welcome her home, that meant they didn't hate her, right? A weird feeling tumbled in her chest at the thought of them wanting to welcome her back and have fun with her. Kyra would welcome her home—but under the auspices of her Lady Orphne persona, which drastically limited everything. Other than that, no one had ever welcomed her anywhere before.

They stayed silent, watching the awakening sky.

"General Bastion demoted me."

Phe's shoulders slumped, and she turned to him, meeting his blue gaze. "I'm sorry." She knew how much he valued his rank and position and his goals to advance his career.

"I knew it was a risk." Roar shrugged. "One I don't regret. If I hadn't been there, you'd be in Djall's thrall."

Phe let her gaze travel the contours of his face, from his

slightly crooked nose to his powerful jaw, then her eyes rebounded to his mouth. She remembered he'd kissed her.

A muscle ticked in his cheek. "I think General Bastion went easier with my physical punishments because he realizes the outcome would've been much worse if I hadn't done what I did."

Phe yanked her gaze back to his blues. *Does he regret the kiss?* She turned to stare at the horizon. "I'm glad."

"What's he doing to you?"

A tremble of remembrance skittered across her nerves. She shook the feeling off. It'd been worse than a public flogging and hanging her from her thumbs for hours, that was for sure. "Nothing I won't survive."

"Phe." Roar let her name hover in the air.

Phe grunted. There was no way she was going to tell him. Bastion kept the punishments private for a reason, and that was fine with her.

Birdsong burst into their silence.

"Is my touch bothering you?"

Phe glanced at their thighs, and heat crept up her neck. Her heart kicked up its pace. "No."

Roar shifted, pulling his leg up and planting it right behind her—knee bent—so he was now facing her. She twisted, wondering what he was doing, and was immediately captured in his intense gaze.

"I'd like to do it again."

"What?" she asked uncertainly.

His gaze dropped to linger on her lips. "Kiss you." He cupped the side of her face, thumb tracing light circles. "Is this okay?"

Phe's heart went wild. *Is this what it feels like without a touch aversion?*

Roar leaned closer, his breath caressing her face. "I'd

like to do much more than kiss," he said huskily. Phe held her breath. "I want so much more for *us* than just kissing . . ."

What was he saying? How was it her mind stopped working? "You want to have sex?" Her voice came out high pitched.

The smile Roar suppressed twinkled in his gaze. "I want to explore being your partner—your lover—in addition to being your friend and supporter."

Phe blinked repetitively, as if trying to clear her sight would make his words make sense. Her heart was swooning her in chest, and her mind was working overtime. She didn't know what to say.

A small smile crested his lips, and his gaze penetrated to her soul. "If you're willing to explore a relationship with me, that is. We'll go as slow as you need. No pressure. No labels. Right now, it's a kiss. Can I kiss you?"

Phe swallowed, her mouth suddenly desert dry. *Relationship with Roar?* She didn't know what to do with that. She'd never considered a relationship with anyone before . . . *don't overthink this.* His question was, could he kiss her again?

Sucking in confidence, she nodded. Heart pumping in her throat.

Roar's eyes smiled as he drew her face closer to his, eradicating the distance between them. He kissed the edge of her mouth softly, then ghosted her lips to kiss the other side. He scooted closer until her shoulder rested on his chest, and then he gently kissed her lips.

His nose touched hers as he angled in for another kiss. This time he drew her bottom lip into his mouth slightly and then released it and ran his tongue over it.

Phe held stock still. Zings of pleasure lit her body on fire, and fear paralyzed her. *What if I'm doing it wrong?*

"Breathe," Roar whispered, scattering tear drop kisses along her jawline. "If this is too much, tell me." His lips moved on her skin. "I'll stop."

Kyra always went on and on about kissing. About how she considered kissing to be the most intimate act—faces close, tongues intertwining, hearts touching.

Seas, Kyra will lose her mind when I tell her.

Roar dipped in again, and this time, Phe timidly opened her mouth and slid the tip of her tongue out, touching Roar's lip—and a second later, his tongue. He deepened their kiss, his fingers slipping into her hair.

Hesitantly, she cupped his cheek, following his lead. Feeling the strength of his jaw, the smoothness of his skin. She mimicked what he'd done with his thumb.

Roar groaned and pulled away. "Phe," his blue gaze scorched her, "kissing you has just become my favorite thing."

A smile curved Phe's cheeks and a warmth—a glow—spread in her chest. Maybe waking up wouldn't be as horrible as she thought.

Maybe the stars don't hate me after all.

ABOUT THE AUTHOR

When Krysta Maravilla isn't squirrelled away writing and reading and eating Nutella, she can be found plotting her next adventure as she loves to explore. With a passion for hiking and a desire to experience different cultures, she has lived in various places throughout the US and the world.

Her love of fantasy and adventure and romance has inspired her to write her own stories, which transport readers to fantastical worlds filled with magic and action where she weaves in themes of healing, friendship, and loyalty.

Sign up for Krysta Maravilla's newsletter if you want monthly updates on *Of Fire and Shadows* series, exclusive content—such as Shadow Tag a cut scene from Sunder, Book Two, her wanderings, and various projects.

Visit her online and subscribe at:
www.krystamaravilla.com

OF FIRE AND SHADOWS

Spark
Spared (A novella)

STAY MARVELOUS